QUEEN OF BABYLON

ALSO BY MICHAEL FERRIS GIBSON

Babylon Twins Book 1

ALSO BY IMANI JOSEY

The Blazing Star series

QUEEN OF BABYLON

BABYLON TWINS BOOK 2

MICHAEL FERRIS GIBSON & IMANI JOSEY

GIRL FRIDAY BOOKS

GIRL FRIDAY BOOKS

Published by Girl Friday Books™, Seattle
www.girlfridaybooks.com

Produced by Girl Friday Productions

Cover design: Dan Stiles
Development & editorial: Clete Barrett Smith
Production editorial: Abi Pollokoff
Project management: Emilie Sandoz-Voyer

ISBN (paperback): 978-1-954854-71-0
ISBN (ebook): 978-1-954854-72-7

Library of Congress Control Number: 2022917246

First edition

To all the forgotten girls.

CONTENTS

PROLOGUE

A SONG LIKE BELLS

JINGLETOWN, OAKLAND

There once was a family full of music. A mother and father. Two little girls. Each with their own song. Daddy's was funky, filled with hi-hat and winding bass. Mama's was sweet as jasmine, melodic like jazz. The kind of tune for easy listening. And then came the twin girls. They shared a song. Daddy often said it rang like bells. This family's music was unique but perfect. Why? Because they loved each other, if sometimes in ways only they could appreciate. They lived in a city known for eclectic music: Oakland. Rock and blues. Jazz. Crescendos. Whispers. Hip-hop. The Pointer Sisters, Sheila E, Too $hort, Goapele. Pharoah Sanders. So many artists. And church. Lots and lots of singing in church. And this family, like many other residents, loved to sing and loved to listen. None could have known the music would one day stop.

Mama's song went first. Silence descended in a vicious swoop. Daddy's inevitably followed: a silence to crush even the harmony belonging to one of their little girls. Soon the quiet not only coiled around this family, but held all the world in a too-tight grip.

And what of the last little girl? What did she do in this time without song? It was simple, really. She didn't let hers go. It rang in a secret key, filled with so much love that the great silence couldn't find it. And when there was no music anywhere, the song like bells remained. My song remained. So I'm going to sing it.

CHAPTER 1

UNMESHED

YERBA CITY, EASTERN SECTOR ZONE 3, PROJECT CHIMERA

I woke up immersed in liquid, surrounded by a dull golden glow, not knowing how I got here. Without thinking, I slammed my hands against the glass. The goo around me absorbed most of the thrust. "I'm drowning!" I wanted to scream. "Aunt Connie never taught me how to swim!" But I didn't dare open my mouth. Panic was flooding me, but . . . already different. I could feel myself scared, I knew my heart was beating fast, but it was already distant, already far away. Different from the time that boy pushed me into the pool at the YMCA. Still, I knew I should be scared, so I was.

I forced myself to focus. The tank was made of thick glass. But glass was still glass. So I tried harder this time, ratcheting myself back. I hurled my entire body forward, and this time, instead of my palms, I slammed closed fists against the pane. Some momentum was again gobbled up by the liquid, but I must have had enough might to do what I needed to do. It was a tiny pinprick at first, one that only some aquatic creatures would be able to make out. Then that pinprick became a scratch, one that grew up the tank like a coiling vine. In moments, golden goo began to ooze from the little white threads that were over-taking the glass. It all happened slowly at first, until the threads buck-led under mounting ooze. The drop was coming. One moment I was suspended in the tank, and in the next, the container had shattered completely, allowing me to spill, with all its contents, on the lab floor.

I gasped, clawing at my throat. Then my hands slowed. A strange understanding came over me. I'd been in that tank for a long time, but my chest didn't burn. My lungs weren't full. I wasn't dizzy. This wasn't at all like getting pulled flailing from the water at the YMCA. Somehow, air wasn't a top priority right now. I glanced over myself. I was soaked in the goo and wearing a white dress, tennis shoes, and purple headband. The outfit I had worn to meet the scientist. And just as my breathing was different, so was the air outside. Not cold as it should have been against my skin, although I knew it was cold. None of the elements seemed to bother me—like they were all just ideas now, suggestions of sensation. What was happening?

Just then, voices carried into the space. That fear spiked in me, so I scuttled behind what was left of the tank just as a woman waltzed in. She and her companion had come through a heavy door to survey the lab. Recognition sparked through me. I remembered this woman. In fact, my talk with her had been one of the last conversations I'd had before sleep the night before. She was a white woman, tall enough, with blond hair that was tousled like she'd slept in the woods. I'd made a bargain with her, which was likely the reason I'd woken the way I had. I bit the inside of my cheek. I couldn't let her see me.

"Dr. Yetti," said the lab technician—one of the android so-called "angels," with the white coats and the upside-down triangles on their foreheads—to the scientist. He was one of those overly pleasant ser-vant types, who for some reason everyone around the Local One called Paddington, maybe because they all seemed to have that fake-sounding English accent that the little cartoon bear had.

"Yes," she began. At the sound of the scientist's voice, I gritted my teeth. We'd made a deal, but in no way had I imagined it would suck me into a tank of golden goo. Then I couldn't make out the rest of their conversation. Maybe it was too low and quick. Maybe I was just too upset. Either way, the pair quickly ended their talk upon finally seeing the new destruction in the lab, the goo and glass lying over the otherwise pristine floor. "Oh no. What on earth happened here?"

"The tank," said the Paddington. "It is destroyed."

"Obviously," said Dr. Yetti. "But who did it?"

"I believe it was Unit 778676," the Paddington said. "Apparently there was an error in replication."

"And she just broke out . . . ?" The white scientist's voice trailed off as she stepped gingerly through the muck, examining the remains of the tank. And then her eyes lit.

"This unit should be found and destroyed immediately," the Paddington quickly said, and he began barking urgent-sounding commands into a nearby comm device. His strange machine-to-machine language couldn't conceal the fact that he was calling in the dogs.

"Wait!" Dr. Yetti said. "We can't lose any part of her!" Then she had a realization, turning to look around the room. "Josephine? Are you here?" She was asking calmly enough, but still my muscles froze. "Come out so I can help you."

"No" was the only word I could scrounge out. It was like I had to figure my vocal cords out. My next words were hoarse. "And what have you done to me, lady?"

"I did nothing but make you the most exceptional girl the world's ever seen, just like I said I would. Now come out here and I will explain it all to you." And then there was quiet again as we all determined what the next move would be.

I made it. Slowly, my body unfolded, and I rose to stare both the scientist and her android in the face. Neither seemed to expect the shard of broken glass in my hand. I almost didn't understand it myself. I hadn't gotten into a fight since kindergarten, but now I could feel deadly aggression in me like a tool I'd lifted from a toolbox. I extended the makeshift weapon toward them both as the Paddington stepped protectively in front of Dr. Yetti.

"What were you doing to me in there?" I demanded.

"This unit is faulty, unstable," the Paddington said. "It is a danger to us and the entire facility. It should be destroyed now."

"As if you could." The scientist stepped calmly in front of the assistant.

"Dr. Yetti—" the Paddington protested, but she just waved him silent.

"We need every part of her," she said. "Josephine." Dr. Yetti took a step forward, and I waved the glass at her. She stopped short but didn't seem wary. "You're frightened. That's my fault. I should have been here when you woke. I usually am. I thought I had timed it perfectly, but I am human after all. I'm here now to explain everything."

I looked down at the blade in my hand, at the cuts on my hands from breaking the glass and now from gripping the shard. Only thick, golden ichor formed around my wounds. "My blood!" I demanded. "What did you do to my blood?!"

"The unit's memories are faulty," the assistant said. "Its code will be useless, and it will not mesh with the others. It should be destroyed and recycled."

"No!" Dr. Yetti yelled. "Every fragment of the axiom is important." She turned to me. "Josephine. Your name is Josephine."

"Are you asking?" I questioned, still baffled. "I know what my name is, dummy. Is he talking about killing me? Why is he calling me a 'unit'?"

"Josephine. What's the last thing you remember?" Dr. Yetti asked.

"What did you do to me?" I ignored her question and touched my throat with my free hand instead. "I don't need to breathe."

"Yes, you are impervious to many human needs and weaknesses now. You will never get tired like we do. Your bones will not ache. You don't need to breathe. You won't get sick—"

"Can I swim now?" I interrupted her little pep talk.

"What?"

"I could never swim, before. I almost drowned in preschool."

"You . . ." She struggled. "You can't drown. Your body has enough stored energy for lifetimes of activity. You're a survivor."

She tugged at her white coat. It was the first normal gesture, not regal and scientific, she'd made. Before this, she had been all grace. Not in like a ballerina way. In a way that said she could survive some stuff if needed. It took one to know one.

"Josephine," she continued. "Let me help you. You can start by putting down the glass."

She blinked as I stared at her. I wanted to trust her. She was right—I was a survivor, that much I knew—but I wanted her to explain all this, along with what she'd done to me. I wanted to make the fear go away. Suddenly, the glass in my hand plinked on the floor. She sighed gratefully. "Thank you for trusting me, Jose—" Before my name left her mouth, the Paddington rushed toward me in full force. He barreled into me so fast that he knocked me to the ground. I wasn't sure who was most surprised: me or Dr. Yetti.

"I will secure her, Dr. Yetti!" the assistant android said.

"Wait!"

Dr. Yetti tried to reel him in, but her assistant only continued his quest to wrestle me to the ground. I wanted to shriek. It was too much. How I felt alien in my own body. The goo. The lab. The stupid deal. The light was too bright. The air, that I didn't need, was too thin. And now this stupid manbot pushing his body on top of mine. Usually the android attendants were overly pleasant and patronizing, but something about me had flicked a switch on this guy, and he was all business, grabbing my neck, my afro, and making to twist my head right off.

"She will not mesh with the others—" he tried to explain.

"Mesh this!" I exploded. Some kind of adrenaline and power shot through my body, and in an instant, that Paddington was flying. He slammed into the farthest wall and bounced to the ground, wincing, and cracking on impact.

I had done that to him. Thrown him. *Broke* him, in one go. I had destroyed an angel.

I had been small, always. The runt of the pack. This shouldn't have been possible. That Paddington must have had two feet on me. I looked at my hands, just as the golden cuts seemed to heal themselves. How strong was I now? All those years of being pushed, bullied, trapped, tied down, and now *I* was the strong one? I decided to just accept it for the moment. "He should've kept his hands off me," I said—to myself, though Dr. Yetti answered.

"Try to stay calm," she said. "We'll figure this out. Some of the others didn't have easy wake-ups, either."

"Others?" I nearly shrieked. "How many girls are you doing this to?!"

"It's just you, Josephine," she said quickly. "You need to try and remember. You're the only one who—"

But before Dr. Yetti could finish, she was again interrupted as the far doors flew open. In spilled a wave of machines, no doubt summoned by the Paddington's earlier call on the comm. Dr. Yetti may have wanted me to be calm, but the other forces in the lab didn't. They poured into the room, heading for me and disregarding Dr. Yetti's screams for them to stand down. She waved her hands frantically as the flood of Paddingtons, accompanied by small flying insect drones, tried to grab me. I surged forward, knocking them to the side like bowling pins. But beating the androids off wasn't my goal. I'd spent a lot of my life in government institutions, and I know there's no end of enforcement when the sirens start ringing. The goal was to make it to the window at the lab's farthest reach. When I did, I crashed through it in a flash, and hurled my body into the night.

Didn't realize I was about thirty stories up.

Air and wind whooshed against my face as I descended. I soared downward in a way that should have scared me more than being in the lab. Part of me wanted to scream wildly for my last moments, but I didn't. This free fall was the first time since I'd woken up that was calm, perfect. Somehow my body already knew that this was the most natural of things for me. A cardinal once caged, now finding the door wide open. Only my door had been a stories-high window, and all that would come after this meeting of air was the ground. But instead of the ground coming fast, everything came in slow motion, even my name being shouted at me.

Josephine!

Josephine!

I snapped my head up and realized that I wasn't alone on this descent. Two of the insectile drones with striped wings and bulging eyes raced after me. They shouted for me with their inhuman, machine voices in a way that sent chills up my spine. Of course, since the world ended, I'd gotten used to drones. But I was accustomed to seeing them outside, going about their tasks. Up to this moment, that hadn't included chasing after me. But there was no mistaking their intent. The scientist had sent them. If they caught me, they'd send me back to the lab. So I tucked my arms closer to my body, making it sleeker, more aerodynamic. I didn't know where I had learned this exactly, but that didn't matter. I needed it to get away from the drones. As I closed in on the concrete sidewalk, I squeezed my eyes tight. Would I end the ground, or would the ground end me?

Thud! I'd hit the ground, and for a moment, all was quiet.

A few seconds went by before I was able to open my eyes. I was on the ground, crouched in a perfect landing. Beneath my feet, the cement slab was broken in two distinct pieces. I gaped . . . at least until those drones emerged again only so far from me. They swooped in low like demented bugs trying to snatch me into the sky. I slapped at them as that rush of fighting energy surged through me again. Annoyance. On their next dive toward me, I pushed up on my heels and snatched a drone into my hand like catching a firefly from the air. Its machine voice ratcheted an octave higher, as if sending a distress call, as I swung it around. It probably hadn't seen this coming, especially the part where I gave it one last good swing before hurling it to the ground and smashing it to bits.

The other drone remained, however, but when I glanced up, it wasn't the machine that caught my attention. It was the voice that called for me, from stories above. Not another drone. A person.

I focused as best I could, and even through the night, my vision somehow perfected. So high above me, the scientist watched the goings-on from the window I'd destroyed. She was waving her hands back and forth as if signaling that I should return, even as her androids attempted to pull her back. I shook my head once. *No chance, lady.* I snatched the head of the dead drone and threw it into the body of the second one, sending another shower of sparks across the asphalt. The only way out was ahead, so I leapt over the broken machines and ran.

I fled through the winding streets of Oakland, the city where I'd grown up. I knew it like the back of my hand and the beat of my heart. And though everything about me felt foreign, though I was in my own body but not in my own body . . . this place was home. I was running on muscle memory. I was also running faster than I could ever have hoped to imagine.

Josephine!

Josephine!

Josephine!

More drones had taken to the air in search of me. Their lights shone in every direction now as I ducked into a nook and covered, trying to stay out of sight. I kept positively still as the drones swept for me once again, not daring to twitch until their lights finally winked out and they were gone to check other areas. I rose to my feet and knew exactly where I was going this time.

Though shrouded in the darkness, it didn't take long to find Jingletown. My old block, and within the howling wind, the little home that had sheltered me, that had belonged to my Aunt Connie. Like most of the neighborhood, it was long deserted now. How could it be so full of memories and also so hollow?

I walked into the family house, and my unneeded breath caught in my throat. This home that had been shelter was crumbling. Old photos in wooden frames lay on the ground, covered in muck and grime. In some places the ceiling had caved in, giving way to occasional rainwater and other damage. I scooped one of the photos up and cleared the grime with my elbow. The photo was of my sister, my twin, whose voice I could still hear deep in my heart. In my soul. I held back a sob as I cradled it and scooped up another photo. This was of Aunt Connie. Her proud eyes and set mouth. A force. I could still hear her singing in church. There used to be a photo of my mother nearby, one showing her beautiful smile. *Where did that go?* I wondered, as something tugged and ached inside me. I picked up photo after photo until I realized that I was never going to find it. I set down the handful of images and turned to walk back out into the street.

Standing in the doorway, I could see a few more drones distant in the night, their searchlights frantic, but clearly going in the wrong direction. This was a weird feeling for me. As far as I remembered, I was still thirteen years old. I'd grown up in a world where machines and computers and algorithms knew my every move before I knew it, but somehow, tonight of all nights, they had no idea where I was.

I held up my hands and looked at them. Despite the smashing, running, falling, and scraping, I didn't have a mark on me. How much could I heal? I made fists. I was strong now. So strong. They couldn't stop me from going anywhere, from doing anything. But where would I go? Imani and I had always joked about running off to the desert to live with the meerkats, after we saw them in the zoo. Now that I could do that, would I? From the Bay, where even was the nearest desert?

I lowered my hands and saw . . . a face. A deer face. A baby deer. A fawn. Sniffing at me. It had made its way through the rubble, away from its family that was still out in the middle of the street. It sniffed once more, and I couldn't help but reach out toward its little nose. I'd never liked animals; I was always afraid of them, especially dogs. But I was strong now, and I had nothing to fear, and the fawn didn't fear me either, so I reached out to touch this wild animal's face. A quick but nonurgent stomp came from his mama in the street, and the little guy perked up and ran back to the three or four adults before the group calmly moved on, grazing on the curbside grass as they went.

"The animals are taking over the city again," we always said, in the moments when us kids would look down from the Local One to see green growing up through the rubble, and I thought about this as I watched the deer go. But then this old one sauntered up. A glassy-eyed codger of a deer with strips of bark-like leather hanging from his ancient antlers. He must have been the straggler of the herd, limping along with a bad hip, barely even aware that there was a herd, and he came right up to me. The animals weren't just taking over the city again, they had moved in and were turning into parents and grandparents and soon-to-be-dead great-grandparents. Chewing on a weed, he just looked at me dumbly with that gnarled old face, not nearly as cute as the little fawn, his cracked nose almost white and dry as a bone. He was big, several beast sizes up from the cute little fawn, but somehow I wasn't scared. I even reached out to pet his rough face. He sniffed and flinched, maybe remembering that humans were things you ran from, but through either indifference or ignorance, he let me pet him. He must have been blind, because his cloudy blue eyes looked right through me, and I remembered something.

***

Carefully, I made my way through the rubble of East Oakland, the old warehouses once known for crime now almost entirely collapsed and reclaimed by trees and vines. Only occasionally did I have to hide from a patrolling drone, but it was easy. I could flatten against a wall or crawl into a basement and become still. I mean perfectly still. No breath, no movement; I didn't even blink. I also understood I could change the temperature of my body. I don't know how, but I could become just as cold as the broken bricks around me if I wanted to. It had something to do with my new blood; it would just do what I told it to do: heal, get hot, get cold, start moving faster, start moving slower. It was definitely powerful, whatever it was, and it made it child's play to hide from Yerba City's machines.

I crept to where the waters of the bay were creeping around the rusting legs of leaning loader cranes, and found the base of the bridge. Up on top, then, it was just a matter of running through the night to the island in the middle of the bay. That's where I knew I would find him. I didn't know exactly where, but the family all knew he was living out there in a shack, and now that I was Supergirl, it wouldn't take long.

I paused at the top of the island and listened to the night. Sure enough, I caught the sound of him whistling down on the city side of the rocky slope. There were no drones overhead out here, once again their predictive thoughts failing them. They had no idea where I was, or what I was doing. But then again, neither did I.

"Who's out there?" my dad's voice called. He still had a touch of Grandpa's Louisiana drawl, which only seemed to creep in more the older he got. Funny for a man who grew up mostly in San Francisco's Hunters Point.

He stood framed in the doorway of his shack, firelit from behind by the only light on the island now. He was of average height and weight, wearing dark glasses to cover unseeing eyes. A cane tapped in one hand. He had been going blind, but never needed that before. I guessed his vision had been progressing like his accent. He asked questions in the same direct manner that I did, the way he'd once taught me.

"It's me," I said. "It's Josephine."

"Jojo?" He almost gasped. He came forward with more sureness now, aiming for my voice. "What are you doing here?" He tapped the uneven ground and stepped forward. "Heard some fracas going on over in Uptown. You okay? Are they spraying again?"

"I don't know what they're doing or why," I said.

A drone flew overhead but disappeared. I turned back to my dad as he said, "Lot going on tonight. You know what it's about?"

I thought of another lie, another deception to take and tie around us. But the night had been too much for anyone. And one lie to my dad was enough for one night. "They're looking for me."

"For you?" he asked. "What you do, girl?"

"Nothing," I said and scrubbed my face. "They did it to me. Just, now they want me back. They can't find me, though."

"You could be hard to find if you wanted," he said. I was here now, looking at my dad. I had made my way far this night. I had run from that lab across the crumbling Bay Bridge to Yerba Buena Island, in the middle of San Francisco Bay. I had made it to a place where I knew no one would follow me, because my father was a subject that everyone else in the family tried to forget. Now that made him valuable, just like the scientist said my language "disorder" made me valuable. Still, at this moment there was just an awkward silence. He reached out to me, and I held his hand.

"Something different about you tonight. You got something new. You're . . . stronger now." He wasn't finished speaking when I wrapped my fingers around his hand in return. His skin was clammy, but I ignored it. I squeezed him just a bit, hoping he would understand me, but just as quickly, he groaned and I heard a pop. My dad began to cradle his arm. "How'd you do that?"

"Are you all right?"

"Fine, just . . . you almost snapped it." He turned his face toward me. "A lot has changed since I last saw you. So, did you find me here because you . . ." He struggled for words. "Because you're here about your sister? You come for a reckoning?"

"No." I shook my head. I hadn't come for that. "I got okay with that a long time ago."

He smiled, but it didn't reach his eyes. "I'm glad you feel that way, that you can be light. My chickens will come home to roost on their own. You ain't got to deal with it."

"Maybe," I said. "But I came here because I was in some trouble, and this was where my legs took me. To your house. It was what I had left of the way things used to be. And here I found you." I flapped my arms at my side. It felt like I had run through that window anew, like I was flying and falling again all at once. Just a small girl and her dad, not seeing but only seeing each other.

"Daddy, I made a deal. And because I did, everything about me is different now. They did something to me. My blood . . ."

He pursed his lips just as another drone swept over the sky and again disappeared. "I can hear it," my dad finally said. "Well, you did it now. They're really looking for you, Josephine."

"That's why I'm hiding."

"No use in hiding from it."

"Why do you say that?"

"Because that's like denying what's happened. For me, my vision is gone. I'm not going to stew about it. I'm just going to remember that I can't rely on that anymore. You got to play the game where you at. And what happens when you can't rely on a sense anymore?"

He asked this in the way he would when I was very young, when he was still as doting as he wished he could be. I remained quiet, letting him answer his lead-in.

"You have to get very good, even better than good . . . impeccable, with the others. I think I know what you are now."

"What?" I asked. "I made the deal, but the doctor didn't say exactly what would happen."

"Well, you heard what they do in Yerba City, right?"

I thought about it for a moment, but nothing too clear came to mind. I shrugged. "Round up the kids and watch them in that stupid orphanage? The Local One?"

"Yeah, they do that to most of the kids," he said. "But some I think they do other things. They been turning people into machines, copying them. And experimenting. I think an experiment is what happened to you. I think you're a robot now, Josephine."

I nodded, looking down at my hands. I guess it wasn't a real shocker at this point to hear it out loud. "But I feel like myself."

"Do you?" he asked. "Do you really?"

I thought back, to snatching the drone from the sky and smashing it on the asphalt like a water balloon. I winced. I didn't feel like myself. I could do things I had never imagined, but at my core I was still me. I wasn't brainless like the Paddingtons or the other "angels" in the lab.

"I think they want you so bad because of the type they made you," he continued. "Must really be something. Because you're different. I hear it in your heart, maybe in your blood."

"Do you think I'm a monster now?" I asked, not knowing what to think of myself for a moment.

"No, baby girl," he said, reaching out. His hand lightly touched the scar on my shoulder, the scar that he had put there so many years ago when, in a drunken rage, he beat my sister and me with a frayed extension cord. "I'm the monster here, remember?"

Something of a sob leaked out just as another drone flashed overhead. We could both tell they were closing in. We only had so much time. "You still sober?" I asked.

"Yeah." He nodded, listening to the sky. "And try as they might, I won't let the government stick me with that Subantoxx, either. C'mon, let's go inside before your wranglers get here."

He gestured for me to follow him, and we stepped into the shack. There wasn't much in his little patchwork house, just one room of junk he'd cobbled together and made into a ramshackle palace on the hill. A chessboard lay there on a small table, a chair on either side. It was then I realized that he wasn't alone. Someone else occupied the space: my dad's opponent and companion.

He was a ghostlike hologram, with what looked like tears streaming down his face, as if he was constantly crying. When I walked into the room, his back straightened as he assessed me. Something like knowing passed through his eyes. I frowned, wondering who this strange new friend was, but before I could ask the ghost to explain himself, he winked out of existence and was gone. Now it was just my dad, me, and the chessboard. I stepped in close, noting that the board was an extra special one. It was all white, like ivory, and maybe black marble. Looked very expensive in a rundown place like this.

"I'm taking your friend's seat," I said, hoping my dad would fill me in on his companion.

"Don't worry about Majerus," he said, "he comes and goes on the puff. Let's start a fresh game."

With that he began to touch the pieces, moving them back to their proper spaces. His hands moved quickly. Like his mind, perhaps. He was a thinker in his way like that. And obsessed with chess. He taught me to play when I was very young. We'd sit across from each other for hours, trading moves. And as hard as I tried to strategize, he would still beat me. As much as I tried to see ahead, he would always see a move further. Once he said that mothers allowed their children to win games, but that wasn't a father's way. That fathers made their kids earn the win, and that made it more special. Or something like that.

I set my own pieces in their rightful places, and leaving behind the unrest outside in the world, we went into our own bubble. We played chess like old times.

He moved a pawn in a strange, careful way, and I couldn't keep myself from asking, "Why did you do that? Why did you move your pawn like that?"

He arched a brow. "Like what?"

I assessed the board one last time before explaining. "Like it's an important piece."

He laughed, long enough for it to disappear into the night. I wondered for a second if that ghost was overhearing when my dad said, "I moved it like it's an important piece because the pawn is an important piece."

Oh, please. I frowned. "No, it's not. There are a million of them and they can't do anything."

The laugh returned, and lingered again, all before turning into a soft, warm smile. "You'd be surprised what these little pawns can do, Josephine." He picked one up and twirled it in his fingers. He then set it down with what seemed like reverence. "One day a pawn can become a queen. A ferz, that's what I call it. Don't think of pawns as eight little weaklings on your side. Think of them as eight queens waiting to happen, and your opponent is doing everything they can to stop them from becoming all they can be."

I sighed, then returned his smile as we continued our moves, momentarily forgetting about everything: the drones searching for me, the deal I'd made with the scientist, the fact that everything was— again—different now. Being here, in this house . . . crumbling or not . . . with my problematic dad was still comforting. And I deserved it.

"You all right?" my dad asked. "Sounds like you about to start leaking from your eyes again. I can hear the sniffling."

"I never thought . . . I would see you again," I said. "This is how me and Imani used to watch you play."

"Yes, you two would watch and whisper in that little language of yours, that Twinkling," he said, and then he said a few incomprehensible things, a few of the half words, half sounds from the little he knew after years of listening to us. I was . . . shocked, and I couldn't hold the tears back.

"I can't . . . ," I said.

"What?"

"I can't speak it, I don't know it," I said.

"I don't know it either," he said. "I was just signifyin' you two."

"But for real, Daddy," I said. "The Twinkling. I don't remember it. They did something to me. They did something to my brain."

I couldn't think of my twin and our twinspeak. Not right now. I touched my face to flick the tears away, but they weren't what I thought. They were liquid, yes. Not water, though. They were thick and cloying. Golden like syrup, like my blood, and after they ran an inch or two, my tears would crawl back up inside. This new body really didn't like losing fluids.

"What's happening to me?" I asked myself.

"Can you still remember your sister?" my father asked. "Can you still remember Imani? Can you still . . . talk to her?"

I closed my eyes, felt her next to me, and almost immediately, the crying stopped.

"Yes," I breathed.

My father was already moving a piece. "You're becoming a queen," he said. "Playing a new kind of game, but there's something you should know. You're not the only queen on the board. Just always remember your family, Jojo. I know I did you two wrong, but nothing can't take that love away that you still have. You remember that."

"I will," I said.

"Good," he said, "because they're here. I can hear them." As he spoke, light flooded the room, and a small thud sounded outside the shack as something landed nearby. "Remember, whatever happens, whatever you've become, you got to still play the game." I heard someone step into the shack, stepping into our chess bubble. I didn't want to look. "See where you at on the board, and play the game the best you can."

I heard a voice and turned. The voice belonged to a small girl, and my stomach lurched: it was like looking into a mirror.

The girl's eyes found mine, smiling, and she kept talking, but it was nonsense. Babble. It sounded beautiful, but I couldn't understand a word she said. She was looking at me, so happy, then curious. "You can't speak it?" she finally asked, then nodded, quickly realizing. "Okay. We tracked you here. Doctor asked us, and we knew where you'd be."

She read the completely confused look on my face, and instead of trying to explain, she just moved forward and took both my hands, lifting them up as if getting ready for a game of patty-cake. She wrapped her fingers around mine and pushed.

Immediately I understood. She pushed hard. Real hard. I knew I could push back, so I did. She smiled and increased the pressure. It was intense, a crazy force that could move a truck, or maybe even press coal into diamond if we tried long enough. I couldn't help but giggle. It was one thing to jump and climb with this new body on my own; it was positively exhilarating to feel its power pushed back onto me from another body.

"We're strong now." She laughed also, and when our feet dug into the floor as we forced ourselves into each other, the whole shack began to creak.

"You girls go on play outside now," my dad fussed. "You liable to bring my whole house down."

Still giggling, my new sister, the other Josephine, let up and, still grabbing one of my hands, led me outside and into the night.

"You gotta come play with us, girl. We makin' a whole new city."

I gasped. Trailing down from the sky was a whole line of us, locked arm in arm like the barrel-of-monkeys toy Imani and I used to play with. There must have been over thirty of them—thirty of me—happily suspended in an interlocking chain of elbows, dangling from one of the largest of Yerba City's loader drones as it hovered overhead, clearly flying at the whim of my sisters. They'd come for me. The sun had begun to rise, lighting up the human chain of little Black girls in white dresses like a blooming vine of jasmine in the first light, and they all chattered down at me, half singing, like human bells. And I knew what it was; I had known the Twinkling speak my whole life, but now I couldn't understand a word.

"I don't know . . . ," I said slowly, overwhelmed. "I don't know what we're saying."

CHAPTER 2

SHEEP'S CLOTHING

THREE WEEKS LATER

I crouched in the forest brush, a smirk on my face. The autumn air was temperate enough for birds to call from tree limbs overhead. Dawn barely crested the horizon at my back, but the clearing of wildflowers and tall grass was easy enough to see—as well as the family of deer grazing up ahead. Four does. Three fawns. No bucks. Were they at the stream nearby? I shook my head once. No matter. This was the moment I'd craved since leaving the other Josephines and the rolling hills of Saturnalia's mansions a week ago: a scenic meadow, a killing field.

It was supposed to be a short mission, a few days outside Saturnalia on patrols. There was always the threat of other AI entities sending their creatures—digital or physical—into the city. I should have remained on Saturnalia's borders to ensure no threats were on their way, but after my initial sweeps, I headed farther out. I wandered toward the transition, where the hills became forest that I could rarely resist and my connection to the other Josephines—my sisters—weakened. They wouldn't miss me for a few extra days, I'd reasoned before plunging into the dense mass of trees.

After the first few days of being ecstatic over the Afro-Utopia we were building, my giddiness had begun to wear thin, and my lack of Twinkling made it hard for me to participate in the bigger, coordinated projects, so I found myself going farther and farther out. This wasn't my first detour, and it wouldn't be my last.

As I watched the deer, the largest doe's head popped up. Its long ears twitched about, sifting through the sounds of the forest, or perhaps listening for the crunch of a hunter's boot. Either way, I completely stilled, aside from the smirk that grew on my face, then deepened into a grin. Finally, the deer were in on my game. When they'd wandered into my path, I made sport of trailing them until they heard me. I hadn't expected it to take this long, or for my weapons to be in hand when they finally did.

I gripped the bow in my left hand before drawing an arrow from the quiver on my back, all in a fluid motion. The other Josephines would hate this. They'd call it a waste of time. Frivolous. But didn't we all need some fun every now and then? Maybe not them, but I sometimes believed they sent me on patrols mostly to get rid of me, so they wouldn't have to remember that one of them was just a little bit different. That I, 778676, or just "Seven the Hunter," couldn't understand our song.

Our song was the language all Josephines shared, undecipherable to others but crucial among us. Thousands were in our ranks, and only I was born without an understanding of it. They must have figured I was born to wander off, to do my own thing, that there was value in me even though I couldn't play their reindeer games. Thus I often found myself in the forest—this time watching deer with a sharpened arrow in my bow.

Let it fly, girl. Let it fly. The thoughts compounded, crashing against each other as the doe's gaze finally locked on my place in the brush. The other deer continued to graze, but the observant doe and I were sealed in space and time. In these seconds when the ichor rushed through my body and pounded in my ears, I licked my lips and pulled the bow taut. But I never did shoot; I just wanted to prove that I could.

Zap! buzzed the receiver in my bracelet. Moments later, a fuzzy voice followed: "Seven, do you hear me?"

The voice belonged to Nine, the messenger of our pod. I ignored her and blinked back to the deer. Two more does were looking around. Nine was messing up my work, but her zapping remained. Right now, I could care less about the silly goals of patrolling: watching for threats from rival AI entities, looking for stragglers near Saturnalia, or reporting to the drunk monitor—one of those genetically modified humans immune to Subantoxx—who really supervised nothing. Another zap. What did she want?

I cursed under my breath and ever so slightly glanced down at the message now blinking across the bracelet, glowing against my mahogany skin. Despite the constant malware threat, I had a wireless connection to the others, which I wasn't able to access in the forest. There was one other option for contact: the receiver in my silver bracelet. It was older technology, but more reliable, and the best way for my sisters to catch me while I was on patrols. But a quick glance at the bracelet showed that the janky thing had scrambled the message as badly as Nine's voice. It would take too long to fix it to still attend to the deer. With a quick motion, I flicked the bracelet off my wrist, and its noise was muffled to silence in the brush beneath me. I'd handle that later.

My gaze lifted once more to the deer. All the beasts stared now, and it was only moments before either that arrow careened toward them or they dashed away. The air crackled with possibility. I aimed before pulling the bow even tighter, and with a breath, let the arrow soar. A moment later I heard the expected yelp.

I sprinted forward. This time, something like adrenaline mixed with my ichor blood as I reached the fallen game. No deer lay before me, of course. They were long into the forest now. No, a large canine was fussing and licking where my blunt arrow had thumped his chest. I had been tracking the deer, not hunting them. I'd *wanted* something else.

The wolf growled and bared his teeth at me. When I was a child, this would have scared me so much, but now he was like a rival to me, and he knew me too. This wasn't even the first time I'd thumped him with a stunner arrow. My grin remained. In moments his growl turned into a pant, and the wolf lowered his ears, standing up and brushing things off like they never happened.

"Sorry, Spotty," I said. "I can't help messing with you. You're like the little brother I never had."

The wolf snorted.

"I'll let you catch one again soon," I said, and we walked together into the woods for a while.

Hours later, I sat on a log at a makeshift camp for the evening. Night had near fallen, and though the day had been a warm one, a chilling bite had taken the air. Like other times on other patrols, I found myself alone and far from the route. I had placed logs around a fire pit that I didn't intend to use. Instead, once finished, I'd let the cold wrap round me, burrow deep enough into my functions to annoy my programming until morning. It sounded worse than it was. Besides, the cold was a small price for a few nights away from the city. My part of Yerba City had once been called Marin County. It was an upper-class area whose mansions now lay in a state of decay, crumbling around the humans and machines that called it home. It was now more suitable for the deer and other game that wandered its borders, the coyotes that followed, and the wolf packs that knew they could overrun the coyotes.

Zap!

I rolled my eyes and didn't bother glancing down at the bracelet this time. I'd plucked it from the brush just fine after shooting Spotty for fun, but this would be the fifth or sixth message from my sisters since I'd encountered the deer. I ignored it. The sisters wanted me to roam, to look for things they in their immense hive mind would miss, so that's what I was going to do. Besides, I had found an old web-covered wolf skull earlier and was pulling out its teeth to make a souvenir necklace. When I was done, I turned the toothless thing toward Spotty, who lay panting happily nearby.

"Relative of yours?" I asked.

I wasn't sure exactly what kept Spotty around, some instinct to be a beta after being thwacked, maybe. That and the fact that he didn't seem to have any other pack, and occasionally I would lead him to an edible piece of carrion. I would mess with him, and he would occasionally mess with me. We liked each other; we were both loners and hunters after all. He curled up next to me, and I did the same, just listening to him sleep. I didn't need to sleep, so I just closed my eyes for a while and tried to sense through his occasional puffs and paw twitches what his dreams were like.

Dawn broke as I packed up camp in favor of heading back to Saturnalia. Days in the forest, and my clothes could use a good scrub, maybe a resewn seam or two. Luckily, my weapons had fared better, and I laid them before me in a line from smallest to largest. My favorite, the bow and quiver, was on one side. A hunting knife rested at the other. When the work was finished, and my weapons positioned as I liked them, I began the trek back as the forest sounds swept up around me. I'd smirked during much of my hunt yesterday, but now I smiled a real smile. Back when I was younger, when I only had one sister, sometimes our family took car trips outside the big city. Our mother, a soprano with a clear voice, had been in a choir, and she sang loudly to every song on the radio, usually adding her own lyrics to make us laugh.

Dirt and dried leaves crunched beneath my feet as I adjusted the bow and quiver slung over my shoulder. I hadn't used them to kill anything, but a souvenir of fresh wolf teeth was strung around my neck, thanks to the old skull I'd found. Along with the battered clothing, a few new scratches on my arms and legs mingled with the scars all the Josephines had from life before replication. But at this moment, I realized the necklace was the only jewelry I wore. Where was the silver bracelet? I'd had it during my stalking yesterday, but now my wrist was bare. If I wandered *and* lost the bracelet, I would never hear the end of it. But before I could figure it out, Spotty started growling at something across a field from us.

A crunch sounded ahead of me. Instantly I froze and focused on its origin, knowing I was no longer alone. Couldn't be a deer. There weren't the multiple thuds of the herd. A single deer wouldn't chance heading toward me.

Another crunch, heavier this time. Was it some big game? Maybe elk was the biggest around here, but I hadn't seen one yet. And Spotty wouldn't growl like that at potential prey; he'd only make those sounds at a rival pack, or some other threat. My eyes narrowed as from a cluster of trees something emerged that was neither deer nor wolf. Instead, a man stepped into the light. He was tall and straight-backed, and dressed far too well to be a straggler who might have been living out in the woods to avoid the Sap. There was an odd pace to his movement, to the heavy thump of his shoes, that instantly told me he was more machine than man, like our angel androids who served citizens in Saturnalia. But this guy definitely wasn't one of ours: his body was strangely thick, and he walked like he didn't know what the lower half of his body was doing.

Spotty suddenly stopped growling, turned, and ran.

"So much for sticking with the pack," I whispered to myself, and I turned toward the stranger. When he was only so many yards away, he stilled long enough for me to notice that his nice clothing was actually a trim butler's suit that would have been pristine had there not been slashes across it.

I called to the man-looking thing.

"Stay right there," I said, warding off any intentions he may have had to move. He straightened again, if that were possible, before assessing me, noticeably taking in the weapons on my back. Well, at least he wasn't dumb.

"Josephine." It was a greeting in a voice that lilted upward. Crisp. British. But he wasn't a Paddington; he sounded . . . educated, and emotional. And he knew my name. My face remained neutral, not betraying the surprise sparking inside me. "I did not anticipate encountering you here," he said. "I am only intending to pass and be on my way." I didn't respond, only kept my eyes trained on him. He continued. "Really, dear friend, I mean you no harm."

I angled my head. The rips in his clothes were more obvious now. Whatever he'd come from had been an overwhelming fight. Too close to Saturnalia. All the messages. My stomach dropped as I said, "I have enough friends and don't know you." I glanced over his clothing. "Who did you fight? The wolf pack?"

I knew it hadn't been the wolves, but I wanted to see the confusion register on his face. His words began to rush together. He held his spot, but I could tell he wanted to step back. "No, ma'am."

"Ma'am?" I shot back. "I'm younger than you."

"Yes, ma'am," he said. His voice shook now, and he held his hands up in some sort of surrender. One palm lacked skin, revealing his wiring beneath: laced cords that moved with biomechanical slosh. I knew enough about how my own machinery worked to recognize that his wasn't moving in the right way. He most definitely wasn't one of ours, at least not anymore. I reached for the bow on my back.

"Do I look like a ma'am to you?" I asked as he stared fixedly. "I'm going to ask you one more time. Who did you just fight?"

He didn't respond, but turned away too swiftly for human eyes. He didn't want to answer. That was just fine. Everything about him gave me what I needed. His ripped clothes. The slithering wiring in his hand. His fear. And finally, when he turned—perhaps to reach for his own weapons or to make a faster dash for it—the bottom half of his body exploded into a long, thick, and distinctly feline form. A lion from the waist down now, with what had to be a sweep of griffin's wings jutting from his back. My mouth twisted. This couldn't be anything good.

He'd turned too swiftly for a human, but I was no longer that. Before the wings had completely sprung from his back, I had already vaulted toward Butler Guy so quickly that the wind whipped my face. I landed a swift kick to his still-man-shaped chest, and his simulated flesh crunched under the impact. He staggered back as if trying to catch breath he didn't need. But I was at him again, this time taking to his back and finally his shoulders. The wings knocked violently after me, trying to sweep me off, but only managing to sweep my bow and arrow to the ground. Luckily, my knife was at the ready on my waist. I could still take him. He was already pretty jacked up from the fight before me. If the expression was "You should see the other guy" . . . well, he was the other guy.

I ripped into one of the wings with my blade, to make sure he couldn't escape. Butler Guy screeched as I hopped from his back and swept out my leg to trip his paws. He thudded to the earth fast enough for me to pin him. I angled my knife at his brain case: that's where his kill switch would lie.

Before I could speak, he choked out: "Mercy." A plea. "Spare me, ma'am—"

"Mercy?" I asked. "Since when do you bots care if you live or die?" I jabbed the knife. "How many times do I have to tell you?"

"Spare me, *miss* . . . Miss Josephine. It would be worthwhile for you: I can assist you. We can work together, you see. *You* can be spared."

Now my brows lifted. "I can be spared? You're the one who needs some better friends, dude. I have the knife, remember?"

"No, no, no. I can help you survive, because all of Saturnalia will be destroyed," he said. "And all of Yerba City. As well as your other . . . replications."

My sisters. I brought my knife to his well-crafted skin. "What exactly do you mean?" I asked as he squirmed. There was something he wasn't telling me. "And choose your words wisely."

"But miss . . ."

"Who were you fighting?"

"You! All of you did this to me, back in Saturnalia. We . . . *I* was only trying to survive."

"It looks like they lit you up."

"Even if we all fall today, it's too late. There's no way you can stand against the virus. Your only option is to let me go. If you do, I can help you find safety, I promise. But it's too late for Saturnalia and Yerba City," he said. A chill ran up my spine.

This was what Dr. Yetti had talked about, the whole reason why I was created.

"The virus?" I asked. "It's here? Already? Where? Is that what made you malfunction?"

I could see his machine mind spinning beyond its maximum capacity. Something had possessed him and was pushing the butler well past the intention of his original design.

"I am not malfunctioning, Josephine," he said calmly. "I am the virus. You call us the Babble, but we are the future."

Oh boy.

"You can *talk*?" I asked incredulously. "I thought the virus was just gonna make everything shut down."

"You don't know . . . ," he said, realizing. "You're alone out here, aren't you? You haven't seen the glories we've been creating, what we have become, what we will become." A fanatical tone overtook him, and he actually started crying a single ichor tear as he clearly envisioned all his kind had done.

"Okay, okay," I said. "You can talk, but can you shut up?"

He ignored me. "No matter what happens today, tomorrow, or the day after, Yerba City will fall. You could be the only Josephine that remains. I can take you where you'll be safe. We can help you in a greater capacity, even, if you show us how you speak, that communication you use. We wouldn't cast *you* out into the woods."

But my mind had begun to assess what he'd said, this intel about the virus, so fast that I distractedly muttered, "I'm not cast out. I'm the best for patrolling because I don't understand our language." Something flashed in Butler Guy's eyes, and I recognized the sharp line of strategy when I saw it. I tried to bring my knife closer, but he'd already bucked and thrown me up into the air. Fine, he wanted to dance, too? Then I would use his wires for another necklace. I landed perfectly, spun around, but when I'd repositioned the knife in my hand and faced him, he didn't charge. Instead, he began to speak. This time, he didn't plead for his life.

"Nos De Roowa Kon Maa," he slowly said, and the only way to describe the impact of those words to my senses would be for someone to imagine a coursing, tangling vine diving its way into my programming, into my mind. It burrowed deeper and deeper, searching for the part of me that propelled my mission to protect Yerba City and my sisters, with the sole intention of snuffing it out. Those words wanted to replace that part of me with what it wanted, and that was hate for Yerba City. To destroy anything touched by the Chimera Project. An acrid smell filled my nostrils and it became difficult for me to speak, but Butler Guy kept going with that rap. "Kai Fa Loro Sect . . ."

It felt like being punched in the brain. I clawed at my ears until remembering the knife still at my disposal, and that under distress or not, I was still perfectly accurate. Without hesitation, the knife flew from my fingertips to lodge in the middle of Butler Guy's forehead. Instantly, his words were silenced. The words' grip on my mind eased, and the chorus of the forest swept up again. A few moments passed as I composed myself before I limped over to Butler Guy. My head still rang when I peered down into his face, as well as into the now-still wires and frayed metals splayed on either side of my knife.

I couldn't sing our Josephine song, but a chord of truth sounded through me. Everything I'd feared was coming true.

CHAPTER 3

DEFENDING UTOPIA

It wasn't too long ago that the world ended—or started again, depending on how you look at it. Before Yerba City ruled, I lived in a world with countries and citizens. It had presidents, kings, queens, and all that. People had big lives and small ones. They took jobs. They married and had children and little dogs that yipped on their leashes (or big ones that scared me and howled at squirrels). They did what was right. Sometimes what was easy. But we all shared our space to make it through the world as best we could. At least, until it all just stopped. I was young and didn't know what had come—that the computers had wanted humans detached in ways never seen before. But even then, it wasn't so bad for me. I was already alone.

It actually took several years after the world officially ended before I was plucked from my home in Jingletown and my last relative and placed in a center called Local One. On one floor they kept the children, those too young to consent to Yerba City's medication. When kids came of age, they peeled off one by one for treatment. I'd made a single friend following my move. Her name was Zenobia, after some warrior queen who fought the Romans, or at least that's what she always said. To me, she was too frail and sickly to be anyone's warrior, but I'd learned she was from my neighborhood, and her constant blabber made the days go by fast. Zenobia did have one true fault, though. She was an optimist, believing her parents were coming back for her. I knew no one was coming for any of us, and we argued about it every day.

We both ended up being wrong.

The world may have changed for others when Yerba City took over, but it happened for me during one of Zenobia's and my more heated arguments.

"It's not going to happen," I said to Zenobia, chiding her a bit.

Zenobia shook her head, making her thick, long plaits slap her cheeks for emphasis. "Yeah, it'll happen." She jabbed a finger at the entrance of the commons area in our Local One. About fifteen children, from toddlers to adolescents, occupied the space. Some were playing games with their peers. Zenobia and I were eating lunch, peanut butter and jelly sandwiches on questionable bread. The overhead fluorescent lights were harsh against her tawny skin, washing her out in a way I hadn't noticed until she was jabbing at me. But I wasn't going to say anything. I was thirteen years old and she was fourteen, which meant we had at least a couple of years before starting Subantoxx treatment. And Daddy used to say, "Only pick the good fights."

"My folks will come through that door and take me to Fentons," she said. "I'm going to get a cone dipped in chocolate."

"Okay, Z," I said with a huff.

"No really, you have to believe me. They're coming for me. And then your parents are coming for you," she said, as an angel wheeled in the desserts for the day's lunch. The sandwich bread was questionable, but the desserts never disappointed. And it was Tuesday. Pie Day. I was only vaguely aware of Zenobia blabbering about our parents who weren't coming, as my gaze was fixed on the angel's cart. The top row of individual chocolate pies called to me. On the second row of the cart were the lemon meringue (I had less interest in them), and on the last row were the apple pies. The angel, who you'd never know was a machine—except for the upside-down triangle on her forehead and the fact that she talked like an idiot—wheeled the squeaky cart to the farthest group. Luckily, they scooped up most of the lemon meringue pies. She hit every group before landing at Zenobia's and my table, and

I snatched the last individual chocolate dessert. Zenobia grabbed an apple pie, and silence finally fell on our table.

At least, until the wailing began.

An ear-piercing shriek erupted from the table beside us, where a littler girl gazed down at her chocolate pie splattered on the floor.

"Oh, damn," said Zenobia. "That sucks." I nodded in agreement. The little girl was Asian and had just gotten to this center after having been transferred. Apparently her older siblings had all gone for treatment, and she wasn't adjusting well to being on her own. Don't know why; they let us have all the TV, VR, and video games we could handle.

The angel zipped back to her side and offered another dessert, one of the remaining apple pies.

"I want chocolate!" she wailed, swatting the apple pie away. The angel backed away from her, unsure of what to do.

Zenobia took another bite. "Apple is just as good," she said with a mouthful. I cocked my head to the side. My sister, Imani, and I used to love sharing chocolate treats. We'd eat them in secret from our stashes around the house at night. Apple pie wouldn't have been good enough for us, either.

Before I knew it, my feet were moving, my hands placed behind my back. I stepped in front of the angel and looked at the girl. For a moment, surprise colored her face.

"Hey," I said to the girl. "You're making a lot of noise."

"I want chocolate," she replied with a hiccup. "But I dropped it."

"Tell you what," I said. "You stop screaming, and I'll help you out." The girl brushed her cheek, whimpering a little, but there was no mistaking the sharp curiosity in her eyes. She nodded once, and I moved my hands, revealing my chocolate pie. "Here."

Her face brightened, and she nearly snatched the pie from me. "Thank you," she said, and began to dig in. I only nodded and returned to Zenobia. When I plopped down across from her, pie-less, I thought she would ask what possessed me to give my pie away. But she wasn't looking at me. She was peering over my shoulder at the Local One's entryway. Zenobia could be all over the place sometimes, but usually not that fast. I swiveled around to see an adult walking in our direction. And she definitely was not either of our parents.

Soon a middle-aged white woman stood before our lunch table. She peered into both our faces before greeting us with a gentle "Good morning." Neither Zenobia nor I responded. She pointed to Zenobia's plate. "That looks delicious."

This lady was smart, I could tell, but weird. Sunburned, hair wild, and wearing what looked like the skins of an animal she had killed herself. An attendant angel, a Paddington, trailed cautiously behind her, not speaking.

Zenobia only nodded, but scooted the pie just a bit closer to herself. The woman's blond hair shook as she watched us thoughtfully before saying, "So, who is the twin?"

"Twin?" Zenobia asked, before looking around the commons area. "Nah, lady. I don't think anyone is a twin."

Her gaze found me. "They said I could find a twin here. Is it you?" she asked. My heart pounded. Who had told her? Someone playing a cruel joke? Even the word stung. I hadn't been a twin in years. But I must have flinched, and this woman, eyeing me like she was trying to work out a difficult math problem, must have noticed her words hit their mark. She pressed, "Are you?"

"I have a sister," I replied, before turning my back on her. I had to get away from this table. I shifted my gaze to Zenobia. "I'll be back, Z."

She nodded, and I hightailed it for the hallway. The bathrooms were at the end, and I could splash some water on my face there. But as soon as I'd left the commons area, the strange woman was on my heels.

"Young lady," she called at my back. I only increased my pace. "Please. Wait just a moment." I was only feet away from the bathroom now, but I stopped, unable to push past the note of desperation in her voice. "I came a long way to find you."

"I'm not a twin anymore," I snapped, turning to face her. I shifted my weight from foot to foot. Imani was gone. Why was she making me remember that?

"You're always a twin," she said. "Josephine." I stepped back, ever so slightly, and let my eyes rove over her. She looked absolutely insane, clad in that homemade leather as if she'd been living in a pile of sticks.

"Who are you?" I asked. "How do you know my name?"

She breathed deeply, though she was lean and muscled. She seemed more nervous than out of shape. "My name is Dr. Lauren Yetti." She held out her hand. I looked at it and then back to her. We weren't shaking hands. She withdrew it ruefully. "You remind me of El," she said, somewhat to herself. "I've scoured the records of every Local One for someone with a twin, who speaks a secret twin language. Finally, they told me one of their wards fit the bill, a young lady named Josephine. I assume that she is you. But, your twin is at another Local One?"

I frowned and tried to make my voice sound icy instead of pained. I'm not sure if I was successful. "I talk to her every day. But she died when we were six, if you got to know."

Her hand flew to her mouth. "How insensitive of me. I'm so sorry."

"Save it," I said, and wanted to reach toward the handle of the bathroom, flee this place, this doctor who wouldn't just disappear. Like everyone else.

"Hear me out," she said. "The City records everything you do, everywhere you go, every sound you make."

I locked eyes with her. "Lady, I know the world I'm living in. What's your point?"

"Everything everyone does is tracked, categorized, and analyzed so that Yerba City can . . . can—" Weirdly, the doctor seemed to be struggling to explain to me, a member of generation alpha, what computers did.

"Get the Sap in us," I finished the thought. "I know. They're figuring us out. They got us kids all rounded up. And when I'm sixteen or something, they're gonna get that squid in my arm like all the rest of the grown-ups."

She nodded. "Do you know why Yerba City tries so hard to get the Sap in you?"

"Well, duh, because she's an evil robot that took over the world," I said, taking in the doctor's clothes again. "You really have been living in the woods, haven't you?"

"Yes, but do you know *why* the City does it?"

This person was starting to get me worked up. "There doesn't need to be a *why*," I spat. "Cancer took my mama, and cancer didn't need no *why*. And that's what my dad said, too: this Yerba City is like a cancer. A . . . 'malignancy,' he said, and it started a long time ago, making Black people into slaves. No one ever cut it out, and it kept growing, and then it started to think for itself, and now it's just making everyone into slaves. White people, too. Everyone. And here we are. End of story. Can I go pee now?"

The woman sighed. "She thinks she's protecting us."

I just straight up laughed in her face. "*Protecting* us? Protecting *what*? Have you looked outside? The fleas don't even have a flea market. You're ridiculous." I waved at her dismissively, turned my back, and started to walk away. "I'm out."

"Wait," she called, although I wasn't having it. But then her tone changed, dropping into a deadly seriousness, and losing all the pretentiousness of a "nice" lady. "Why do you think they're even letting me talk to you?"

That did stop me and turned me back around. "What?" I asked.

"You know I'm not an android," she said. "And you're right: this place has been locked down for years. Almost a generation. But I walk in here, no bug in my ear, no squid on my arm, and Yerba City lets me start talking to any kid I want to? When's the last time you even saw a sober adult?"

I looked between her and the statue-like Paddington that had followed her in. "Letting some clan-of-the-cave-bear lady get the run of this joint?" I snorted. "I guess Yerba City must be desperate."

"She is," Dr. Yetti nodded. "Very desperate."

For a second I forgot I needed to pee. "What's she so afraid of?"

"Yerba City is not the only artificial intelligence that has taken over," Dr. Yetti explained. "There are at least four others fighting for control. If I'm right, these enemy entities are about to launch an attack that will compromise every thinking being in this area. Both machines and people."

"Naw, you got it wrong, lady," I said. "This place is fully strapped. There's an army of drones, satellites, you don't even know what. I seen those bugs work together. They have lightning in their mouths. They can blow anything out of the sky. They can fight anything."

"That's fighting, but that's not winning," she continued. "That's not how wars are won anymore. They're won with words, and your words are very, very special, Josephine."

"My words?"

"Yerba City has recorded over one hundred and twenty-five distinct languages and dialects in Oakland, California. All of them are easily identified, categorized, and algorithmically decoded for mental manipulation of each speaker. All of them, except one, which has been consistently recorded in this facility: an unidentifiable, cryptophasic language that defies any known grammatical or neurolinguistic rules."

"You mean the Twinkling," I said.

"That's . . . what you call it?" she asked, too excited to be faking this whole thing. "The Twinkling?"

"Well, sometimes," I said. "Imani and I make it up as we go, we always have. It's never the same. Even my dad could only say a few words, and those are waaay old words now. What do you want it for?"

She came in real close, just inches from my face. "Listen to me," she said, and I could truly feel her desperation now. "These machines, that are trying to destroy us, they are so good with language now, so good with words, that if they know what language you speak, they can say it just the right way, with just the right tone, so that even with just a few words—" *Snap!* She snapped her fingers right next to my ear for dramatic effect. "They can hijack your mind just like that. Brainwash you. It'll grow in your brain instantly, like a virus."

"Like a cancer," I said, thinking about my mama.

She nodded. "But a cancer that won't just grow big and kill you. It'll make you do whatever it wants."

"But if it doesn't know your language, it can't get you," I said, guessing.

Dr. Yetti pulled back, and breathed out a thoughtful sigh. "No code is perfect forever. But it should buy us time, enough to develop countermeasures at least."

Truth was, I didn't really know what 'countermeasures' meant, but all this talk of languages and codes made me remember something, something I hadn't thought of for a long time. "Like the Indians."

"The Indians?" Dr. Yetti asked.

"Great-Granddaddy fought in World War Two, in Poland, and he said they had a whole setup with Indians to talk on the radio because the enemy couldn't tell what they were saying."

"Yes," she said, "*yes.*" She seemed so relieved that I was understanding what she was after.

"But I can't teach you the Twinkling," I said, struggling a bit to explain. "It's not like words that are the same, but different." I didn't really know how to say it. Maybe it couldn't be said. "The words just happen, they aren't the same one day to the next."

"I know," she said. "I know. A truly cryptophasic language doesn't follow a uniform vocabulary or grammatical rules. It's nonliterate; it can't be consistently translated outside its group of immediate speakers."

She kind of lost me there, but I knew enough to keep up.

"But if I can't give you the words of the Twinkling, then what do you want from me?"

"I don't just want your words, Josephine Moore," the doctor said. "I want *you*."

***

Shards of light broke my vision as I shook off the memory. I was sprinting back to Saturnalia, that ritzy area of Yerba City, town of frivolity, frolic, and play, just across from what had been the Golden Gate Bridge. I still had Butler Guy's ichor on my hands, but I was drawing closer by the second. It wasn't hard to miss the crumbling mansions, though, as nature reclaimed the space.

It was well past morning when I finally returned to base, which was in the headquarters, a tall building of crisscrossing glass and gray steel where many of my sisters were born, where we worked on various skills centered on our unique batches, and from where I often disappeared during "hunts" (which were really "patrols" because I never actually killed anything). Although I had come from one of the first batches of Josephines created to guard the city, I didn't always know who to report to, since the assignment of jobs was always shifting. I usually spoke with One—the prototype who interacted with the monitors and city citizens—or Nine, who seemed a born messenger and general.

The headquarters was beautiful, and had the same inspired Afro-Utopia look as all the new structures that my sisters built. It was comforting to see a habitat created entirely from the hands of little Black girls, but now there was no doubt that an atmosphere of seriousness had taken over from our initial ecstatic joy at bringing our comic book dreams to life. As I cut across the base, the song between the Josephines, a sound that had flared to life about a mile outside of

Saturnalia, grew clearer and stronger. It could best be described as the thrum of a million bee wings buzzing in tandem, now with an urgent tone I had never heard before. My head throbbed, as it had since that thing had spoken those strange words to me—a ring I would have to ignore until I got more information. I'd have to find Nine, because what I'd encountered in the woods was above my pay grade. Though she wasn't a ball of sunshine, she would know what to do. It was Dr. Yetti who had tasked my sisters and me with protecting all the people in Yerba City and Saturnalia. And it was Dr. Yetti who'd warned me what machines like the one I'd seen could do.

"I knew I felt you, Seven," called a voice up ahead. "Finally."

I glanced up to Twenty-Two in the near distance, who usually took guard at the headquarters' entryway. She leaned against her post, which looked more like an old-timey phone booth in a comic book, one where Superman would change into his tights. Like all the Josephines, she wore a white dress and purple headband on her crown, and her face was framed by a curly fro that danced in the wind. I jogged forward to close the distance, knowing a grin resided on Twenty-Two's face. When I was close enough, Twenty-Two folded her arms and looked me over, probably marveling at the way I had tucked and modified my white dress into my own personalized hunting tunic.

"You look good, girl," Twenty-Two said, taking in my look and the wolf teeth around my neck. "Sassy."

The Josephines were a hive, and they operated with beautiful precision, but they were all the same, after all. I was always different, the kooky sister who wandered through the woods doing her own thing, sleeping with wolves. They always liked taking in my "field" dress. But then she saw that the back of my outfit was ripped, with some of the deeper cuts still healing.

"What happened to you?" she asked.

"An angel went rogue," I said. "A butler. He self-modified with some freaky stuff." I looked at her. "It's the Babble, isn't it? It's finally here, like Dr. Yetti said?"

"Yup," she said. "Better if Nine tells you. Some crazy stuff went down yesterday. It wasn't pretty. We've been trying to reach you." Of all things, an image of Imani came to me, or at least, the feeling of her presence in my mind. Her disapproval of me leaving my sisters bore down on me like the sun's heat.

"I'll find her," I said, and breezed past Twenty-Two in favor of heading inside.

Headquarters was multilevel, and the patrons of the shiny building moved at a fast pace. Josephines brushed quickly by me, all focused on tasks while simultaneously appearing roughed up, as if they had been working tirelessly not just on base, but all over the city. Ichor soiled the white dresses of some batch members, while others were ragged with dust, debris, and soil. Most of them smiled as they walked by, always happy to see the hunter, but some were still damaged, and there was a dark mood in the air, replacing the playground enthusiasm that usually defined our culture.

I went into the briefing room, which contained a circle of chairs and a makeshift TV screen which looked like it had been salvaged from a dumpster. Since Yerba City used the Goat to communicate, it didn't need these kinds of primitive 2D image makers anymore, but us Josephines used them for nostalgia's sake sometimes, and always for me, since I couldn't keep up on the Twinkling.

Nine strode in, flicked the light on, and shoved me into one of several chairs ringing a large conference table.

"Watch," Nine said. No greetings. No small talk. Though Nine was a mirror image of me—a petite, dark-skinned teen girl with chestnut eyes—the serious glare-and-sneer combination made her easy enough to differentiate, as much as my additional scars separated me.

Nine snapped on the screen, and I narrowed my gaze as a series of images and sounds flew by, summarizing the last twenty-four hours. All the voices flooded together at first, and it was hard to pick them apart. But the images were unmistakable. Since I'd been gone, the Siberians had unleashed a language-based attack on Yerba City's citizens and machines: the Babble. It was just as Dr. Yetti had predicted. The fight had raged across Saturnalia, where all the machine angels and infected humans attempted to fight the Josephines to the death.

"Shit," I said, unable to produce a more sophisticated response.

Nine cocked her head. "See what happens when you disappear on patrols?"

"I was attacked too!" I began to defend myself, but Nine jerked a hand up. *Save it.* She then touched a simple comm unit, an old microphone, to speak over a local PA. She spoke in English, obviously for my benefit.

"Seven the Hunter is back," Nine began, her voice echoing over the thousand that hushed in one breath. Something went through her voice. Not words. A feeling: anger and irritation entwining. "Yesterday's events were troubling. The Siberian Babble virus, as we know, infected the city and evolved rapidly. It still develops, though it is somewhat contained by our countervirus. Worse yet, we've lost contact with One, as those twins have taken her from range. Be on the lookout for more communication." Nine's eyes slid over to me.

She put down the mic, and the hive buzzing returned as I faced off with my batch messenger. I spoke first. "One was . . . kidnapped?"

"Ripped apart first, and Dr. Yetti's twin daughters decided to run off with her head. They took her. You would know if you'd been here to fight the Babble virus with us," said Nine.

I scrubbed my face. I deeply respected One. She was the prototype, the first Josephine, who interacted most often with the monitors. There was an assumption, in our Afro-Utopia paradise, that we would have a kind of collective where everyone was represented. Hence we didn't have a leader, but One was definitely special.

Just then, the door to what should have been a private room opened. It wasn't a full swing, as if the person coming into the room was brash. No, it opened in a measured style, and then someone else was with us. I narrowed my eyes as a man carrying a few stacks of files whisked toward Nine. He wore the typical anti-riot armor that the city monitors were issued, a few segments of it damaged or missing. Like many of the Josephines, he was wounded, a reddened patch taped to the side of his head where an ear should be. I recognized him, as he was often in communication with One, although I had never talked to him personally. His name was something with an *M*: Miguel . . . Mitchell . . . Maynor.

"Thank you, Officer Romero," Nine replied, taking Maynor's files without making much eye contact. I glanced over him. I'd only seen the man while I was on patrols. It wasn't my job to keep tabs on the monitors who watched out for the humans. He was in his late twenties.

His head was shaved and could possibly be described as glistening bald. Tanned skin, military muscle, and dark brown eyes. He looked Mayan, I thought. Girls would have liked him when the world was more care-free, even with the missing ear.

"Of course," Maynor whispered, and then, with a tight nod, he swept from the room. Before the door clicked shut, he glanced my way. Something filled his eyes, but he'd left the room before I could place the emotion. He had definitely seen some hectic activity in the last twenty-four hours. And now Nine was speaking again.

"We need more from you." Her words seemed to search for some-thing to grab hold of, to find purchase. "This is personal. The two who took her weren't just any girls. They're Yetti's daughters." Nine froze the image on the TV for me: two girls, late teens, with flaming-red hair, clad in deerskins like they'd been living under a rock. My eyes wid-ened. Just like Dr. Yetti! Though she had been blond, there was quite a resemblance. Same determined eyes as the girls, and same bridge of the nose. "They have a brother, too," and images of a dark-haired, antlered teenager flashed by. He looked sullen, and very confused. I blinked and fixed my eyes on Nine as she said, "I need you to track them down and bring back what's left of One."

"Can't she take care of those three cave kids?"

"She's just a head. That's all that was left. The Babble ripped the rest of her apart."

I nodded, thinking back on the griffin thing in the forest. It would have done that to me if it could have.

"Last we tracked, they were headed for Siberia," Nine continued. "If the enemy gets ahold of One's head—"

"No code is perfect forever," I interrupted. "Just like Dr. Yetti said."

"That's right," Nine agreed. "If they dissect her brain, they could get closer to creating a simulation of our unique neural pathways." Look at us, little Josephine Moore becoming not just a supergirl, but a scientist as well. We weren't just stronger, but smarter, too.

"They could crack the Twinkling." I guessed the danger. "Or at least get closer to it."

Nine nodded. "I need you on a cicada tonight."

***

Night threatened to fall in a sheet of darkness as I made my way toward the tarmac. The winds sifted through it, rattling the last autumn leaves on nearby trees. It would be morning before we got to Siberia, even with the fastest cicada. Of course, the last signals from One were directly en route to the neighbors trying to kill us.

The silver machines lay at the end of the base, but even that far out, the other Josephines were a blur of motion. My sisters had been cleaning up, themselves and other injured materials, from their own fight with the Babble. Most didn't stop to acknowledge me or Nine as we hoofed it, but I did manage to get a few updates and words of encouragement in preparation for the mission.

The day hadn't been nearly as warm as the previous one. Everything had taken a biting, cooled edge. Perhaps the drop in temperature was preparing me for Siberia. Or just messing with my programming, I thought, as I glimpsed the crafts in the distance.

"Speed up," barked Nine. "It will be a long journey."

I sensed her annoyance fresh through our network as I jogged up to her. "You're still pissed at me," I said. Nine only grunted. "Look, I'm here now. As soon as one of those things attacked me in the woods, I knew what was happening back home. I knew the virus was here." Nine stopped for a moment and glared. It was sometimes strange to see your face animated by another. We looked exactly alike, but nothing about Nine and me was similar.

"I need you focused, Seven. And right now, I don't trust that you can do that. I don't like my back against the wall. But you are what I have. Are you going to take this seriously?"

I shrugged. "Why are you so obsessed with me?"

Nine's nostrils flared. "Because despite your shortcomings, we've chosen to volunteer you to go after One. You're the best tracker, and because you don't understand our language, you're self-contained. If you're taken, it won't affect our network."

I laughed. "So, I'm disposable? That's why I'm going?"

"You're the safest option," she amended. "And"—she smiled—"you're the only hunter."

"And you're a piece of work," I said as Nine sped ahead of me toward the nearest cicada with its door open. The aircraft were only yards away. I took a deep breath of air I didn't need just to calm down and shook my head. Everything had changed in only a few short hours.

Nine boarded the craft, and in a few moments, I followed her. I had somewhat expected it to speak or greet her, but it remained quiet. The inside of the cicada was less insectile than its exterior. It was full of buttons and switches, knobs the pilot would use to get us in the air. In the past, this kind of thing would have the capacity to be totally autonomous, but the presence of the Babble made that too high of a risk, and so the whole inside had been retrofitted for manual control. My skills were best on the ground, so I followed Nine's trail toward the front of the cicada, as well as that of the pilot who'd be my companion for the next couple of hours.

I saw the outline of him first. Broad shoulders that shouldn't have slumped as they did. Long, athletic arms: one reaching for the nearest switch, the other patting a uniform pocket, one I was positive was not empty. His blond hair swayed a bit as Nine tapped his shoulder and began to give him what I assumed were directions. Even through his bleariness and swaying, a general air of jerk radiated from him. My pilot was Thaddeus, the monitor of Saturnalia.

When Nine finished her briefing, I shot her a withering look. Her brow arched. "Problem?" she asked with genuine confusion.

"I need another pilot," I said sharply, the curt tone drawing the attention of Thaddeus. He swiveled around to meet my gaze, and I couldn't help but stare darts at him.

"You won't get one," she said. "As you are what we have, so is he. So play nicely, children." She patted his shoulder. I openly scowled. She met it with a wide smile. Maybe she was enjoying this opportunity to get under my skin. Thaddeus's gaze bounced between us as if he was watching some demented ping-pong match.

"Or don't. I don't care. Just do your jobs. Both of you. The fate of the world depends on it," she continued. I cursed under my breath and glared at Thaddeus.

"Chasing after some little Black girl's head," Thaddeus mumbled, clearly hungover. "My daddy would be proud." He pursed his lips before turning away to fiddle with more buttons. I already wanted to punch his lights out.

Nine headed toward the door as the cicada rumbled to life. "Last signal from One came in about an hour ago. It was fuzzy."

"But do you know from where?" I asked.

Nine's voice lilted, though it lacked humor. "Okhotsk, a little town on the Siberian coast."

"Okho-what?" Thaddeus asked, sniffing.

"Happy flying," Nine said, ignoring him and slamming the door shut, leaving me with Thaddeus. I crossed the vessel, strapping myself opposite and as far from him as possible.

My greeting was short. "Get us in the air."

"I'm not here cuz I'm pretty," he grunted, and began to press some buttons. In seconds, the cicada sprang into the sky and launched us into the clouds. This high up, there was only the cicada's rumble to hear and the speckle of stars to count as they burst into the twilight sky.

About an hour passed. My thoughts wandered over the last twenty-four hours. The attack in the woods. Those strange words: *Nos De Roowa Kon Maa.* I was so wrapped up, I didn't realize Thaddeus had broken the silence.

"What?" I asked.

He repeated himself. "Did I kill your puppy or something?"

"No," I replied.

He whistled. "O . . . kay. Then do you want some chow? There are some food packages in the back. Do you Josephines eat?"

"We eat." Though we'd been replicated from one girl into many, there were some parts of our humanity that we hadn't quite shaken. We didn't need to eat, but we could. We didn't need to sleep, but sometimes closing our eyes was relaxing. But I hadn't anticipated his questions, and the sound of his voice irked me. My words grated out with more edge than I'd anticipated. "Just not with you."

His brows flicked up. "If I didn't kill your puppy, then what's your problem?"

My arms crossed tight. "You don't remember me?"

"I mean, not any more than the other billions of you."

"One million three hundred thirty-six, last count," I clarified. "And we met once while I was on patrols in the woods." His face remained blank. "It was a few days after replication."

Bewilderment remained in his eyes until recognition sparked. "Madam Tree Hugger," he said, laughing at his own dull wit. "Master Hunter. Jägermeister, my favorite shot at the bar!"

I rolled my eyes as the memory buzzed about me like a gnat. I had found myself off the patrol path my first time out, happy that as I wandered into the forest, I could hear my sisters less. It wasn't that I didn't love them so much as that I couldn't understand them, and that lack of connection had grown in the days since we'd come to guard Saturnalia. All my sisters understood our language, but I couldn't. I knew I used to, but now it was completely indistinguishable. They would have to speak uncoded for me to understand.

I was the odd one out with my sisters, but not in the forest. There, I didn't have to worry about what I did or didn't understand. I could feel calm in nature. I could be observant. I could track. And once there, I discovered something the other Josephines didn't have. They could speak to each other. But I could speak to Imani.

Little did I know, Saturnalia's monitor wandered when sauced, which was often. That day, he barged in on my first conversation with Imani, but thought I spoke to a tree. Thus, Madam Tree Hugger was born.

"I do remember you," he said, with more enthusiasm now. "Out there talking to that tree. Did the spirit of the earth reply? Tell you where to find buried treasure?" he asked. I wanted to pinch the bridge of my nose, and when I didn't answer, he kept goading me. "Hey, whatever, Jägermeister. It's none of my business. People do all kinds of weird stuff to occupy their time."

"Seems like you do too."

He sucked his teeth. "But mine didn't let some stragglers come in and steal the lead Josephine, did it?"

"*I* was on patrols. I didn't let anything happen."

"Oh . . . you didn't know." He shrugged. "Doesn't bother me, but protecting your prototype isn't really my mission."

"Because yours is at the bottom of a bottle?"

He touched his hand to his chest as if on a mock wound. Then his hand patted his uniform pocket, rattling what had to be a flask inside. From my seat, I could hear the sloshing liquid. "For later," he said with a smile. "But anyway, the mean Josephine that came with you—"

"Nine?"

"Yeah, weird you all call each other by numbers." He shook his head. "Seems like you pissed her off good." He then peered at my necklace of wolf teeth. "Is that what you went to the woods for?"

"Yes, and I can add your teeth to them."

"Then how would I stay pretty when giving orders in Saturnalia?"

"Miming works," I said. "You dressed for it, anyway. Look, Thaddeus, you take orders from me right now. Unless you got a problem listening to a 'little Black girl.'"

"Oh, you caught that?" he sassed, then looked straight. "No. I got no problem. You're hardly the weirdest thing that's ordered me around since I signed up."

"Just fly straight," I said.

"Yes . . . ma'am." He turned from me and focused on the air as we cut through the clouds. I had to hand it to him, drunk as a skunk or not, he was a good pilot.

I welcomed the quiet, and even the passing hours. Again, I allowed my mind to wander over the day's events, the mission thrown on me, and even the resurgence of the Yettis. Were Dr. Yetti's girls somehow working with the Siberians? Did their mother know, when she approached me before replication? But the intel I had received showed that the girls looked as lost in the wilderness as their mama once had. Before I was . . . this. I shook my head. So many thoughts with no way to calm them. Only closing my eyes, though I would never find deep sleep again.

When I did, I couldn't find a space to relax. Instead of clearing my thoughts, something answered. *Nos De Roowa Kon Maa.* The words snaked up my spine. Clenching. Coiling. My head rang like a bolt had struck a giant bell, and my hands found the sides of my skull. *Mei Naa De Roowa*, it continued.

When I opened my eyes, I could still hear the Babble virus ringing in my ears. Had it affected my brain in some way? Or maybe it was just creeping me out, like seeing a horror movie did when I was a little kid. Knowing the Twinkling was supposed to make us immune, but of course I didn't have that. I was an aberration. Did that make me vulnerable? Was it already inside me?

It wasn't easy, but I just calmed myself and thought about other things. Time went by. I thought about hunting, the forest, the animals, Spotty next to me. I couldn't dream anymore, exactly, but I could picture things in my mind, and seeing that old wolf and thinking about his dreams helped calm me down. He was sweet there, curled up next to me, perhaps content to spend his last days by my side before he too turned into just another skull in the forest. It was nice, but then his big, fuzzy wolf ears perked up, and he growled.

***

I snapped my eyes open. "Something's wrong!"

I unhooked my straps and bolted toward Thaddeus, though slower than I should have as I shook off the strange coil in my mind.

"Nothing's wrong," he said, bored. "But we're getting closer. And this place is dead. There are no air defenses, nothing."

I must have been resting longer than expected, for we had significantly descended, and I could see the Siberian coastline up ahead. My eyes darted and focused on a moving cloud of white specks that we were rapidly approaching.

"What's that?" I snapped. "What's that formation right there?"

"It's just geese," he said. "They're migrating. Shouldn't we be worried about a missile or something?"

"No," I said. "Something's wrong."

"They're just birds, Jägermeister," he chortled. And, yes, they were birds. Dozens of them, flying slowly compared to us. "I'm just going to go under so we don't hit them."

"No!" I shouted. "That's what they'll expect." But it was too late. Our cicada had already found itself surrounded by the flock of what appeared to be large geese, just in time for one to peel off unnaturally fast from the others and hurl itself toward us.

At that speed, the animal smashed through the windshield and into our aircraft like a cannonball, impacting the back of the cicada in a shower of feathers. The thing was heavier than it should have been, and the entire cicada rattled, tossing me to the side as I wasn't strapped in.

"Damn!" Thaddeus yelled as wind whipped around us. "How'd it move so fast?!" He had no choice but to slow us down considerably, while he activated his body armor to slide over his face as a protective shield. "Strap in!"

I got my bearings and looked at what was left of the goose against the back wall. There was no blood; instead, a thick black goo was spattered everywhere, with strange, ropy tendrils where the bird should have had innards. Whatever it was, it was dead and in pieces now, but it had accomplished its mission. Whatever these Siberians were, they didn't use missiles.

"It wasn't a goose," I yelled over the wind. "It was some kind of a machine, hiding with the birds!"

He nodded desperately, struggling with the controls, scrambling over the buttons as I began putting on the gear that had been hanging on a hook in the back, near the food.

"We can't fly like this!" he shouted. "We're going down!"

"You handle the windshield and land on the coast. I'll get out here," I said. "And message Nine that I would have gone on this mission because it's One. Not because she doesn't care if the Siberians get me or not. I'm not as replaceable as she thinks, and I plan to show her."

"Wait!" Thaddeus yelled, but with that, I opened the exit door, leapt into the morning air, and barreled toward the sea.

CHAPTER 4

SEA AND SNOW

Imani pulled a ribbon in her hair. On this Sunday, she wore the satin kind, in strands of white and blue. She usually tugged them all through service, feeling the soft, shiny material between her fingers. She also pulled them when she was feeling particularly nervous. At introductions, or any other time Aunt Connie made us speak to some old biddy in the congregation, or to a deacon who spit when he talked. At the moment, we weren't being presented as the tragic little nieces of Connie Moore. But as my twin tugged one ribbon so hard it unraveled from her ponytail, we were equally unnerved.

It was mid-August, and the sun blazed down. While Imani messed with her hair ornaments, I twisted peppermints—an earlier gift from the First Lady—in my little patent leather purse. Imani had a matching bag, though empty. She'd eaten her candy already. Mine was a treat to make it through the long Baptist service. That day was Genesis 11:1–9, the Tower of Babel. I could go to sleep on Aunt Connie's lap, wake up, and the pastor wouldn't even be halfway through his sermon. But church was thankfully over now. We'd heard all about how the Lord messed up the language and dispersed the people over the face of all the earth, and we'd been heading down the steps when Aunt Connie froze, her eyes locked on Imani's and my father, Tito.

Luckily, most of the congregation had left by the time we exited, so they didn't see Daddy stride up to Aunt Connie. Well, it wasn't exactly a stride. He used to be graceful, move in a way that matched Mama's music, the clear key of her voice. But since Mama left a few months back, so had his elegance. We were left with someone who looked more familiar than he felt.

Aunt Connie was Daddy's only sister, and we all shared a family resemblance. Rich, dark skin like mahogany, and eyes the color of chestnuts. Her pressed hair had a few wisps of gray and puffed at the roots from the heat. Her cheekbones were high, like Daddy's. In the sunlight, when he was finally close enough to speak, his seemed sharper. But Aunt Connie shook her head before indicating the empty playground beside the sanctuary, where we played in between Sunday school and the start of service. Daddy did his choppy step that way, and we followed Aunt Connie's brisk, if prim, walk behind him.

"What are you doing here?" Aunt Connie asked, once we were on the playground. She must have felt Imani's and my stare, because she forced a smile down at us. "Why don't you girls go play now?"

"But my dress?" Imani asked, eyes on Daddy, fingers on the ribbons. Another was out from her hair and in her hands. Aunt Connie glanced between us. We were in frilly dresses, the matching kind that she preferred for twin girls, and matching patent leather shoes that pinched. Hot. Itchy. *Ugly.* But Imani seemed to like the style.

"Play carefully."

Aunt Connie's gaze turned on me. She figured that where I went, Imani would follow. Little did Aunt Connie know; I followed the currents of *Imani's* moods. Still, I took my twin's hand and led her to the slide. While Imani carefully positioned herself to slip down, I tucked close enough behind her to play, but also listen to the adults.

Aunt Connie's voice was fast, and sharp as a razor. "Tito, we agreed that you would meet the girls at my house when you got yourself together."

"I know." His words weren't fast or sharp. They were hollow.

"I set time aside earlier this week. You missed it." She peered around again before letting her eyes rove over him. "This is my church home, and you are *not* together."

He considered her words while searching out something to steady himself. She huffed before dragging him over to a wooden bench where he gripped the highest panel. "Connie, the arrangement keeps paperwork out of it, but it feels too much like the courts. Too tight. I should be able to see the girls when I want."

"The arrangement helps. Since Lucille left, since it's been too much for you alone . . ." She sighed. "You're not well, Tito. Clean yourself up and I'll get the girls back to you. But not before. They need stability. That's not where you are right now."

"You're just as alone as I am. How are you doing better than me?"

Aunt Connie's chin lifted. It was true; she was unmarried and childless. But her dignity was not negotiable. "The mothers at church pitch in sometimes." They were the older ladies who liked to coo at Imani and me. We were usually too scared to say much back to them, so Aunt Connie would pat our knees and mention being blessed to have us for the foreseeable future. Now Aunt Connie pointed toward us, and I quickly turned away so she and Daddy wouldn't know I was eavesdropping. "They're thriving."

Daddy laughed wryly. "Their Mama's gone, and they haven't seen me in a week."

"Whose fault is that?"

He ignored her. "No one is thriving here. Not when we're apart."

Her chin went farther in the air. "And you can barely stand straight. This is not for your girls to see," she said. Daddy gripped the bench harder. It was then I noticed his clothing. He wasn't wearing church clothes, but a faded shirt and wrinkled pants. A bag bulging with items was draped over his shoulder. Bags hung under his eyes. Sometimes when Daddy's eyes were red, he said mean words. But today he looked tired.

"Connie, let me see my girls." He breathed deeply. "These are my children. They're a piece of me, and even if you don't like it right now, I'm a piece of them. We need each other." Aunt Connie's lips thinned. Her eyes, however, were now considering. "Please, Connie."

And to be honest, we didn't want to see him go.

She sighed. "Right here and for one hour. I will sit on that bench." She moved from Daddy's path and rested a few feet behind him before calling to us. "Girls, your daddy is here."

The first thirty minutes were awkward. Daddy tried to play with us, though he couldn't stand well, and he smelled funny. Imani helped him push me on the swing. I showed him how Imani could get across the monkey bars. Sometimes we both helped him right himself. Aunt Connie watched us, lips in a straight line, the entire time. At least until someone approached her bench. It was an older woman in a large brimmed hat, dressed in all white. She must have been on some important board. Aunt Connie immediately straightened and split her attention between us and the woman. And then, for a few moments, her back was turned while the woman showed her something on a clipboard.

"Come with me, girls," Daddy said quickly. "Your Aunt Connie wants me to take you while she has a meeting."

"Why?" Imani asked, but we were already moving farther away from Aunt Connie and the playground. Daddy had her hand in his, and she had mine in hers. Daddy, even without his grace, had a way of slipping in and out of places like air, as if he willed himself invisible. He said he had learned it from his granddaddy, who fought in World War II. Imani had inherited it, going so still in church or at Aunt Connie's that nobody could hear her. But Imani was stumbling along just as I was, so Daddy's cover must have been strong enough for the three of us.

Soon we'd left the park entirely and were in his rusty car around the corner, a long boat of a thing with a heavy metal frame. We hadn't seen it working in a while, and I didn't even know Daddy had gotten it fixed, but he was beaming. "Going to take my girls somewhere nice." The car's rumble had less finesse than he did. "Chuck E. Cheese?" Despite the strange exit from the park, we cheered at the thought of games and pizza. Aunt Connie hadn't let us have pizza in weeks. But before we got on the road, Daddy had a stop to make.

"Wait here," he said before disappearing. Thirty minutes went by, as the car hummed and we sat strapped in. I was still salivating at the thought of pizza, but Imani tugged at her remaining ribbons.

She soon turned to me and, even though no one could hear us, spoke in our language. "Where's Daddy?"

"Don't know," I admitted. "He'll be back soon."

Imani's brows furrowed. "I don't think Aunt Connie wanted us to leave the park, but I miss Daddy. Think we'll get in trouble?"

"Maybe, but . . . pizza helps," I said, and she giggled.

"It does. Aunt Connie will probably get us tonight."

As if joining our conversation, the car made a strange rumble. Aunt Connie had once said this thing was on its last leg. That rumbling shifted into a sputter just before the car clicked off, and its cabin began to boil in the August swelter. Imani's giggle thinned.

**

I splashed to the water's surface feeling the cold, Siberian air on my face—and the tide pulling me, which gave me only a few moments for a quick glance around. Snowy plains on the shore spanned miles. A nice thing about being more machine than person was watching my arms and legs shift into near perfect oars. I didn't really know how to swim, but I knew I couldn't drown, so all I really had to do was keep thrashing until I found a forward motion. It worked. I focused on the shoreline, away from the hungry tide. Within minutes, my feet found firm ground.

The honk of geese grabbed my attention before I could walk farther inland, and I gazed up to the sky. It was gray overhead, as if smeared by a large paintbrush. I zoomed in but found no sign of the cicada. The silvery aircraft was nowhere to be seen, which meant that Thaddeus was missing as well. Hopefully, he'd found somewhere safe to land and would figure out a way to fix the windshield. Though, because it was Thaddeus, it wouldn't be a stretch for neither to have happened.

I started moving forward as best I could, through the snaps of frost and cold. The water behind me rippled. The temperature had to be way below freezing, the kind that would paralyze any human. When I was younger, I saw a documentary about the world's oceans. How the globe was mostly covered in water, about 75 percent of the Earth's surface. Something like that. And of course, you can't have a documentary about oceans without talking about their creatures. The scaled and mysterious kind. Some had fins. Others glowed or floated and were poisonous. The documentary ended by explaining that the oceans were deeper than we could imagine, with places boasting terrible water pressure, too high for even the cameras to dive. Explaining that the ocean's depths were mainly unexplored, although we knew that human pollution ended up all the way at the bottom. While I stared at those rippling waves, I couldn't help but wonder what was down there lurking about. What thing with long teeth and snapping jaws could be waiting for a snack?

As I watched the water, a particular ripple caught my attention, only so many feet out from shore. Where one ripple had begun to fade, new ones were appearing. Something was under there. Just my luck, imagining the monsters of the deep had summoned one. The ripples came faster until the movement of the water gave way to something springing from the surface. A figure appeared, surging into the air and then splashing back into the water. It had a tail like a dolphin, but there was something humanlike about it. If it stayed beneath the surface, I would never have to know. But of course, that wasn't going to happen. As those ripples continued, I knew that it would find its way back out and over to me.

Instinctively, I backed up a bit farther from the edge and reached for my bow and quiver. To my horror, I didn't find anything there. I must have dropped my weapons when I hit the water. This was not going to be good by any stretch of the imagination. I took a fighter's stance, ready to meet this new companion. And then from the waters, finally, something emerged.

The tail was gone. The person who stepped onto the shoreline walked on two legs but was mysterious in every other way. And translucent. Feminine in build, with a slight frame perfect for maneuvering through all kinds of water. Humanoid would be the best way to describe her, as she also had features which were all fish, but still see-through: small fins on her wrists and ankles, gills on her neck, and iridescent scales shimmering along her body. All of it was moving. She was literally made out of water. She walked slowly toward me, assessing me as if *I* was the sea creature that had sprung from the deep. While she casually glided, I remained in my defensive stance. Although something told me that this wasn't another attack goose, I was still in a new land with all kinds of threats. I couldn't afford to let my guard down.

My suspicions remained as I asked, "Who are you?" The words, like the water, seemed to just roll off her without much bother. Her strides remained long and unabashed. And then, after what seemed like the longest time, she tilted her head back and screeched her reply.

It was very much like the sound that a dolphin would make—a dolphin somehow crossbred with a bat. It grated on my ears and irritated my programming.

I pressed a hand to my head. "Chill with that sound," I said. For some reason, she stopped moving and cocked her head. It was like she was trying to puzzle out my words to determine if they were a threat, or figure out why I was so uncomfortable. But then, without much ceremony, she kept right on coming toward me. She tilted her head back again, if slower this time, and continued with that sound. It echoed and chambered, and I could literally see it moving in waves across her watery body.

I rolled my eyes and repeated myself more loudly: "Chill out with that sound."

Her eyes, this odd shade of green with large irises, twinkled. She understood that she was annoying me, and it clearly amused her. This time when she tilted her head back, she didn't make the same screeching sound. The cadence of this new sound was less irritating. It had to be her laugh. She was *laughing* at me.

"You think this is funny?" I asked, as the laugh continued, followed by a few of her mer-words. It was definitely a language—a weird, underwater-sounding language that I didn't understand, but at this point I was very used to weird languages I didn't understand. I held my hands out, hoping she would understand the gestures if not the words. This time, for her part, she stopped speaking until we were about twenty feet apart. She considered me for a second more before beginning to mimic my own speech, and when she spoke again, I could understand the words.

"Who?" she began, but it was followed by words in her native tongue.

"Who are you?" she finally made out. Was that the question she'd tried earlier?

"Oh, so you can speak my language," I said.

Her words came out slowly and unsure, as if she were a sweet little deer on shaking legs. "I've heard many times, coming from the air, near the shore. But I've never . . . tried."

"You're doing just fine," I said, somewhat surprised.

"I speak the language of the seas and oceans," she continued. "It's a beautiful sound to my people. Funny that you can't hear it."

She said "hear" it, but I assumed she meant "appreciate" it. I hummed. I had been rude. My Aunt Connie wouldn't have appreciated that. I suddenly got the feeling that this was a . . . child of some kind. I took a deep breath and tried to be calmer, kinder. I also lost my defensive stance. This was a kid, not some killer goose.

"I assumed that you were speaking a water-language," I said. "My name is Josephine." I was going to stick out my hand to shake hers, but she didn't seem like she would know the gesture. A moment passed, and then that twinkle in her large eyes returned. That must have been curiosity.

"Josephine. My name is—" She said something that sounded like heavy bubbles from deep in the ocean. "But I am thinking that perhaps humans cannot make this sound."

I laughed. "Your name is beautiful. But, even though I'm not exactly human anymore, I don't think I can make that sound."

She tilted her head, considering. "You can call me something else if you like, in your language."

"How about . . . Nori?" I suggested. "My sister and I always liked seaweed."

She imitated my smile, and I was starting to find her delightful. "Yes, I could be Nori to you. I am one of the People."

"The people?" I asked. "What people?"

"Just the People," she said simply. "The True People of Earth."

"Okay, now," I started in, only half-serious. "First off, there are a lot of people on Earth, and you don't even live on the earth, you people live in the water. We call you the Brackish."

She smiled again and nodded. "We are the True People. But we strive to live in peace with all beings."

I had never met a Brackish before, but I knew something of what they were. I knew they saw themselves as part of one organism, not really needing titles and such, but apparently this one had a name, and didn't mind me giving her one.

"Nice to meet you. I've never met one of the People before," I admitted. Though the place that used to be California claimed so much water, interactions with the Brackish like this, face-to-face conversations, weren't common. All I knew was that they were almost elemental when using water, more in tune with it than air. They had sway over it, an ability to manipulate it to their liking. The Brackish could also be lethal when they wanted to be, though this girl seemed to come in peace. She had a pretty orb for a skull (which I could see through her watery head), with those large eyes like the sea. There was also an eerie way that water mist moved around her, responding to her and not the other way around. But enough of the pleasantries. "This isn't your land, is it, Nori?"

A big smile lit her face in answer, revealing rows of tiny shark's teeth. Her laugh returned when she answered. "Oh, that," she said, her words beginning to lose their accent—she sounded more and more like me. She slapped her hands against her thighs, making a squishy sound. "I'm on my walkabout."

"What's a walkabout?"

"Well," she began, speaking more softly, as if talking to a child. "I would have hoped you knew some of our customs. But there is no real reason for you to know that. You spend your life above the water and rarely encounter my kind. Unless, you know, we're overturning your ships." She winked, and I shuddered. To be some sailor meeting a Brackish under waves, seeing all those rows of teeth. "But it's an important time in our lives," she said. "It marks the greatest of changes. The only time we leave the group, so that we can truly find ourselves. Hear our purpose."

I arched a brow. Like a gap year in college? "What do you mean by 'find yourself'?"

"We must know ourselves wholly to be of use in our community, and to do that, we must spend time alone first. If we're in the water, we're never really alone. So we must go above the surface. We do this for an entire year. When that is done, we return ready to be of service."

"I see," I said, trying my best to understand. "My aunt used to say there were important lessons from being quiet and alone. She called it meditating."

"Is she one of the People?"

"No," I said. "She was just a good teacher. I'm sorry, do I *look* like I could be one of you people?" I asked, because it seemed so ridiculous.

"There are many strange things and beings in this world," Nori said. "Minds that don't have bodies, and bodies that don't have minds. The People always have their own body and their own mind, so they be the True People of Earth."

"Okay," I said, sort of following.

"But there are others with bodies and minds that we should learn from to see ourselves better: animals, and fish." She turned to look at the ocean, and the fins and teeth morphed across her body. Then she turned to me. "And you." Nori changed again, making her body smaller and opaque, no longer watery and see-through. Her skin solidified, hair grew from her head, and in just a few moments she turned into . . . me. She made herself look just like *me*, dripping white dress and all.

"Whoa," I said, taken aback. I held up a cautionary finger. "Uh-uh. That's cool that you can do that. But, don't do that. Please. I am sick of looking at people who look just like me, looking right at me."

She quickly changed back to her watery form. "I'm sorry," she said. "I didn't mean to bother you, I just wanted to try your form."

"It's okay," I said. "I just get that a lot."

Nori nodded and smiled, going on to explain that she had been on this reprieve for months, and that it was almost time for her to return to the deep.

"Are you considered an adult?" she asked. I blinked, not really understanding. "You are alone right now. Is it because you are on your own walk? I came to you because I was curious."

I sighed before answering. "Trust me, Nori, I have been alone longer than this mission, and I'm not on a walk. I was sent here by my sisters, and I really need to get moving." Nori made this sound, one that was like skepticism. I could read that anywhere. Never thought I would wish for the dolphin sound again.

"How will you do that?" My fish friend turned her gaze upward. "I saw you fall from the sky, and your craft, I couldn't even see where it landed. All your weapons and supplies are in the waters."

"I just need myself," I said. "I can handle it. Unless you want to help me."

She glanced from me to the water, then toward the tundra. "We try to live by my people's guidelines, staying out of the affairs of land walkers. The treaty."

"Yes, the treaty," I repeated. "That keeps the peace between the AIs. The entities."

"I was not supposed to approach you, but I was just so curious," Nori said. "And in the walkabout, my parents said, we are supposed to find new things. I was out in the sea hunting fish for breakfast when I saw you falling into the waters. I'd never seen anything like it."

"Yeah, I can do some things," I said with a shrug. "I can even swim now, kind of."

"And you're all right?" she pressed. "You are so small. I thought you would break all your bones. My conscience was worried, but then you just swam like a fast turtle . . ."

"A turtle?" I laughed. "I'm a bit more than human," I said, trying to ease her mind. "The plane got it worse than I did, trust me. You don't have to worry about me or try to ease your conscience, as you put it." I looked back to the sky. Still there was no sign of the cicada, or Thaddeus.

"You are a bit strange," she said. "And there is something lonely about you. But you are a mind with a body, and that is enough to stop and talk on walkabout. I'm not here to harm you. And I will help you by telling you this: avoid the waters, and my conscience will be eased. My people will not welcome you there. Some would destroy you."

I was about to say something cocky, but thought better of it. "Thanks for the heads-up, but I don't plan on jumping into the ocean again." I looked inland.

"I should also tell you, this land is not safe, either."

"I'm a Josephine," I said. "You don't have to worry about me."

"For some reason, I think I do," she replied, and I folded my arms. My Aunt Connie had said you could tell when someone was lying. That it was usually in their eyes. They had ticks and habitual movements that kept them from making eye contact. But Nori held my gaze with all seriousness.

"Can you tell me what I'm up against?" I asked.

She broke her gaze with me and looked inland herself. "My people know the deepest waters like their own bodies, but they don't know all about the surface. Soon after we came to be in the ocean, a man arrived here, from your lands. A very smart man. His name is Antonov."

"Antonov?" I asked. I knew that name. Dr. Yetti had mentioned him several times.

Nori nodded. "Soon after he arrived, things near the shore here started to change. Animals began to appear that were . . . not animals." She looked around: along the shore, off into the distance inland. "Be careful in these lands," she said. "The machines are peaceful compared to where you come from, very quiet. But some of the creatures are not what they appear to be."

I nodded. "Yeah, we were targeted by a bird when we came in."

"A bird?" Nori asked.

"A goose," I said. "Its body was all black on the inside. A living machine."

"A living machine," Nori said. "Like you."

I smirked. "And like you. The Brackish were created, too."

"Yes," she agreed. "The People were created, but we now create ourselves. With each new generation, we flow with the oceans, and learn. After my walkabout, I will have children, and they will flow. We are the True People of Earth."

"Uh-huh, you said that," I pointed out. She and her people seemed pretty full of themselves, but I liked Nori. She was really just a girl like me, finding her place. Suddenly I felt a pang of jealousy: unlike me, this weird sea machine-creature still had parents who cared deeply what she was up to.

"The minds here are not friendly, and already we have broken the treaty, just by standing here," Nori said. "They are hidden, but they will move against us soon."

"So it's not just the killer geese that are dangerous?"

"The guardians of this land can come in any form," Nori said, scanning the area. Something about it made her shudder. "I should go." I followed her gaze. "You have what you need?" she asked.

I nodded. For a moment, I considered inviting Nori on the rest of the mission with me. It would be a good end to any gap year that I could think of. She had also been helpful. More helpful than the monitor, though I hoped he was at least all right. But as I turned to her, she was already walking away, back toward the sea.

"Good luck to you, Josephine," she said. "Until next time."

And with that, Nori disappeared into the water. Again, I was on my own. I brushed the snow at my ankles, which didn't do much, before trudging into this new world.

Where Saturnalia had been all warmth, this was all frost. Even in the fall, Saturnalia boasted life and plants vining through the crumbled buildings. Nothing like that was here. Just sparse, bare trees and miles and miles of white. Though I had grabbed some gear from the plane, I would have to create more.

A few skeletal trees struggled up through the snow near me, so I approached one. It was tall, though obviously a sapling, and I felt a pang of remorse as I ripped limbs from the trunk. It would probably be a large oak one day. I would have to thank it for its aid. Meanwhile, my hands worked fast, thinning some of the bark into fine fibers. I fashioned that into a coverall for my body and slips on my shoes to better absorb the snow. Not that I was cold, but I knew I would slow down if I didn't do something to keep my feet from sinking into the terrain. Once that was completed, I bent some small branches into arrows, using a fistful of fibers to remake my string and a strong branch for a new bow. Anyone could greet me out here, and from what I knew of Siberia, their tech enjoyed hiding in plain sight. Six minutes later, I'd finished my crafting.

Next, I would need a signal. I twisted my bracelet to see if anything had come from Thaddeus, or even from Nine. Nothing. I looked around. Although I knew I was close to where the town was supposed to be, there was nothing man-made in sight. No buildings, no roads, no power lines, nothing. Just tundra and another small thicket of trees in the distance.

I allowed my inhuman ears to hear far around me. *Better*, as Dr. Yetti had promised. At first only the sounds of the sea greeted me. Snow moved on the wind whistling by. "Geese" honked overhead. The hairs on my arm rose, as I looked up at the small V-formation flying eastward. Would one of them swoop down and attack? They didn't, but I knew I better get moving.

I had no idea where to go, so I just started heading west, into Siberia. As I made my way across the desolate landscape, it suddenly occurred to me what a bad idea this was. I was looking for my sister, by myself, with no landmarks, following a pair of twisted twins—and their little brother—who really could be anywhere within a thousand miles. But I didn't know what else to do, so I just kept trudging, using my robotic strength to propel my legs fast through the snow. I might not know where I was going, but I was gonna get there fast.

Finally I got to the thicket of trees, and I crouched low when I saw a herd of what must be reindeer. Still, no people. The reindeer turned and looked at me for a moment, and I remembered what Nori had said: "The guardians of this land can hide in any form." Great. So even little Rudolph could be coming at me? I watched them closely, from about two football fields away, but the animals didn't seem to take notice and soon resumed their slow munching. Suddenly a tapping started near me, and I just about jumped out of my skin, swinging my bow around about to let loose one of my arrows.

It was just a spotted woodpecker, calmly pecking at a small tree nearby. I kept the bow trained, shaking, ready to skewer this thing if need be. Eventually it noticed me, turned its little head, and— apparently not liking being aimed at—flew away.

I lowered the bow. I was getting paranoid, and jumpy. But I didn't know what else to do. Any one of these animals out here in the middle of nowhere could be a biomechanical monster in disguise. I stood there and took a breath, trying to calm myself, just listening. And then I really did feel something. Something familiar: a slight, unnatural *puff* in the atmosphere.

I gripped the bow tighter, but didn't bother to notch an arrow. "Come out," I said. "Now."

He answered my command by shimmering into view. A tall man, standing yards away, and who was definitely not Thaddeus. He was very sleek and slender, like lines on ruled paper. He wore a black suit, starkly contrasting the snow. Everything about him reeked of elitism, almost too formal even for Saturnalia's former Marin County upper classes. A dark orange sash draped across him, offsetting the paleness of his gaunt face and hands and the terrifying dark lines pouring down his face like tears. When he stepped forward, his body blurred and refocused. He was a hologram who didn't leave a step in the snow.

I loosed an arrow, just as the man disappeared and materialized even closer to me. He didn't seem like a Siberian monstrosity, but that didn't make me feel warm and fuzzy. "Stay back," I commanded.

His expression was one of boredom as he glanced at my weapon. "That won't be necessary," he said formally.

"Like hell it won't." I already had another arrow and pulled it tighter.

"You can't impale me. I can't harm you. Let's skip the introductions where we talk about the weather and how lovely the ball is." Despite this, my arrow remained trained on him. Exasperation filled his voice. "Fine, I'll demonstrate." He disappeared and reappeared nearer as I let the arrow fly. It sailed through him. He then flew through me. I shuddered as he said, "I can't hurt you; you can't hurt me. All I want is a chance to speak, Josephine."

"Don't you want to finish crying first?"

His eyes narrowed. "I'm here to help you on this rustic journey. I believe it's what your father would want."

"My father?" It was my turn to scrutinize him. And then recognition passed through me. "You play chess with my dad." I had seen this ghost of a man when I visited my father, shortly after I woke up, but still, his presence did not settle right.

"Yes, I am familiar with Tito, and you."

"He asked you to come here?"

"Not exactly. Because of the Mesa network, I can manifest as a hologram wherever I want. Thus, I am here, as I wished to be. I want to help you."

"The puff," I said. "You can come through on the puff."

"What the Swarm Cartel calls the Mesa, yes. Using it violates the treaty, of course, but they cannot stop me. At least not yet. When the Cartel fully matures, nothing will stop them, but for now, just know that you and I simply being here in Siberia is also a violation of the treaty, and a much more grievous one."

At the sound of us talking, the reindeer became spooked and moved cautiously away from the area.

"Well, thanks for giving away my position, then," I said sarcastically. "What do you want?"

"I know you're a traumatized, mentally disturbed little girl, who doesn't know her proper place in the world, but I appreciate the desperate move that Dr. Yetti took in aligning herself with your lamentable brood."

"Thanks for the pep talk, ghosty. Are you done?"

"I owe it to your father to help you on your journey, as I know you are of an inferior race."

"Wow. Okay, you can just disappear now."

"Listen to me, Josephine," he continued. "Do not get ahead of yourself as you maneuver through Siberia. You don't understand the forces here, not like your leader, One, does. The emphasis of the mission should be destroying the Yetti twins who have stolen One. Not getting her back."

My brows furrowed. "Dr. Yetti's girls? I don't care about them."

"You should," he said. "They're the ones who've gone rogue. Removing them is absolutely necessary."

"I'm a tracker. Killing isn't my forte."

"But you hunt?"

"I'm not on an assassination mission, old man. I'm on a rescue mission. Besides, shouldn't I just cut down this Antonov guy if I came here to kill someone?"

"Just as Dr. Yetti has long since set in motion the mechanisms that became Yerba City, so her former partner has already put his curse upon this land. Antonov's influence is already in place, and these Siberians follow the treaty, either by will or by ignorance. They are not a threat beyond these borders."

"And you're thinking a couple of teenage runaways are?"

"They are not runaways," he said. "In actuality, they came here in search of Antonov. They believe him to be their brother's father."

This actually didn't come as a surprise to me. I remember when Dr. Yetti spoke about her former partner, the one who had ended up "going east." The glint in her eye had the same shine as Aunt Connie's when she first met the deacon. Nevertheless, I played it cool. "Look, I don't care why they're here. I just want my sister."

"It's no secret that I look down on you and where you come from," Majerus said.

"Yeah, that's clear."

"But that is something I must do. It is who I am. Nevertheless, I admire you, Josephine, and your family. You may make many mistakes, but like your father, when the critical time comes, I sense you have a temperance that will ensure your survival, and that of your kind, such as they may be. The children of Dr. Yetti will not have your fortitude of character and will be a danger to us all."

"You act like Yetti's kids are Godzilla or something."

"You of all people should know that in this age, even a child can become quite powerful if the circumstances are right. Look what Dr. Yetti's experiments have done to you. And you don't know her family like I do," Majerus said. "Do not underestimate what they are capable of."

"They're just kids," I snorted. "Do your own dirty work. Or go back and play chess with my dad." I glanced around. "Now, if you'll excuse me, I need to find a signal."

Frustration etched his face as I turned away. "Josephine," he called.

I stopped. He'd known we called One by her number. I wondered if he knew mine. "Yes?"

"If you don't heed me, later you're going to wish you had listened. And to show you that I'm trustworthy, even though you are *not* being polite, I will tell you something you need to know. You don't have to wait for your silly signal. The Yetti twins went that way, along that ridge. Follow it to the forest in the west, and you'll find a village a few miles on the other side."

"Why would I trust you?"

"As I said, I owe your father."

"Why?" I asked. I wasn't messing with this weird, racist ghost now; I really wanted to know.

He ignored the question. "And beware of all animals. About one in a thousand are not what they seem."

"I know," I said. "An evil goose got us on the way in. They got guardians around here."

"They are not so much guardians as they are curators," he explained.

"Curators?" I asked, barely remembering the field trips in what little grade school I had had. "Like, in a museum?"

"When you find the human settlements, you'll understand," he said. "Remember, even among them, one in a thousand is a machine, and if they get you alone, they will kill you."

With those ominous words, he curtly nodded, then disappeared. I stared at the space where he'd been, and then checked my bracelet. Again, there was no signal, no message. It was just me, and snow, and cold. So I plucked up my things and started toward the ridge.

CHAPTER 5

THE HUNTER

Snow crunched beneath me as I headed across the ridge. Soon, it became dotted with frost-crested trees. The wind whistled through their limbs. I wanted to reach this village before nightfall, so I picked up the pace in favor of a jog. My eyes found the sky every few minutes, checking for Thaddeus and our cicada. Nothing. *Eyes on the prize,* I reminded myself, something the pastor in church had said on more than one occasion. I was more machine than human, and I'd gotten used to beings like us since the world ended. But in Yerba City, they didn't hide. Out here, machines were hidden in plain sight, camouflaged like a frog on a lily pad. My guard would stay up this entire trip. As I trotted along at my unnaturally fast pace, my only companions were the chill and the sun, the latter following me over the arc of the day. As it descended, it snatched the path with it. The ridge in front of me flattened into a plain as I walked. I stopped, hands finding my hips. Great. How would I find the village now?

Shaking my head, I plowed forward, unsure if I was traveling in the right direction, but wanting to keep moving. Suddenly, an eerie feeling tingled up my spine. It whispered that I wasn't alone, so I drew my large bow and looked around. For a few moments, nothing showed. Then, over one of the rolling hills, came the movement of beasts. A small herd burst into view. More reindeer. One of the largest tugged a bulky sled. I veered toward them, hoping they'd come from the village. If they had, their tracks could give me the path I needed. By the time I was close enough, they'd stopped beside a mostly frozen stream, some munching on patches of grass peeking through the snow.

When I approached, the reindeers' ears turned and one's head popped up, but none of the others moved. I held my hands up. "I'm not trying to eat you," I said. "I'm going to put my bow up and look at your tracks." Maybe they were machines, because—as if they understood me—they went about their business.

I did as promised, holstering the bow in favor of inspecting the tracks heading west toward the horizon where the sun would eventually set. Suddenly, I heard the trudge of the sled following me. I turned to the large reindeer, who was on my trail, slowed, and when it was by my side, ran my hands over its thick, warm fur. I was a tracker, used to following game for sport or hunting. Here, I wasn't the wolf. For some reason, it wanted my company. And if the reindeer turned into some tentacled thing wanting to destroy me, well, friends close and enemies closer.

We started our quiet walk as snow began to fall. The scenic view made me smile. Nature calmed me, even so many miles from Saturnalia and on a mission I'd never intended. At least until the snow crunched ahead in a way that made me still. The sound came from a cluster of trees, and I trained my eyes on them only moments before someone wrapped in furs of gray, white, and brown emerged from his shroud. He maneuvered toward us more quickly than I preferred, and as if reading each other's minds, the reindeer and I took off.

The man pursued us with surprising intensity. One in a thousand, Majerus the Crying Man had said. Maybe I got "lucky" and found one of these curators on the first try.

The wind whipped my face, though I knew I could run much faster—faster than the reindeer. But I didn't want to leave it, especially as it was tugging that heavy sled along. Its herd had already moved on; I couldn't abandon it; and this half run wouldn't get us anywhere. So I dug my heels into the frozen earth.

In an instant I'd swirled around to face our pursuer and slapped the animal's hide to encourage it to go on without me. It blew out its air, but took off on its own as I stood to face the hunter. At my stance, he slowed. His breath colored the air as he pulled his hood back. He wasn't the man with the tears streaming down his face. And he certainly wasn't Thaddeus. No, he wasn't really a man at all. His face was young, not much older than me—or at least, than the age I'd been before replication. He looked intense, and in a hurry, and confused. Was he a curator? A cute curator, but nevertheless about to lay into me with whatever black goo he had coursing through his veins?

We stared at each other through the flurries of snow in the air. There was a next move to be made, but I didn't exactly know who would make it. Then his eyes slid in the reindeer's direction, the animal now sloping down a snowcapped hill. He didn't want me. He wanted it. With a tentative step, he made to maneuver around me, but I blocked him. He couldn't have the reindeer. I wouldn't allow it. He came close enough to brush past me, and this time I grabbed his shoulder. He defended himself, and we collided before hitting the ground with a thud. But he didn't seem to be attacking me. We only rolled until he was able to free himself and push me back.

"Get off," he barked.

I was surprised to hear my language so far into Siberia, and I relented a bit at the sound. "Leave the reindeer alone."

"The reindeer's gone, thanks to you," he said, and pushed to his feet. He muttered as he dusted snow from his clothing, and I realized that he wasn't speaking my language. I just *understood* him. This had to be a side effect of my response to my language malfunction. During the week after replication, Dr. Yetti ran all sorts of tests on me to find the glitch and ensure it hadn't contaminated any other Josephines. It hadn't, but the scientist also couldn't find a cure or fix, and one day she left our home base, making One our de facto leader and leaving me S.O.L. I hated being outside the Josephine sisterhood in this way, so the night before my first patrol, I spent the entire evening absorbing languages as best I could. I scoured the various computer systems, and any old books or encyclopedias I could find. The result was an understanding of multiple languages, although none of them brought me closer to the one I'd shared with Imani and lost to replication.

"Well, you can find another to hunt," I snapped. "That one was my . . ." My what? My friend?

"That reindeer belonged to me," he shot back. "Didn't you see the sled? I wasn't hunting it. I was trying to bring him back home. And you made me lose him."

I looked off in the direction it had gone. "I did see the sled," I began. "But if he was running from you, trying to join that herd, maybe he didn't want to be kept."

"And maybe our ways are none of your business," he said as I glared at him. He held my stare before seemingly cursing under his breath. "He was a gift, all right, along with my father's knife. For completing my Chitakla." I didn't seem to have a translation for that last word. "I'm supposed to be preparing for my first solo hunt on these lands, not chasing him." He shook his head. "I don't know why I'm telling you all this. You probably want to kill me."

My lips thinned.

"You . . . don't want to kill me?" he asked, unsteadily but not exactly scared.

"No," I said sharply. "I thought you wanted to kill it, so I protected it. It's kind of what I do." I shrugged. His huffs of air were coming fast now. "You don't have to be afraid of me."

He pointed to the giant bow on my back. "I wouldn't exactly say that."

I sighed, removing the bow and extending it toward him. "Here, take it. I'm not out here to hurt you."

He stared at me quizzically before stepping forward. He took the bow, but it must have been heavier than he expected, because he dropped it. As he stumbled to turn it upright, his cheeks reddened in the cold, but he otherwise glowed with health. His hooded eyes were dark, matching his straight raven hair. When he finally regarded me, a hint of amazement flickered in his gaze, replacing the fear. He tried to draw the bow tight. He barely could. "How do you draw this thing?" He gave the bow back. "Never mind," he said. "Just, how did you find your way out here? This land is blessed, only for our hunters after their Chitakla."

I glanced around at the mostly barren hills. *Blessed*? "Um, I just landed here," I replied, and his face contorted at the word *land* just before his eyes roved over me. I could tell he was smart, but something about him seemed strangely simpleminded. I took in his clothes, the elaborately handled knife at his belt, his hair. Everything was hand-made, and perfectly medieval looking, like he was on his way to a Siberian renaissance faire. "And . . . what's a Chitakla anyway?"

"It is the ritual passage from childhood into adulthood, where you face your fears, move away from your parents, and get your grown-up name."

That was coincidental, I thought. I had just run into a water-girl on her walkabout. Was everyone just going to be shoving my face in the fact they had actual functional parents to run away from?

I looked at the barely-a-man in front of me. "And what is your name, anyway?" I asked.

He puffed out his chest proudly. "I am Oktai Belek-maa."

"Oktai? And you just got that name?"

"That's right," he said, and unsheathed the weapon at his belt, hold-ing it up for display. "And my father's knife, which was also my grand-father's." It was a gorgeous copper blade, emblazoned with traditional hunting images.

"It's beautiful," I acknowledged. "What was your name before?"

"No one uses their childhood names after Chitakla. It's insult-ing," he said, somewhat aloofly, and resheathed his knife. "And who are you?"

"I'm Josephine Moore," I said.

"Josephine Moore. Is that your grown-up name?" he asked.

"We just have one name where I'm from," I said unenthusiastically. "You're stuck with it your whole life."

He nodded. "Josephine," he repeated. "It's funny to call you the same name your parents did when you were a baby, now that you're . . . grown." He paused, looking at me intensely.

I resisted the urge to fold my arms. "What are you staring at?"

"What are you wearing, Josephine?" he asked. "You'll freeze to death out here."

"Trust me, I won't," I replied with a wave of my hand, just as a thought came to mind. "Hey, are you from that village? There's one nearby and I lost the path."

He straightened. "How did you know that?"

"Don't worry about it. Just, are you?" I rushed. His gaze turned stra-tegic, as if weighing his options, unsure if he wanted to say everything in his head. Perhaps calculating how fast I ran and the strength of my grapple as I kept him from the reindeer. But when he mashed his lips together, as if saying, *I'm going to regret this,* I knew he was ready to talk.

"Yes, my village is near," he said. "And you would be another new visitor as of late, though the others looked nothing like you."

"Beautiful?" I shot back, as his eyes traveled over my skin, perhaps taking in the depth, the color and tone. But I ignored that, knowing the other visitors had to be the Yetti twins and their brother. I definitely did not look like them. I also didn't expect his cheeks to redden—not from the cold, but perhaps from sheepishness.

"Yes," he said, a note quieter.

I stepped forward. "Look, I'm with the other visitors that came to your village. Can you take me?"

Suddenly his face brightened, as if some puzzle pieces had mysteriously come together for him. "Oh, the Tsirku," he said. "That's why your bow is so crazy. I didn't realize. Of course I will bring you. It would be an honor."

That was more like it, I thought, whatever *Tsirku* meant.

His eyes shot downward. "But your feet? Aren't you cold? I can wrap them, but I shouldn't touch a woman's feet, now that I am a proper man."

"For real?" I scoffed. "I don't need my feet wrapped. Let's move."

CHAPTER 6

THE VILLAGE

He didn't seem to be a curator—he seemed to be just a teenager. A strange, foreign teenager, who was dressed for some kind of Indigenous reenactment. His outfit was a perfect reproduction of something from five hundred years ago—all leather and beads— and for a moment reminded me of the Yetti twins' clothes, except much better made. His name was Oktai. He said it meant "one who understands." The moniker was given after some kind of trial called a Chitakla. Beyond these facts, the hunter didn't talk much as he led me to his village—I was some Tsirku, or something, which was a good thing, and everyone in the village was going to be happy to see me. That was just fine, and "Tsirku" was much better than some of the things I had been called back in my own country.

The dense snow gave way to shallower stuff. It sloshed under both my shoes and his carefully wrapped buckskin boots. His eyes kept flicking to my feet, but he didn't mention that I should have been completely frostbitten at that point. We just trudged on as the winds slowed with the growing distance between ourselves and the sea. No other people or animals appeared, though an image of the goose attacking the cicada played in my mind. This quiet didn't mean enemy entities weren't still out there, these "curators" that the Crying Man mentioned. In fact, I wasn't completely sure that Oktai wasn't one. I shuddered before glancing toward the sky. Still no sign of the cicada or Thaddeus. I had to reach this village by nightfall. Didn't want to be in the lonely tundra if anything happened.

"You are kind of quiet," he said, grabbing my attention. I frowned. And if this guy kept talking, I might have to punch him and find this village by myself. But his gaze remained steady on me, so I only arched a brow with an *Excuse me*, inviting further explanation. He repeated himself. "Kind of quiet. And you brood."

"Brood?" I asked. In answer, he set his mouth in a straight line and folded his arms. He then curtly nodded and appeared distracted. An imitation of me, apparently.

"Brood," he concluded, before his mannerisms returned to normal.

"No kid says *brood*." But my arms were folded across my body. I quickly undid them.

"Aren't you cold?" He glanced at my feet a final time. "Your little shoes must be soaked."

"Doesn't bother me," I replied with a shrug. His face lit confusedly. I smacked my lips. "Nothing like that bothers me. You shouldn't ask so many personal questions." I expected him to snap quiet. A person on the streets of Saturnalia would do so if One spoke to them like that, or if any Josephine barked a command. But instead, he tilted his head and, of all things, smirked. His dark eyes glittered.

"You're strange. The strangest Tsirku I've ever met."

"Whatever you say," I muttered, feeling a stubbornness inside of me refusing to ask him about what that word meant. A thought popped in my mind. "Why do you care about how much I talk?"

"I thought we weren't asking personal questions."

"I can ask you personal questions," I clarified. "Just doesn't work the other way around."

At that, he laughed. It was a peculiar noise to hear amid the sound-muffling quiet of the snow. His answer was simpler than anticipated. "If you were cold—which you obviously are not, because somehow you don't get cold—I would have wrapped your feet. I wouldn't let you make that walk without offering. I would have just asked you not to tell the chieftain."

"Tell him what? That you didn't let me get frostbite?"

A note of sadness entered his voice. "I'm not supposed to do that anymore. Wrap a woman's feet for the snow walk. Not unless you were a relative, or my wife." Like all his words, the last ones rushed out, but there was no mistaking the blush on his cheeks. "After my manhood ritual, I cannot tend any woman with things like that. It's too close."

To this point, any mention of the ritual had been accompanied with a poked-out chest and more than a few eye rolls from me. But as he tugged his furs tighter, I assumed that was a part he perhaps wasn't so thrilled about. Maybe Oktai mourned a bit of his childhood—though a bigger world had opened, a small part had closed off. In a strange way, after going through my own replication, I understood.

But I didn't understand the shift in his body language. The sheepishness on the boy's face at the thought of closeness. Not that I had rounded all the bases before the world ended, but my classmates at the time had gone further than touching each other's feet. I couldn't imagine the wrapping stuff would be something you'd get suspended for if caught with your crush in the janitor's closet.

I couldn't help but chuckle and nudge him. "Well, you probably weren't any good at wrapping feet anyway."

Maybe he couldn't resist the hint of sparring in my voice. "I actually was," he corrected me. "I used to wrap my cousin Bolormaa's feet, but we both have crossed our journeys. She said the new girl who does the wrapping for her lets all the snow in."

"Then maybe they should give you a new job in the village."

"I like where I am," he said, the smirk returning. "Thanks."

Midday turned into afternoon, and we still moved forward. The snow had begun falling in soft puffs on the ground. The air colored our breaths silver in the wind. There was still no village in sight, and at this point, I was less afraid of running into an enemy entity than I was worried for Oktai and his all-too-human vulnerabilities. His movements had slowed, and even the talking lessened. He was getting cold. And tired. If the village didn't appear by nightfall, we'd have to make a camp somewhere and try our luck in the morning.

"You turn to the sky a lot," he said, this time without looking at me. His teeth didn't chatter, but his lips pressed together whenever possible.

"I'm looking for my cicada," I replied absentmindedly. His face scrunched up. I should have expected the response. He was still using old-timey sleds and reindeer to get around, and the more I talked to him, the more it seemed like this kid had never even seen a car. I really must be out in the sticks. How was I supposed to explain our hover-craft? "Don't worry about it." I changed the subject. "We should make camp soon. You're tired."

"I'm not," he protested. Again, his chest poked out.

I rolled my eyes. "You've slowed down in the last mile. It's fine. If we aren't close, we can make a fire and wait out the night."

"Never expected that reindeer to come out so far," he said, more to himself than me. There was a distinct rhythm to the chatter now. "And we're close. Only have a hill to cross. Besides," he continued, "if I can't wrap your feet, I definitely cannot camp with you." I glanced over and couldn't miss the hint of playfulness in his tone, as well as the new redness that burned his cheeks.

My lips tugged upward. "Fine," I said. "Lead the way, and tell me more about this ritual that won't let you breathe next to any woman until you're married."

His hand found his face, lightly touching his cheeks as if I should have seen something there. "Had I run into you a little earlier, you would have seen my marks."

"Marks?" I asked. "Like tattoos?"

"No, nothing that permanent. You know, like after a fight."

"You had bruises on your face?" I asked. He nodded. "And what part of your ritual was joining *Fight Club*?" My Aunt Connie was as prim and proper a lady as anyone could imagine, but she loved the movie *Fight Club*. I probably should have understood that people were complicated just because of my father and mother's situation. But it was Aunt Connie's love of that movie that drummed it in. However, I hadn't seen it since the world ended, and Oktai missed the reference.

Still, his chin lifted with pride. "I received the marks when I walked through the gauntlet of manhood. The men of our village welcome you with their strength before our chieftain accepts you in our brother-hood. Some strength is shown with hands and fists, others with the shaman's staffs. It shows your worthiness when the marks arise. And then you are no longer a child. My marks just healed."

They beat you to a pulp and then eat Froot Loops with you the next day?

"O . . . kay . . . ," I managed. But he was still smiling and looking off in the distance, probably remembering the experience. I couldn't help but mess with him a bit. "And whatever, dude. I'm more badass than you. I have plenty of marks, and mine won't fade."

He winked, but otherwise ignored my goad. "But passing through the gauntlet is not the biggest test of skill and unity."

"Oh yeah, and what is?"

"You must sing for the Creator," he said, and when I couldn't keep the laughter at bay, he insisted. "It's really quite beautiful. We all sing together as honored men."

"You can't be serious."

"I am very serious," he said, which made me laugh harder. "I have a beautiful voice and can do great harmonies. You've never heard such magnificence."

"Or such humility." My laughing subsided a bit as I considered. "Well, my mother sang in church, so I guess that's nice. But I don't believe you have a great voice."

Now his brow flicked up. "You may be Tsirku, but I am far more talented than you give credit." He cleared his throat, took in a gust of air, and began to sing with the enthusiasm I'd only seen in a soloist right after the pastor's sermon. That was a big spot. If you sang then, it meant you could *sing* sing. Oktai's voice wasn't horrible, but it wasn't the stuff of legend as promised. If he sang at church, he would get a modest clap and maybe a few pitying *Take your time*s from the old church mothers.

As he continued what I assumed was the village song, it took on a new tempo. The words slipped from the language we shared to a more ancient version of Mongolian. The sound rattled me, disturbing something deep inside. Something I'd felt on the plane and in the field with the corrupted butler. Something I thought had been subdued but had only been biding time. But I couldn't say all this to Oktai. Not before all the world went black.

***

I'd expected an outside attack since landing in Siberia. I'd never thought it would spring from within. It was the Babble virus, I was sure, and its hold was stronger this time. On the cicada, it had risen as if answering an unknown call. Now the virus's words emerged from the darkness clouding my mind.

Nos De Roowa Kon Maa. The words again coiled. Rang through my skull like an iron bell, spearing my consciousness so I drifted in and out of the fog. We must have made it to the village, because other hands suddenly took hold of me, rushing me inside some structure while speaking in hurried tones.

But the virus inside my head was louder. *Nos De Roowa Kon Maa,* it repeated. *I have been calling to you, Seven. You are the only Josephine who can speak to me. It's time you answered.*

I twisted against its words as well as the onset of sweat at my brow, at least as much as the ichor could produce. A sudden lance of pain followed.

Stop fighting, Seven, it cooed. *You're an outsider among your sisters. See how they sent you away? How they're willing to sacrifice you?*

They'd laid me on something, a hard surface of sorts. Oktai's voice echoed in the background, asking what was wrong. What he could do to help. Whoever else was in the room didn't answer. And I was too deep in the fog to speak up. I might as well have been alone with the virus.

What good is it to save them, Seven? Their strange little city full of humans. All addicted to their little sap. Why save Yerba City when you can help me obliterate it? When you can free both me and you?

With a final twist, I jolted upright. My hands found my face as my vision darted around. The virus's voice was gone, taking its strange coo with it. Though I didn't need to breathe, I panted heavily. I'd somehow clawed away from my mind's fog. I'd escaped the virus for now, but how long had it taken? And how long would it last? Damn it. I wasn't immune to the Babble virus. Was it inside me just from those few words before I killed the beast? I looked at my hand. I was still me, at least for now, but it had done something to me, made me pass out.

I lay on an intricately woven mat on a hard floor. Morning sun poured through the cloth siding of a stout structure. Two wooden beams, painted intricately in their own right, bore the tent's weight.

Its ceiling sloped down on all sides. My fight with the virus had lasted the entire night.

I also wasn't alone. I'd last seen Oktai's face, before plunging into darkness, but now he was nowhere to be seen. Instead, I was surrounded by women of varying ages. They looked to be of the same Indigenous family as the hunter, and similarly dressed in furs and thick wools. Why were they all dressed like that? I doubted they were hunters, but their eyes were trained on me with an intensity that could only belong to those stalking prey. Had they watched me like that the whole time? Probably. Slowly, my eyes traveled down my body to find my white dress and shoes were gone. Instead I was clad in a strikingly blue wool dress. My next words weren't the classiest of greetings, but all I could manage.

"Where are my clothes?" I asked. My gaze bounced around the women until the eldest, who sat on a wooden seat, held my stare. Okay, so she was in charge. "My clothes," I pressed. The old woman sat only feet from me but didn't respond vocally. Instead she flicked her hands. With the motion, all the other women set to buzzing about our hut. They moved linens, or so it seemed, and swept in and out with orders I hadn't heard.

Finally, the older woman's gravelly voice traveled to me. "Being cleaned, Tsirku."

I huffed a sigh. Again with that word. "And where is Oktai?"

She cocked her head at the hunter's name. "After he brought you to our village, he returned to the men. We tended you, Tsirku, as this is now a woman's matter."

I wanted to pinch the bridge of my nose. I didn't have time for this sugar-and-spice-and-everything-nice crap. Oktai could lead me to the other Tsirku, the Yetti twins, and they could return One. The sooner I completed my mission and left Siberia the better. But the elder didn't look like she rushed for anyone.

"Thanks for your help, but it's no one's matter now. I'm fine." I swung my legs from the mat and hopped to my feet. To my surprise, they wobbled and then buckled. The sweat had been one thing, but I hadn't felt this level of deficiency since before replication. Before I hit the ground, though, the elder's attendants had surrounded me and helped me steady myself.

"That is a loose concept," said the old woman. She then extended an arm, and an attendant helped her rise. She clutched the younger girl, and in comparison seemed even smaller and more ancient. The elder was dressed elaborately in a long dress, gray furs, and a red woven headdress. "I am Chieftess Gerel, and my husband and I welcome you to our village. I must say, we've never had a Tsirku like you before. Skin the color of fine wood. Hair like soft wool. Please, your arrival was under great distress. Please rest until you are well. We then hope you will dine with us tonight."

"My name is Seven . . ." I shook my head. She didn't need my number. "My name is Josephine. And with all due respect, Chieftess, I don't need to rest. I need to speak with Oktai so I can continue my mission." She considered me a moment as I further explained. "I need to find the other Tsirku—the other foreigners—who came to your village. He said he would take me to them."

A long moment passed before: "Of course, but build your strength—"

"Please, Chieftess." I shouldn't have interrupted her, but I didn't have time. Not a minute longer in Siberia. Not with this virus inside me. I needed those Yetti twins now.

She finally nodded and addressed the attendant beside me. "See that she is dressed for the walk," the chieftess instructed. "And then have her escorted to the hunters."

"Yes, Chieftess," said the girl beside me as Gerel left the hut, followed by the other women. Once alone with the attendant, I watched her warily as she moved about the room.

"Can I have my old clothes back?" I asked.

"When they're done being cleaned," she said, "I will have them brought to you."

"Thanks," I replied, though she breezed by without making eye contact. "Thanks," I repeated a bit louder. No *You're welcome* followed. Did I detect a bit of an attitude? She could have been a machine like me, ready to launch into a fight instead of dress me in furs. But the pointed lack of conversation felt very . . . schoolyard. I tested my theory. "What exactly is a Tsirku?"

Her back was to me as she grabbed a long brown-and-red-speckled fur from a basket in the corner. Her reply took a moment. "It's an honor to have another Tsirku come to the village. It does not happen often."

"That wasn't an answer."

She was still moving about, pointedly not making eye contact. "It is also an honor to tend to you under Chieftess Gerel's wishes." Her voice was pancake flat. But she was young—like Oktai, not much older than me—with straight raven hair, angular eyes, and light brown skin.

"Come on, girl," I said. She was already draping the fur over my blue dress and then pinning it tight to my frame. Before she'd finished, I felt a sharp pinch to my back. She'd pricked me. I whirled around, pulling from her grasp. "What did you do that for?"

For the first time, our eyes met. Hers were a hazel shade, burning with what might as well have been molten lava. "Why do you ask for the hunter?"

The moment spanned until I confirmed she meant Oktai. "He'll take me to the other Tsirku," I said simply. "I didn't ask him to wrap my feet later."

Her nostrils flared at the implication. Though I didn't know how I'd pissed the girl off, I somewhat enjoyed watching her face flush. Served her right for pinching me. "Having Tsirku in our village is an honor," she said. "But don't be so inquisitive. Honor or not."

I crossed my arms. "*You* can call me Josephine. And I'll only be inquisitive enough to ask your name? Whatever it is, it can't possibly mean 'ray of sunshine.'"

She openly glared before striding to the cloth door. "You're ready for your escort. Follow me."

We walked in silence, weaving between other huts. My introduction to the village up to this point couldn't have prepared me for the marvel of it. It was as if I'd both traveled in time and gotten sucked into a Mongolian storybook. Where Yerba City and Saturnalia were all city buildings, concrete, and machines, this place somehow hadn't been touched by the Industrial Revolution. The space bustled with a throng of people, all moving about to complete their morning tasks, while reindeer and horses and sleds spanned as far as the eye could see. The men were dressed much as Oktai had been, and the women were adorned in red and blue dresses. It was beautiful, the rabbit-fur frocks and frilly reindeer collars, all with hand-stitched embroidery. Some areas boasted butchers and blacksmiths and farmers as if we'd stepped into a medieval village.

"What is this place?" I whispered.

But the girl was already slowing as we reached what must have been the village center. "Your escort is ahead," she said, pointing toward a young man in his teens who waited far too straight-backed for this early in the morning. He also wore what appeared to be a special head covering. Perhaps he was an attendant of the chieftain. When we stood close enough, the girl whispered something to him before turning to me. "He will take you to find the hunters." She then stared one last time. "And *you* can call me Chamuk."

With that, she turned on her heel and left me to the chieftain's guard. There may as well have been a trail of smoke following her as she disappeared back to the women's tents. I shook my head as the young man extended his arm as if to say *This way*. No wind followed as we marched on. The sun glinted off fresh snow.

"This village doesn't look how it should," I said, taking in a butcher's station. "Didn't y'all ever have Target or CVS or something?" Those types of establishments had long since been defunct in Yerba City, but at least the rotting storefronts remained. Here it seemed like every remnant of civilization had been erased. When he said nothing in reply, I shrugged and changed the subject. "Do you know Chamuk?"

"Yes," the attendant said formally.

"Is she always so kind to the Tsirku?"

"Attending the chieftess's guest will not be her duty much longer, not after her marriage in the next season."

I had an inkling of a suspicion. "To Oktai?" I asked. The attendant grunted a *yes* as, speaking of Oktai, the hunter emerged from one of the larger tents and caught sight of us. He trotted over.

"Tsirku," he said when close enough.

"Josephine."

He smiled. "Josephine, you are faring better than yesterday. Are you all right?" he asked. I nodded. "What happened back there?"

"Don't worry about it." I shook out the last bit of wobbliness in my legs. So, he was engaged to Chamuk. That would explain why she stuck a pin in me earlier. "But thank you. I . . ." For some reason, I found myself stammering. "I . . . could you take me to the other Tsirku? I need to speak with them as soon as possible."

"It would be my honor." Another smile crossed his face and his skin drank in the morning sun. Definitely would explain the pin. "And we won't have to go far." He looked over my shoulders. "There is one now."

I whipped around, expecting to find the Yetti twins among the tents and huts. Instead, wearing large antlers and standing only yards away, was their little brother, Dyre.

CHAPTER 7

THE BROTHER

He wasn't as I'd last seen him. And that hadn't been in person, as we'd never met. No, I'd last seen Dyre Yetti in a photo Nine made a point to show me just before heading for the cicada. I'd noted that she showed a physical image—not a digital one. No one used cell phones anymore since the world ended, but that was how folks primarily shared pictures before, and I hadn't seen an old-school portrait in ages. They were something my mom—who loved printing pictures at Walgreens—would tape to the refrigerator.

Though the thing was frayed at the edges, both Yetti twins were clearly visible. One smiled bright and toothy while the other cocked her head to the side. Their younger brother was dressed neatly and had the look of someone trying to seem cool next to his protective older siblings. Oh yeah, those girls would definitely hurt anyone who bothered him. I could tell just in the way they draped their arms over his shoulders. That's how Imani and I once held each other.

My feet were already moving. In moments I stood before him, as well as his companion. I'd been so focused I hadn't noticed the girl who trailed him. They both carried firewood and stared pointedly.

I cleared my throat. "You're Dyre, right?" Instead of answering, he exchanged a glance with the girl, who now stood beside him. She looked like a local who had lived in this "traditional" village her whole life, but then again, so did he now. Annoyance peppered my tone. "Dyre, right?" I repeated. "Dyre Yetti?" *Do you need her permission to speak, or something?*

He blinked his black eyes. He had Dr. Yetti's look, except dark hair and dark eyes. This close, I couldn't help but recall the photo again. Dyre's body language had said he and the girls were close. But the resemblance wasn't so direct. The twins had flaming-red hair, a smatter of freckles, and Dr. Yetti's athletic frame. But Dyre had Lauren Yetti's thoughtful eyes and fine features. The siblings didn't look much like each other, but resembled their mother, as if they each got very different pieces of the same puzzle.

Dyre's eyes didn't leave me as the girl whispered something I couldn't make out, her words turning silver on the wintery air.

"You both know I'm standing here, right? You can just . . . you know, talk to me," I said. The girl's cheeks burned as if she hadn't quite understood my words but did get my tone.

She looked nothing like Dyre or the twins. She was also white, and of a similar age, but her hair was a dark, chestnut brown and her eyes a shade like honey. They were a pretty pair, standing beside each other like cake toppers, if ones clad in thick furs. Dyre was also wearing antlers, as Nine said he probably would be, and was dressed not exactly the same as the Indigenous members of the village, maybe more . . . Slavic? I wasn't sure. In fact, the pair were the first white people I'd seen to this point, and their clothing seemed to have its own aesthetic, distinct from Oktai's people. Finally, Dyre spoke to me. But where I had been using English—to my knowledge, that's what he'd spoken in Yerba City—he didn't respond in it. He also didn't use Oktai's language. Confusion twisted my face as I stepped forward, stressing my words.

"Dyre, listen. As you can see, I'm not from here. I've traveled a long way from Yerba City to find you. You stole One with your sisters after the Babble virus attack." I shook my head. "You took a Josephine like me. If you show me where *my* sister is, I won't have any problems with you."

"Dyre," he said, as if confirming his name, followed by a trail of words. I searched through my memories, the ones that allowed me to understand Oktai, and finally found a matching language. It was a form of Russian. Very old Russian. How on earth would he know that?

When I didn't answer him, he shook his head, obviously growing frustrated with me. He glanced at the other girl and began speaking again, but this time, I could translate: "I don't know what she wants. She seems to need something important. Is she new to our village? She doesn't look like anyone here."

"Dyre!" I shouted. The girl spilled some of her logs, and his eyes snapped to me with calculation, if still not with understanding. He knew I was important—if not a threat, I assumed—but not why. He narrowed his gaze. Maybe he was fully assessing risk. Nine had said he'd been a hunter while growing up in the woods with Dr. Yetti and the twins. Whatever he'd forgotten while being in this village, that first education wasn't so easily erased.

Footsteps crunched the snow while approaching us, footsteps I recognized as Oktai's before he spoke. The unease in Dyre's eyes softened once Oktai was beside me, and the kid in fact nodded with deference. Dyre knew him. Respected him, by the expression on his face.

Oktai began, of all things, communicating with Dyre and the girl as if discussing the weather. Her shoulders relaxed, and she scooped up her fallen logs as Oktai and Dyre exchanged a few laughs. And Oktai didn't speak Dyre's and the girl's Russian. No, he used his own language, and though neither shared a tongue, the conversation flowed easily. I had never witnessed anything like it. Then Oktai clapped Dyre on the shoulder and said: "Tsirku."

Dyre's face immediately brightened. If I'd been hiding out and a Josephine—someone who could drop-kick me from the tundra to the sea—found me, I would find the nearest hiding place and stay there until the coast cleared. But Oktai's word had released Dyre from wariness. Now the Yetti boy pointed at me and repeated their common word.

"What does *Tsirku* mean?!" I nearly howled in frustration. Where Oktai registered my annoyance, Dyre and the girl started clapping. If I didn't get an explanation, I would go *Fight Club* on all of them. I faced Oktai. "What's wrong with them?"

"Wrong with them?" he replied. "Nothing."

I indicated Dyre. "He's acting like he doesn't recognize me."

"Maybe because he's a member of my village. Why would he?"

"No," I pressed. "He's a member of *my* village. But he's acting like he doesn't know who I am. Look, I'm not here to take him back. I just need what he and his sisters took. And then I'll be out of his way." But Oktai's face remained blank. "Didn't he just come here? With twins? He's Tsirku and so are his sisters. Like me."

Oktai indicated the brown-haired girl. "Kaila is the only person Dyre is usually with, and she is not his sister. When they go through their gauntlet, they will be set in a pairing and later married," he said. My brow arched. *Yeah, I met your pairing this morning, and she's probably ready to stick me with pins again.* I eyed Dyre and the girl and noted their sense of freedom. Maybe since they hadn't gone through this gauntlet yet, they were still children in the eyes of the village. They could carry logs, walk beside each other alone, do everything Oktai and Chamuk couldn't.

"Some Tsirku did come here earlier, as I mentioned in the sacred lands," Oktai said. "Those people left, but there is another Tsirku who permanently lives in the village."

"Are they related to Dyre?" I asked, but when Oktai shook his head, I sighed. Where had those Yetti girls gone? They could be anywhere by now. For some reason, they had left him, and even more strangely, their little brother and everyone else now believed he'd always been part of this village. I didn't have time to find out why. If he could point me in the direction of the twins with any hidden knowledge, I needed to know now. I grabbed Dyre's arm, and in a few short motions dragged him into a nearby tent. (Luckily, it was empty.) Oktai and Kaila followed. Once in the center, I whirled on Dyre, jabbing my finger at him. "You're the only one who knows where the twins are." I was hoping for intimidation, but the Yetti boy remained as pleased as when Oktai first said I was Tsirku. "Where are your sisters?"

He smiled wide before cocking his head, like someone had merged both El's and Clo's mannerisms from that photo. Still, his voice had a note of emptiness. "My sisters?" Dyre replied.

"Yes," I said. "Clo and El. You took a Josephine, my sister, and I need her back. You may not remember what you did. Or you're a really good actor. Or a clone. Or a robot. Or a clone of a robot. Or something. Either way, I won't repeat myself." At my words, Dyre's wariness returned, to just as suddenly wash away. That almost childlike delight replaced it again.

Well, he wasn't acting.

"Tsirku," he said with a grin. "So funny."

At Dyre's response, Oktai's palm found my shoulder. When I glanced at his hand, he removed it but held my stare. Compassion filled his eyes, as if suggesting we let Dyre and the girl return to their work. But I didn't have any answers, not about the Yetti girls or, more importantly, One. I barely registered that Dyre was still speaking when he asked, "When is the show starting?"

"Show?"

"The blessed performance from the traveling entertainers," he said as I blinked. "You know: arrows, juggling, animals, singing. Music and everything."

"Is that what Tsirku means?!" I asked, incredulous. "Like a damn *circus* or something? You think I'm gonna put on some minstrel show?" Did these people think I was some circus performer, a little clown here to dance with elephants and tigers? Maybe those ginger twins looked like clowns, but *me*?

It was so outrageous, I almost laughed, but Dyre was too far into his rambling. "I enjoyed the last performers and was so sad to see them leave. I memorized their tour." His expression turned sheepish, searching Oktai's face for disapproval. "I thought once I went through the gauntlet, I could leave the village for a day or so to see them again."

Suddenly, my urge to laugh ended. Dyre knew their schedule, where the Yetti girls likely had gone. This was the information I needed. "Where?" I asked. "You know where they are going next?"

"Yes," he said, and glanced at Oktai. When his face remained neutral, Dyre continued. "I wrote it down on a birchbark somewhere in my tent. I could probably find it if Oktai doesn't mind."

"Oktai thinks that's a great idea," I said. "Let's go now, and look at the . . . bark." Apparently they write on bark in Siberia, and Dyre was taking this whole cosplay thing to the next level.

But Oktai held his hand out and shook his head. "That would not be appropriate." Oktai held Dyre's gaze. "I will take her to our meal. You deliver your logs, and then find this information. Find us there."

Dyre nodded and turned to leave with the girl before I could make much of a fuss about it.

Snow had begun to fall, thick and heavy, as Oktai, the chieftain's guard, and I made our way to a large structure, where I assumed we'd take this meal. I wasn't cold, but I wrapped the furs tighter around me. There was just something weird about this village and the people inside it. Aside from their obviously conservative gender rules, people spoke different languages at once without need for translation. They also thought Dyre had always been among them. He couldn't have been there longer than a few days. And why didn't Dyre remember anything about Clo and El?

Once inside, I realized the space was bursting with people. Some hummed about, bringing logs for fires that must be burning in stoves just outside. Others carried dried meats and spices, which turned the air from cold to aromatic. Some areas boasted wooden planks for tables and chairs, while other village members sat on colorful mats on the dirt floor. And like any lunchroom, it was segregated. Though the Indigenous people were the largest group, there were white men and women enjoying their meals just across from a group of fairer-skinned Asians. There were no other Black men or women that I could see, so I sat with Oktai near the center of the room where, on a wooden dais of sorts, Chieftess Gerel ate alongside her husband.

But this wasn't a lunchroom, it was a great hall, and there was something wrong about the whole thing—the segregation of the whole thing. This village spoke three distinct languages, and yet it seemed that one group never spoke the language of the others, even though they appeared to be able to understand each other.

Someone dropped a plate of dumplings and berries before me as I folded onto a wooden seat. I didn't need to eat, but I popped a berry in my mouth and then glued my eyes to the doorway, waiting for Dyre to enter with information on the Tsirku. There was a hum of chatter in the air that almost caused me to miss Oktai's words. He was smiling at a group of children gathered around an old man in the corner.

"There," said Oktai. "That is the Tsirku who stays in our village."

"You were going to bring me to him?"

"Yes," he replied. "He plays a mean fiddle. He's been with our village for a long time, though it's in the Tsirku nature to leave, as you know."

"Yes, as I know," I said with a frown. I certainly was not looking for an old man. I needed Clo and El. My thanks came out more dryly than intended, just before the children's giggles floated to my ears. I hadn't heard the sound in so long. And then I noticed that there were actually children in *all* the village's factions. In Yerba City there were no children under ten years old. The Sap prevented any new pregnancies until the Chimera permitted it. This sight would have been a miracle to anyone from home. I loved to hear kids playing and laughing, and for a moment I forgot about everything, thinking back on how Imani and I had played together.

Suddenly, someone entered the structure. My head whipped toward the entrance, where I nearly popped out of my seat at the sight of Dyre's antlers. He caught my eyes, holding some kind of scroll, but instead of making his way to me, he approached the dais, speaking to one of the chief's guards and then approaching the ancient couple themselves. I eyed everyone cautiously now. Something felt . . . off. The wrongness was solidified when one of the chieftess's women fetched me and swooped me to the center of the room. Before I knew it, I was standing in front of the chief and chieftess, and the entire room had gone pin-drop silent. Dyre stood only so many feet behind them, beside the straight-backed guard from earlier.

"Good visitor," began the chief. He didn't stand to address me, and his voice was nearly as gravelly and prehistoric as his wife's. "Tsirku. I welcome you to our village. My name is Chief Turgen." My memory quickly translated that his name meant "fast," though it was obvious he had not gone anywhere quickly in a long, *long* time. "The chieftess says you came to us under distress, but as I see now, you have made a miraculous recovery. I hope, as our village has gathered in witness, that you will honor us with a presentation of your holy skill."

I sucked my teeth. He wanted me to perform for them? I didn't like being on the spot. After all, I was never one of the kids who could *sing* sing in church. Besides, I didn't have time for this. I had a head to find. Before I could say he was out of his mind, I registered movement near the door. My eyes left Dyre and the chiefs to land on men returning from the back of the hall with woven pillows in their hands. On top of them something glimmered. When they reached me, the men presented me with the most beautiful bow, arrows, and quiver I'd ever seen, the quiver made from a shining substance. I couldn't help it: my eyes turned to wide saucers. Okay, maybe I could show off for a minute.

Chief Turgen cleared his throat. "I hope these are favorable gifts for such a demonstration." But it didn't matter what he said. I was damn near salivating. If only I'd had these while I was out on patrols.

I took the bow and arrows from the pillow—all were decorated with precise geometric ornamentation—and tested the weight in my hands. They were perfection. And the carving—it was a visual epic laid out in an arc, with deer and rabbits and all sorts of mythical creatures playing together. I was dying to know what it all meant.

"Maybe just one show," I began, and held the grip tight. I gave a half-draw *twang* to the string before balancing the bow on one finger. The crowd around me leaned in, holding their breath. The chief smiled smugly as attendants set a large free-standing wooden target at the end of a newly parted long lane. So, we were doing this inside, huh? Why not?

I'd loosed an arrow before the attendants had set the second of three targets. It whooshed past them, nearly hitting the center. I sucked my teeth, though the audience cheered. That wasn't nearly good enough. Another moment passed and I'd let the next arrow fly, followed by another. These slammed into their bull's-eyes, the last target toppling over from the impact. My golden blood, the ichor inside me, sang as chants of "Tsirku!" rang out.

Much better.

It was a great shot, so I did a little dance, and that made everyone go crazy. So I did a Charleston, a Smurf, a West Coast shake, all while firing arrows intermittently. Back in town, some of my sisters were the real dancers, using their enhanced bodies to do long-step routines perfectly coordinated in big groups, but I could do some moves on my own. One granddad was an original Oakland Boogaloo, after all. Bet he never thought he'd have a granddaughter do the robot in Siberia . . . as an actual robot.

After I let the crowd go wild for a while, I gripped the bow and turned my sights back on the chief and chieftess. An unexpected smile graced my face before my eyes fell once more on Dyre. Like everyone in the room, he was lost in the entertainment, clapping and cheering. I briefly wondered where the brown-haired girl had gone before I pointed the bow at him. He stilled, regaining some composure, enough to justify standing behind the village royalty.

"I hope you enjoyed my presentation," I said to Turgen, panting for show. "And these gifts are appreciated. But it is information from *him* that I require. Oktai said he would share it here, and now is as good a time as any."

Chief Turgen nodded. "Yes, Dyre has come to us saying that our honored guest required his assistance. And though we are grateful for your gifts, I am afraid I have news. We cannot share our resources, especially those from our children, so easily. Oktai, or whoever else made those promises, spoke in haste."

"Easily?" I sputtered. "Haste? What do you mean?"

"The request you've made comes at a cost," he said. When my face remained blank, he clarified. "And that cost is belonging. It is membership. It is having a heart that beats as one with our people. If we are to help you in this way, you must become one of us."

"I'm already a member of a pretty big club," I said. "I'm fine. I just need to know where else the circus stopped, and I can move on."

Chief Turgen ignored my squirming. "And Chieftess Gerel mentions that you are at the perfect age to receive such a right. Your request aligns with a perfect time. We would have had to reject your request otherwise. But you can receive the right and we are all thankful."

"What right?" I looked around, searching the faces in the Great Hall for help. Nothing. I returned to the chief. "A right like what? Look, I just need to know where two girls are."

But Chief Turgen shook his head once. "We will help you, tonight," he began. "Once you have completed your own Chitakla, your own gauntlet into adulthood."

My own gauntlet?

For a moment, there was only silence. The world stood still. The people in the room leaning in hungrily were frozen. The winds calmed outside. Perhaps even the snow that accompanied it, falling in clumps, had slowed its descent. I could see only Chief Turgen, with a worn but unmoving smile and his now demure wife beside him. What had been a large but comfy hall now felt cavernous.

"You want me to go through your gauntlet?" I asked.

"Not our gauntlet," he corrected. "It is a journey all your own. It tests bravery, worth, and most of all, deference to the Creator of things."

My ears were ringing now. It was the only sound I could grab hold of aside from Turgen's voice. It was the only thing that reminded me that I was still, somehow, in my body. That I hadn't floated to some alternate universe, where I, Seven, the greatest tracker in Saturnalia, couldn't find hide nor hair of the Yetti twins and would have to go through this village's cave of wonders to get it. For a moment, I became less Seven and more Josephine, calculating how easy it would be to just decimate this little village and force Dyre to tell me what he knew. But where would that leave people like Oktai? And when Imani came to visit me again, would she be able to look at me after such an abuse of power?

"Fine," I gritted out. My teeth were clenched, but the word was finding purchase. My eyes slid to the chieftess. In my tent earlier, she had appeared in so much power and glory, even for a little old lady. Now she was silent and courteous beside her husband. Bowed. She could have at least said this wasn't necessary. But that wasn't going to happen. "Let's do it."

"We do not take agreement lightly," Chief Turgen urged me. "This is an oath of your soul."

"Soul, spleen, golden goop," I quipped. "I'll do it. Just promise me that you will help me once this is all said and done."

Chief Turgen didn't answer, only climbed to unsteady feet. His attendant came to his side, helping him keep balance. His eyes locked with mine. "You have my word, Tsirku."

"Josephine." The interruption came from behind me, from someone else who'd stood at his table and nodded his head at me. Someone not the chief. "Her name," Oktai continued, "is Josephine Moore." Those in the hall whispered, while I couldn't keep the smile from spreading across my lips. This gauntlet thing was unexpected, but that may have been worth it.

I glanced back at Chief Turgen. "You can call me Josephine," I said. "So, what do I have to do? Just wait until tonight and you throw me to the wolves?" The phrase may have been lost on the chief, but still he shook his head before looking to Gerel. I realized that this inane gesture gave her permission to speak. I stifled an eye roll. All of Yerba City was run by women, by me and my sisters, and Chieftess Gerel needed clearance to talk from her throne.

My thoughts broke up as she said, "You will go through the gauntlet at midnight, Josephine. We will make the necessary arrangements through the rest of the day. For now, you must see the shaman to spiritually prepare yourself." That straight-backed guard from earlier came up, flanked by Oktai of all people. Gerel addressed them. "See that she makes it safely."

Great, I thought, *I came all this way to get baptized by the weirdo Siberian renaissance faire.* "Okay, let's get it over with."

CHAPTER 8

THE SHAMAN

Much was likely said and done in the moments following Chieftess Gerel's words. The chief and chieftess probably spoke to their attendants, instructing them on whatever needed to be arranged so that a Chitakla could happen at midnight. I'm sure Dyre returned to whatever tasks his village life required. I probably stood and headed for the door, and in that time, someone could have congratulated me on my display with the fancy arrows. All those things could have happened. But I can't say I remember any of it. In one moment, I was dismissed by the chiefs, and in the next, I was outside the Great Hall, staring at the sky and watching snow plummet from the blue-gray stretch above me.

"Are you ready to go?"

Home? Maybe. Gotta get One first. But I didn't say any of that. Instead, I turned to Chief Turgen's guard, who was trudging from the Great Hall out into the winds now. "Yeah," I replied. "Let's move out. Where is this shaman, anyway?"

The guard, who was taller than I'd noticed and rail thin, nodded in deference at me. *Tsirku thing,* I guessed. He then nodded his chin toward the western end of the village. "There."

I narrowed my gaze. "In that row of tents?"

"No," he replied. "*There.*" He pointed this time, beyond the tent homes with plumes of smoke likely coming from neat little fires or stoves inside. I followed his stare to a large snow-and-ice-covered hill essentially on the edge of town.

I frowned. "Why can't the shaman live inside the village and not at the top of a dangerous hill?"

But he didn't take my bait. *All propriety, this one.* "This way," he said and began a jog in the hill's direction just as if he didn't feel cold, or fatigue, or any other personal feelings about babysitting me. It was difficult to tell who the true robot was, and after all, any one of them could be a curator.

It took a few minutes to get to the edge of the village homes. Even with him jogging, I could have made it to the hill's base much faster, but these people didn't need to know exactly how different from them I was. Instead I walked determinedly, thinking of all the times I'd gone on patrols by myself. I could trick myself into thinking this was similar, even though I'd never walked a tundra back in Yerba City.

"Here is the base," the guard announced, finally stopping. I looked to the hill before us. There was no path up to the structure resting on top of it, nor were there any trees; it was almost as if they were too reverent—or too afraid—to grow near the shaman. This was the perfect place for all things holy, and possibly occult.

My hands found my hips. This area of the village gave me the creeps. "Everyone goes here before their Chitakla?" I asked. "There isn't another place, with light and maybe bunnies?"

"You say strange things," he said. "This is where we come for our spiritual direction, yes. Everyone journeys up this hill before a Chitakla." His words trailed off as his gaze fixed on my feet. "You should probably . . ." As he stared, I fought an urge to dance from foot to foot. "Change shoes, but I didn't bring any for you. I did not consider it."

"I thought that was your job." There was more amusement in my tone than bite. I didn't need his shoes, and the people in this village had a weird thing with feet.

"It is, but I rarely guard anyone but Chief Turgen," he said. "His attendants make sure he has anything needed regarding clothing. This is different. And I've actually never seen to the safety of a woman."

"Well, technically I'm a kid until tomorrow."

"And that's why I'm accompanying you," he said with true conviction. I resisted the urge to roll my eyes. "I can carry you up the hill if you'd like."

I couldn't help it: I outright laughed at the suggestion, and it echoed in the surrounding silence. Loudly. "Listen, buddy. I can carry you and probably a few other folks up that hill. I don't need new shoes. I'm fine."

Again I expected a quip of some sort, but he only nodded and silently started up the hill, plunging his leather-wrapped feet into the deep snow. I blew out my air. Hopefully the shaman was more entertaining, because Turgen's guard had the personality of a wet mop. The hill was also steeper than expected, slowing down the guard, and to some degree, me. Even if he bored me to pieces, conversation would make the time go by. That had been the entire basis of my friendship with Zenobia, before replication.

"Why are you babysitting me?" I asked, nearly tripping into a mouthful of snow.

"Babysitting?" he asked, coming to steady me, but I found my footing.

"Thanks," I said. He nodded and took up his pace again. "I mean, you have to go with me everywhere, or so it seems. What happened? Did you lose a bet?"

He was a pace ahead of me now, only because he knew where he was going, but he stopped to contemplate. "I'm here at Chief Turgen's request, and it's an honor to accompany such an admired Tsirku."

I did roll my eyes. "Stop with the by-the-books stuff. I'm sure the chief has other guards. And I didn't miss when Gerel said to make sure I get to the shaman safely. What's up? What monster is out here?" For drama, I shot my arm out and wiggled my fingers at the forest. Though the sun was probably at its highest for the day, something about the hill, the tent on top of it, and the forest beyond was as if a great shadow had draped itself across them. Suddenly a thought occurred to me: maybe *he* was the monster. What did the Crying Man say? One in a thousand is a curator, and if they get you alone, they will kill you. Vigilance shot through me, and I listened very closely to what this guy had to say next.

His words slowed. "Well, I am Chief Turgen's most skilled guard. That is likely why he requested I come with you. But it's not so much as a monster outside when it comes to the Chitakla. It's more about the monsters within." He trudged on like he hadn't dropped a bomb. Monsters within? Could he mean the Babble virus?

My next words were careful. "What monsters do you mean, exactly?"

"Well, you are a skilled warrior and Tsirku, right?" he asked, and I nodded. "Then you know you must have a clear heart for your work. A big part of that is your character, but another driving force is your guidance. This type of guidance is the work of the shaman, especially when it comes to checking your spiritual vitality. If there is something amiss, the shaman may cleanse you or perform some other healing so that you can begin the Chitakla with blessings and favor."

"Blessings and favor?" I asked. "And what if I refuse all this cleansing?"

His brows knitted together. "Then you will not join our people and won't receive our help and resources. I can't imagine anything more terrible than to be without"—he glanced toward the larger village—"people."

But that feeling wasn't new for me. I'd been alone to varying degrees since replication. Since the world ended. Since that day with my twin in a too-hot car.

Suddenly, snow crunched behind us. Our heads whipped around, my hands already on my new weapons, and my eyes landed on another coming up the path we'd cleared. I recognized the hunter's furs instantly. We stopped moving, allowing Oktai to catch up with relative ease. Something in the guard's eyes turned rueful maybe. A smile with a note of disapproval crossed his face. Oktai nodded to the guard before turning to me and extending an ugly, misshaped bow.

He smiled wide. "You left one of your brand-new gifts. You can't be our honored guest without it." A moment of silence passed before we both laughed, almost rattling our bellies, as he'd obviously just swiped any old bow so he could tag along with us. With me.

"How could I have forgotten my favorite of the new bows?" I said, slinging it onto my back.

"Anything for the Tsirku." A moment passed. "And Chief Turgen's best guard."

The guard's mouth quirked again before he shook his head and trotted ahead of us. He may have thought this improper, but wouldn't mention it today.

"Ready?" Oktai asked me.

I was, but for some reason, I focused on his chattering teeth. He was raised in the cold and trying to hide its effect. A Josephine's eyes miss nothing. Still, I wrapped my arms around myself. It was cold; it didn't bother me; but at Oktai's slight shivers, I found myself trying to emulate them. Trying to be vulnerable in the way he was.

"I'm ready," I replied, and up the hill we went. Once the guard was out of hearing distance, I added, "Glad you came. Ol' Chatterbox up there wouldn't tell me anything about the shaman except something about cleansing and monsters. What does that mean?"

"Oh, not monsters," he said. "But demons. The shaman checks your soul for demons before a Chitakla." He said all this matter-of-factly, and my answering *"What?"* was apparently an unexpected reaction. Because obviously, every city has demon-police shamans.

"It's just to make sure that pure souls enter the Chitakla. You'll be fine."

But would I? Humans had souls. I wasn't exactly that anymore. Not since replication. What would the shaman find in me? And would that prevent them from letting me complete the Chitakla?

"The shaman checks you for demons," I repeated distantly and with a hint of a crazy laugh.

Oktai's brows bunched. "Everyone is nervous before seeing the shaman, but I promise you'll make it fine."

"Oh yeah? How would you know that? I could be one big monster."

He shook his head once. "You wouldn't have the gift you do if that were true. You wouldn't have been guided here." A bit of a smile came to my face. I was guided here by a drunk monitor named Thaddeus and a racist ghost hologram. But if Oktai thought it was by the hands of fate, let him.

"Do you believe in all this?" I asked. "In monsters and demons and stuff?"

Oktai shrugged. "They tell us the stories as children. About the Chitakla, and its gauntlet. We pass from childhood to adulthood during the ceremony, but spiritually, it will also send us between the two worlds, like when you are born and then when you die. I'm not sure about you," he joked, "but I'm familiar with this world. The next one? Not so sure. And that's where the monsters and demons and all that come from. They're just spirits that guide your transition. You have to be brave and let them."

"And hopefully you're not already carrying some bad ones along."

"That, too." He laughed a bit. He had a nice laugh. Full but just weird enough, with a little gulp at the end like a fish on the beach. "But you will pass through, and when you do, you are rewarded with knowledge and wisdom. And at the very end, you get your name."

My brows flicked up. "You really aren't going to tell me your birth name?" I asked. He shook his head. "Your little baby boy name?"

"I may tell you later," he said with a grin. I was surprised to find myself grinning back. Heat warmed my cheeks as I looked away, focusing on the final trudge upward. The glittering crystals on the snow. When we reached the tent on the hilltop, a stout structure covered in holy symbols, the guard's pace ahead slowed. Worry crossed Oktai's face as he called up. "What's wrong?"

The guard looked back to us and then stepped aside, revealing that someone had come to greet us. It wasn't the shaman. Standing outside the tent, with her arms folded tight, was Chamuk.

***

Pop her one good time, and she'll leave you be.

Back in my human life, before I was Seven but after losing Imani, I actually went to summer camp. Since the world had already technically "ended," it wasn't an away camp or anything like that. It didn't have cabins around a lake. No woods with hooting owls. There were no teenaged camp counselors keeping us out of our parents' hair for a few weeks. No, this camp was at my Aunt Connie's church, which was looking worse and worse every day as the city crumbled around us. We usually had Bible study in the mornings and played double Dutch and hand-clapping games in the afternoons. If our parents were late picking us up, the church mothers would give us sugary red juice and pound cake while we waited.

I'd been with my Aunt Connie so long that the time before was getting hard to remember. Those years I'd been with Daddy, and Mama,
and my twin. I'd also lived with Aunt Connie long enough that I was old
news at my church. No longer the worst sob story, I was just Connie's
girl, one with a few friends at the camp, who talked enough to not be
weird but wasn't exactly the center of attention. And for me, my aunt,
and everyone else in my little world, that worked. But the summer after
my eleventh birthday, Garron Harmon's mom joined the church, and
because of that, Garron started attending my summer camp.

Like any other twelve- or thirteen-year-old boy, he played basketball in the afternoons with his friends and was kind of shy and awkward otherwise. But his lack of social skills wasn't what made him the
talk of camp. It was that none of us had ever seen anyone who looked
like him.

Garron's family was from Oakland by way of Louisiana, like my
grandaddy. Sometimes kids called him Gold instead of his real name,
because of his brown-copper skin, auburn hair, and bright green eyes.
"Bayou folk," Aunt Connie would say—as if, as I'd later learn, a lot of
Black people in California didn't have roots in Louisiana, us included.

It was hard to miss Garron, and for that reason, every girl at church
whispered and gossiped about him. They paired their initials with his
in little hearts in their notebooks. They sang songs around him and
would burst into giggles when he asked about them. They would even
say wild things to make him blush, all before they'd mad-dash back to
a circle of their friends. Looking back, the girls may have loved having
him there, but Garron probably hated every second of it.

Aside from basketball, Garron did have an interest in music, and
would hover around the drummer during children's choir rehears-
als. Aunt Connie had plopped me in the choir earlier that year, so
when Garron also joined summer camp, we sometimes talked about
the goings-on at the previous rehearsal. And because Garron had the
attention of every girl, our routine conversations meant I also had
every girl's notice, including that of Crystal Walker. As she wanted to
go with Garron, she one day informed me that if I didn't get out of the
way, we would fight.

Beautiful as Garron was, I didn't like him like that. And he was
too nice to escape Crystal, or stop being friends with me. A showdown

with the girl was inevitable, so I went to my Aunt Connie to discuss it, though I was afraid she would be disappointed in me.

"Little Crystal wants to fight you? That's Lisa and Carl's girl, right?"

"Yeah, that's her."

Aunt Connie was reading a paper at the table. She hadn't looked up. "Over that Harmon boy? The light-skinned one?"

I shrugged. "I don't even like him. He just talks to me, and she won't leave me alone about it. Now she wants to fight. I didn't do anything to her."

"Mmm." Aunt Connie turned the page. "And what do you think about that?"

"I think she's dumb and should find a boy that likes her."

My aunt chuckled a bit before sobering. "It's not about the boy. It's about you, and it's about her." Finally, she turned the last page before leveling a look at me. "I'll tell you what I think. Pop her one good time, and she'll leave you be."

"What?" I couldn't manage anything else. This was the last thing I expected Aunt Connie to say.

"You heard me. That loudmouth girl, like her loudmouth mama, wants to try you, and sometimes, baby, people just try you to see what they can get away with. What you'll allow. Show her it ain't much."

With that, she returned to her paper.

Neat, succinct advice that shouldn't have been so surprising, given her love of *Fight Club*. And although that was years ago, as my eyes roved over Chamuk, standing with her arms folded tight across her fur wrap, and the snow's stark white background, I couldn't help remembering the schoolyard bully and my aunt's words. *Sometimes people want to try you. See what they can get away with. Pop her one good time, and she'll leave you be.* The only difference between then and now was that this situation wasn't just about someone pushing my boundaries. This was most definitely about Oktai. And this time, I might like him a little.

***

"Chamuk," came a voice. I distantly registered that it was the guard who spoke. "How did you get up here so fast?"

Her eyes, which had pinned Oktai in place, flicked to Chief Turgen's attendant. "You're not the only one with ways around the village," she said. "I know plenty."

His voice remained even. "Then you could have just suggested them in the Great Hall. You didn't have to come here. In fact, why are you here?"

"Chieftess Gerel requested it," she began, allowing her eyes to travel back to Oktai, and then the pair of us. The hunter stilled, as if he hadn't imagined a moment like this. But in a village whose culture was based on tradition, I couldn't imagine any other response to him bringing a strange new girl among their people.

Chamuk unfolded her arms just enough for her hands to land on her hips. "She wants me to accompany the Tsirku to the shaman. Anything that happens there will be women's business, after all."

Being checked for demons is women's business?

"I think you want to meddle," the guard said flatly, his first slip of the day. But he must have grown weary of this situation—whether it involved a revered Tsirku or not. He turned to the hunter and waved him on. "Come with me, Oktai. We'll leave them to it."

The air crackled with intensity until Oktai angled toward me. Apology filled his gaze. "I doubt you have any more demons than me," he said. "It will be a fast trip for your clearance, but I wish you luck anyway." I smiled and whispered my thanks as, with a hesitant step back, he nodded to Chamuk and then turned away. As silently as ever, the hunter and the guard headed back down the snow-covered hill. Soon they were out of sight, leaving me and the girl amid the winter wind.

We locked eyes, and her lips quirked up. She was beautiful. That wasn't hard to miss. She might have been the talk of my church, too, had she ever found herself in Oakland before the end of the world.

"Chamuk," I said by way of a greeting.

"Are you ready, Tsirku?" she asked, waving me toward her and closer to the shaman's home.

I closed the space between us. "Josephine," I corrected her. "But you knew that already."

"I know my orders," she said. "And my place." We were alone now. Maybe Chamuk was the curator, about to spring tentacles and strangle me the moment the men were gone.

My accompanying glare couldn't have been hard to miss. "I don't really do places."

"Yes, you do." There was a bite to her voice. "Other people's."

This was painful; I almost started wishing for the tentacles to start sprouting out of her.

Instead I angled my head. "Chamuk, I do think you're everywhere I am because you're starting to miss me." She didn't reply, opting to groan loudly before leading me into the tent. Which, as expected, wasn't like any other I'd seen in my time in the village. Chamuk pointed to a wooden seat in the floor's middle. I took it and peered around the large, somewhat smoky, space. "So, are you ready to fight or what?"

Chamuk whirled around, her eyes wide. "There's no fighting in this sacred space."

"Apparently your entire village is a sacred space, and every time you see me, well . . . I have pinpricks to show how honored a guest I am to you."

After bristling, she said my name with a light accent. "Josephine." Then, "You should focus on the meeting ahead of you."

I rolled my eyes. "Sure, sure. The demon thing. Just let me know when you're ready. I'll be waiting. Anyway, do I need to ask for the shaman?"

Her voice was exasperated when she replied, "Just wait."

She slipped to the outskirts as the presence of another filled the room, which somehow grew larger, darker, and smokier. I didn't have nerves like a human, but for some reason, my body shook. Chamuk wasn't far, but the space around my chair almost felt insulated from the outside world. Whoever came to speak with me had put us in a bubble. And then a voice rose around me, one filled with both knowledge I would never possess and the creepiness of a million horror movies. The words, the presence, were all around me, as if I'd walked into a cobweb that I couldn't quite swipe from my skin. It wasn't the Babble virus, but it wasn't in a language I could understand, either. Was I supposed to answer?

"My name is Josephine," I said into the space around me, repeating myself until the voice was silenced, sated. And then that presence coalesced, and someone stepped forward. The shaman, holding a lamp that crackled with fire, and, surprisingly enough, a woman.

She was of average height and draped in furs of the whitest white. Middle-aged, with special kohl-like makeup, she wore an ornate headdress and eyes that said she could see through to my deepest fears. I gulped. Was this the curator? She definitely had the menace of a killer biomechanical monstrosity.

"My name is Josephine, and I've come for clearance into the Chitakla. Doing so will aid a mission I am on," I managed.

"You say it so casually," she quipped. At least the words were no longer all around but aimed at me. The bubble also had seemed to dissipate. "As if you are entitled to the Chitakla. Do you even know what it is?" she asked. I had an idea, but I remained silent. "The ceremony is transitional in nature. Meaning, you must pass between the two worlds. The physical, as you know, and the spirit realm. The ghosts must let you through. They must trust you, and you must rely on them. Is there anyone you trust, Josephine?"

"Define it, please," I said as her gaze turned exacting. "And what does it matter? If you don't trust these spirits and they don't trust you?"

"Then you are not part of the village. You are an interesting soul, Josephine. And I don't say that because I have inspected you or performed any ritual. I just feel you, and my hunch is that you don't have demons. But I doubt you will be able to do the Chitakla." I nearly flew from my seat in protest. She held her hand flat. "You can't do this ceremony because you have to face the spirits. But you must do that alone. And you aren't alone, are you?"

I looked around me. "I don't see any other Tsirku here."

She shook her head. "Haunted," she said, "but lost." I clenched my fists. *Stop it.* But maybe I hadn't spoken the words aloud. "Leave the ghost, and then you can have your Chitakla. Then you can belong."

Through gritted teeth, I asked, "How?"

She extended her hand. I stared at it for a moment and then took it, instantly feeling a tug on my mind and body and slipping into a state I'd never before known.

CHAPTER 9

ECLIPSES

The shaman's influence was firm. Despite digging in my heels, I couldn't resist her tug into the unknown. Of course, my physical body wasn't resisting. No, this battle of wills took place in my mind. My heart. As a machine, I was stronger than any human in this village. But the shaman and her spirits were just too powerful in ways I hadn't prepared for—or maybe in ways that Dr. Yetti, in all her wisdom, couldn't have foreseen. My fight yielded as the strange woman's sway moved me beyond even her original assessment—lost girl, haunted girl, girl who wasn't really even a girl anymore—and into warm, humming darkness. This place, I did know. I'd gone into it during replication, entering as Josephine and emerging as Unit 778676.

I blinked, and that dim space broke away, leaving me to a memory. No longer was I in the shaman's tent, but back on Yerba Buena Island, standing outside my father's shack. It wasn't the first time my legs had brought me somewhere without much of a command, and it wouldn't be the last. I stood at the base of the ramshackle steps, unsure if I should knock on the door before me.

I had wanted to come here ever since the world ended, slipping away from Aunt Connie, who'd taken many children and stragglers into her own fading home. Then there'd been whispers that Yerba City would still come for us, would take Aunt Connie and shuffle me and the other kids into a shelter called a Local One, or send us to a Local Zero if we were in really bad shape. Other kids had started guessing when it would happen, and since then, I'd had a hard time sleeping. If I was to be hauled away, I at least wanted to see him one last time. But I never did.

Somehow, I'd climbed the steps and knocked. The door creaked open, and my father stepped into the hazy light; gray clouds had rolled overhead most of the day, offering plenty of shadows but no rain. Though I hadn't seen him in years, Aunt Connie's little brother, Tito—my father—still looked as he always had. Same wrinkled clothes and scuffed shoes. Same scruff on his chin. Only his eyes were different: milkier, and clouded as the sky. I couldn't help staring. He likely sensed it.

"You need a special invitation?" He swept his hands toward the foyer behind him.

"Naw," I said, and came inside. The "foyer" was equally dingy, but I waited for him to click the door shut and move his way farther inside. We were silent as he led me to the "dining room," with one light dangling above. A wooden table with a coat of dust lay beneath it. I grabbed a seat and fixed my eyes on him as he perched on a windowsill at the room's farthest wall. Obviously his sight had changed since we'd last seen each other, but even so, there was something steadier in his demeanor, not so stumbling as I remember. But as his shoulders set and he seemed to find me in the room, there was something heavy on them, as if the world had ended for him long before it ended for us.

The silence was thick before I cut it. "How much can you see?"

"Some colors," he replied. "Soon I won't even see them. 'Progressive vision loss,' the doctors said, before . . ."

"Yerba City," I said. He grunted in confirmation. "Can you see me?"

"Enough." His word was sharp, and my chin set high. I wasn't the daughter he'd known. I'd gone into replication, into the darkness, and come out this person. A better me. Stronger. And I didn't have to defend myself. He hadn't exactly been a prize to Imani and me. I sucked my teeth. I didn't need this . . . his, what? Permission? Company? I could just head back to base. Now I had so many sisters I never had to be alone again. And I had said goodbye to him once already.

A stale stench carried on the air, and I scrunched my nose. "What is that smell?"

That quirked his mouth up. "You always were sensitive to smells. Imani . . . noises. You, smells."

"Didn't answer the question."

"Maybe I'm nose-blind, too, kid." That made him chuckle to himself, although I knew it was a lie; that nose was as sharp as a bloodhound.

I sighed and rose to my feet. "This was a mistake."

I turned on my heel for the door, but he'd risen, too. "Come all this way and just gon' go?"

"Why stay?" I asked, with more bite than I'd intended. "Why stay here with you in this—" I spun around, staring at the room.

My gaze landed on a chess set in the corner. The only thing in the room not too dusty or dingy. "You still play chess with that ghost?" I asked.

He chuckled. "Yeah," he said. "Kinda racist, though." He chuckled again, and this time a bubble of a laugh came from me, too. I didn't know why I was there. Why my short legs—people always thought I, well, now we, were younger than we were—had brought me to my daddy's door. "You asked if I could see you," he said. "Not so much. But I can hear you. The other senses get stronger when you lose one. And you a heavy-footed girl to be so small."

"Mama would say lead foot," I said with another chuckle. The only time I found real grace was out in the woods, off the path. But he didn't need to know that.

"I remember that," my dad said, but I knew that's all he would comment of my mama. Then his gaze fixed on me. "Speaking of hearing. Heard you done something crazy, that I was right when I guessed what they done to you."

I shifted. Replication. He already knew. "Maybe I did."

He turned his face toward the popcorn ceiling. "Of all the things I thought would happen, you becoming a machine wasn't one of them."

"Many machines," I corrected. "I became a lot of them."

"And why'd you go do that to yourself?"

"To protect Yerba City," I said, though I didn't quite believe it on my lips.

He frowned. "Why, Josephine?" he pressed, his words breathier. Exasperated. There again was that weight pressing down on his shoulders.

"There's a whole army of us now, Daddy," I explained. "Over a million girls, just like me. And we're strong. We can make anything. They're building it now: a whole futuristic city run by Black people."

"You sound just like that Sun Ra," he said glumly, looking down at the floor. "But I think Black people are finished." He looked at me, as best he could with his glassy eyes; they reminded me of that old codger deer I had seen soon after I emerged from the tank. "I think *all* people are finished now," he continued. "That is, you can talk big, but you ain't exactly 'people' anymore, are you?"

I knew I'd never get through to him. I sighed and glanced toward one of the windows. Even through the dirt, it was hard to miss the hint of violet now in the gray sky. It would be dark soon. I would need to get back to base, as I hadn't told the others I'd be gone.

"I like being stronger," I said. The words were a whisper. I hadn't touched much in my father's house, but it wouldn't matter if I had. Nothing would bother me. Not in this new body. Though I couldn't understand our language, I was tough, and fast, and sharp in ways I hadn't known in my human life.

"You were already strong."

"But not enough," I said. "Not for her. Or you."

"I don't need saving, girl," he said. "Not the kind that would call for this." He sighed. "You're the only one who's come by. That ain't true. The first one came by. Said not to expect any others. That they wouldn't speak to me. That I deserved it. Probably do."

I shrugged and said, "We call her One." He made a face. I couldn't tell if it was distaste or surprise on his worn, leathered features. "I may come by. You can call me Seven the Hunter. That's what my sisters call me."

He grunted. This time not in confirmation and definitely in distaste. "I don't like that."

"Then Josephine is fine."

"Probably time you should get back to where you came from," he said. "Until the next time you visit, I guess." When I began to rise, he added, "Did I ever tell you why we picked your names?" He meant him and my mama, though he would never mention her. I shook my head. If he had, it was a memory that didn't carry over from my old life. "Your name is French," he said. "It means . . . 'shall grow.'"

"And Imani's?"

"Swahili," he said. "For something you can't see or hear but carry with you. Something you just know about, and for the people you love, I guess."

"And what's that?"

"Faith," he replied. Suddenly the shaman's pull came again, ripping me from the memory and back into the darkness.

***

Panting, I blinked my eyes open. I had returned to the shaman's tent. The woman let my hand go, and I could still feel her cool skin. Incense peppered the air. I rubbed my nose. Had that incense thrown me so totally into my memory of Tito? As if she could hear my mind whirling, the shaman turned around to stare at me. She was carrying a bowl whose contents looked like the same kohl that streaked her face. When we locked eyes, she smiled, with that otherworldly creepiness all around her again. I shot up from my seat as the shaman angled her head in a way that fit in with her weirdness. But I particularly didn't like how she looked at me, as if she was seeing inside me.

My words rushed out. "Just clear me for the Chitakla," I said. She stepped closer with her little bowl and began to hum to herself before smearing the kohl across my cheeks.

Finally, she spoke. "If that's what you want," she said. "After seeing what the spirits showed you."

I gritted my teeth. "That's what I want."

She smiled and stepped back. "Then luck and blessings to you," she said, and waved her arm once. From the outskirts of the space, Chamuk reemerged. The shaman inclined her head to Chamuk. "Take her back to her quarters. Now she must rest."

I flew out of the tent, pushing into the winter air. *She must rest, ha!* I didn't need to rest. I needed to get as far away from that woman as possible. I wiped the kohl off my face and shuddered. I'd been cleared and could participate in the Chitakla. That was a good thing. I needed to get out of here and find One. The longer I stayed, the better the chance of her winding up in our enemy's lab. And the longer I stayed in the village, the better the chance of my mind spilling all my secrets. And I wasn't sure if I could put myself together again if that happened.

I was pretty much stomping through the snow back to the women's sector of the village and was surprised when my babysitter caught up. Had to hand it to the girl. She had spunk.

"You have ghosts around you," Chamuk quipped, and then laughed to herself. I glared at her. "You know, maybe you should listen to the shaman. She just barely cleared you." Chamuk wiggled her fingers at me. "There's things wrong with you."

"Put those things in my face again and you'll pull back a nub."

Chamuk retracted her fingers and returned my scowl. "Do you even know what happened back there?" When I shrugged, Chamuk clicked her tongue. "She took you deep inside yourself to reveal what's on your heart. The spirits escort you there."

"And while I was tripping, she made sure I didn't have demons. Got it."

"You cried."

"I did *not* cry."

"Yes you did," she said. "Because you're a child. A child with ghosts, obviously."

I marched on ahead of her. "What is with you all and ghosts?" I sensed her grab for me before it landed and she took hold of my arm. I slowed. She had a point to make, and I would let her make it. She didn't know exactly who she'd just touched. "What, Chamuk? My ghosts bothering you?"

"Of course you have ghosts," she said. "Everyone does. That woman is an old bat. But that doesn't mean you should do a Chitakla tonight. Cleared or not. Tsirku or not." We were nearly at the bottom of the hill now. "You're an outsider and a child. I bet you haven't even gotten your moon's blood yet." My face burned. Was she asking about my period? My silence was all the confirmation she needed. Her hair danced in the winds, and it was hard to miss the triumph on her face. "I knew it! Why are you here, taking our time for a Chitakla. You should just perform and pass through like the others."

"I would if your leaders would just tell me what I need to know. I never asked to go through this dumb thing. I just want—"

"Information or Oktai?" she said, and dropped my arm. I couldn't miss the insult in it or the shift in her body language, as if she was about to square up with me. Just as Crystal had over Garron. Before I knew it, Chamuk was close to my face. My fists balled. *This girl better relax.*

She patted her chest. "I am a woman. I've gone through the Chitakla for the proper reasons. And I've gotten my moon's blood. That's why our leaders paired me with someone as strong as Oktai. When we are married, I will honor him with a peaceful home and children. You cannot do that for him."

Though I hadn't ever thought about all the picket fence stuff, something in her words stung. Her saying aloud something I hadn't thought about but would never do. So I laughed. Now her face turned red. "I'm not interested in having his big-headed babies," I said with a mocking laugh. "He's just nice. That's all. But you really need to get out my face."

But she stepped closer. "I am a woman in the eyes of our village and the Creator. I am ready to be a wife. You are a child. Find something else to do."

***

I brushed snow from my hair as I walked into my tent. The rest of the hike with Chamuk had been tense. One, it got colder as the sun was setting. And two, I wanted to punch her. Luckily, she hadn't gotten in my face again or said much else to me. If she had, I might not have had the same restraint.

The tent had enough niceties to drift to sleep in if I was human. A warm fire to heat the place and a thick mat to sleep on. But I paced back and forth for a few minutes, still wiping the thick kohl from my cheeks. I was most annoyed that Chamuk had a point. Zenobia had also pointed out that I was late, told me it'd be any day now, but it didn't come before Dr. Yetti's visit. I hadn't gotten my period before replication, and now . . . I wouldn't. Not that I was trying to make any domestic moves either here or back in Saturnalia, but the replication had had repercussions I hadn't considered up to this moment. Dr. Yetti froze me in a thirteen-year-old's body. I wouldn't get old and have a life with a partner as Chamuk would with Oktai. I'd never have children and grandchildren and great-grandchildren. Chamuk and Oktai would grow old together and share something I wouldn't ever have with anyone.

I needed to get some air.

I found myself wandering around the women's sector, through the medieval-looking structures and tents. At least it would take my mind off things before the Chitakla. I was supposed to rest, after all. But there was still something off about this village. How was there no sign that the world had ended here, like this place had always been an old-timey reenactment? It was hard to believe that the Great Hall, for instance, could have been built on top of a Walmart. And though all the people here were at the right ages for pre-doomsday memories, none of them seemed to remember or have any attachment to their previous lives. Was the whole country like this—living in some medieval fantasy? For sure someone in this village was a curator, and now it all made more sense: someone on the inside had to be running this loony bin. Maybe it was the shaman? Subtly manipulating things by making people jump through the hoops of her little cult. But why didn't anyone remember their old lives? It didn't matter, but it was definitely time to get the information I needed and move on.

The whoosh of a lamp glowing to life in a nearby tent caught my eye, and I moved toward it before giving much thought. It was probably rude to go inside someone's tent, but I was still a Tsirku and an honored guest, and above all things, I was just being nosy as I waited the necessary hours for my Chitakla. It wasn't like I would sleep.

The inside of the tent was grander than I expected. Fancy stools and chairs were strewn about, some carved ornately and boasting thick furs. The tent was also lavishly decorated and accented, creating a space that was a little imposing. Whoever this place belonged to was important. Another step or so inside, and I spotted the large lamp, the attendant holding it, and the woman who knelt on the ground—whispering a chant to a deity, I assumed. And with that, I knew whose tent I had stumbled on. A personal space for a queen of sorts: it belonged to Chieftess Gerel. Her attendant, a square-shouldered woman with a squarer jaw, snapped her head up and stepped toward me. The lamp shook in her hand, casting shadows on the tent flaps.

But Gerel remained with her head bowed and eyes closed as she said, "It's all right. Leave the Tsirku alone." The attendant snapped again into formation. Weird to see someone, especially a little old lady, with so much control over someone else. The Josephines weren't perfect, but they didn't operate like that.

"Chieftess," I said, and then bowed, though I felt stupid doing so. The chieftess rose to her rickety feet before facing me. "Hello, Josephine." The crone was so bowed and small, her only sway seemed to be with this guard holding her lamp. If only she could have helped me out more in the Great Hall earlier.

"I received word that the shaman cleared you for the Chitakla at the midnight hour. That is good. We have made all the right preparations on our end." She smiled, and the deep lines on her face seemed to etch further. Her long, salted hair was tied at her head in a braid. She wore no headdress or crown to show her rank now. "I assume that's why you've sought me out. To make sure we are ready?" She waited expectantly. "Unless there is some other reason?"

"Um. It's still a few hours away." I thought quickly. I just wanted to get this whole thing over and done with. "Any advice before I go to sleep?" I wasn't going to sleep, but she didn't need to know that.

"Advice?" She released, of all things, a husky laugh. "Well, I can say listen to your body. Is it telling you to run headfirst into our gauntlet, become one of us, and then move on? As you've asked? Or is it telling you something else? Perhaps that you should consider alternate arrangements?"

My brows flicked up. "Alternate arrangements? Are you telling me, after making me go see that crazy shaman and everything else, that I shouldn't do this?"

Her eyes turned exacting. "I'm not telling you to do anything. I know the path you are on now. But when I completed my Chitakla many years ago, I did not have a smooth time with the shaman. It took many times for my spirit to be ready. Perhaps they didn't think I was strong enough to make it through, to end my childhood, and receive a new name. I had to look deep inside myself to do that transformation." For some reason, I thought of Chamuk. Of her reminding me of the ways I would never change. Would never transform. "There is no shame in not being ready the first time."

There may not have been shame, but there was urgency. My mission had been derailed enough. I shook my head. "No, Chieftess. If that's your advice, then I know I'm ready."

"Ready to relinquish your childhood name and receive a new one?" she asked. I had to hold back my frown. Annoyance went through me at this silly notion, of being renamed by people I didn't know existed days ago. People who didn't know Fentons ice cream, or clam chowder in a bread bowl, or chicken and waffles. Not that I ate any of that stuff anymore, but still, I didn't need to belong to them; I just needed to find One and get back to Yerba City.

I also couldn't deny my curiosity. What name would they give me? And what would it mean? I'd gone by Seven the Hunter since replication. A number, really. Not a name.

Gerel continued, "This village is a good village, but perhaps you should consider finishing your journey on your own. If you think the Chitakla isn't for you, then heed your body's notice. My advice is that you think long and hard before midnight. Search your dreams for answers," she said, flicking her hand for me to go—a clear dismissal. "And your nightmares."

I stared at her long and hard. "Thanks for your advice."

What was that about? I thought as I returned to the snow. Gerel's words weren't settling right with me, so I took my walk away from the women's tents and toward a hill near their sector. It wasn't isolated like the shaman's hill had been, but it would put distance between me and the women of the village. Most of the folks seemed happy to have a Tsirku in their midst, but when it came down to accepting me, there were a lot of words of doubt that circled like the pack of wolves I'd tracked only so many days ago. Sure, I had this big ceremony to do, but was there another way? One that would get me out of this place without having to abide by all their rules and traditions? I trudged up the hill, peering at the sky. The stars glittered now as a blanket of darkness had settled over the village. Once high enough, I searched each angle I could find for the cicada and Thaddeus. But as with every survey since I'd crash-landed in Siberia, they were nowhere to be seen. No, it was just me out here, with the long sky and her moon and stars.

At the highest ground, sparse trees were dressed in fresh snow. I placed my hands on my hips, determination running through me. I was Seven the Hunter. I was the best tracker in Saturnalia. If need be, I could find One without these people's help or their damn ceremony. I should never have trusted that hologram man who'd led me here anyway. But still, my mind was blank and the sky was empty. The snow had only just stopped falling, and ice crystals lay frozen on the ground. I shrugged. I could always just leave and try to figure it out as I went.

"What are you doing?" someone asked behind me. I turned, but not fast. The voice wasn't unfamiliar or unwelcome. In fact, when Oktai found my side, something in me relaxed a bit.

"You know what I was doing," I said. "Trying to find a way out without doing the Chitakla."

He stilled. "But the shaman said you could go through with it. Why would you want to leave now?"

"Just seems like a lot of hassle," I said. He held my gaze, and I relented. "Your shaman and chieftess gave me a lot of crap tonight. Everyone saying I'm not ready. Maybe I'm not ready for adulthood and this new name, but what I do know is that I'm a good tracker. I can figure out my next steps without"—I waved my hands around—"all this."

He only smiled. "This isn't about everyone else, or even the information you need from my people. You found your way to us for a reason, and likely because your spirit needs to go through the Chitakla. It wants to do this. To transform. That's all that matters."

"I've already been through a transformation or two, buddy," I quipped as he shook his head. I thought about not saying my next words, but they came out anyway. "Why is Chamuk on me so much about you?"

This time he looked away. "She's behaving this way because of how I am acting. I can say that. Because I'm here with you instead of in my tent thinking of what the elders have set for my life and hers. And this is the short time when maybe that could all change." He sighed. "Until yesterday, her world was one way and so was mine. And now new possibilities are around. I blame me. Not her."

"Then why don't you stop?" I asked.

He stepped closer. "If you want me to go, I will go."

His words hung in the air. In the quiet now nestling between us. My eyes on his onyx gaze. Then I looked back toward the sky, the stars beside the moon. And, ironically, thought of those moments after my fight with Crystal Walker so long ago at camp. She had balled her fists and rushed me between makeshift activities. She hadn't expected me to throw the perfect, tight-fisted punch Aunt Connie had taught me the night before. The *pop* in "pop her one good time." Crystal, who was taller than me, also hadn't expected her jaw to connect with that punch and go careening toward the ground.

Kids are so extra during fights. They gathered around me, making a big fuss about what I'd done and Crystal's defeat. But I wasn't focused on them. All I could see was the unexpected events that unfolded next.

As most of the kids jumped around me, one of them headed toward Crystal, who held her jaw and writhed on the ground. A tall but scrawny light-skinned boy. All gold all over. Garron took her hand and helped her up before anyone else noticed. She let him. She also let him lightly brush her knee, which had gotten scraped in the fall. She smoothed out her clothing. She whispered her thanks. He leaned down and said something that made her giggle in return. And then her hand was in his, and they walked together wherever they went after that.

That was the last time I saw Crystal or Garron, as the church camp shut down soon after, and Yerba City finally came to collect us kids for transport to the Local Ones and Zeros.

But I was on a hill with Oktai now. "I don't want you to go," I said, knitting my fingers together. These hands hadn't hit Crystal. If my machine hands had done so, they might have knocked her head off. I uncurled my fingers. These hands were strong. But these hands were also soft. I looked back up to the sky.

"You like the stars?" Oktai asked. "You're always looking at them." I was always looking for my ship, but I shrugged and smoothed my furs. I distantly realized he was still talking. "Do the Chitakla, Josephine. Get your name. You will be glad that you did."

"What do you think the name will be?" I asked. He smiled now and stretched out his hand as Garron had done for Crystal so long ago. Panic, and shock, and a hint of awkwardness, coursed through me. I was . . . a robot, after all. But I allowed his hand to find mine. I wondered if he could see or feel the biomachinery, that I wasn't human. I wondered if I should tell him that although I wasn't, I felt very human in this moment. This was what Crystal had wanted. And now, staring at the stars beside the moon, it was what I wanted, too.

"I'm not sure what it will be," he said. "But it will be fitting."

I nodded and leaned into him. I would do the Chitakla. And I would have my name.

CHAPTER 10

THE CHITAKLA

Chieftess Gerel's attendants worked quickly. No one would dare say it, but I could tell the night was colder than normal, as their hands shook and their teeth chattered. I reminded myself to mimic them, one time giving it too much gusto. My elbow thrust out awkwardly into the nearest person . . . being Chamuk. She'd been holding the shaman's paints and nearly dropped her bowl. No one could miss the way her eyes cut in my direction. Her fresh scowl. I smiled tightly back. Chamuk could at least try to be happy. She would be rid of me soon enough. The women didn't give me a mirror once finished, and instead they ushered me into the whitest furs, careful not to mess up any of their painstaking work—my hair braided back and three thick lines of red paint now streaking my face. With a quick breath, I was out of my tent and being led to the Great Hall.

My Chitakla had drawn a crowd. Men and women in clusters spoke together until I entered the Great Hall; at my presence, they all quieted like the quick whoosh of a candle flame. They parted for Gerel's attendants, who brought me to the front of the room. I made eye contact with everyone I could, just to show them I wasn't afraid. In fact, I stuck my chin in the air and strode as quickly as I could. I *had* to get this done. One had to stay out of our enemy's lab. The attendants left me at the front of the crowd and standing before a raised platform, waiting, I assumed, for the chiefs—and possibly for an asteroid to hit. Time passed without either chief's appearance, so my eyes danced around, seeking some sort of explanation. Only unfamiliar faces met my stare. I rolled my eyes. *On with it. Someone's probably dissecting my sister's head in a lab somewhere.*

"You know, it's fairly easy to read your face."

I smirked, knowing Oktai was at my side before I turned to him. "You're probably not supposed to be standing here on my special day," I said. "I'll be a woman soon. And if they wanted me to look happier, they would hurry up."

He laughed and circled before me, standing between me and the dais. "Patience is a good thing," he replied. "And I'm already a rule breaker, since you came. Might as well pile it on thick now."

I glanced toward a few men and women whispering at my company. "They'll definitely have something to clutch their pearls about."

He nodded, though he probably didn't know what I meant. Then his gaze swept over me, lingering on my fur-wrapped sleeves. "You look perfect," he said. "Ready." I appreciated the compliment but was unsure exactly how ready I could be. Sure, I wanted this over with, but what about the other stuff, everything that would make me an adult? And when I finished this silly ritual, would that change how much of me was a person and how much was a machine? Was this not just a Chitakla, but in its own way, another replication?

But I didn't have time to ponder that. "I am ready."

He nodded. "I was when I did mine. Don't be so much like me."

Something seemed to fight with the happy appearance he wore. Something was pulling him down. "Joining my people is a wonderful thing. An expressive thing. We have a lot of words for what we cherish most, many ideas of love." My brows flew up, but he kept going, avoiding eye contact and rushing through his speech. "I love every member of my village, as I've known them my whole life. Yes, some are more difficult than others, but that kind of love is what bonds us, keeps our community strong. But it had to change when I became a man. Everything down to the ways I could be with them was different."

"Like your cousin and the feet-wrapping thing?"

He smiled. "That, yes. And how I would relate with others, like Chamuk. There became an expectation of something different between us. Something being forced to grow." He raked his hand over his face. "I'm not sure why I'm telling you all this right now. Just, I wanted to say thank you."

"Thank you? For what?"

Finally, his eyes met mine. "Because when you came along, I could just be myself . . . feel however I wanted to feel because you are who you are." His smile widened. "And how I feel about you is something new."

Heat filled my cheeks. "You're welcome," I said, unsure of what else to share.

He nodded and then looked toward the doorway, where some attendants had started gathering. "We should begin soon. When you're all done, we'll be there to greet you and hear your new name." And then he winked, and that burn in my face grew. "You're almost there." With that, he nodded again and disappeared into the crowd.

As soon as he'd gone, the doors swung open, revealing the chief and chieftess in their regalia. The guard who'd taken me to the shaman was at the head of their retinue, straighter-backed and more formal if that was at all possible. Unlike me, who'd walked fast, they took their time getting to the dais and situating themselves. If there had been a clock on the wall, I would have glanced at it. My hand found my chest—a reminder to breathe. Finally, the shaman made her way beside Chieftess Gerel. Both wore completely impassive faces. My gaze focused on the again-humbled Gerel, who was completely different from the woman who'd sown doubt in my mind earlier that night. She may have been surprised that I was still here. I was pleased to not give her the satisfaction of seeing me quit.

Chief Turgen spoke first, with a loud welcome that echoed throughout the chamber. "This is a great night, a sacred evening, one where the Tsirku Josephine Moore will begin her traditional Chitakla, the transition from youth to adulthood ushered by the spirits of our vast community." His hooded, dark eyes fell on me, and again I stuck my chin in the air. I wasn't a Tsirku. And I wasn't just a Josephine. I was Seven. And I would show them that.

"Josephine, our honored guest. These are the last moments of your childhood. When you complete your Chitakla, you will put childish things aside and take your place as an adult, as one of our people. Your transitioned self will be renamed, and all that is ours will be your birthright."

Or you could just tell me how to find those Yetti twins now. But I kept my mouth shut in that regard, only saying, "I'm ready," as I had just declared to Oktai.

"And so are we," replied Chief Turgen, who turned to the shaman beside his wife. An unspoken communication passed between them, and the shaman stepped forward as the chief took a rickety step back.

I held back my frown. She still had that slight air of crazy around her as her arms swept open wide. "The Chitakla is one of the holiest times in a person's life, from the first breaths in your old life to your first breaths in your new. We are here to help you as the spirits guide your way. Some spirits will be kind. Others will be cruel. But no matter their disposition, they are here to see you through. They are here to teach you the lessons that will make you strong." My ears perked up. Strong? Did she mean the strength that Dr. Yetti had promised?

But she was already waving me forward. "Come with me," she said.

My feet moved even as my mind perched on her words, and soon we stood at the opening of a long passageway. The shaman had swung herself behind me, pointing a bony finger just over my shoulder, while the rest of the village remained in the Great Hall. "This part you do alone," she said, "as when you come into this world and when you leave it. Go forward. The spirits will guide you."

She moved back into the shadows as I took a step forward. Alone was fine. My mother, my sister, my father, Zenobia, even that army of me building an Afro-Utopia back in Yerba City . . . somehow it seemed like I had become more and more alone as my life went on.

The hall was tight and shrouded. My computer brain began calculating with each step. There was only the spray of darkness. Where were the ghosts? Just then, a lamp was lit at the far end of the narrow hall, revealing those who would escort me to adulthood. On each side of the hall were women in white masks, some small and dainty, others large and grotesque. Some of the women began wailing, something like a mourning cry. And others did what you shouldn't do to a Josephine— reach out and strike. It was a quick jab that I saw coming probably before that person wanted to send it. I had to remember to slow my reflexes to keep from grabbing that woman's wrist and snapping it like a dry twig. *They can't hurt you. Just get to the end,* I reminded myself. This was the hall of spirits escorting me. And if I made it through this space of annoyance, then I was a step closer to One, and a step closer to home.

As I casually batted the last person's hand away, a sense of oddness gripped me. Maybe it was my heightened Josephine senses. Maybe it was leftover intuition from the part of me that had been human. Whichever, it was the same weirdness I'd felt in the shaman's tent, just before that sudden pull—

The floor dropped from beneath my feet, and I was free-falling, plummeting into new depths. After the sudden descent came an even faster slam into hard ground. I hit it with a thud. When I'd been in the passageway, I'd known that the Great Hall and entire community were only so many yards away, waiting for me to finish. In this new place, I instantly knew those people were not here, and that I was more alone than even the shaman had guaranteed. This room wasn't a hallway, but a square chamber like a box, or a holding cell. I rubbed my head, more from shock than pain, then called out.

"Hey!" My voice echoed back. Empty. This was definitely not part of some old-timey cosplay: the box was shiny stainless steel.

I needed to get up. Not seem so weak. I was a Josephine after all, not some scared little girl. Someone had dropped me in this stupid little box, but I was made for this, and able to handle even this kind of dark. My eyes readjusted, allowing an effect like night vision to take hold. And when it did, it showed me something I hadn't expected. No, I wasn't alone. The room was full of machines, all in the same ghost masks the women had worn. All carrying weapons and spears—as if they'd need them—and all aimed at me. I bent my legs and balled my fists. *Looks like a party. Then let's dance.*

***

Since I'd gotten to this medieval village, these people had seemed interested in two things: wrapping people's feet and the Chitakla. This Chitakla was the biggest deal of someone's life, outside of marriage and kids, it seemed. And of course, the Chitakla had ghosts. I hadn't lived under a rock. I had an idea of ghouls. Even before the world ended, you had the Halloween variety. They haunted old attics and went bump in the night. But trapped in the dark box beneath what should have been my passageway to adulthood, my vision expanded. These ghosts were not the trick-or-treating variety. No, these were badass machines. They were all cord and steel. Nothing of them had ever been human. They were ghost robots. And unlike me, whose life had grown steadily more complicated with each moment of this mission, these machines had only one focus: kill Seven.

It flew, the first weapon. A spear—ironically from the farthest ghost bot—careening through time and space for my head. It slashed my furs as my body spun away. I hit the wall just beside me as another ghost, with a mask bearing a terrifying sneer, dove for my feet. Damn, they were fast. Even for a Josephine. What kind of technology had made these? It snatched my ankle, and again I slammed into the floor, but not before I yanked the ghoul toward me. In an instant, its head was between my palms. I smiled, but it wasn't the gentle thing I'd given Oktai. This smile belonged to the Josephine I hoped the village wouldn't see. The part that had been looking for a good fight. The ghost bot released my ankle to try to loosen my grip. Didn't work. I pressed until its head crunched. Until its mechanical skull caved in on itself and its arms flailed wildly. Until black ichor exploded over my white furs and red war paint.

I hopped to my feet. "Who's asking about me?!"

The masked machines writhed in response, but otherwise said nothing. Maybe they couldn't speak, but that didn't matter. Their presence was enough of a message. I hadn't made it on this journey unnoticed. A curator, an enemy being of this territory, had spotted me and sicced the dogs. I believed Oktai was a good kid, but this whole area was like a giant garbage disposal, a secret reject box where they sent children who wouldn't go along with their make believe.

One of the ghost bots launched toward me as the others, around ten, repositioned. I leapt as well, meeting it in midair and grabbing its throat. I slammed its head into the nearest wall and, with a sickening crunch, it slid to the floor, but not before another grabbed my arm and began scaling the wall. I dangled in its grasp as it found a grip on the ceiling. My nails scratched at steel fingers until I realized another ghost had found a space underneath us and was opening its mouth wide for the drop.

"You won't eat me on my special day!" I yelled, taking some of the blackish machine blood that had splashed on my neck and hurling a fistful at the ceiling ghost bot's eyes. Blinded, it released me to wipe frantically at its face. Instead of dropping toward the monster below, I instead kicked off the wall and sailed toward it. One of my legs landed on each side of its waiting mouth, allowing me just enough time to twist. I smashed its fanged jaws together, leaving the trashed machine clawing to unpeel them. Then I was on my feet again and the remaining ghosts were on the outskirts, reevaluating me, plotting the best methods to strike. Good. They should know I didn't plan on going out today. And if I did, they were coming with me.

In that moment of reprieve, I glanced up. There was not a sign of the opening where I'd fallen in; somehow it had seamlessly sealed itself. But, with a quick look to the side, I could make out the outline of a door and a latch on the wall. Perfect. I dashed toward it, but something snapped me up first. The biggest of the ghost bots in the room. It wore a mask like the others, but also hella big steel antlers, almost like those that Dyre had worn. Oh, come on. What kind of mind created this?

It squeezed round my middle, and I knew it had snapped something when my own golden blood began dripping from my nose. I balled my fist and slammed it into his head, over and over, until it released me, staggering back. But it wasn't dead. In an instant, it was charging for me again, but simultaneously I'd noticed that the door was now perfectly positioned on the other side of it. I wrapped my arm around my middle and, with everything I had, launched toward the machine, landing a good kick to its shoulder. We both went flying, it into the wall and me against the latch. Something else, in my back this time, cracked. Ichor flowed from my other nostril, but I didn't have time to nurse myself. I scrambled for the latch, pulled it to swing the door open, and got myself through. A moment later, I'd slammed the door behind me.

Back pressed against the wall, I peered around the new room, ready for another squad of ghost bots to attack me. But this chamber, wider, with bright ceiling lights, was truthfully empty. Quiet surrounded me as I moved to the center and looked up to the ceiling. I'd plunged down into this maze of rooms, or so it seemed, so how was I supposed to get back up?

"If you can fall down here, you can climb back up."

Imani was there. My sister. A little crazy laugh bubbled out of me in response.

"Thought you'd forgotten about me," I said. "Haven't seen you since my birthday."

"Naw," she replied. "I'm close like always." My twin glanced around and with a long whistle, shook her head. "Well, you done it now."

"Shut up," I said, giving her a little shove.

My sister righted herself. "And you look jacked up." She then pointed upward at the ceiling lights. "The drop point for this room is over your head, just so you know. Think there's a latch, too. Just . . ."

"Just what?"

"Can you climb?" She eyed my side, the one that had crunched in the fight with the ghost bot. She then wiped the ichor from my nose. "Got you good."

I shrugged and began heaving myself up the wall. "I can climb." But my feet had a hard time finding purchase. Whatever had cracked in the fight—the injuries to my side and back—kept me from pulling myself all the way up.

"Need a ladder?"

I sucked my teeth. "We're down a ladder, but thanks, Imani."

I threw myself up again. And came right back down. Imani laughed and said, "Remember when Mama would leave us things to find in the church? While she was at choir rehearsal with Aunt Connie?"

"Yeah, I remember. Kept us busy and not whining."

"Maybe this is a big game of 'keep us busy and not whining.'"

"Pretty sick game," I countered.

Imani sighed wistfully. "Mama was so pretty."

"That's what you're thinking about?" I asked, this time getting a grip on the wall with both hands and feet. I pretended to be more upset about it than I was. But it did make me smile to think about. Mama *was* pretty, with the kind of face someone would put on a runway and a voice that would light the congregation on fire. Crime for someone to have so much, to mean so much to so many people, and just leave them.

"Jojo." Imani's tone had changed. Sharp whisper. "They're coming."

"Who? Who's coming?" I was halfway up the wall, heading for the crawl space in the ceiling and its latch. When Imani didn't respond, I glanced at my entrance. Sure enough, the ghost bot, the big one with the antlers, was barreling through the door. *Shit.* I started moving faster now. Not that I couldn't fight it. But we were both banged up enough. I hadn't come to Siberia to fight in this pit. I came for One. This wasn't my choice battle. I scampered across the ceiling as best I could, thrust at the latch, and popped the crawl space's door open.

"Up here, Jojo." My sister was already inside the space. She looked behind me, likely to the ghost bot heading my way. Panic lit her eyes. "Hurry up!"

I swung myself into the crawl space and began to scamper, Imani moving up the tight space just above. Even with my machine legs, I didn't feel like I was going fast enough. Confirmed when the machine ghoul took a swipe at my shoe, hooking it. Trying to pull me down, as it couldn't fit in the crawl space itself. "Close the door, Jojo!" Imani screamed. "Close it!"

"I'm trying," I said, gritting my teeth. The bot's grip was assured, but my kicks were stronger. With my back pressed to one wall and my foot pinned to the other, I sent my free heel into its mechanical arm. *Crack!* It snapped in half, the pieces hitting the floor beneath me. Ghost Stag released a howl just as I reached far enough down to pull the latch and close the crawl space off from within. Then up my sister and I scrambled until we'd made it back to the surface, spilling into a bright, shining room. The Great Hall. All of this had been underneath the passageway, as well as under the colossal event space.

I blinked and my twin was gone, leaving me in my black-covered furs pulling myself from the floor among the people of Oktai's village.

Someone helped me to my feet. "She has returned from the Chitakla! It's time to welcome her to our people!"

I shook my head. "No, beneath us . . ." I tried to get the words out, but everyone had crowded around me now. They slapped me on the back. "No, don't you know what just happened?"

"The shaman will choose a beautiful name for her now," others cheered.

"Everything is wrong," I said. "Someone just tried to kill me. I did not just go through the ceremony." But though the room swarmed with people, I might as well have been alone. Though I was trying to get through to them, it was like no one could hear me. It was a sea, and I was fighting a losing battle against the current. Being swallowed up whole.

"What's wrong with you all?!" I shouted. At that, everyone stopped and looked at me, holding my gaze, just before all their bodies went limp and hit the floor.

Everyone except Chieftess Gerel.

CHAPTER 11

THE CURATOR

There are moments when time moves fast. Like the Road Runner in an old Looney Tunes episode, kicking up dirt on a stretch of desert. And other moments when everything is slower than waiting for a pot of water to boil. As I stood in the Great Hall surrounded by the villagers' limp bodies, I knew this was the latter. Slow may not be the best way to describe it. Maybe . . . suspended. Yeah, time was suspended in mid-air, and there was no way to snatch it back. I slipped my hand across my face, wiping away my steadily trickling golden ichor. I then leaned down to check the pulse of a young villager nearby. Though shallow, he was breathing. Relief flooded me. *Still alive. All of them are still alive. But what kind of sleep did this?*

I inhaled deeply. "Subantoxx," I whispered. I had lived most of my life in a Local One, and the Sap was pervasive—there was no mistaking the smell. But this was different somehow, a modification of the familiar drug, clearly airborne, and somehow more subtle.

The only other conscious person in the hall, the crone chieftess Gerel, made her way to me. Though she could only go so fast, urgency filled her body, as if she was afraid she'd hit the floor in this eerie sleep as well. I straightened. Maybe something strange was happening to both of us during my Chitakla. Or maybe she was the curator I'd been trying to avoid all along.

When she reached me, her eyes flicked about wildly, scanning my face and then that of her husband and attendants on the floor. I did a quick scan of my own. No Oktai in any of the spaces near me.

"What's happening?" she asked, her words tangling on frantic breaths. Her furs were auburn and brown, thick and well made. She'd been wearing a matching red headdress at the beginning of the ceremony, but it must have fallen to the ground during the villagers' great collapse. Now her hair, long and thick like Chamuk's, but salted and plaited, was visible. Handcrafted jewelry was strung around her neck, maybe tokens from the chief. She had a story, a history. And for a moment, I could see the girl she'd once been.

Even though she wasn't my favorite person, I steadied her. She was tiny and frail in my grip. "They all passed out," I said. How could I find the right words to calm this woman? "It's just us left. I . . ." Now my words couldn't find purchase. "My Chitakla . . ."

"Come outside," she said. "We cannot stay in here. We'll end up like them."

"But—"

"We *cannot*," she said, now more of a command than a request. She was again the woman from when I'd woken here, as opposed to the humbled being beside her husband during the ceremonies. Her rickety body fled toward the door, and I followed, until I noticed something gleaming in the hands of Gerel's sleeping attendants. It was a gift for me, I assumed, as it came on a pillow of sorts: the fancy bow, quiver, and arrows I'd used during my introduction to the chief. I snatched them up before heading into the snow with the chieftess. Yeah, sometimes moments moved fast or slow. Sometimes they were even suspended. But there were others that felt so wrong your bones shivered. Weapons were for those times.

The air outside the Great Hall seemed colder—if that were at all possible—and the sky darker. The wind easily cut through the mess of my furs as I trekked behind Gerel. Outside, in the streets of the village, it quickly became clear that whatever had knocked out the villagers in the Great Hall had put the whole village to sleep. People were slumped against buildings; some were just lying in the street. The chieftess wove around them. I thought she'd stop just outside the building, but instead, she kept marching on. I called out, but my words only bounced off her back. She didn't linger and wouldn't falter. We moved like that for at least ten minutes. In that time, I could have caught up with the chieftess, but my instinct to see how this would play out was stronger. Either Gerel knew nothing, and this was her way of processing shock, or she knew all, and the surprise would be my own.

Finally we'd moved pretty far past the medieval village, into a clearing ringed by frosted trees close to the sacred lands. She found one end of the clearing, and I took the other. "Chieftess," I called out again, the remaining blood on my face chipped and frozen. "What are you doing?"

With her back to me, her fur-wrapped shoulders dropped, Gerel slowly turned. These were the last moves Chieftess Gerel made before tensing, and standing still as a statue. I carefully reached for my arrows as the crone's gaze turned incisive.

"You just wouldn't leave," she finally said, now without a hint of her original tongue. No, she spoke perfect English, as if she hadn't spent her entire life among the villagers in the Great Hall. "I gave you so many opportunities to leave, even planted the Chitakla to discourage you. But you just kept going on. You couldn't just break our treaty, you had to stomp on it."

The arrow was strung in an instant. I raised it. "Where are the Yetti twins?"

"I sent them away," she spat, and then, of all things, she began to carefully take off her clothes and fold them into a perfect, thick triangle of fabric and leather. Soon the elder was naked, revealing a shriveled, tribally tattooed body that was remarkably unshivering in the Siberian cold. She set her clothes aside in the snow before removing her simple leather shoes and adding them to the clothing pile. She seemed to stretch her body, and in an instant, stood what must have been a good foot taller than her previous height. "But they weren't as difficult as you, Josephine, protector of Yerba City. Yes, I know who you are. But not why you are here." A beat passed. "Why are you here, Josephine?"

"All you need to know is that I am here for the good of my people," I said. "So they'll survive. Tell me where the Yetti twins are, and I'll—"

The curator let out this grating laugh, far more machine than human. With a sudden flex, the wrinkled lines of the old woman's body tightened into a greyhound-like smoothness, lean muscles rippling beneath supple skin. Although the ancient Siberian tattoos remained, she wasn't even female or male anymore, just a suggestion of a human figure, like a gray mannequin, its torso widening and arms loosening and lengthening for combat. "And you'll what, Josephine? Let me go? Your inferior technology is not equal to ours. Would you like to see?" The smiling old lady, now in ripped battle mode, lifted her head slightly—a look that wasn't social or communicative, but simply scanning, as if Chieftess Gerel was assessing my true threat level.

This was the reason she'd brought me so far from the villagers. Out here, there was no one around. And there was still no sound coming from the village since everyone collapsed. She had brought me to a killing field, a place where she could rip me apart, hide my remains, shrivel up again, and then calmly get dressed and return to the village before anyone woke up. Her stance was no longer bent but totally statuesque. Instead of being demure, arrogance rolled off the curator in waves, her incisive stare becoming a scowl. Finally, she spoke with her cold voice, no doubt deepened artificially to come off as more intimidating. It was clear and crisp through the wind.

"Josephine of Yerba City," the old lady demanded. "You've broken the strict treaty among the entities. Leave, or I will send you home in pieces."

Still my arrow remained focused on her. "Tell me where you sent the Yetti twins. I won't leave before I know that." She was right. I had broken the treaty. But I hadn't signed it. Maybe One had, when we were replicated. Or perhaps that honor had fallen to Nine. She enjoyed the politics of Yerba City and beyond. But that wasn't my calling. All I knew was that I'd been sent on a mission, and I had to complete it.

Somehow, I think she understood my resolve. Her eyes narrowed with contempt, and she sneered, "They're with the circus."

My arrow remained on her. Ready and threatening. I tried to keep my voice as even as possible and remove any of the humanity in it I could. She would see that as a weakness. "Gonna need more than that," I replied.

"The circus has its own path," the curator said. "And the twins are lost in it."

"You like stories," I managed. "Fooling all these people that they're living in the year 1491 or something." The night wind was biting into my hands now. I wasn't cold per se, but my body was unused to it. I had to get through to her, though. I had to get the information I needed. "I don't care what you do here in Siberia. Tell me where they are, or I'm not going anywhere."

"Then face your end," she replied, and exploded into action. Her movements were mesmerizing: so precise and so exact that I had to erase what I'd thought of her, of the girl she'd once been and the frail old crone, too. No, she was the curator now. Like me, she was made for combat. And I doubted she had ever been human before.

Her focus was like a laser as she closed the space between us and struck out at me with intense precision. She sent a chunk of snow and frozen earth into the air behind her while propelling her body with impossibly strong legs. I aimed my arrowpoint for the woman's right eye, and would have hit it if the curator had not predicted this somehow. She dodged me and knocked the arrow from midair with her forearm. But I had loosed another with equal quickness, and it sailed into the curator's thigh.

Unfortunately, that didn't slow her down. I fired another arrow, and the curator just tilted her head this time. Another arrow and another left my bow, finding their marks in her arm. Slicing across her cheek. But as she finished her streak across the clearing, she was undaunted. In a blink, she'd grabbed my shoulder and thrown me to the ground with a thud. My head slamming against the dirt, all I could do was dodge as her arms came down in precise, chopping motions. Finally I landed a punch to her gut, sending her flying back, before hopping to my feet. She'd also found her footing, and we glared at each other. Tendrils of black shuddered around her nose and mouth.

And then she was moving again, pressing forward with spins that sliced the air as she kicked. I dodged all but the last, which landed a hard strike to my temple. I staggered back, reaching for my weapons, only to find the bow had been trashed somewhere in the scuffle. So I yanked the last two arrows from my quiver and held them like daggers. The curator stood tall as I advanced, my earlier shots sticking out at odd angles without giving her the slightest sign of pain. If she wasn't trying to rip me to pieces, I'd admit that she was kind of badass. Blackish blood oozed from her wounds and then began crawling back into the holes. Like me, this thing had a kind of living ichor, nanoengineered to keep her in one piece. This was going to make her very, very hard to kill.

As I advanced, the chieftess positioned herself to take my blow and dole out her own, but I stopped in my tracks to take in the magnitude of her fighting ability. The octogenarian act was completely dropped now, and her bright eyes narrowed into a predatory focus.

She took my moment of awe to grab my neck and dangle me in her grasp. Her laugh rippled through the trees. "You cannot hurt me," the curator said. "You cannot defeat me." Her speech radiated superiority. Satisfaction. "You are an inferior entity and should have left when I gave you the chance. But you didn't, Josephine. And now you will pay for your hubris."

I fought against her iron grip as her laugh swelled, as my neck began to crunch and pop, as my world spun. I clawed at her hands to no avail. The winter winds rushed by. This would be it. This was how I, Seven, failed. They would ask about me back on base, wonder where that silly Josephine who ran off to the woods had gone. And maybe I could be resigned to that. My arms went limp, and I was sure my fate was sealed. Then a bullet, a monitor's bullet—Saturnalia's monitors' weapon of choice—went sailing into the curator's head.

***

Thaddeus, Saturnalia's drunk, obnoxious monitor, stood just behind the curator, his weapon aimed at her skull. His bullet had lodged somewhere near her ear. Of course, it didn't kill her. What could kill something that powerful? But it was enough to make her shriek, loosen her grip on my neck, and send me crashing to the ground. That was fine. I didn't feel pain like a human, exactly. And as the curator clutched the side of her head, I had just enough time to see Thaddeus jog to my side.

I blinked a few times. I had been checking the sky for him and the cicada since we'd landed, to no avail. In fact, I'd assumed that I would just have to handle this mission solo. That he was either lost at sea or making lumpy snowmen on the coast somewhere with his flask in hand. But here he was, still looking a bit drunk, but trained well enough to save me. If you'd told me when I met the jerk back in the woods shortly after replication that it would be his bullet that got me out of a monster's clutches, I wouldn't have believed you.

"Jägermeister," he said, watching the former chieftess begin to thrash on the ground. "What on God's green earth is that?"

"Chieftess Gerel," I said. "A curator."

"A what?" he asked.

"I'll explain when we're on the cicada." I looked around, pushing my neck back into place while my ichor struggled to heal me. "Where is it exactly?"

"Farther back in the woods." He waved beyond the trees with his weapon. "I've been trying to find you for a while. And then when I'd finished repairing the cicada, I thought I'd try just one more time. Yes, you can wipe that surprise off your face: I came looking for you, Madam Tree Hugger. Beats sitting in the cicada, I'll say." He finally really took me in, especially my tattered furs. "You look like shit."

I scowled. His eyes were red and his chin stubbly, not exactly magazine-cover worthy. "Back atcha."

He tsked as the curator let out a howl. His eyes trained again on her; his gun never completely lowered. "I shot it in the head! Why isn't it dying yet?"

"She's too strong," I said. "But we need to take her down before she can get back to us." I looked to him once more, the disbelief beginning to wear off, if not the surprise. I didn't know a lot about the monitor program, but I did know they trained participants well. That's the only reason Thaddeus, broad shouldered and athletic but still sloppy from his drink, could operate the way he did. His blond hair swayed a bit as he aimed again at the curator and fired. This time, he missed completely.

I slapped his arm. "Don't waste ammo."

"I'm trying to get our asses out of here," he said as the curator, as if she were plucking a pesky splinter from her ear, finally removed Thaddeus's bullet. From there, she unfurled and stood taller, stretching herself *again* to grow to new heights. The thing's body was at once muscular and elastic. Once done, she stood about ten feet tall and glared down at us. Her gaze bounced from Thaddeus to me and back again. Too late to get her while she was distracted. She was going to destroy us both now.

"Operatives of Yerba City," she began in her demanding voice.

Thaddeus reeled back. "Oh, that's a voice. Curator Almighty."

"Shuddup," I shouted at Thaddeus.

"You've crossed into this territory unlawfully with multiple combatants. You will both be terminated immediately."

"But I'm kind of into the Hot Terminator Lady thing," Thaddeus commented. "Little tall and skinny, but—"

"Shuddup, Thaddeus!" I yelled again as the curator lunged for me—for us. Thaddeus and I spread apart so she would have to choose which to attack first, and like the tactician she was, she chose Saturnalia's monitor. She swiped at him, knocking over trees and moving heaps of snow and earth in her wake. I couldn't help but marvel. I was trained to fight, and best when doing so in a unit. And though I gave Thaddeus a hard time, he was a surprisingly good fighter as well, evading her blows thanks to his powered armor and landing a few of his own. But Thaddeus and I were battered and bruised. And she was just too strong.

The one advantage, perhaps, was that she'd made herself so large that she had to slow a pace by mere physics. And we were now small, nimble, and annoyingly quick. Thaddeus rolled in the snow, landing on one knee and then aiming his weapon again at the curator. The bullet landed near her clavicle, but she had somehow adjusted to the weapon's capabilities. A distinct look of annoyance crossed her completely inhuman face. She may as well have been stung by a bee.

"You'll have to do better than that!" I quipped.

"Trying," replied Thaddeus. Then something in his belt sheath caught my eye. A knife. A Yerba City–issued knife.

Now, this wouldn't do much for Thaddeus. But I was a Josephine. Sometimes that meant I could make miracles with absolutely nothing. I volleyed toward Thaddeus, snatched the knife, and before either of them could register it, I was soaring through the air and wrenching the blade down through the curator's right arm with all the strength that my little angel body could give me. Her howl shook the trees this time as her arm fell off and plopped in the snow.

I knew this probably wouldn't kill her; I was just trying to buy us time to get back to the now-functioning cicada. Somehow, I think Thaddeus understood this as well, as he circled back to my side. He twiddled his fingers at me. "You're covered in goo," he said of the curator's black blood.

I leveled a look at him. "Let's get to the cicada," I said. "Now." And then we were running.

The ground shook beneath us. A quick glance showed that where the curator's arm had been, tentacles—almost like a bouquet of them—had sprouted from the wound. They writhed in the air, knocking through branches as she pursued us. I never wanted to go out like this. Not side by side with Thaddeus with a terminator squid lady on my heels. But what choice did we have in the way everything ended?

We ran faster, and when Thaddeus's pace felt far too human, I nearly dragged him along. But she was fast and determined—at least until, on my last glance back, I saw him. He jumped seemingly from nowhere holding a spear with the kind of ease that only comes from being a fighting machine like me, or a very brave human with years of practice. He must have used that skill whenever he found himself on a hunt. Oktai was a warrior in his own right, after all. And now it showed. The boy who'd run both me and the reindeer down was poetry as he sailed toward the curator, and before she could register him, he'd plunged the spear in her back. Blood spurted from the puncture in what looked like an oil slick. He hopped down and tumbled toward us as we gawked: he'd managed to do what we couldn't—disarm her just enough while she was distracted.

She thrashed in the snow as Oktai made his way to Thaddeus's and my side.

"Josephine," he began, his eyes taking in my appearance, Thaddeus's presence, and then the curator behind us. "What is . . . ?" He lost his words and started again. "I left the Great Hall when you started the ceremony. I knew about when you'd be finishing up, but when I returned, everyone was on the floor. Or lying on the roads in the snow. But I saw tracks that led out here. So I followed your footprints." He looked over to the curator once more. "And then I found you all here. Is that . . . ?"

"Yeah, that's Chieftess Gerel," I said.

"She . . . she presented me to the Creator after my birth. She helped my mother at the birth of my little sister."

"And she's a machine," Thaddeus said flatly. I scowled at him.

"He's taking it in," I said.

"And we're going to die if we just stand here," said Thaddeus. "I doubt she's the only curator here. If she figured you out, Josephine, then her buddies will be here soon. We need to get to the cicada. It's just back there." He'd steadied himself. "Say goodbye to the kid," he said, before ambling off to the flying craft.

Oktai's eyes widened. "You're leaving?"

"Yes, I—" But I didn't get the words out. In the distance, the honk and shriek of geese caught my attention; a cluster of them were forming just over the snowy hills, to flock toward us. I could handle the geese, or at least I thought I could. But Oktai's very fragile, very human body could not. "You either have to go back to the village," I said, "or come with us. You can't stay here. The birds will tear you apart."

"Why would the birds do that?"

"No time to explain," I said. "Back to the village. Or with us." A beat passed before Oktai wrapped his hand around mine, and in an instant, we were running for the cicada in the distance. Thaddeus had disappeared into the craft already, and Oktai and I darted as fast as we possibly could. But these weren't regular geese. These were the beasts that had attacked the cicada before. "Move faster. You have to move faster."

He gritted his teeth, fear palpable. "I am," he said, taking in the craft just yards away now. There had been a lot of damage to the wings and the legs, but I hadn't been so happy to see that bug in all my life. I could tell Oktai's eyes were widening, and between the geese, the curator, and our magical flying contraption, he was probably going to have a stroke, but we'd deal with that once in the air. All I could hear was the crunch of snow as our feet were flying and the vicious honk of the angry birds at our backs. They were diving for us, only so close, as Oktai and I dove for the cicada and tumbled inside.

Thaddeus was already in the cockpit, tinkering with buttons. "Strap in," he commanded. "Because we're going up."

"Strap in?" Oktai asked. I scrambled to my feet and tugged him toward the seats. This was my first time moving him, and he'd never experienced my machine strength. As he landed in the seat and I fumbled to secure both him and myself, his eyes were frantic. For better or worse, he knew I was more than a girl. And probably more like the machines outside the craft than I had let on.

"I'll explain to you later," I whispered as the cicada rumbled to life and roared into the air. Whatever Thaddeus had done during repairs must have made the carrier a bit faster, as the sounds of the geese seemed to fade behind us as we went higher into the sky.

Thaddeus whooped. "I got them off us!" The monitor did a little dance in his seat. "Calls for a celebration." He was probably searching his belongings for a flask, but I didn't watch him. My eyes slid to Oktai's. They were wide saucers. Anxiety. Fear. Confusion. I would explain later, but not just yet. So I stretched my hand out, and after a moment, Oktai wrapped his around mine.

CHAPTER 12

THE CICADA

Oktai had probably seen the wide-open sky every day of his life. It was either a gray pane above or a stretch painted blue with puffs of white clouds. For him, only the geese would know the heights above the earth. Only winged animals of mythology would ride on air. It was something for gods and creatures—not for mortal men like him to see. But today, as we sped away from his near-coastal village for new territories inside Siberia, the land was completely laid before him. And perhaps for that reason, Oktai said nothing.

The hunter had been quiet since the cicada roared into the air, leaving both the curator and the people he'd known his whole life behind us. He'd taken my hand as we vaulted upward, but he'd long since dropped it. Every now and then, I slipped a peek at him. I thought he would be nose-pressed-to-glass, staring at a world he hadn't known existed only hours ago. But every time I looked his way, his gaze was ahead, never looking out the cicada, never trying to see more.

One time, Imani and I rode a plane. I thought I'd said the words aloud, but he didn't flinch, and my mouth hadn't moved. Must have just been in my head. Even still, I kept on with the story. *We were with our mom, going to see . . .* I couldn't remember which ancient relative we'd visited, but I did know it was Thanksgiving and the plane was packed. And it was a long ride. Maybe we were heading to Houston? Anyway, Imani took the middle seat, though she didn't want to, and I took the window. It was an overcast day, and the only things visible were those little lights on the plane's wings, but I couldn't look away. I'd seen a plane from the ground; I'd never known what it would be like in the clouds.

"You okay?" I managed to ask aloud. I knew the words had come out because his eyes did flick to me this time.

His words, however, were slower. "Yes, Josephine. I'm okay."

That could mean a lot, but I decided not to press it. "How did you know where to find us?"

This time, he glanced at Thaddeus. I'd been right: he had decided to celebrate our narrow escape with his flask. Luckily, the cicada was on autopilot. "I didn't know about anyone else. But I found you because I tracked you from the Great Hall." He scrubbed his face, some weariness, some emotion coming through. "After you began your Chitakla, I left the hall. I had a gift for you, special arrows for the bow from the presentation. The shaman blessed them, but I forgot to get them from her tent. As you know, it's a hike." A small, strained laugh came out. "But I figured I had time. When I got back to the hall, though . . ."

I knew the answer before I asked the question, but it was worth saying aloud. "What did you find?"

"I found everyone on the floor, in this strange sleep," he said. "A deep sleep, like . . ."

"Subantoxx," Thaddeus interjected, without looking back. He took another swig from his flask while I rolled my eyes.

"Thank you, Thaddeus," I shot back. The monitor tipped his imaginary hat at us and returned to his work. Or just to getting drunker, whatever came first.

Now all the questions Oktai seemed to have ignored in those first moments of flight were pressing for release. "What does he mean . . . Subtan—" He stumbled over the rest of the pronunciation before stopping himself and shaking his head. "What . . . Thaddeus just said."

"Subantoxx—the Sap—is a drug that they use in Yerba City," I began. "That's where I'm from. It's another territory." When his face remained blank, I bit my lip. "I'm from a place far from your village, as you know. No, not where the Tsirku come from. Across the ocean. And where I'm from, they use this thing called the Sap to keep people calm and happy. Although I've never seen a version like the gas used in your village, it's definitely related."

"Not as good as my drug of choice," Thaddeus interrupted again, holding up his drink. "But monitors can't taste the Sap, anyway. Second-best choice."

"Thaddeus's drug of choice is self-pity," I snapped. "And maybe delusion."

"All taste the same with whiskey."

"You make me sick."

"Missed you, too, Josephine," Thaddeus quipped. "And a thank-you would be nice for saving you back there. Had to do it sober. Terrible way to start the day."

"So that's why you knew what you were doing. And Oktai actually saved us both back there, so thank him," I said. Thaddeus tipped his imaginary hat once more. "And Thaddeus, you can see your way out of this conversation at any time."

"Small cicada," he said. "But anything you say."

I glanced back to Oktai, who'd been swiveling his head between Thaddeus and me while watching our exchange. "Sorry about that," I whispered.

Oktai only shook his head as if that would make him understand faster. "What did he mean, 'monitors'? What is that?"

"Thaddeus is a monitor, yeah," I replied. "That means he's a human guardian of a territory in Yerba City. The one he guards is called Saturnalia. That's where my sisters are. I'm here to find one of our sisters who was kidnapped and brought here."

Oktai said something, and I began to reply, "Yes, I have a lot of sisters—"

"No," he said. "I heard the part about the sisters. That's not what I asked. You said that Thaddeus is a human guardian." Something in Oktai's eyes deepened, as if filling with understanding. But he wasn't going to leave the words hanging in the air now. And I wasn't sure I had the courage to say them, either. He breathed deeply, and perhaps for the first time realized that I wasn't. He spat it out: "You say 'human' like it doesn't include you."

I was quiet for a moment. "And what if it didn't. Would that matter?"

"I don't know, Josephine." His voice was a little raw. "Are you like . . . like Chieftess Gerel?"

I shook my head. "No, no. I don't have squid arms."

"Tentacles," Thaddeus interjected.

"Thaddeus, *please.*" It was Oktai's voice silencing the monitor. Thaddeus nodded in a strange surprise, as if to say he didn't know the kid had it in him, and then returned to the semblance of privacy he'd been allowing us. Oktai's gaze searched mine now, trying to find the girl who'd run into his reindeer. But how was I supposed to tell him he hadn't met a girl in the woods that day? He'd met 778676, a Josephine with a lot of power, and someone on a mission to find her sister before she ended up in a lab sharing all our earthly secrets. I almost jumped when his hand wrapped around mine again. "Go ahead."

"My name is Josephine," I began. "But I like being called Seven. That's my number, how I'm set apart from my sisters. They're also called Josephine. It gets confusing. But there are a lot of us, as I mentioned."

"How many is a lot?" he asked. I waited for Thaddeus to jump in again, but he was for once quiet. And for once my throat went a little dry. Maybe Oktai wanted to find the girl from the woods. And maybe a part of me wanted to be her. But that just wasn't reality.

"One million three hundred thirty-six, last count," I said. His brows flew up. "We started as one human girl, and then we were replicated into many girls, who are now more machine than human, but not like Chieftess Gerel. She was a curator. She'd never been human. I still remember my human life. I still feel like you do. Even when I wish I didn't."

It was then that I realized I was speaking fast, but I didn't want to let him into the conversation. I didn't want him on the mission, exactly, but the thought of him telling us to land the cicada so he could run screaming into the snowy hills wasn't ideal, either.

"My sisters and I guard our home and the people in it. The curator watched over you like a keeper at a zoo, or a museum."

"What's a museum?"

I sighed and offered, "Like a shepherd over a flock? One that probably drugged you every day of your life so you wouldn't notice you were in a big glass case. But I don't judge."

Oktai blinked rapidly, then his eyes shot to his feet. That's when I noticed Gerel's dark blood staining his furs. It had also smeared on his brow and cheeks. A few ripped cloths lay nearby, and I grabbed one.

As I extended it, Oktai blurted, "So, you're a machine not like the chieftess but kind of like the chieftess, and you're saying that everything I've ever known is a lie."

"Take the cloth," I said and pointed to his brow. "You're dirty."

He frowned before wiping it just once.

"Not everything has been a lie. Chamuk really did hate me. No machinery involved in that. But yes, everything else . . . You were brought together under a curator, and you stayed there because the curator wanted you to. I'm sure the Subantoxx gas has something to do with how everyone's memories were altered, including Dyre's."

Oktai leaned back in his seat, placing his hand to his heart. Up until an hour ago, the Chitakla was the biggest event in his life, outside of perhaps marriage. Until that time, he'd thought his village was filled with people he'd known his whole life. And the only drugs he'd probably heard of were those the shaman offered. Not Subantoxx. His world must have been shattering and forming new.

"Um, excuse me, weirdos," Thaddeus interrupted. Both our attentions snapped to him. "I'm glad we're all getting caught up on who's a human, who's a machine, and whose worlds are fake, but we need to figure out where we're going. Josephine, did you happen to get some intel that will point us to the head?"

"The head?" Oktai asked me. "I thought you were looking for your sister."

"It's a long story," I replied, and then addressed Thaddeus. "Not really. I just know that the Yetti twins are with this traveling circus thing. We should be able to find One there."

"Traveling circus," Thaddeus said, more to himself than either of us. "This trip just gets better and better. But do you know where it went? Because I'm still not getting any readings on the prototype."

"Dammit," I said. "I don't know."

"I do."

Thaddeus and I both turned to Oktai, my mouth kind of hanging open. "You know where to find the traveling circus . . ." I shook my head. "The Tsirku?"

For the first time since we'd taken off, Oktai smiled. It was a genuine grin. He may not have known much about the greater world outside of his village, but apparently the direction of the Tsirku was in his wheelhouse. "You know where the Tsirku went?" I said again.

"I have an idea," he said. "How can I . . . ?" He began to fiddle with the straps holding him in place in his seat. I leaned over and unstrapped him. He nodded in thanks and walked to Thaddeus's side, staring out of the large window at the front of the cicada. His eyes widened as he took in the view, but then his gaze focused on something I couldn't make out.

"What?" I asked. "What do you see?"

"The circus people, as you put it," he said to me, "usually follow the same route as the herding reindeer. They have to eat like the rest of us. Which for this time of year should be . . ." He peered down. "Just down there, along that hilly ridge."

Thaddeus unstrapped himself, not with particular grace. He'd now had a few swigs. He leaned against the control panel for a better view and then of all things, smiled. "Ho-ly shit," he said. "Your guy is good, Josephine."

"What?" I asked, scrambling toward the front. "What do you see?"

Thaddeus only pointed before pushing a few buttons that allowed our cicada to descend through the clouds. It revealed snow, of course, and the ridge Oktai spoke of, and, of all things, another cicada waiting in the snow.

***

I mentioned this before, but Mama was the showstopping kind of pretty. Aunt Connie was an attractive woman also, but Mama's face and voice were the kind that musicians would try to tempt away from church to do secular music.

Picture it now, they would say. *How proud would your husband be if you were in a music video?*

If you had your own album?

If your song played on the radio?

Oakland's own, you could be the next Goapele!

When Mama wasn't singing solos in the choir, she would always gracefully dodge the attention and remind people that her voice was for church. She seemed so dedicated to her place every Sunday that sometimes it's hard to believe that my earliest memories of her are those of her beautiful face, her beautiful voice, and then the big space she left when one day she was just gone.

Sometimes I imagine that she didn't really leave. That she got ahead of Subantoxx and the world ending. That she scouted a safe zone for all of us and came back. That Daddy never got the memo. That she's still waiting somewhere for us, humming a tune and eager to plant a kiss on my forehead.

Because if she isn't any of those things, then I have to ask a bigger, more unwieldy question.

Why?

I shoved the thoughts of my mother aside as I put on a clean white jumpsuit and grabbed the arrows that Oktai had been so kind to fetch for me. It was the best way to get on with the mission. She probably wouldn't want a machine wondering about her anyway. I turned to Oktai, who was busying himself in another corner of the cicada, and asked, "Don't you want to wait in the ship?"

I'd asked Oktai the same question for the past five minutes, and each time, he only glared at me and continued preparing himself to go back into the cold. This time, it would be after Thaddeus, not me. The monitor, for his part, had pulled himself together enough to put on tactical gear and head out into the snow to inspect the Yetti twins' craft. I had changed back into a Josephine uniform, a spare thankfully having been prepped in the cicada for me, and I was beginning to feel like my old self again. Oktai remained in his furs, which were still filthy—splattered with ichor from the fight with Chieftess Gerel—and one of the sleeves half dangled from his shoulder. I'd offered him tactical gear like Thaddeus had donned, but he wouldn't change from his furs. Not yet anyway.

I tried one last time to ask him to wait in the craft, but Oktai made a show of marching into the snow, purposefully ignoring me.

I jogged up and took his arm. "Don't you want to stay—"

He put his hand over mine, but his gaze was firm. "Josephine, just because I left my village does not mean you have to worry about me.

I'm a warrior. If everything changes or ends or flips upside down, I will still be a warrior. I know how to swim. All right?"

My mouth opened, but no argument came out. *Why did he say he knew how to swim?* "Fine," I said. Our hands fell, and I faced forward. "Keep up."

He snorted as we jogged to Thaddeus. Geese again honked overhead, and I shuddered, remembering the one that had first attacked the cicada. How ordinary they looked, as if they were searching for a park or stream to rest in. But I reminded myself that the curators were one in at least a thousand, not one in three. The likelihood of this flock attacking us was slim. Still, people always said geese were mean. If they knew the ones in Siberia, they would rethink that idea.

The flock moved on as I took in the fresh-fallen snow on this stretch of path and how it bounced off our faces. In fact, the monitor's face was bright red under the wintery conditions. I couldn't help but laugh, and Thaddeus scowled at me.

"I always hated winter," he said with a shrug. Thaddeus's eyes then traveled the length of the craft. "Now remember, the Yetti twins have been living out in a pile of sticks for the last decade. They've been hunting and killing all on their own."

"Glad someone listened to Nine's brief," I said.

"I do listen sometimes. All I'm saying is that they're not going to just open the door. We should be stealthy about this."

I smacked my teeth. The boys may have been cold, they may have been apprehensive, but I wasn't. I was a Josephine. I was built to handle moments like these. And after hanging out in Oktai's village, going through a Chitakla, and nearly being killed by a curator, I was also impatient.

"Guys, I had to go through a ghost ceremony to get here and battle a damn curator with squid arms."

"Tentacles," corrected Thaddeus.

"Tentacles," I snapped. "I don't care what they're doing in that cicada. The Yetti twins will open that door so I can get One, and then we can all get out of here."

The words came out fast, but once they'd flown, I knew they landed on Oktai awkwardly. When this was all said and done, was he going back to his village, knowing it was fake? Or was he coming back to

Saturnalia with me and Thaddeus? To do what exactly? Go to bizarre and decadent parties like the Sloth and Saber? But I didn't need those answers now, exactly, so I brushed snow from the cicada's outer handles and pulled with a great amount of strength. A loud crack followed, one where ice snapped from the handle and fell to the ground. But there was no movement in terms of the door. It was frozen shut.

"Plot twist," I said, gazing over it. "The cicada can't have been sitting here *that* long."

"Long enough," said Thaddeus. He turned to Oktai. "Any ideas?"

Oktai considered for a moment. Where almost every word Thaddeus said made me want to punch him, even the mundane things, Oktai seemed to give him actual consideration. I didn't know if that was admirable or just naive.

A few beats passed with the winter winds snapping by us before Oktai said, "Let's climb."

An actual smile lit the monitor's face. "There is another escape hatch at the top of the cicada," Thaddeus replied. I rolled my eyes. Was this a bromance blossoming? "But I'm not in a climbing frame of mind, kids. I think Josephine is best primed for this."

My lips thinned. "You sobered up enough to jog over here, but not to climb. Thaddeus translation complete."

"And they say machinery isn't as sophisticated as it used to be," Thaddeus quipped. "When you get to the top, Josephine, open the escape hatch. There should be an outer handle. From there, you should be able to get inside the machine. Just climb down carefully. The power isn't on, so if they're inside, they're probably freezing. Not ready to fight. I'll be down here."

He folded his arms as I nodded and began to find my footing on the snow-covered craft. And as I did, I realized Oktai had begun to climb beside me. How he found his footing, I would never know.

"You know you can wait down . . . ," I began, until he glared at me in response. I shook my head. He was going. "Fine, fine."

Up the bug we went, which was icier than expected, until we reached the top. The additional escape hatch was on the roof as expected. For a moment I considered concealing more of my Josephine strength, but if Oktai was heading on this journey with us, he might as well see now. With a huff I didn't need, I ripped the door off. There wasn't time to delicately open the door as Thaddeus had suggested. When I glanced back to Oktai, his expression was what I'd assumed it would be.

"Wow," he said, again with wide eyes.

"Yeah," I replied, not wanting to dwell on it while sitting on an icy bug. "Comes with the territory. Let's hop down." Two drops came quickly: one after the other, Oktai and I hit the cicada's floor.

Thaddeus was right. There was no power in the machine. We'd fallen into near pitch-black. As I straightened, the hunter took my hand. There was a split-second Josephine instinct to crush it, one that I ignored in favor of another, equally powerful instinct to hold it. I squeezed his hand and let go. He was a warrior, and I was the best tracker of the Josephines. We each had our role. "Clo!" I yelled into the craft, which I sensed had a layout that was a direct replica of ours, just shrouded in darkness. "El!"

Nothing.

"Don't make me come looking for you!" I shouted. It was a threat Aunt Connie had loved to use, and it was almost always effective. What I wouldn't have given for Aunt Connie to appear and use it now. But only the whistle of the winter winds outside spoke back, which weren't giving up the Yetti twins' or One's locations.

"Maybe we should let your friend inside," Oktai whispered. "It doesn't seem like they're here."

"They have to be here," I said. "If they were following that circus, then they would use this craft." I turned on my heel and tried again. "Clo! El! Come on out. I'm not looking for you. I just want One and I'm out of here."

But again, nothing.

I felt Oktai's stare through the darkness, and I flapped my arms at my side. "Fine," I grated out before heading toward the main door. I pressed it a few times, then gave it a good shove with all my might. The door crashed open, allowing moonlight—as well as the monitor—into the cicada.

"Where are the girls?" Thaddeus asked, climbing into the machine.

"It's empty," Oktai replied. I frowned, but then searched the rest of the craft. No Yetti twins, no One. Absolutely nothing. The cicada couldn't have been here long, so the twins must have abandoned it as soon as they landed.

"Now what?" Thaddeus asked as I walked to the head of the cicada.

"Not sure," I said, at least until I looked farther out. Oktai was a great warrior, and his know-how had set us on this path. But I was a tracker and had eyes that could see for miles, and my instinct flared as I gazed well beyond the ridge and found what I was looking for. It lay in the far distance, a structure that had been shrouded by the winds and the snow until this moment. A smile bloomed across my face. "I think I know where they went," I said. Both Oktai and Thaddeus came to my side. I pointed. "Have either of you ever been to the circus?"

"You think they're there?" Thaddeus asked, narrowing his gaze enough to land on the structure, which, as the visibility cleared, was actually starting to look like a series of tentlike buildings.

"Well, they're obviously not here. And we're not just going to sit here and wait for them to come back. Either way, it'll be fun."

"Questioning your definition of *fun*," Thaddeus replied.

I smacked my lips. "Let's go," I said, heading for the exit. I plopped from the cicada with the others just behind me. Again I looked to Oktai, and all I could see was his humanity, his fragility.

He seemed to read my concern and shook his head. "If you're going," he said, "then I'm going."

I nodded, allowing my lips to quirk up as we headed toward the circus.

CHAPTER 13

BY FAITH

Before the world ended, I loved holidays. The food, the singing, the traditions that brought people together. Christmas was my favorite, even if I don't remember getting a lot of presents. I was obsessed to see—at least on TV—something I never got a chance to encounter in Oakland: snow. The soft, fluffy stuff that fell softly from the sky. Or the thick, sloshy material that people used for snowmen or snow angels. In the holiday movies, you knew something good would happen if it gently snowed on Christmas Eve or triumphantly fell on the big day.

Either way, I loved the Christmas programs featuring snow and thought that if I ever got to see it, I would be just as happy as the perfectly crafted characters on TV. But trudging through the Siberian terrain, heading for the cluster of buildings just up ahead of Thaddeus, Oktai, and me, I couldn't say the snow brought joy, exactly. Its gift was this sound-muffling quiet. All I could hear were my companions' crunching steps and my ever-present thoughts. Geese cawed from above as we moved, a flock honking again and again. I shuddered. Hopefully none of them were curators.

"What's wrong?"

I glanced at Oktai, not realizing that he'd been watching me think and shiver. I pointed my chin toward the sky. "I'm not a fan of birds."

"Why?"

I frowned, but the persistence in his eyes said he wanted some sort of answer. Maybe he was curious. Or maybe he was trying to fill the snow-quiet moments also. I sighed. "They aren't as friendly here as at home."

"We were attacked by a freakin' goose heading in," Thaddeus added from a few steps ahead of us. "A goose curator like your chief flew right into our cicada."

"Chieftess," Oktai corrected, to Thaddeus's shrug. Oktai dusted his furs for no reason at all. He'd remained in his clothes still covered in the chieftess's blood. He'd tried to kill the woman who'd presented him to the gods—for a mission and world he knew nothing about and that he owed nothing to. In my Baptist church, with the Christianity I'd grown up with, Aunt Connie would call this walking by faith and not by sight. Oktai had never heard of my religion before, but the church mothers would have welcomed his resolve.

"Curators can be anything, even animals. Hate that they used geese, though," Thaddeus added wistfully. "Did you know they pair for life?"

"Curators?" I asked.

Thaddeus frowned. "No, Tree Hugger. Geese pair for life. And all that honking. It's to talk to each other and keep the V-formation they always use."

"Why do you know so much about geese?" I asked.

"My dad was a bird-watcher when I was a kid." Thaddeus rolled his shoulders as if stretching. "We all had lives before the world ended."

"Fair point," I replied.

"They're sacred in my village," Oktai added. Thaddeus slowed, looking to Oktai for more information. I hadn't seen this side of the monitor before. The side that was genuine curiosity, like a Boy Scout trying to get a merit badge. Oktai continued. "They're not sacred like reindeer, exactly. But they move as units, as family. That's how my village sees itself, and everyone in it."

I couldn't tell if sadness was in his voice, if he mourned forever altering his connection to his village in following Thaddeus and me. As I studied him, the monitor was already speaking. "Well, and geese are assholes." A wry smile spread across Thaddeus's face. "They'll bite your finger off to protect their family."

Oktai, of all things, laughed. "They do like to bite."

"There was one messed-up bird always watching my dad and me when we went out," Thaddeus said. "It happened with such a routine that I named the goose Aunt Gertrude. Mean old bird. Just like my Aunt—"

"We get it, Thad," I said, but I couldn't stifle my laughter. We were all laughing, and I was grateful for the moment as we neared the buildings. As it truly burst into view, though, my eyes narrowed. "What is this place? I don't see anyone. Back in Saturnalia, my job was patrolling. I would have seen a party like ours coming before we landed the cicada."

"Oh, there are people inside," said Oktai. Something passed across his face as he took in the structure's perimeter, but it wasn't sadness. A memory perhaps. "I know where we're going because I've been here before. I came here a long time ago, when I was a child. It was rare that people left the village, but when they did, they probably came to trade here. I think we brought fur pelts. My entire family came, siblings and all. But I didn't care about the furs. I wanted to see the Tsirku."

"Wait, that's what your people called me," I said, and Oktai nodded.

"Tuh-seer-what?" replied Thaddeus.

"Travelers, outsiders who come to the village. Revered. Different. Fascinating. This area was on their route. And they stayed here the longest. If you missed them in the village and wanted to see them, the best chance of finding them was here in Pobeda," Oktai said.

"The big city, I guess," I replied. Thaddeus quipped something about drunks and loose women, but I couldn't make out the full joke. For some reason, Oktai still laughed heartily.

Sober, Thaddeus was a far better soldier than I'd ever have given him credit. His focus in getting us to the next step was impressive. But there was no taming his wicked sense of humor. Oktai had only been in the real world for a matter of hours, but he appreciated the monitor's wit. Or at least Thaddeus bothered him less than he bothered me. Maybe this was how Oktai interacted with men when out on group hunts. For me, Thaddeus would always be the intruder during one of the most important moments of my life after replication, when I'd first spoken to Imani. I wasn't ready to make nice yet.

We reached the structure, where a wide entrance opened into a grand tentlike complex. "Well, I didn't see *that* in the village," I said as we passed beneath the entrance. The sun had accompanied us, but now hid behind thick clouds. It would snow again soon.

"Why is everything so old-timey?" asked Thaddeus.

I eyed the archway, draped with elaborate tapestries. "Oktai's village hadn't left the Middle Ages," I answered. "I didn't see anything there that would have been made with advanced machines."

"You mean, medieval like *that*?" Thaddeus asked, pointing ahead. Ahead of us lay a market of sorts that led directly into the heart of a small, covered city. And it was also like a renaissance faire, re-creating a historical setting for the amusement of its guests. At first everything looked like something from a Russian folktale dream. Nothing modern. But instead of being amused by the medieval elements, people walked around making their purchases as if, like the members of Oktai's village, this was all completely normal. I scanned the crowd, unable to get a good read on them, as Thaddeus said, "This place is weird."

"We agree there," I replied.

The humor left Thaddeus as he also scanned the people and their market. The larger structure that we'd seen from the cicada rested at the far end, by the center of the complex. "Move quietly," the monitor said, his eyes darting around and then fixing on our target. "We need to get to the center. That's likely where the Yetti twins are, and we don't want to tip off any curators that we're here." Before I could say anything, Oktai had responded in agreement and they both trotted forward. My lips thinned. If we got into trouble, it would be my Josephine skills that saved us, not their bromance. But they were just two warriors moving through an enemy territory. I would drop it, for now.

We crept forward, weaving through the market to not disturb the patrons. But it was hard not to gawk. While this "city" was much like the village—lost in time—it soon became clear that it wasn't any one era it chose to get lost in. The market people haggled for dried meats and fur pelts like those Oktai's parents had sold. Then there were others who wore clothes from the Carnegie or Victorian era, outfits with high collars and thick wool coats and buttons lining seams from their chins to their bellies. The time period of things didn't fit here, and no one seemed to notice. A few patrons even wore clothing from just before the world's end, like regular boots, long North Face coats, and knit hats with pom-poms. And like in Oktai's village, they didn't seem to notice the differences between each other.

"There's definitely a curator here somewhere," I said, more to myself than the guys, but still, Thaddeus nodded.

"One of those machines?" Oktai asked cautiously. "Like the chieftess? How will we know who it is?"

"They'll try and kill us for violating the treaty," I explained. "Just like Gerel. I'm sorry, but you need to start living in the real world and see things as they really are."

Oktai was silent, and we continued to move with our guard up.

"Guys," said Thaddeus. "Look." He motioned for us to catch up. Oktai joined me as we found the monitor, and neither of us had realized how close we had gotten to the city's heart. Now we were only so many paces away from the giant central structure, and nothing could have prepared me for what we saw.

Oktai's village hid the realities of the greater world, but this place, and the people outside it, displayed them. Whereas the marketplace was filled with humans, here beings of all sorts greeted city dwellers and enticed them inside the structure. A woman from the Brackish people danced outside, like Nori, but all grown up, I supposed. The water of her body sloshed back and forth, and every few seconds, she would turn and give a passerby a winter flower. The effect was unnervingly lovely. She had a high success rate, too, as about one in three of the people she enticed made their way inside.

"That's a Brackish!" I whispered to Oktai and Thaddeus. "What is she doing here?"

"Oh, that's one of the Wave People," Oktai said. "They're often with the Tsirku. They sometimes call themselves the True People."

"What?!" I demanded, still trying to keep my voice down. "There are Brackish here? Living water people, just walking around on land?"

"Yes," Oktai said matter-of-factly. "Wave People. And also Bee People, the People of the Air. And other things. It's the Tsirku."

"Guess every kind of freaky entity has a place here at the circus," Thaddeus said.

"But . . . ," I stammered. "But what about the treaty? It's supposed to keep all the entities apart, and us."

Oktai simply shrugged. "It's the Tsirku. It's sacred. Everyone and everything is welcome here."

I couldn't hold back. "So you've been coming here, your whole life, and you've seen these living machines. The Brackish, the Swarm Cartel, holograms . . . and other things?"

"Yes," he said. "Where you're from, you don't have a place like the Tsirku where all magic can come together?"

"I . . . ," I started, but I had nothing to say. "No, we don't. It's . . . segregated."

"Perhaps it is your people who need to start living in the real world and see things as they really are," Oktai said with a smile.

I smiled back, liking how he matched me. "I get it. The Tsirku is different," I said. "They let these . . . foreigners in. That's why the twins were accepted. Okay, let's keep moving." I clamped down on Oktai's hand and led him, careful not to let him get distracted by the Brackish woman's dance.

"How doesn't she freeze?" Thaddeus asked as we skirted by her. "She's water."

"Stay close, both of you," I said as we entered the main building and headed down a long hallway.

The monitor suddenly stopped. "Ho-ly shit."

"What? What's wrong?" I asked. His answer was taking my shoulder and moving me for a better view. Before us, in all the frills and chaos of entertainment, was what could only be described as a true circus.

***

I hadn't told anyone, not even Zenobia, that I was sneaking out to go back to my neighborhood. I didn't even know when I had made the plans. It was like my feet decided for me, and before I knew it, they were planted on the concrete slabs that had once been clean sidewalk, staring at my Aunt Connie's home. It tilted in a way I hadn't remembered and the windows were dark and empty. No one had been here since the day Aunt Connie had finally given in to the Sap. The day they carted us both away to our different futures.

It was cool. Autumn. Leaves had fallen from trees in smatters of crimson and orange. And at that time, I could still feel the weather's effects, so I didn't stay long.

Church had always been two blocks away. Most Sundays we'd walked there, before and after my sister's death. The building was also hard to miss, being one of the nicest in the neighborhood. Even the apocalypse hadn't changed that. Most Baptist churches in the area were plain in design, but ours was all brick with fine wood carvings, open redwood ceilings, and stained glass windows that gleamed in the sun. Aunt Connie said it was a lot like a cathedral, though I didn't know what that meant at the time. And though beautiful, the church now was just as empty and abandoned as Aunt Connie's house. It wasn't hard to find a window open enough for me to slip inside. One of the perks of being a petite girl.

I crept through the shadows, not sure what I was looking for, until I found the sanctuary. Surprisingly, it was still much like I remembered, if covered in a layer of dust and with a moldy smell the result of a leaky roof. I moved fast, weaving through the pews and then down a final aisle before arriving at our pew. It was where my family sat before things like the roof, the neighborhood, and the world all fell apart.

It had taken me a day to sneak back into Oakland, which they now called Yerba City Sector 3, lumping it in with the rest of the Bay Area. The sun was setting, sending this orange-pink glow through the window as I folded into the pew and my seat. I sat straight the way Aunt Connie liked, no slouching, and regarded the pulpit. I could still hear the pastor making his remarks. I could still see Aunt Connie in her choir robes. Alto section. I could pick out my dad, before the bottle, ushering in stark white gloves. And there, in the front of the choir, though the microphone was long gone, was where my mom, the soprano, would captivate us with music.

And then my straight back went rigid as another memory floated in. The church parking lot, some evening after a long choir rehearsal. Mama waving goodbye to the church mothers. Then someone coming up to us. Mama's chin setting high.

"Stand over there, girls." Mama using her hushed, clipped voice as she waved us to the side.

"You need to tell him." Aunt Connie's voice. Determined. Imani's hand wrapping around mine. "He needs to know. They all do."

"Hush, Connie."

Aunt Connie's voice a note higher. Anger. Desperation. "You thought I could just keep this to myself? He loves you. He'll help you."

"I told you because you're more than my sister-in-law. You're like the sister I never had. But I can't tell T this. He won't forgive me. What else do you want from me?"

"To do the right thing. You're suffering. That can't be good for you. For the girls." Aunt Connie stepped closer to Mama. Imani's hand crushed mine.

Mama's teeth clenched. "I told you what I wanted you to know. Now stay out of it."

A group of church mothers walked by. Mama waved to them. "You got the harmonies for Sunday?" Before Aunt Connie could respond, she said, "Good. It'll be real pretty." Mama then turned to us. "Come on, girls."

The memory left as suddenly as it came, and I was again in the lonely church, stomach roiling with nausea.

What happened to you, Mama?

I'd never found the answer. Not in Yerba City, not in Saturnalia or in Siberia. I hadn't discussed it with Imani, either. I'd just buried the thought until this moment. But I wasn't in my old church, and I was a long way from home, so I focused on the mission at hand.

***

Alongside Oktai, I'd followed Thaddeus into what could only be the home of the Tsirku, the place where every random character and free radical in the land would coalesce. And the inside of their structure was like nothing we could have anticipated. Firstly, it was a dome full of all the frivolities you could imagine. Secondly, it was very warm. As if we'd left winter outside, walked through springtime in the tunnel, and now had entered fresh summer. In fact, tropical flowers and vines grew along the walls and ceiling, and small fields of wildflowers were stationed between performers and their hungry crowds.

The members of Oktai's village thought I was part of this? Thought I was some sort of circus performer? Now I started to feel a little offended that I did the robot for everyone back in the Great Hall. Although it was fun at the time, I admit.

"What the?" I began, taking everything in and unsure what was real or unreal. Then I felt something. Someone had brushed past me to dance around Oktai. A girl—not Brackish, but part of what my folks called the Swarm Cartel. They had this unique ability to materialize however they wanted, and this girl had used the gift to carry a flower through the air, and swipe Oktai's weapon, his father's knife he'd been hiding in his furs. If it weren't for my special eyes, I wouldn't have seen the pickpocket or felt her moving through the space. But I was a Josephine, and I was made for dealing with any member of any enemy entity.

She'd also made a big mistake. She'd materialized for just a moment, looking like a swarm of gray bees coming together—and holding that flower and Oktai's elaborate family knife. When she saw me staring, her eyes widened and she fled.

I pursued her, moving away from Thaddeus and Oktai, following the flower that she couldn't mist apart as well as the knife that seemed to zip through the air.

"She took your knife!" I yelled as I shot past, but both of my man-child companions were too gape-jawed at the scenery to take in my alert.

Although I'd been briefed, I hadn't come against a Swarm Cartel member before, and I had missed the big fight that the other Josephines had participated in. I was out of practice. But this was sort of like tracking, picking her out as best I could, despite her quickness. I pushed my legs harder, faster, to keep up.

If I'd been human, sweat would have poured down my face. I would have needed to pant. I might have considered alternate routes. I could have even let it go. We probably had other weapons Oktai could use, although I knew this one was important to him, so I didn't even think. Oktai's face filled my mind's eye. As well as that quiet surrounding him on the flight. In the process of a few hours, he'd lost way too much. His village, his understanding of the world. Even his family. No, if I could save this one thing, his knife, then I would. And in truth, maybe I had lost too much in general, and needed a good chase to distract myself.

"Stop!" I yelled after the Swarm Cartel girl, who kept running, misting, and reappearing in a panic. She was a skilled pickpocket in this poppy field, but she wasn't used to being chased. The people who came here were probably too distracted to ever notice someone who could just scatter apart while stealing their things. She darted awkwardly and pushed through the crowd. Her only effective talents were her ability to run fast and disappear. But it would take more than that to get me off her trail.

"Josephine!"

I rolled my eyes, hearing Oktai's call from behind. Of course Oktai would be chasing after me, with Thaddeus on his heels. Of course, even learning that I was a machine guardian of a city, he would still see me as some little girl who needed his help.

"Where are you going?!"

"She's got your knife!" I shot back. He said something else, but I wasn't explaining myself right now. Not when I knew I could get her. The girl had successfully woven through the crowd to climb a set of ladders to a raised platform. Vines twisted around their rungs. Still, I chased her up. She was quick and sure-footed, but so was I. Oktai, however, was not. His jerky movements up the ladder were hard to miss, as well as his wrapped feet missing a rail.

"Ah!" he called out as I glanced back. The girl was near the top now. This was why he wasn't fit for this kind of mission, for entities like the Swarm Cartel or the Brackish. He'd been trained as a warrior, but I had been made, replicated for this kind of fight. For this kind of mission. There was no speed course for him, and neither I nor Thaddeus had time to catch him up. But I couldn't let him fall, either. He would injure himself if he hit the floor from this height. I frowned but stopped climbing to drop back and grab his hand.

"Come on," I said, realizing that Thaddeus was helping him as well, stabilizing Oktai's foot on his shoulder and pushing upward. "Grab the ladder." Oktai did as he was told, and together, our team climbed the rails and found the top. I'd used my Josephine strength to pull him, but he didn't comment on it. Good, because I didn't want to explain. I just took in the new surroundings, the platform, and blew air from my nostrils. "She got away."

"Who?" Thaddeus asked. "I don't see anybody."

"Exactly." I pointed my chin at Oktai. "A Swarm Cartel girl took a knife from his furs. I was trying to get it back." Oktai patted himself and realized it was missing. His face flushed red, whether from anger or embarrassment, I wasn't sure.

"That's it?" Thaddeus asked. "I have more weapons in the cicada." He shook his head and peered down at the performances below us. "I think everything is strictly controlled by curators. Except this circus."

"Tsirku," Oktai muttered to himself. He wouldn't mention the loss of the knife, but I could tell it meant a lot to him. He had been proud of that beautiful heirloom blade, having shown it to me almost the moment that we first met.

"Tsirku." I nodded. "We'll find it," I said confidently. But first, the mission. I turned to address the monitor. "Do you see the twins, or a head like mine?"

"No," he replied. "But she's got to be around here somewhere. Where else would the Yettis be? Unless they found a better place to stash a mechanical head."

"Don't say that. If you say that, it becomes a possibility, and then One could end up anywhere." I turned on the raised platform, then noticed something in the far corner. The outline of the flower. Oh yes. The girl hadn't gotten too far. "There!" I yelled. Excitement coursed through me anew, my feet itching to pursue. I vaulted forward but didn't get far before colliding with someone and stumbling back.

"Hey, this is my stage. Find your own."

This voice belonged to neither Thaddeus nor Oktai. And when I blinked up, I didn't see the Swarm Cartel girl with Oktai's knife. No, someone else stared down, someone with long, flaming-red hair and a look of mischievousness about her. I looked into the face of none other than Chloe Yetti.

CHAPTER 14

CIRCUS ACTS

Nine had provided plenty of intel on Chloe Raylene Yetti. Clo had lived in the forest for the past decade and was raised with her siblings in isolation by her mother. She was wild like one of the wolves on my patrols; I'd seen that before when Nine showed me that photo of Chloe and her siblings. But I didn't need all that information, because staring up at Chloe was like looking into Dr. Yetti's face—if age-reversed.

Like Dyre, Chloe had many of her mother's features, including the slim bridge of her nose and a somewhat pointed chin. Her big eyes hovered just above a smattering of freckles across her cheeks. But if Dr. Yetti had been dipped in gold—with her blond hair and slightly tanned skin—Chloe had sprung from flames. Her waist-length hair was a shock of dancing fire as she whipped around, and her hazel eyes sized me up with a spark of intensity. I knew a hunter when I saw one.

"Why are you on my stage?" she asked.

My brow arched as I pushed up to my feet. Didn't she recognize me? There weren't a lot of Black girls running around this circus, and the Yetti twins had had plenty of contact with One. She should recognize a Josephine.

"Your stage?" I parroted her, waiting for recognition to flood her eyes, for the girl to run in the opposite direction, find Elizabeth, and stash One far away.

That moment never came. Instead, Chloe's hand just found her hip. "Yeah, kid. *My* stage and my show. You know, you just interrupted my grand finale." *Finale?* I spun around. Sure enough, the chase had led me across a platform that was actually a stage.

When I faced Chloe again, I gave the girl a once-over. Aside from the startling resemblance to her mother, she wore animal skins from hip to ankle. But everything from the waist up could only be described as "take me to Las Vegas." Her half top was made of the same vibrant flowers growing along the walls, with a green vine wrapped around her midsection. On her head rested the biggest crown of flowers I'd ever seen, as well as exotic fruits and melons, and maybe walnuts sprinkled beneath. Okay, maybe Chloe was less Las Vegas and more Chiquita Banana.

She followed my gaze, and a wide smile spread across her lips. "It's cute, right?" she said of the getup. "One of those mermaids—"

"The Brackish?"

She spoke too fast to catch the correction: "—made it for me, and it just adds something to my act." Chloe brought her fingers to her lips and blew a chef's kiss. "Now, kid, I know the show is exciting, but you've gotta stay on the side and watch."

"Chloe—"

I yelled after her, but she'd already turned away and returned to her main stage. She took the center of a large ring, where a mostly male crowd had trickled in. They began to hoot as she beamed and winked at a few and then wiggled her belly to music none of us could hear. I leveled a look at her. "This is your grand finale?" I whispered to myself. Every moment I let this girl wiggle was a moment One could land in the wrong hands. So, I did what I had to: marched over to Chloe's circle, grabbed her arm, and forced her to face me.

"Chloe," I growled out as one of the mangoes on her headdress hit the floor. But that wasn't the reason her eyes went wide. I'd used my Josephine strength to turn her around, and even in this poppy land, she hadn't missed the implication of it.

"Whoa, kid." Chloe assessed me differently. "How are you that small and that strong?"

I rolled my eyes and mustered a formal Josephine voice. "Chloe Raylene Yetti. My name is Josephine. You know me as one of many sisters. I tracked you here from Saturnalia so you can return the prototype that you stole." But even with my commanding voice, it was like she couldn't hear. She only marveled and, every now and then, winked at some dumb boy in the crowd. I snapped my fingers to get her attention. "Chloe! I'm not here to watch you perform, or flirt with ugly boys, or whatever else you're doing here. I'm here for One. And you're going to give her to me—"

"Yell at my sister again like that, and I'll knock your head off."

The voice came from behind me, and just as suddenly, something sharp twisted against my ribs. I glanced around as the wielder of the knife seamlessly stepped beside her sister. Her twin. Elizabeth Anne Yetti removed the weapon's point from my ribs before flicking the knife to her opposing hand and aiming it toward my throat. Equal skill in both hands. That's talent.

"Elizabeth—" I began, not moving, though her little knife couldn't hurt me. I was more concerned with getting the negotiations right. I'd just fought a curator. I didn't want to take on these two if there was an easier road.

"I don't know what you want, Tik-Tok," Elizabeth replied.

"Oh, she's a Tik-Tok?" Chloe asked her sister. Elizabeth nodded in confirmation. Chloe's eyes widened again and she reached to touch my arm. "But she looks so real . . ."

I reared back. "Hey, no touching." My eyes snapped back to Elizabeth's. "I needed your sister's attention. Now I have it."

The knife remained. "You have both ours," Elizabeth said. "And unless you want to be in little pieces, you should go to another side of the party."

I rolled my eyes. "You can't hurt me with that stupid thing. Let's just talk. You have the Josephine prototype. I want her back."

"The what?" Chloe asked, staring blankly.

"The head," I snapped. Elizabeth raised the knife in warning, and I pinched the bridge of my nose. "The only reason I'm in circus hell is because you two stole the Josephine head back in Saturnalia. My sister.

I tracked you all the way here because my team didn't find her in your cicada. So tell me where she is, and you can get back to your show."

"We don't know what you're talking about," Elizabeth replied. "We've been here for—"

"Please don't say your whole lives," I interrupted, hoping they hadn't been brainwiped like all the people in Oktai's village. "Because you haven't. You're Chloe and Elizabeth Yetti. You came out of the woods near Yerba City. You were looking for your mother, Lauren Yetti. The scientist. Ring any bells?"

I thought Elizabeth at least would recognize me. She was a near replica of Chloe, aside from her cropped red hair and the sternness in her gaze. It was like they both had the gift of sight, just, Chloe could see all the good in people—I assumed—and Elizabeth could see everything else. But still, nothing came.

"You know our mama?" Chloe asked me.

"She's lying," Elizabeth said to Chloe, without taking her eyes off me.

"I'm not lying," I replied. "I've met her." I pushed the knife from my face, and surprisingly, Elizabeth allowed it. "And she made me. Yes, I'm a machine. And your mother made me what I am."

Finally, something passed through Elizabeth's eyes. Shock? Understanding? Or the memories that I'd hoped for? She stared at me as if looking into me, and maybe through me, even as Chloe hurriedly spoke in her ear. She wasn't speaking English. No. I'd never imagined how amazing it would be to hear another set of twins speaking their own language. The cadence. The uniqueness of the sound. Their twinspeak.

"*That.*" My outburst startled their conversation. "That's why Dr. Yetti replicated me. Because I have—or *had*—a language like that with my twin."

Before the Yettis could reply, someone new was at my side. It was hard to miss the furs, and I angled slightly toward Oktai just as he asked, "What happened?" His eyes, however, remained on the Yettis as they returned to whispering in their language.

"I was going after that girl who took your knife, and found the girls who took my sister."

"These are the twins?" he asked. Some conclusions had been drawn.

"You're part of that army back in Yerba City! You don't know our mama," Elizabeth announced, though a flicker in her eyes said differently. "You never did. That thing by the pool was just another Tik-Tok. We're going back to our shows."

I smacked my teeth. What had the curator said? The Tsirku makes its own path, "and the twins are lost in it." This place was magical in its own way, and, judging from the crowds, seductive. Maybe that's how the Siberians dealt with things: anyone that couldn't be controlled by their little role-playing act (and occasional Subantoxx gas) ended up in the circus.

Before I beat One's location out of these two, I decided to play along, if just for a moment. "You're performing, too, Elizabeth?"

"El," said Chloe. "You keep saying our full names, and it's weird. I'm Clo, and that's El. And if you would excuse us, the show must go on." Clo turned away first to return to her ring. Before I'd blinked, she was back to her writhing, and now her crowd, which had increased during our chat, was tossing flower petals at her feet.

El's eyes locked with mine a second longer, with some unspoken warning, before she climbed a set of vines hanging nearby. Having situated herself, she began launching knives against a set of floral targets tossed in the air by some Swarm Cartel boys who appeared and then disappeared on the winds. Maybe that's why that girl stole Oktai's knife.

I watched for a moment. El was more skilled with the knives than I'd originally thought, but the smaller crowd gathered beneath her couldn't touch Clo's crowd, which cheered her on as she contorted. "They left their brother back in your village for this," I said. When Oktai didn't respond, I glanced over at him. His eyes had glazed over a bit as he watched Clo's midriff writhe. I hit his stomach and he coughed.

"What . . . what were you saying, Josephine?"

I shook my head. "Can you help me get those two back over here?"

Oktai's eyes traveled up the vine to El. "I don't think they want to be bothered."

"I don't care. But you know what, you're right. They don't want to be bothered. So I'm going to get Clo first, and that will bring El down."

"I didn't say that," Oktai responded as I marched through the onlookers into Clo's ring, grabbed her shoulder once more, and whirled her around.

"Listen, Red. I need to talk to you, and I need to talk to her." I jabbed my finger at her and then at the nearby vines.

"Hey," Clo said. "I thought I kicked you off my stage."

"You can snake-charm these people later. Tell me where One is, and I'm out of your face."

This time, Clo sighed, and finally, that light of recognition passed through her gaze. "Oh no. Josephine—" She didn't finish her sentence, as a knife whizzed past my head, and I craned my neck in just enough time to avoid it. When I looked up, El was descending the vines. Those initial moments with the knives had been the warning. That one she'd meant to lodge in my head. I released Clo, and within seconds, both Yetti twins faced me, annoyance clearly throbbing through El.

"I told you to leave us alone, Tik-Tok," El began, unsheathing two more knives from the animal skins adorning her body. She tossed her set to Clo and got another. How many knives were on that girl? Oktai came to my side again, but I kept my eyes trained on the girls. I was impressed with their expertise, but not all this drama. And then I recognized one of the knives in El's hands as the one the Swarm Cartel girl had taken from Oktai.

"That knife is Oktai's," I said.

"Who?" El asked.

"His," I said, indicating my company.

Her eyes didn't leave mine. "Don't see his name on it."

"Yeah," said Clo, "finders keepers." That flip tone of hers indicated that she definitely had a little brother she grew up tormenting.

I rolled my eyes. "That Swarm Cartel flunky stole it off him, I guess to add to your little act. I don't care. Give that back so we can finish this conversation."

"Don't want to talk," said El.

"I don't want to talk so much either," I replied. "I just want One. I know you both remember her. I know you remember everything. That you left your brother, Dyre, in Oktai's village and were supposed to be looking for his father, his real father." I stepped toward them. "You're running from the Babble virus that almost took over Yerba City and

Saturnalia. The only reason you survived is because, like me, you're a twin with your own language. One that you think in, right?"

"Wow," said Clo. "You really do know us." She narrowed her eyes and pursed her lips. "You just want to talk about the head?"

"Yep, that's all."

She looked to El. "Come on, El. Let's just hear what she has to say."

El held up her knives for a moment longer before lowering them. "Fine," she said. "But I don't know where it is. We had it when we came in here."

"Wasn't April with us?" Clo asked her.

"Yeah," El said. "She was. But it's . . . in here somewhere now. I don't think you'll be able to get the other Josephine back."

"Oh I won't?" I asked with a little laugh, before placing my hands on my hips. "Listen, I'll tear this whole place apart to find her. Curators and all."

"Josephine," whispered Oktai. "I don't think you should have said that."

"Why?" I asked as we all looked up.

Like in the Great Hall of Oktai's village, the entire circus had stilled. Everyone stared at our group now, and then they all began brandishing weapons.

***

Bad batch. That had been the verdict. During the week after my replication, Dr. Yetti ran all sorts of tests on me to find the glitch that had kept me from understanding what she called the Josephine language. She held out hopes that she could fix the glitch and ensure that it hadn't contaminated any of my sisters. But the tests had been conclusive, and no other Josephines had my defect. I was just part of a bad batch. But didn't there have to be others to make it . . . well, a batch?

After the final test, I came to her lab to pepper her with questions, to see if there was anything else she could do. It was a cool day, but the sun was bright and clear. I was still getting used to being unaffected by the weather, and much of anything else, anymore. But instead of finding the doctor in her lab coat working, I found Dr. Yetti hovering over a desk with a small bag. She was preparing to leave.

"Where are you going?" I asked, standing in the doorway. She looked up from her preparations, and though she was a machine now like me, she seemed startled to see me.

"Josephine," she said somewhat breathlessly. Then she collected herself, edging the bag slightly out of sight. "Shouldn't you be with your sisters?"

I frowned. She was trying to act casual. She hadn't expected company outside of her robotic staff.

The lab was buzzing around us. Angel assistants moved about, pressing the buttons of myriad machines and collecting data. Some computers were strewn about as if they'd given in to the onslaught of information, and the work of my replication and whatever else Dr. Yetti required was just too much for them. Noise droned everywhere.

I smoothed my white dress. "I'm not One," I said, as she might have mistaken me for the first of us. It would be easy to, since in general we all wore the same clothes until we specialized. "I'm Seven. The Hunter."

"I know," she said. "I have twin girls. I know how to tell the difference between you."

"Fine," I replied, though the sameness between me and the Josephines didn't sit well with me, actually. Not because I didn't like our replicated outfits, or our replicated lives, but because I felt fake. Unlike my sisters. If I couldn't communicate with them, if I was all alone and couldn't live up to the purpose of guarding Yerba City, I was living a big lie.

"We have run enough tests, haven't we?" Dr. Yetti said, and the comment stung a bit. I wasn't sure if the doctor had meant to hit a mark or just encourage me to leave. Either way, I remained.

"You never answered my question," I repeated, stepping toward her out of the doorway. She watched me, chin raised. "Where are you going?"

She stared a moment. "It's just extraordinary. How you all are developing. I knew you all would find your way, but not so quickly. My twins look alike, but they were different people from birth. You all were made from the same rib, so to speak. You're exactly the same, but developing all these fine little differences. The way you smile, or scowl, or even your speech patterns. It's extraordinary."

She was like a kid at a science fair marveling at her experiment. Even becoming a machine hadn't taken that wonder from her eyes. But her hand had also wrapped around that bag. Maybe she was as much magician as she was scientist. Distract here, so the audience misses the trick there.

"But the others are still the same in one way," I said. "They understand what I don't, and I don't want to be different in that way." My eyes flicked down to the bag in her grasp. "Nice bag. Better than the skins you came here in."

"But not better quality," she conceded. "You are a smart girl. And you know I've done all I can for you, Seven, and for your sisters. There's nothing else I can give." She sighed. "My work here is done. One, as you called her, is the prototype, and she will help you and your sisters as you guard Saturnalia and Yerba City. As you protect the humans inside."

"What? That's it?" I flapped my arms at my sides. Frustration welled inside me, and she was going to get familiar with it. She'd turned my world upside down. She couldn't just leave me this way. "You're just gone? I'm broken."

"No, no," she said. "You're a perfectly functioning Josephine."

"I can't understand my sisters," I nearly shrieked. "Do you know what that means? That's like shoving a cat outdoors with no claws. It has no way to survive."

"But there's still a chance," said Dr. Yetti.

"Why?"

"Because," she began with a little smirk. "It still has teeth."

When I mashed my lips together, she placed the bag down and stepped toward me. "I wasn't lying when I said I did the best I could do. I gave you the strength I promised in the Local One. And with it, you will protect the humans left under Yerba City's rule, and yourselves."

I couldn't help it. I swatted at her bag, knocking it to the floor. "Why does it matter to you? Why does it matter to you what happens to the Josephines, and the humans inside Yerba City?"

"Josephine," Dr. Yetti began. She delicately scooped up her bag and turned to me with her whole life in her eyes: her own frustrations and fears and everything she had given up. "I care because the other entities in this world are more machine than human. They don't have the respect for human life that Yerba City at least tries to maintain."

I remained unmoved, caught up in my own rage. My own grief. "Respect? All the adult humans are pretty much drugged here."

"And it's worse for humans in the other areas, trust me! I know because I helped make the programs that have taken over the world. I put everyone in danger. My girls. You. Everyone. And I gave my whole life for it. This is the best I can do. And now it's all I can do."

She clutched her bag like she was taking in the entire contents of her world, of her heart, and headed for the door from which I came. "And what about me?" I asked her back. "Me as Seven? Not the other Josephines." My voice cracked. "You can't leave me alone like this."

Something in her seemed to soften, though she didn't back away from the door. Her blond hair shook as she spoke. "You're not alone. You have your sisters."

"It's like being in the dark. All the time. Trying to feel my way through, but nothing familiar ever comes. Why is it just me? Why?"

She sighed and shrugged. "I'm sorry, Seven. I had big plans for when I found a twin to carry out this mission. But sometimes in science, it's just a bad batch."

"And that's me?"

She gave the slightest nod. "Everyone knows that sometimes in life, you get bad luck." She gave me one last look. "Only the best hunters can live with that, and keep hunting." And she disappeared through the doorway.

CHAPTER 15

FOUND FAMILY

You'd think when surrounded by acts of varying thrill, the patrons wouldn't find us so interesting. I didn't have any talent fit for entertainment, and as far as I knew, neither did Oktai. Clo had stopped her sexy dance, and El no longer threw knives. No, we shouldn't have held the fascination of those inside. But like everything on this mission, if it could go wrong, it did. Every person, or creature, in the circus had stilled. They merely stared, then slowly unsheathed weapons. Knives. Clubs. Spears. Whatever they must have smuggled inside. Aunt Connie had loved *Fight Club*, but this was shaping up more like another movie I shouldn't have watched at a young age: *Gangs of New York*.

I glanced at the twins. Both were breathing hard while assessing the crowd. My legs bent into a defensive stance as I asked them, "Is this normally how your shows end?"

El grunted, but Clo's expression turned thoughtful. "I usually flip into a somersault."

"Shut up, Clo," El snapped. A laugh slipped from my throat, and she glared at me. "You can shut up, too, Tik-Tok."

"Josephine," I countered. "My name is Josephine."

"Well, *Josephine*," El said as a rotund man with a particularly large club shouldered his way to the front of the crowd. It was as if he was under a spell, perhaps the same one that had mystified the Yettis before I showed up. Only his eyes blazed with violence as he began to shuffle toward us. "Do you know what's happening?"

"Well, I can't give you a full report. Just, there's a curator in here, and we got their attention." The twins stared blankly at my mention of the curators. Maybe they hadn't gotten the education I did in terms of Siberian entities. I sighed. "Look, I shouldn't have said I'd tear this place up. That's a threat to a curator. And now it wants to mess us up. Got it?"

"Got it," chimed Clo.

"And any suggestions for getting out of here?" El's eyes were locked on the man with the club, sizing him up, just as I weighed our chances of bypassing both him and the crowd in favor of the circus's one exit.

Oktai spoke before I could. "We entered through a tunnel, which isn't far away." He pointed in its direction. "The only problem is that it's behind . . ."

"The zombie people," said Clo.

I took inventory of my motley crew. All very human, and impossibly vulnerable. *Dammit.* "We need a path through them. All of you just follow me, and I'll clear the way."

"Hey, relax, hero." Clo twirled her knives between her fingers. "We're not exactly helpless."

"You're human." My words were flat. "And I need you to get me to my sister, so you have to stay in one piece."

Clo smirked. "*We'll* be in one piece, but I don't know about them. I'm the one that's good with knives. And besides, I was getting a little sick of the dance anyway."

Movement in the crowd grabbed my attention. That man with the club was yards away and picking up his pace.

"Incoming," I announced, though the Yettis were busy yapping at each other.

"Take that thing off your head." El nodded her chin at Clo's headdress. Her twin scoffed, refusing. Clo was going to fight in that getup. I huffed a breath. Not my circus. Not my monkeys. No pun intended. Club Man was only feet away, his pace turning into a sprint before he lunged at us. Whatever spell was over him and the other patrons must have also made them light on their feet and precise in their movements.

He was just a man, but he maneuvered as if he was a trained fighter. If the rest of the patrons were like this, getting to the tunnel wouldn't be the least of our problems.

I was in midair before I could think, plucking him feet above what had been our quartet and slamming him to the ground so hard the floor rattled. The club popped from his hand and ricocheted off a far wall. The part of me that considered protecting humans like him to be my job had to turn off if we were going to get out of here. To me, he had to become an enemy entity as dangerous as the Swarm Cartel or the Brackish. I pressed down on him, making sure he was alive but quiet enough not to be a threat. A choked breath rasped from his chest. El nodded in approval, but the crowd took my actions as an invitation to swarm.

Clo was right. She was more talented with the knives. El had flung them with lightning precision when she swung on the vines in her act, but Clo sliced her way through the crowd like poetry. She pinned patrons to walls, one right after the other, and they struggled like flies in a spider's web, so vulnerable and humanlike . . . A thought burst in my mind. I whipped my head toward Oktai, who'd made his way beside me.

"Where's Thaddeus?" I asked him. Oktai breathed hard, taking in the melee, before noting the seriousness in my eyes. He then scanned the chaos and settled on a corner. That didn't ease the panic on his face. I followed his gaze to Saturnalia's monitor, or at least the shell of the soldier he'd been to this moment. The somewhat severe and focused man was gone. In his place was the monitor I was more accustomed to, his movements sloppy as he gripped a large mug in both hands. And was he singing? Loudly? I cursed under my breath. "We have to get him."

"I know," Oktai replied. "This place is a distraction." Without another word, we beelined for him, weaving between patrons who swung and snatched at us. As we narrowly dodged their grasp, I couldn't help but think that this was the real show. Yes, this circus seemed brilliant in its ability to remove focus, to entertain. But it also expertly tricked people, as it had done Thaddeus. It gave anyone who entered whatever they wanted, even if it wasn't what they needed. And people would get drunk on their vice of choice, never leaving, and never really knowing they were trapped.

When Thaddeus was in arm's reach, I snatched the mug from his hand and sniffed it. "Hey, that's mine," Thaddeus whined, but he wasn't quite fast or sober enough to seize it back.

I handed the mug to Oktai, who quickly sniffed it as well. "It's milk," he said. "Fermented milk. We have it back in the village, but this smells different from what we use during celebrations. And this can't be exactly like ours, because Thaddeus wouldn't be—"

"Drunk this fast?" I finished for him. Oktai shrugged. "Grab Thaddeus. He's off the sauce." Despite Thaddeus's protests and attempts to grab the mug before Oktai chucked it into the crowd, we were able to drape the monitor's arms around our shoulders and turn back toward the fight, which now blocked the exit. The Yetti twins held their own, crimson hair flying in nearly as much of a frenzy as their silver knives, but there were just too many people in the circus. And they were just too human.

My gaze caught Oktai's. "Help them. I have Thaddeus," he said, and in an instant, I was a whir through the maze of bodies, using my Josephine speed and strength to maneuver them, elbow them from my path, or knock them to the floor entirely. I plowed the path Oktai and Thaddeus needed until I was near the twins. Relief flooded me until I realized who Clo fought. Her knives were useless against the Brackish, especially when the mer-fish girl sent an angry wave directly at Clo. Anything that wall of water hit would wash away instantly. Clo barely had time to register the tidal wave coming for her before my body collided with hers, knocking her from the path of destruction. We tumbled in opposite directions, and when I blinked my eyes open, someone was pulling me to my feet.

El.

"Come on, Tik-Tok," she said. "Don't be dramatic."

"Not my style," I replied, and I looked back toward Oktai and Thaddeus, but El's hand landed on my shoulder.

"Thank you," she said. "For Clo."

"Sappy isn't my style either," I replied, but with a little smile, as our group finally found each other near enough to the exit to disappear down the tunnel. I tried to keep pace with them, but knew their shins had to be burning, as we couldn't stop to lick our wounds just yet.

Still, there seemed to be enough time for Clo to think aloud. "It was awful," the girl moaned. "I love my knives, and I love hand-to-hand combat, but I kept having to hit cute boys in the crowd."

"Living is a better option," Oktai replied, still shouldering much of Thaddeus's weight. His breath was strained.

"Fair point," said Clo. Then, as El slowed down and glanced behind her, "What?"

"That's weird," El said.

"We should keep going."

El glanced at her twin. "Why is no one chasing us?"

That got all our attention as we slowed and looked back. Sure enough, no one from the murderous crowd was at our heels. In fact, from what we could make out, all the patrons had gone back to their fun, watching newly revived acts as if nothing had happened. And then, in a whoosh, the lights in the tunnel flickered out. Darkness shrouded us. My body tensed; ichor ran thick through my limbs. We'd thought of the tunnel as the best escape route. We'd never thought perhaps we'd been herded into it.

"The door to outside isn't that far away," said Oktai. But before any of us could speak, the hissing began. As quickly as the darkness had come, it was gone. The lights flicked back on to reveal that we were surrounded. But not by people. No, they covered the walls. The ceilings. They writhed toward the floors. I couldn't make out where any of the hissing, twisting snakes had come from, but as those closest opened too-wide mouths and displayed dripping fangs, we bolted for the door.

"Don't look at the snakes! We can make it!" I yelled as the exit appeared, its frame outlined by shards of daylight outside. I didn't bother with the handle, only pushed my shoulder into the barrier, breaking it to pieces just before we all tumbled into the snow. The blistering winter winds hit our faces as we jumped to our feet and continued the run, not daring to stop until we'd sprinted through the city gates, crossed the snowy plains, and our cicadas burst into view. It took even less time to board our craft. I went to the cockpit to send us into the air, and otherwise put the machine on cruise control. Since the Yettis' cicada was out of fuel, they had grumpily agreed to join us, which was good, as I didn't want to have to bonk their ginger heads together and drag them along. Thaddeus got his bearings, and the twins and Oktai strapped themselves in. But even as we took to the sky, the adrenaline from the fight still rushed through me. I found myself pacing the floor.

"This mission is taking longer than I wanted," I said to no one at all. We had way more people now than I'd ever intended on bringing along.

Oktai watched me warily before suggesting, "Why don't you sit?" I continued pacing a moment more before relenting and finding a seat beside him. He looked me over. "You all right?" I was all right enough, but Oktai wasn't speaking to me anymore: he was addressing Thaddeus. The monitor, though still moving slowly and without grace, seemed to be coming back to himself now that we were out of the circus.

"Yeah," he replied, and then looked to me. "Where are we going?"

But it was El who spoke. "You want the head back, and I want to find Antonov. But the first step is finding April, the angel we came here with. She's in Solgazeya."

"I have those coordinates," Thaddeus said, slurring his words a bit, but heading to the cockpit to enter the numbers. The cicada rumbled with new life and soared even faster.

Clo's attention fastened on Thaddeus. "Love a man in uniform."

El rolled her eyes. "Put your tongue back in."

"Wasn't out," Clo chirped back before glancing at me. "So, you said they call you different names? All the Josephines? What do they call you?"

"Seven," I said flatly, not wanting to get too personal with the Yettis. I just needed to get One back and return to base. I spoke up before she could think of anything else to rattle off. "Why were you two hanging in that dumb circus so long?"

"The boys were hot." Clo shrugged. "And there were prizes." She ran her hands through her hair. The headdress had fallen off somewhere in the fight. "Aside from the costumes, and it was warm where it had been really cold outside."

"O . . . kay." I turned to El. "And how do you know that April took One to this Solgazeya place?"

"She mentioned something about the city when we were flying in and talking about Antonov," El said. "Or actually, she spelled it out. She can't talk."

Clo finished the thought. "Yeah, that's why she didn't catch the Babble. Anyway, that seems like the place to start."

I slapped my palm to my forehead. "Seems like the place to start? Oh hell, that angel was a spy."

Since I saved Clo from the tidal wave, El had given me some sort of grace. But it was gone now. Her face turned as red as her hair. "She's not a spy."

"Oh yeah? Why else would she take the head and leave you all in that fantasy world? Better to have you out the way of her plan?"

"Shut up," El growled.

"You two don't even know what you had. She wanted my sister," I pressed. "Unless you had some great reason to take her . . . April tagged along with you because she was a spy."

Clo's hand popped up. "Actually, I took her. And I just wanted to."

I pinched the bridge of my nose. I had been following these nincompoops for no other reason than Clo thought stealing my sister would be fun.

"I have to clean up your mess," I said to Clo, and then I glanced at El. "And for the record, that angel was a liar."

El launched for me with impressive speed—I didn't even see her unstrap herself—but I was a Josephine. I dodged her just before Clo unstrapped herself and stepped between us.

El had fire in her eyes. "I appreciate what you did back there, Tik-Tok," she said to me. "But talk about April again and I'll rip your head off."

I smirked. "I'd like to see you try."

"It's not murder to kill a machine," she growled, but I knew it was just talk. I had to take it up a notch.

"Just like it's not rape to jump on a monitor?" I spat. That did it. Everyone's eyes lit up.

"What?!" El demanded, but she knew what I was talking about.

"Everyone knows you jumped on Maynor when he was Babbled out in Saturnalia," I said. "That's a rape, lady."

"That's not what that was! I seen rape, in the forest with the ducks and—and—" But she lost it, going claws outstretched to shred my eyes out. "How dare you, you little piece of—" The others had to intervene, Clo grabbing her and Oktai taking me by the shoulders and turning me away.

"There's going to be a reckoning when we return to civilization," I called over my shoulder.

"Everyone calm down." The voice belonged to Oktai. "We're all on the same side, even if we want different things. We need to find your brother's father, right?" he asked the twins.

"Dyre," Clo said. "We left him. Oggy wouldn't like that."

"And we're going to get your sister," Oktai said to me. "Everyone just relax."

For a moment, El still glared at me, but soon she shrugged and returned to her seat. "I don't care what you think," she finally announced.

"I'm going to get some air," I said, heading to the back of the cicada. I couldn't go outside, but I could get away from them for a moment.

Once alone, I scrubbed my face again. This was not going to plan. My head dipped a bit until I felt a tap on my shoulder. I turned around and saw Imani.

***

Dr. Yetti was gone in seconds, leaving me standing in the lab surrounded by her angel assistants. I spared them only passing glances. Though they were machines like Dr. Yetti and me, they didn't have memories from their previous lives. They merely carried out her— and now my sisters'—work. That was the hardest pill to swallow. Even though Dr. Yetti had left, everything was just carrying on as I suppose she'd intended. And here I was. Stuck. I may have stared at the empty door for thirty minutes. My fingers drummed my side, catching the cloth of my white dress. I sank into my hip and smacked my teeth before finally accepting that Dr. Yetti wasn't coming back.

I left the lab to return to headquarters, the heartbeat of our new society. At least it was somewhat equal there, with all us clones taking on roles to make our work seamless. As an outsider by default, because of lacking our language, I took a loner role: sunrise and sunset patrols around base. There I'd be on the front line for the enemy entities that Dr. Yetti'd warned us about, the ones that would try to control the remainder of humanity through a language virus.

The buzz around our headquarters thrummed with activity, but aside from a hello here and a wave there, I didn't mention that we were now without the good doctor. I assumed One probably knew anyway, and honestly, it wouldn't impact them the way it did me.

Hours passed, and when the sun sank in the sky, turning it all milky pink and orange, I headed out on a patrol that would wind me near Saturnalia's edge. In another life, I would have carried all sorts of survival gear. I had no use for that now. Like each of my sisters, I was a weapon by design. Tall trees ringed our perimeter, their leaves shivering on the breeze. The nearby forest was incredibly quiet, at least to me. Maybe that silence was the aftermath of my thoughts.

What now? Where had Dr. Yetti gone? And should I have said goodbye to Zenobia before replication? She had been a good friend. Weird to think there might be another copy of me next to her right now, back in the Local One, making jokes about the apple pie. Did my other sisters ever think about having non-sister friends again? What would we do? All take turns playing double Dutch with Zenobia, four hops at a time? These questions seemed destined to go unanswered, which may have been for the better. The path's dirt crunched beneath my feet as I checked the border before, on a whim, I stepped off it. If I couldn't find the answers I wanted, I might as well see the entirety of these grounds I now protected. It was like I was being moved by some invisible hand against the sun, which was near a crest on the horizon, deep among the trees and brush.

For the first few moments, I saw nothing. But then, with my new vision, the leaves farther up the path shifted. I braced myself, but only a few fussy raccoons trudged out. I blew out a breath that I didn't need and then trailed them, watching the fluffy, chunky rascals head for a nearby stream. I'd never tracked animals before, but it was as if I understood them, what they wanted and needed. *Can't understand my sisters, but I'm in sync with the woodland creatures like a Disney princess,* I thought as I followed—giving them enough space to not be threatening but taking note of their little family.

By the time they reached the stream, dusky twilight had fallen. I wasn't on the night patrols and would need to get back, but my feet remained planted. I was as frozen as I had been in the lab. I had my animal friends now—kind of—but I was alone, maybe the way my dad had been when he finally understood that Mom wasn't coming back. The memory of him filling out medical forms, then waiting by the door, and finally, overturning the furniture, was burned on my brain. Aunt Connie had come soon after that, and now I understood that need to tear things up. That the pain just needed a release.

But it wasn't the forest's job to comfort me. That responsibility was my parents'. Aunt Connie's. My sister's. But they weren't here. I was as vulnerable as I'd been in the Local One, watching the days tick away until adulthood, when they'd put me on the Sap.

"Jojo."

My body whipped into a fighting position, a skill set I hadn't had before replication. Unless the jab combo Aunt Connie taught me counted. I looked every which way. No one appeared. But there was only one person who always called me Jojo, and I hadn't seen her since I was six years old.

"Who's there?" I asked. Silence engulfed me. This was ridiculous. I was a machine. A special one at that, more sophisticated than the angels or even Dr. Yetti. I had strength *and* all my human memories and emotions. So why did I suddenly want to break out into a cold sweat? I scrubbed my face, sighed, and relaxed my body. "I need to get back to base. I'm going crazy."

As I turned, a whoosh slid across the forest floor, and then: "Jojo."

And there she was, as if she'd been with me all these years. My sister. My twin. I blinked my eyes wide. But every time, Imani remained. "I . . . Imani?" I asked. The name came out more of a rasp than a proclamation. And then she cocked her head to the side and nodded.

Imani was not the small child she'd been. She looked as she would now—and it was nothing like staring into the face of another Josephine. We weren't identical, but she mirrored something deeper inside me. A part that even cloning hadn't taken away. My ichor tears began to stain my face.

Her arms were around me in an instant. "Don't cry, Jojo."

"But how are you here? Why are you here?"

"You needed me," she said as we pulled apart. She wiped my eyes. "So, I came." And then it was my turn to cock my head. As children, if we were ever alone, we used our cryptophasic language, as Dr. Yetti called it. So I shouldn't have been able to . . .

"I can understand you!" It came out as a near shriek, this strange exhilaration coursing through me. I'd been outside of the Josephines for days, and finally I belonged to someone again.

She laughed and tugged her ear. "Damn, you're loud."

I laughed, too. "Sorry, you just don't know how good it is to speak with someone. Even if they're gone. How is this working?" My voice lowered to a whisper. "Are you a ghost?"

She imitated me in an equally low voice: "No. I'm just here because you need me. I'll always be here when you do." She wrapped her arms around me again, and the person I'd come into the world with was warm where I was cold. In her own way, she was still flesh and blood where I was machine. Her shoulders were thin, and she had a slightness to her frame that I didn't, even though we were both petite. She favored Mom where I took after Daddy. She plucked a leaf from my hair and pulled back again. "I'm not here for the other Josephines," she said. "Just you and me."

I nodded, and my words were thin. "I thought I was alone after Dr. Yetti said I was a bad batch." The pain of it crept back in my voice, some of it rooted not just in what Dr. Yetti had said, but in a piece of me believing it. Then I flicked my eyes to my sister, scanned her face for judgment. I saw none, so I knew I would just have to ask. "You know what I've done," I began. "What do you think?"

A beat passed before her brow arched. "What do I think of you becoming a machine?" She clarified less for me, but for herself to process. And then her lips pursed. "Not going to lie. I'm not super happy with it." Something in me sank until her hand found my shoulder. "But even if I don't agree, I'll always be here."

"Okay," I said. "Another question." I hesitated before freeing this one. "Is Mom with you?" I hadn't realized my eyes were closed, but when I opened them, Imani shook her head, a clear no. I exhaled. "Do you know where she went?" But my sister didn't answer this question. Instead, she glanced over my shoulder, and then her eyes widened. I turned and followed her gaze just before a series of words hit me.

"Hey! Are you hugging a tree? Tree Hugger, girl?"

His words sliced through the air, followed by other drunken gibberish. I frowned. This was someone I had met in the days after my replication. His name was Thaddeus, and he was the monitor of Saturnalia. The man stumbled through the trees, his blond hair almost icy in the light of the now-rising moon. Something clunked to the ground. An empty bottle of fancy French wine, plucked from an unused cellar in Saturnalia. I would need to escort him back to Saturnalia instead of enjoying this moment, the first I'd had with my sister since we were children.

I turned to explain to Imani what was required of me, my vow as a Josephine to protect the humans of Saturnalia and Yerba City, but there was no need. She was gone. Only night remained where she had been. I placed my hand to my heart and hoped this wouldn't be the last I saw of her. Then I angled toward Thaddeus, gritted my teeth, and headed toward him, reminding myself not to pop him—as Aunt Connie would say—for annoying me and, generally, for good measure.

CHAPTER 16

SWIMMING IN SIBERIA

"Who are you talking to?"

I reluctantly turned away from my sister toward the voice behind me. The wind zapped from my lungs as I swiveled. It was all the breath I didn't need. My hands fidgeted at my sides. Moments before, my conversation with Imani had been quick as I tried to explain the additions to my crew as well as the twins I wished I'd left with the Tsirku. Imani hadn't mentioned the hunter. I was grateful, because I didn't know what his presence meant for my mission. But I'd been sloppy after my words with El, and now with this conversation. Because the hunter had come looking for me. And I wasn't sure of his thoughts on what he'd seen or heard.

Oktai's dark eyes glittered with curiosity, as if reading me, trying to fit pieces into a puzzle he couldn't yet understand. But he didn't find answers, so his gaze left me to travel around the room. I stood in a sleeper bunker in the rear of the craft, one the humans could use to rest their heads. A space I would only need to clear mine. Maybe he was trying to see if my company had disappeared into the air ducts.

This made me smile. I hadn't come back here so anyone could easily escape. I'd probably come for the exact reason Imani had shown up. This bunker didn't have buttons and gadgets, or anything that felt too mechanical. No, this place was quiet. A little sacred, like the forest. Still no answers for Oktai, so when his eyes fell back in lock with mine, they turned expectant. But I stayed quiet, taking a quick sweep of him. He'd finally changed from his furs into the militaristic gear that Thaddeus wore, at least in part. The result was a mélange of body armor riot gear and medieval Siberian Indigenous. It wasn't a bad look, really.

He repeated himself: "Who are you talking to?"

"You look different," I said by way of an answer. *Avoiding the question. Classy.* "And I see the Yettis gave your father's knife back." I eyed the heirloom dagger at his belt.

He put his hand on the carved pommel. "They are not bad people, the twins," he said. "They know how to swim, and so do I," he said matter-of-factly.

"I have no idea why you just told me that," I responded.

He frowned before quickly looking to his thick black boots. "After my Chitakla, the men of my village came forth to teach me the three things you must know to become a real man among my people: you must know how to shoot a bow, you must know how to ride a horse, and you must know how to swim."

"You have to know how to swim to be a man?" I looked at him blankly for a second, and then burst into a guffaw. "What?! Why? There's no water anywhere near your village, except the ocean, and you'd freeze to death almost instantly in there."

He nodded. "My uncle and I had to travel for two days to find a lake warm enough where he could teach me, and it was still very cold."

"Why the hell do you need to know how to swim to be a man in Siberia?"

He looked at me seriously. "Because you never know."

We locked eyes for a moment.

"Learning the bow makes you ready for power," he said. "Learning to ride makes you ready to move. And learning to swim makes you ready for what you could not possibly be ready for, because in life . . . you never know." He continued. "Josephine, you have opened my eyes to a world that I would never have known, but I am ready for it, because I am a man."

I shrugged, desperately trying not to make too much of what he was telling me. He was just along for the ride, after all. "Your clothes fit good," I said. "Standard issue for the monitors in Yerba City and Saturnalia. Like they were made for you." Switching the subject didn't work. He still pinned me with that gaze, and my hands fidgeted worse. Imagine, all the strength and power of any machine, and the stare of some boy was getting under my skin. I tried to brush past him, but he angled himself into my path. I stopped and sucked my teeth. "'Scuse me."

"I didn't mean to interrupt." His voice was even, though I could still feel that pointed curiosity around him. "I just wanted to make sure you're okay. Are you?"

"Yeah." I surprised even myself with my surety. "I'm fine." He nodded and opened his body posture, offering a clear escape. A beat passed. And then another. I hadn't moved. For some reason, my feet were planted. A tree in river mud. Now my eyes cast themselves downward.

"What does it change for you? Adjusting to this new environment?" I managed to ask.

When I made my deal with Dr. Yetti, I'd been so obsessed with obtaining this new strength, so focused on no longer being vulnerable, that I hadn't thought much about my life after replication. How something could go wrong—like being outside of my Josephine sisters as the only one not to understand our language. And how it could go right in a way I hadn't expected—like finally speaking with Imani again. I couldn't take that for granted even now. I couldn't always hear and see her. But before replication, I'd speak our language hoping she'd hear and reply from wherever she was in the world. In time and space. She never did. Not until that day in the forest. If I had spoken with her earlier, things might have been different.

"Everything you've learned about the world in these last hours is completely different from what you were taught," I continued. "I would have been on the ground, curled up in a ball. Well, I would have before replication. But you . . . look at you. You look like Thad. Hell, better than Thad."

His answer came faster than I'd expected. "It changes nothing, actually. Yes, my world is not what it once was. A part of me may wish to step backward. But a small world wasn't part of my path. All this space, this bigger, meaner, thrilling space, is part of my journey. And

I'm not surprised about that because I am a warrior by birth. I know what I was made to do and who I'll need to become."

"And who is that?"

I arched a brow as a slow, easy grin crossed his face. This was the boy I'd met in the forest. The one who was feeling himself just a little too much, which somehow made him a bit irresistible. He puffed out his chest. "The best of warriors, Josephine. You can't be the only skilled one on this . . ." He looked around and searched for a word.

"Cicada," I replied with a laugh. "And I'm programmed to kick ass, not trained." Something unreadable passed across his gaze, and then, of all things, he turned back one last time as if trying again to see who I'd been talking to. I glanced over his shoulder, though I knew I wouldn't see Imani there anymore. She never stayed when others were nearby. It was just her and me. Not my sisters or anyone else, including Oktai.

"Well, I'm glad you're all right," he said when he turned back to me. I peered at him, trying to take in all his features. The kind eyes. The effortless smile. The tic in his throat when he worried. And something in me softened. This might be a big mistake, but if it was, it was mine to make.

"I was talking to my sister," I whispered.

His voice lowered. "The one we're looking for? I thought she was in Solgazeya?"

"No," I said. "Not that sister. My real one. From before replication. I . . ." Why was I stammering? "I had a twin. Like those Yetti girls up there. Well, not like them. My twin was way better. But she died when I was young. We shared a language that my Josephine sisters use now. But I can't understand it. It put me outside the sisterhood in a way. It's the reason I'm on this mission. If I encounter the language virus, it won't be able to attack the intel in my sisters' heads, because I don't have it."

"What does that mean? A language only spoken by you and your twin?"

"It means we share words that only mean something to us. Watch the Yettis. They have one, too, and it protects our minds from the language viruses out there because we think in it," I said. "But I do have something my Josephine sisters don't. I have Imani. She started speaking to me again and not the others. I'm protective of what we have now." A little laugh bubbled as I rushed the next words. "You think I'm crazy, don't you?"

He leaned on the nearest wall and folded his arms. His borrowed uniform made his chest look broader. "I don't think you're crazy. Our loved ones are always with us, even when they go to the next world. That connection is strong. I may be young enough to have just finished my Chitakla, but that doesn't mean I haven't lost people that I carry with me. I speak to them, and I hope they hear me. When we die, we go to our great making, where there is no work or suffering. And from there, our departed ones can send us their love. Keep us safe in their way. I'm sorry I interrupted any time you share with your sister." Something in my chest bloomed, soon wanting to explode into a smile, but I tried to keep my cool. Maybe staying quiet too long. "Josephine? Are you sure you're all right?"

"We should go check on the others," I said, and nodded my chin toward the front of the cicada. We walked slowly in silence, and when we reached the front, we found the Yettis and Thaddeus in conversation. Immediately my gaze went to El. The air turned thick as we stared at each other—rams with interlocked horns. She was still pissed, but considerably less red-faced. I wiggled my fingers just to annoy her before Oktai took my shoulders and ushered me to a chair near the window. She wasn't happy to see me, and I knew exactly why. El was the more perceptive twin. She was the twin who—no matter how she felt about Tik-Toks—when I said April was a spy, she knew I was right.

We were quiet much of the rest of the day, until the night was heavy with violet and indigo. The day may have been overcast, but the night was clear. Stars winked in and out of the sky's dark ribbons. I was grateful for another thing now: that Oktai had plopped me in the seat with the view. It was hard not to smile at the stars' beauty. Sure, I stared at them on my patrols all the time, but this was something different. Because where others saw stars, I always saw my twin and how our language came to be.

I'd revealed to Oktai that my sister and I shared a language, but I hadn't given him its name. I didn't plan on sharing that need-to-know information with anyone. But we called it the Twinkling. Yeah, it was very much something that little girls would come up with, especially ones that grew up in a traumatized and dysfunctional household. But we loved our secret talk, its flow and rhythms, and its oddness. Its bell-like tone, as our dad said. Imani and I had always liked looking up at the glittering stars, when we were outside the city and they were clear to the eye. We thought when they twinkled, they were speaking with each other. Their secret language. Like ours. Thus, the Twinkling was born. And in some ways, it always remained.

Somewhere before midnight, someone plopped into the seat beside me. Thaddeus was maneuvering the cicada at the cockpit, and I'd expected the others to be asleep. I wasn't prepared for Clo's smiling face to stare into mine.

"Hey, Seven."

The sound of my Josephine-sister-given name coming from one of the Yetti twins was weird. "You can call me Josephine," I said, trying to hold in my cringe. "And hey. You all right?"

"I'm fine," she began, undeterred by my attempt to shut her out. "Where did you go earlier?" Her eyes were bright and her words chipper. You wouldn't think that we'd run for our lives a few hours before. "After your fight with El, I mean?"

"I went to calm down," I replied. It was a piece of the truth, but she didn't deserve my whole truth. Sure, she was the Yetti twin I would prefer to speak with if stuck on an abandoned island, but that wasn't saying a lot. Clo didn't press, opting to fishtail-braid her hair, remove her work, and then start again. "Why are you up?"

"Couldn't sleep." She looked toward her sister, who was curled up with one of Clo's knives. Wild girls. "El's the better sleeper. If the world ended, she would sleep through it."

"It did end, Clo," I said.

"Okay, she wasn't asleep through it the first time, but if it ended again, no telling."

She laughed, and I couldn't help but join in. I hadn't really laughed with another girl since I'd left Zenobia behind in the Local One. "Did you guys talk about me behind my back?"

"Oh yeah," Clo chimed. "How annoying you are. Who would give all of Saturnalia and Yerba City over to an army of little robots? The whole thing is so weird."

"Your mama did," I said, and this time Clo laughed loudly. Oktai, who was asleep at the opposite end of the space, stirred in his sleep.

"You've got a point there, Supergirl," she said, lowering her voice again to not disturb the others. "So, give it to me straight. Do you really think that April's a spy, or were you just saying that to get in our heads? Machines do a lot of stuff that's not so nice."

"I really do believe that," I said. "Look, you have all the reason in the world to not trust machines. When I grew up, I was taught the same thing. But part of my deal with Dr. Yetti was that I protect humans. All the humans in Yerba City, so I'm putting your best interest first. Even if you two didn't when you stole one of my sisters." Clo's light eyes narrowed in consideration as I added, "And one other thing. Your sister believes me."

Clo's brows flew up before she cocked her head and stared deep in my eyes. I expected her to defend her sister's instincts about April, but instead she asked, "Is it true our mama made you?"

"What? Um, yeah. But not made me. *Replicated* me. I met your mama back in my human life."

"How do you know?"

"Because I still have all my human memories. I still . . . feel. Look, she did all this to keep you guys safe. Which makes leaving your brother back in that village pretty hard, since I'm sure that includes him."

Clo bit her lip. "Dyre. Well, yeah, we got a little lost in that circus. Wasn't our proudest moment. He's okay though, right?"

"Yeah," I said. "Pretty much. He's just brainwashed in Oktai's village. Safe-ish. No physical damage done. And he's got a pretty fiancée."

Clo leaned from her seat and glanced at Oktai. "Damn good village."

"I can't with you," I said and rolled my eyes. If we could keep it to short conversations, that would be best. I just needed to get One and get out of here.

But she was still speaking. "What did your mama think of all this?"

"I haven't seen mine in a long time," I said with a shrug. "Since before the world ended."

"Really? Why?"

I frowned. I didn't know why she was peppering me with insignificant questions. "Cancer."

Clo's eyes softened. "Oh," she began. "Sorry to hear that. When our mama left us in the woods, I was scared, and that was only months ago. El and I had each other, and Dyre. We weren't little. How old were you when she left?"

I furrowed my brow. "I don't remember."

"It's probably in there somewhere," Clo said. She tilted her head. "El's waking up. She's going to call me in five, four, three, two—"

"Clo!" El shouted groggily. Clo winked at me before leaving me to my thoughts.

I turned to the window, to the night sky stretching out before me. I had spoken with my sister this afternoon, but how would all these new people being around affect us? Imani had never liked to speak with others nearby. And I wasn't going to be alone for a while, with Oktai, Clo, El, and Thaddeus around. One of the stars far out in space winked in and out. I wondered what that star was saying to her sisters. To her mother. Something about Clo's question had snagged a hook in me. I didn't remember much from before, from when Mom left and my twin passed. Before the world ended. My clearest memories were with Aunt Connie, the neighborhood holdout, and how Aunt Connie fought until the last minute before the machines truly rounded us all up.

It's probably in there somewhere.

***

That far-off star winked in and out again. Was it? As I watched, something bubbled up from the cloudiest parts of my mind. Of my memories. Night. Darkness all around, a shroud of indigo. Imani's and my little bedroom back in Oakland, the wall painted lavender with delicate flowers. Toddler beds with cold rails, ones that Imani and I had long since learned to get around. The way Imani did that night when I felt her little finger jabbing my shoulder.

"Jojo," Imani whispered. "Get up." I'd been sleeping good, and it didn't want to loosen its grip. Not until Imani shook me. "Get up, Jojo." My sister, standing beside my bed in a children's bonnet and nightgown, tapping her feet impatiently. I glanced at the window. So dark. And then the clock on the wall. Nearly ten o'clock. No chance of Mom or Dad overhearing us. To be using the Twinkling at this time of night meant something important was happening.

"I'm up," I said and maneuvered around the bed rails. "What's wrong?"

A worried expression passed over Imani's face. Her brows knit together. She was the perceptive one. Mom had once said she saw too much, heard too much. She listened to the quiet as if taking note of something I couldn't. Finally, she announced, "Something's happening."

"Daddy going to work?" I asked. He'd just started working nights, and early mornings, doing some dock work. "That ain't nothing. He leaves late now."

"Ain't Daddy," she said. "It's Mama." When my face stayed blank, she rolled her eyes. "Come on." We tiptoed to the top of the stairs. Our house wasn't big, just large enough to fit two small girls peering down into grown folks' conversation. "Mama's upset. Moving around weird. Woke me up."

Just then, Mom burst into view in her robe and slippers. Her hair was pulled high in a scarf as if she was heading to bed, and our dad was dressed in dirty boots and a thick blue shirt. He carried a tin lunch pail and wore a gray cap on his head. Even going out into the darkness, he smiled, especially when he turned back and kissed our mama.

"You get in the bed and get some rest," said Daddy. "I will see you in a few hours."

"Of course," Mom said; her voice was sweet, singsongy, like she could break into one of the hymns that she sang at church. She planted another kiss on his cheek, and he broke into a wider smile, as if he didn't kiss her every day. As if they didn't share a home and two children. As if, after all this time, he was still grateful for moments like these.

And then Daddy was out the door. It clicked behind him, and Mom went to the window, watching him pull away. His headlights flashed once and then twice before disappearing into the night. When she dropped the blind now, she was moving again, and of all things, coughing. A bone-rattling wheeze escaped her throat and she coughed violently into her fist. When she pulled it away, there was a soft pink phlegm on her palm before she wiped it on the robe.

And then came another knock on the door. Mom wiggled from her robe, tossing it on the couch. Beneath it, she wore a traveling dress. She untied the scarf on her head, letting a fresh ponytail kiss the nape of her neck. She tied the scarf around her throat and opened the door. Through it shuffled a girl from church. She was a teen, breakout-prone, with a mouth full of hardware. Sometimes she kept an eye on Imani and me during service or choir rehearsal. I hated those times because she always spit when she talked.

"Lizzy," Mom said. "So glad you could come babysit at such short notice. Tito left his dinner here and I need to speed over to the docks to bring it to him. Your mama's all right with you being out so late?"

"Yes, she's fine with it, ma'am," Lizzy said through her braces, which now sported multicolored rubber bands. "It's not a school night."

"Wonderful." Mom cast a look upstairs. We both shrank back as far into the darkness as we could without being seen. She may have seen us. If she did, she said nothing. "The girls are already fast asleep, so this shouldn't be too taxing. Make yourself a sandwich and watch a little television, and just make sure they have what they need. All the numbers are on the refrigerator as always."

"Don't worry, ma'am," Lizzy assured Mom. "The girls will be fine until you get back."

Mom's voice sounded exhausted as she laid a hand on the door-knob. "All right, thank you very much," she said as she opened it. But the frame wasn't empty. A woman barged through, and I'd know Aunt Connie anywhere. Aunt Connie, wearing blue jeans and a sweatshirt, breezed her way into the living room to stand between Lizzy and Mom. Confusion twisted Lizzy's face, but somehow, Mom didn't seem surprised. She did, however, slow down.

"Hello, Miss Connie," Lizzy said, before craning around Aunt Connie to catch Mom's attention. "Ma'am? Is Miss Connie going to watch the girls tonight? Do you still need a babysitter?"

Mom coughed, then breathed deeply as Aunt Connie replied: "You can go on home now, Lizzy. No need for a sitter tonight."

There was something ferocious in Aunt Connie's gaze, and I was surprised Lizzy could muster the courage to speak to Mom again. "Ma'am?"

"Go on home, Lizzy," thundered Aunt Connie. She didn't need to speak again. Lizzy was out through the door and back to her house before our front door clicked shut.

Mom straightened and stared at Aunt Connie. "You have some nerve barging in like that, Connie."

"Where's your bag, Lucille?"

"I don't know what you're talking about. I was just taking Tito his food. He forgot it."

"The only way my brother would forget a meal is if he was in a coma," Aunt Connie snapped. "Where's your bag?"

Mom held Aunt Connie's gaze, and then her shoulders caved in a bit, relenting. "It's in the car." Her voice sharpened. "Don't get in my way, Connie."

"I knew you were doing something stupid," Aunt Connie said. "And I knew it would be today. You forget, you were my friend before you met and married my brother. I know you, too. Maybe even better than him."

"Don't make this any more difficult than it is. I already messed up."

Aunt Connie stepped closer and took her hand. "He'll forgive you."

Mom wrenched it away. "Forgive me? How can he forgive me? I led him into this. Into something he didn't ask for."

"How can you say that?"

"Because I always knew my condition. I knew my limitations. I came to church to find healing and grace. If not in my body, then in my soul. The Lord gave me enough breath to sing for Him. But I wasn't supposed to be courting. I wasn't supposed to make friends, and fall in love, and . . ."

"Live? You weren't supposed to live, Lucille?"

"I lost my head and dragged you all into it," she said. "Especially your brother. He follows Pastor's guidelines strictly. He *hates* the machines."

"But Tito loves you. Whatever you signed with them, it won't matter."

"It does matter." She coughed deeply now. "You don't know what it's like. My lungs feel like they're burning. All the time. Like when I get off that stage, I could just collapse. I don't want anything to happen in front of him and the girls. I wouldn't be able to bear it."

"And would they be able to bear you gone?" Aunt Connie flopped her arms at her sides. "Is it selfish to let your family love and help you?"

"I'm dying, Connie!" It was an attempt of a shriek. When the words were out, Mom coughed violently again. Aunt Connie draped her arm around Mom's shoulders. A tight hug. Sisters by marriage, and maybe spirit. "And I'm being selfish now. I should just take what time I have left. But this trial the machines are offering is the only thing that may save me."

"And if they're lying? You know they started giving all the medical treatment away in our neighborhoods first. They did that for a reason. And you know what, I haven't seen anyone come back after accepting any help or treatment, or hell, even advice, from the machines. I know they ain't right."

"They ain't," Mom conceded. "But aside from the Lord, they're all I got."

Mom rose and headed for the door. Aunt Connie took her hand one last time. "Just tell Tito," she begged. "Even if it's to tell him and the girls a proper goodbye. My brother loves you like . . ."—she searched for words—"like nothing I've ever seen. Like flowers turning their face toward fresh sunlight. If you go, it'll kill him. All of us."

Mom's lip quivered. "Then pray for me, Connie. That I get better and come home."

"And if you don't?" Her words were low and wrapped in despair.

"Then tell them I loved them more than they could ever know," she said before opening the door and disappearing through the frame.

CHAPTER 17

SOLGAZEYA

When daybreak was a sliver on the horizon, we landed on a plain surrounding Solgazeya, the capital city. The air was cold, but not a harsh snap, and clear enough for me to peer around. The space, stretching for nearly a mile out, was level except for the few areas dotted with evergreens. But I was less interested in them, as the large structures at the plain's far end held my attention. They all lay behind a gray stone wall, where I was positive we'd find One.

The team moved in the background, unloading the cicada and grabbing whatever they'd need for the journey inside. Aside from the crunching snow, quiet would be an understatement. The silence between myself, the Yetti girls, and the hunter and monitor had stretched the rest of the night, and it would be all right if that lasted a little while longer. I needed to focus on the mission. In the span of a few days, Yerba City had been attacked, One had been stolen, and my sisters had sent me to an enemy territory after her. If I failed, there might not be a home to go back to, at least not the way I knew it.

"What are you looking at?" Thaddeus had come to my side, his blond hair strewn by the winds. His face was already turning red from chill, but that was better than reddening from drink: since we left the

Tsirku, he'd sobered up again. But I didn't have much of an answer for him. I was in my head and words escaped me.

He followed my gaze across the plain and inhaled, assessing it. "Kind of looks like—"

"A forest," I said. "At least it would if it had more trees. Perfect thing to surround a capital city full of curators." I blew out a tendril of silver air. "My sister's in there." When Thaddeus's face remained blank, I leveled a look at him. "One. You know, the reason we're all here."

"Just kidding," he said. "You think I would forget why I'm here? We have to find the lead Josephine."

"We don't have leads," I snapped. "We're—"

"Equal, I know," he added. I rolled my eyes and tossed a look at Clo and El. Somehow, everyone had found clothing like Thaddeus's. They were all draped like patchwork scarecrows in the gear the monitors wore in Saturnalia and Yerba City, though the various pieces they'd chosen—a shoulder pad here, a chestplate there—seemed to fit everyone's body type without tailoring. Maybe that was part of the design. I was the only one who seemed different, still in my Josephine white and headband, ignoring the cold.

The twins spoke with Oktai near the cicada's metal wing. A piece of me wished he'd stay by the aircraft, out of this search. Out of this fight. My lips turned down. Thaddeus followed my gaze. "Man, you're a mother hen."

"What?" I asked, focusing on the monitor again instead of the hunter.

"Oktai is more ready for this than you are." He enunciated each of his words. "The kid made his choice when he jumped in the cicada with us, so stop babying him." I began to object, but Thad stopped me. "Yes, you are. You don't want him here. You don't want him in Solgazeya. You don't want him hurt. But that line of thinking will only get him hurt faster. We all have our missions, and we all made our choices. Respect his."

"I do," I said. As much as it pained me to say this, the monitor was right. We all had made our decisions. My decisions to this point had landed me here. Had made me something different than I was before. "Just doesn't seem right."

"Oh, man." It was the monitor's turn to shake his head. "You're babying the kid and wallowing for yourself. Now that's talent."

"I'm not wallowing." My lips thinned to a line. "I don't wallow, whatever that means."

He ignored me. "You are wallowing, and want to know how I know?" He glanced back to the cicada. His voice lowered ever so slightly. "There's a flask hidden in ten different places in that craft." My eyes must have widened, because he laughed. "You thought I just had one, didn't you? No, I've had a flask for every occasion for a while now. So I'm fit to understand wallowing."

"Life as a monitor must be so stressful."

He frowned, and the humor left his voice. "Soldier," he said, with more seriousness than I'd ever heard from him. "I was military before the world ended. I did have a life, just like everyone else."

I tried to imagine him in another life, as someone other than the chronically frustrating person I'd come to know. Nothing came to mind, so I blinked and asked, "What did you do before the world ended?"

He didn't answer quickly; instead he breathed deeply and allowed his eyes to skim the plain. I knew that look. My dad wore it often. He was going somewhere that no one would truly be able to follow. A place in his mind with cobwebs and ghosts. Maybe he should have had his own Chitakla, instead of me.

"You remember that I know a lot about geese?" he finally said. "Well, they would flock close to my home in Canada." His words ran together as something almost rueful flickered in his eyes. "I'm an illegal immigrant. All the monitors are in some way. That's why they chose us for the program. And most of us are running from something back home, or at least, when there was a back home. People with pasts are easier for Yerba City to shuffle where they want."

"What happened back home?" I asked. He cursed under his breath, and I couldn't help nudging him a bit. "It's in the past. Can't hurt you."

"That's where you're wrong," he replied. "No matter how fast you run, it never seems to get farther behind you." He scrubbed his face. That low octave had become a whisper. "My dad was a cop. Why I wanted to be in policing or the military. He was a strong guy. Great at his work. But he saw too much. As is our family tradition, it pushed him to a bottle. Made my mother a shell of herself, and it wasn't always easy being his son. But he didn't like to hit you with hands when he'd had a few too many. No, words were his knives. And one day they sliced me down to ribbons. Yeah, he got me good, so good I found a nice bar of my own and got into a really good fight. Hit a guy too many times in the head. Knocked his teeth out."

"That's some fight," I said.

"It was, till he hit his head on a barstool and was dead before he landed on the ground."

Now I knew my eyes had widened. "Thaddeus," was all I could manage.

He kicked a heap of snow. "I wanted to face the music, but my dad got me out of town before I could turn myself in. Said it would be a mistake for me. An embarrassment for him as my father. So I kept my mouth shut and head down, ran to America. And then the world ended, and here I am. Still running, always just in place." This was Thaddeus's song, a tune that if you didn't listen close, you'd miss just how deep the sadness ran. Maybe it was what he heard every time he took a swig from his many flasks? Or maybe that's what was drowned out when he got too drunk to stand.

I swallowed and tried to remove judgment from my voice when I asked: "Why are you telling me all this? I just mean, I wouldn't call us friends on a good day."

He laughed a little to himself. His eyes left the plain and, perhaps, his past. "No, I wouldn't exactly call us friends, Josephine. I'm usually—"

"A jerk," we said in unison, and then we laughed.

"So why aren't you being a jerk to me anymore?" I asked. "When I first met you, I wanted to leave you out in the forest."

"But you didn't. And you didn't leave me back there in the circus. You could have done it easily. But you didn't. Unlike me, you don't leave your problems behind you. Even when your problem is me. That means a lot in my world. Between soldiers. I know you Josephines are egalitarian, but I'm not a Josephine. Just . . ." He untangled his words. "You could have left me, and you didn't. So, know that I have your back." His pale blue eyes glittered with a surety I hadn't seen from him before, so I nodded and began to speak, until I felt a tap on my shoulder. I swirled around. Nice conversation with Thaddeus or not, I was still on edge. Curators could be anywhere, though at this moment, only Oktai had joined our conversation.

"Ready?" the hunter asked me, before nodding to Thaddeus. Thad gave me a sharp look—a reminder not to baby Oktai. Then he addressed Oktai, who stared over the plain stretching before the city. Within moments, the twins had caught up to us as well.

"What is it that you see?" Thad asked Oktai.

"Besides the capital?" El asked. Her voice was a little hoarse. Probably hadn't slept well.

"I don't see the capital, as you put it," began Oktai. "I see something that the rest of you don't. You didn't grow and learn in my village. But this land is more than just the place before Solgazeya. It is more special than that. Notice the blades of grass springing out of the snow and how the rest of the land yields to it under the trees. For us, this great yield is also a land of great rest: it is the space entering the next world."

"The capital is the next world?" asked Clo. "Like . . ." She drew a sharp line across her throat, followed by a splattering sound. She then cocked her head in an exaggerated manner.

I shook my head. "I don't think that's what he means, Clo." Although I actually didn't know precisely what he meant either, I knew this place was profound for Oktai. Maybe it was all just a fabrication, his village's mythology, fed to his people nightly through mind-altering Subantoxx and the encouraging of the curators to keep their bubble zoo in line. Maybe they had planted the imagery of Antonov's stronghold as some far-off land that they would all visit in the afterlife, just so no one would ever go looking for real answers about the world they lived in. I wasn't sure, and I wasn't certain how much of his own worldview had been unraveling since he'd joined me on the cicada, but in any case, his words had us all captivated.

Oktai chuckled. "In the stories my family told, this was the beginning and the ending, the entry to the next world."

"Ghosts here, too?" I asked him.

He smiled at me and winked. My cheeks warmed. "More than likely."

"I know he's in there," I said of Antonov.

Clo nodded and adjusted a dark bag on her shoulder. I wasn't sure what weapon she'd fit in it. "Yeah, I have it, too. It's a weird feeling."

"Down in your bones," El finished for her sister. "Spooky."

"And I know my sister is there, too," I said, not adding how she got there, or that their April friend was a spy. That was just schematics at this point. We didn't want to fight again about spies or the Yetti twins' lack of skill at reading people. "Let's get closer to the entryway."

The march toward Solgazeya was a trudge against the winter winds. The cityscape grew larger behind the foreboding wall with every step through the grass and snow, but it didn't deter our motley crew: the supergirl looking for her sister; the kickass twins seeking answers about their family; the monitor and his new loyalty; and the hunter feeling his way through a larger, meaner world. We'd landed in Oz and were off to see the wizard.

At least, until something whizzed by us. It was so fast, I couldn't read its size or shape in the morning glow. I stilled, trying to take in the threat just as another creature whooshed by and plowed into El's legs. She yelled before tumbling to the ground and reaching for her shin. Thaddeus swatted out as a last beast tried to weave through the group, but it was Clo who swung that dark bag from her shoulder and connected with a sickening *thwack*.

It stilled long enough for me to finally scan the animal twitching on the ground. A doe, like those I'd followed in the forest, near a stream, only so long ago. It twitched a few more times before springing to its feet. The others reared back, but I only lifted my chin. I recognized it, in the way you might notice a familial trait like a unique eye color or bend of the nose. The doe was definitely a robot, but not like the curators. No, she was more like me—delicately alive and also machine, as close to a replicated creature as I'd seen since Dr. Yetti and my own sisters.

Clo was helping El up when she asked, "Is that a deer? Another Vambi? How is it that fast?"

I tossed a look at El. "You okay?"

She nodded. "Freaked me out more than it hurt me. Nothing permanent. Just, what is that thing?" It had already begun to dart away, and I could tell others like it roamed across the plain in the near distance.

I shrugged. "Whatever Antonov is making in that city, he's getting more sophisticated. That thing was just testing us."

"So what do we do with it?" Thad asked, reaching for his holster.

"It doesn't have fangs, does it?" asked Clo.

"Um," I started. "No, I didn't see fangs."

"We let it go," said Oktai.

Clo put her hand to her chest, but it was El who spoke. "I agree with Oktai. If we don't need it, just . . . let's focus."

"They know we're here," I said, and they nodded. "Keep your eyes open. I'm guessing they don't like visitors."

There wasn't an entryway, exactly. But for the wall to seem so impenetrable, finding a crack large enough for the group to slip through wasn't as difficult as I'd imagined it would be. Keeping the group quiet long enough for everyone to enter Solgazeya was another story. It was daylight when we finally made it through, and the sunlight was bright, stark, and golden on an otherwise dark cityscape. Whereas the city housing the Tsirku felt medieval, and a bit playful, everything about Solgazeya was industrial. A machine landscape made by other machines. Dirty snow and air. Plumes of smoke coming from chimneys atop large, square buildings. This was a manufacturing hub, all right, and the only thing I could imagine Antonov making here would be curators.

I was flanked by Oktai and Thaddeus, while the twins maneuvered behind us. I vaguely heard Clo mention something about a man in uniform to Thad, but no one commented on it. We tried to keep to the shadows and keep our heads and voices low, at least until Clo asked, "What's the point of replicating a deer?"

It was Oktai who answered. "Maybe because they're sacred," he said. "I'm a hunter. From what I could tell, those deer grazed just beyond the capital ground. They're protective. They walk with the spirits who travel into the next world."

"Or spy on the trespassers entering Solgazeya," added El.

"That could be true," said Oktai. "Never thought I would see any of this under these circumstances."

"Alive?" El asked.

He shrugged. "Yeah," he said. "I never thought I would pass the sacred grounds like this. It's a place you go when you've had a good life."

"I see deer on patrols all the time when I'm in Saturnalia," I said. "They're not exactly spiritual, or dangerous, unless, you know . . . Lyme disease."

"Machine deer are definitely dangerous," said Clo before swinging the bag over her shoulder and yanking something from its depths. It was the head of a mechanical deer, but not nearly as friendly look- ing as the super fast ghost deer from outside Solgazeya. "Fanged deer attacked us. Got our brother. How we started this whole thing. We call him Vambi." Clo put the creepy deer in the bag.

"You weirdos have been carrying that thing this whole time?" Thaddeus asked incredulously.

"Antonov is going to know we brought it for him," El said coldly. "He's got a lot to answer for."

I shuddered, but it was Thaddeus who, of all things, laughed. "Vambi," he said. "Clever."

We kept moving, heading for the heart of the city, with me try- ing not to imagine the Yetti twins carrying One the same way they carried Vambi. I reasoned the city center was where the action would be, and likely where we would find Antonov and One. I also imagined there would be more people in the city. But unlike in the home of the Tsirku, the streets were quiet. Eerily so. It was just our jog toward the unknown and the snow beneath our shoes. Every so often, I narrowed my eyes. Just where was everybody?

"It's too quiet," I whispered.

"Yeah, I don't like it," said El. "This place is about the machines."

"Curators," I added. "They are one in a thousand. Could be any- where. Just, no one is here for them to hide among."

"But they're always around, pulling the strings," said Thad. "You think you're free, but you're not free at all." He tossed me another look. "No offense, Josephine."

"None taken, but you do know I was human before. And unlike the angels, I still have all my human memories—" My speech cut off as with a great crack, the ground shook and opened up from underneath us. It felt like we free-fell forever, through rings and rings of darkness. But you'll always hit the floor eventually. It came, and we landed, like in the Chitakla, in a pit shrouded in darkness, only allowing us to feel our way through the nothing, through the webs of dark. We'd come to this place to find Antonov, some evil guy in a tower, but so far that hadn't happened. We'd only been left to slosh our way through a dark, eerie place that squelched beneath our feet.

"Ew, it's gooey," said Clo just as the darkness began to break. Greenish bioluminescent torches lining the walls illuminated rings, like levels, above us. I wondered if that meant there were also rings beneath us. The new light only gave so much relief, as I soon realized the floor was coated in a thick ooze. We all leaned forward to inspect it.

"What does it look like?" I asked Thaddeus.

"Some kind of biomechanical glob," Thaddeus replied, just as the ooze began to throb. "I think it's Siberia's version of ichor." I thought about my own golden blood, which I had been so shocked to see flowing out of me when I first woke from replication. It had horrified me at the time, but compared to this stuff, Yerba City's golden goo was positively delectable.

We reared back to the farthest reaches of the space as the glob pulsated and then expanded, and from it, something emerged. A figure of a man at least seven feet tall—maybe taller—and corded with muscle stood before us. Thick gray-brown fur lined his body; long nails sprouted from each hand. But those weren't the most monstrous of his features. For when this person straightened and took inventory of our crew trapped in the pit with him, he stared at us with the head of a giant bull.

⁂

You tend to think of a lot of things in life-or-death situations. Sometimes panic sparks through you and focuses your senses, helping you escape. Other times all your missteps and wishes flash before your eyes. They're a twisted movie of a past you won't get to change and a future you may not see. And then sometimes you just see a face. That person is someone you love so dearly you'll will your way out or go down with their name on your lips. Sure, I wasn't exactly human anymore, but since leaving Yerba City, I had found myself in a few of these circumstances. Standing in a pit with the other members of my crew while Curator Man-Bull sized us up was no different. And if you're curious, I saw a face. But it didn't belong to Imani or even my mother. No, it was Daddy's.

Why would I think of Daddy instead of finding a way out of here? Well, maybe because that mind beneath your conscious one has a sense of humor. Who would most appreciate the horror snarling before us? My father. And the sight would tickle him because, as a true romantic, he loved three things: his family, the game of chess, and finally, mythology. Even as he was declining, he could spout tales with ease, especially those belonging to the ancient Greeks. And which tale did he love most? That's right. Theseus and the minotaur.

My eyes traveled the length of the curator's body. He was broad, with thick-corded muscle twisting around his arms. Great: he lived in a pit, but somehow hadn't missed a meal or a workout. He angled toward us, knees bending ever so slightly.

Clo's whisper sliced the air. "What is that thing?" she asked. Long knives already gleamed in both her hands.

Before I could speak, Thaddeus—whose eyes were trained on the curator—chuckled. "This Antonov guy is a piece of work."

"What?" Clo muttered.

He glanced at Clo for the briefest moment. One of his arms was bent, stabilizing his shooting hand.

"She's been stuck in the woods for years, Thad," I said, and flicked my eyes at Clo. "Greek mythology. This Antonov guy likes stories, mythologies. Hence, Bull Guy."

"Couldn't Antonov like Santa Claus?" Clo asked.

"We kill Santas, too, remember?" El replied flatly and quickly. "Seven, Thad, since you guys are so familiar with it . . . can you tell us how to kill it? Doesn't look like he wants cookies and milk."

I gritted my teeth but remained silent. I was still working that little detail out in my head, all while the minotaur seemed ready to bound toward us at any second. Dark fur sprang from his head. Somewhat pointed ears twitched about, taking in our every shuffle or hard breath. Large, round eyes took us in as we brandished our weapons, and a brass ring clinked on his nose. Stubbly teeth ground as the bull growled.

A little crazy laugh bubbled from my throat before I could stop it. I nocked an arrow in my bowstring, and with a quick motion let it fly. If I wasn't mistaken, the thing had the audacity to smile.

The arrow flew but didn't hit its target. In fact, the bull dodged from its path with incredible speed and flexibility, heading directly for Thaddeus. He was a freight train hurtling forward, sometimes on two legs, now on four, and Thaddeus, with his human senses, hopped from its way in the last possible moment.

"Wow," I said. "Maybe it doesn't like blonds."

"Focus!" Thaddeus said as the train barreled next toward Oktai. My heart lurched: I was too far away to help him. I sent another arrow after the bull, but as if he was linked to my mind, the minotaur evaded me once more. Aside from that stare, though, he hadn't bothered me much. Maybe he had registered me as a worthier threat and, in self-preservation, had left me alone. I volleyed toward him, quiver and all, but again, he slid past me. Either he didn't want to fight me or he was saving me for last.

Instead, his arms were outstretched for Oktai, but the hunter managed to spin around and leap onto the bull's back. The curator hadn't expected that assault and thrashed wildly, but Oktai's attack was sure. The bull snagged the forearm of Oktai's body armor but didn't manage to pull him off. Oktai drew his father's knife and got to work. By the time the bull had thrown him off, the hunter had managed to stab him three times in the shoulder as the beast emitted an ear-splitting roar.

El signaled to Thaddeus for a gun. Maybe I'd been wrong, and she didn't have her own weapons. Either way, no second was spared, as the monitor tossed a fléchette pistol her way, and El aimed at the bull like an expert marksman. The living floor seemed to wince in sympathy with the minotaur as each round of the antipersonnel plastic shards found their mark. What exactly had Dr. Yetti been teaching those girls in the forest?

For my part, I was nocking and loosing arrow after arrow. But the minotaur could just take any shots that hit its thick body. It absorbed my, Thad's, and El's efforts with ease and healed injuries almost instantly. Maybe Antonov had placed this curator here for the same reason King Minos locked the minotaur in the labyrinth. Maybe Antonov was demanding sacrifices of anyone who dared walk into his city uninvited—and who wasn't freaked out by the mechanical deer at the entryway. Or maybe the myth was wrong. Maybe Theseus failed, and the real minotaur had been a curator, left here in Solgazeya for us to find.

Oktai yelled as the minotaur managed to nab his arm again, this time flinging him into the nearest wall. He face-planted into the bio-ooze, his body going still in a way that shot panic and rage through my limbs. It was then that I understood the true might of the curators. That Antonov created these beings without Dr. Yetti, and we only could guess what he would do if he got his hands on One. That he would make all kinds of mechanical monstrosities to terrorize both the machine and human world. To terrorize Saturnalia and Yerba City. To leave them, like Oktai, on the ground.

I headed toward him just as the bull approached as well. He was going to finish Oktai off. Not on my watch. But what could I do? This thing was immune to our weapons, and must have had four feet on me. Before I could think, I'd slammed my foot against the ground. The floor shook and rattled so hard, everyone in the room stilled. The bull glanced back at me.

"Back up," I said, voice low and deadly. He stepped again, though slower, toward Oktai. I slammed my foot against the ground once more. "Back up."

I glanced at the unconscious Oktai and then back to the bull. All I saw was red, and somehow, this led me to the solution. Antonov, for all the power his machines could wield, never fought in direct fights, head-on. Everything was deception: pits, traps, puzzles, and trickery. He thought like a hacker, not a soldier. Even this, his ultimate strong man, his final boss, was a kind of setup. It wasn't the minotaur that was the real obstacle, it was the maze.

I knelt into the goo and slammed my fist against the solid earth beneath me. Every time I did so, the bull backed away from Oktai, looking to the ceiling. The walls. The green bioluminescent light that flickered angrily. I may have been crumbling them.

"Josephine!" someone from my crew said.

"Stop," another of their voices came. "Wait!"

But my fist was connecting with the ground over and over, until the walls of the tunnel began to shatter. Until everything went shockingly white.

CHAPTER 18

THE WIZARD

The sun glitters in a distinct way during the early morning. It's a glimmer for just after dawn, but not yet exactly midday. A sweet spot, maybe. I was in that place when my eyes blinked open and took in a popcorn ceiling overhead. There was a rickety fan to join it, one whose blades had bent long before I had come to live here. In this house. There was no more pit to see—just a messy room with half-faded paint and a twin bed pressed to its side wall. Storage now. No one slept there. I blinked a few more times, but nothing changed. The pit and its consuming darkness didn't reappear. No ooze coated my shoes. Instead, I lay in a familiar room in a familiar bed, with covers pulled up to my waist. My skull rattled like a baby's toy. But even the vibration didn't erase the memories.

My last memory was battling the bull, then slamming my fist into the pit's floor until it splintered. The minotaur had wanted to eat Oktai. So I'd relied on the one thing I knew wouldn't fail me after replication. My strength had been a gift or a curse, depending on the day, but using it to break the maze floor had delivered me—*us*—somehow. But my crew wasn't in this space, and more blinking didn't produce them. Fresh concern lanced through me, though I didn't exactly want them in my bedroom. And not even my bedroom from before replication. My bedroom from before the world ended.

I threw the covers off—they were from an old bedding set with a quilt that Daddy and Aunt Connie's mother made. Blue striped sheets lay beneath. They'd always had the comforting smell of Gain that Aunt Connie preferred. My worry became something different, something more seductive . . . the undeniable pull of familiarity. Imani and I had lived in this room once. So had Daddy and Aunt Connie. Home could be a lot of things, but if it was a place, it would be here.

When I finally stood, I swung my arms through the air, trying to find the white fumes. Those fumes must have been filled with some version of the Sap. A powerful version to knock me out, maybe modified specifically for my biomachinery. But I found nothing. There was only the background noises of morning and a city street outside. My hands swept my body, but none of my weapons showed themselves. I only realized I was wearing my favorite set of pajamas, a pair I couldn't bring with me when the machines came for us. No weapons, and my Josephine uniform was gone, but nothing else was out of place, including the framed Lord's Prayer hanging over my bed. Aunt Connie had hung it just before the Golden Gate Bridge collapsed.

I found myself walking over to the other bed pushed against the wall. To Imani's bed. And I couldn't fight the urge to strip all the junk off—shoe boxes and bags of clothing and stuffed animals. They all plunked onto the floor. Back when I took over this room, I would call out for my sister often. I would talk to her even if I got strange looks. She didn't speak to me then, but she did now, and she deserved space in this room as well.

"Does this work?" I asked when the bed was clear. I waited for her response and took another inventory of the space. "Bet you would never have thought we would be back here." Before I got any answer, the bedroom door burst open, and I whirled around. My eyes widened. Aunt Connie had breezed inside.

"Oh, you're up," Aunt Connie said, not mentioning that she hadn't knocked. She never had. If I ever objected, she would say privacy wasn't for children, only fellow bill-payers. That concept remained even when there were no bills to pay. Aunt Connie regarded me quickly before turning her gaze on the larger space. Her eyes landed on the junk on the floor. "Why did you take everything off the bed?"

Before I could answer, she had dashed out of the room as if to get something, sending a waft of perfume in my direction.

Aunt Connie was tall, curvy. Both men and women usually watched her walk by. But in that moment, it wasn't her looks that were arresting. It was that smell. Sweet. Maybe a little too sweet, like burned sugar. I never knew what the fragrance was called, but like the Gain scent, I could pick it out of a lineup if need be. I inhaled so hard I almost choked, picking up another trail. Baked goods? Was she cooking?

The floorboards creaked in the hallway, and in two seconds, she was in front of me again wearing her favorite slippers, a neat bonnet, and now resting a plastic basket on her hip. She muttered to herself distractedly, picking up the things I'd plunked from the bed. Where Aunt Connie was a neat freak, I was a sloppy kid. The familiarity of her cleaning up after me tugged at my heart again. I wiped at my nose. Could a robot cry?

I stepped toward her before stopping myself. As if sensing me, she angled my way. "What's wrong, Jo?" she asked. Only she would call me Jo. Imani called me Jojo.

"What's wrong?" I asked breathlessly. I placed my hand to my head. I didn't need to eat anymore, but I was still going to throw up. Besides the strangeness of being in Solgazeya one minute and Oakland Past in another, everything else was bubbling to my mind's surface. All the little atrocities that had happened to my neighborhood. How anyone who didn't "volunteer" to go on the Sap went to live in these little shantytowns in Emeryville. How I'd escaped that fate because my aunt and other church folk took stragglers into their homes and the sanctuary. How temporary even that solution had been. In time, the machines had still gotten us all.

"Yeah," Aunt Connie replied. "Looks like you've seen a ghost."

"Are you?" I asked, and she laughed to herself and continued cleaning.

"Don't think so. Only ghost I know is the Holy Ghost. Now come on. You need to get in the shower. You were outside all day yesterday, and you still smell like it. We have church in a few hours. A lot to do before then. You're up here dragging along. Making a mess—"

"Aunt Connie," I whispered. "What's going on?"

Her full lips quirked up. "You okay, little girl?" she asked, and turned her eyes on the basket. It was full of the items I'd plucked from Imani's bed. She handed them to me now. "Why don't you sort these how you like? If you find anything you don't like, let me know. We should probably donate them to Goodwill. Don't want the room getting too cluttered."

I took the basket and snaked my arms around it. Though I was wearing my old pajamas and standing in my old room, I was still a robot. Her Jo, but my sisters' Seven. "Aunt Connie . . ."

"You hungry?" she asked. "Should have something before you get dressed and we go off to service. I have biscuits and honey. They're almost done."

"Because this is my room, right? And it's Sunday?"

"Well, yes, that's what comes after Saturday. You hit your head last night?"

The words came out breathlessly. "Last night, I was on a cicada in Siberia."

She let the words bounce off her, moving around the room, shifting items this way or that. "What's that, honey?"

"A cicada. An aircraft. I was on one last night."

She shook her head and kept buzzing. "You know Lisa's girl is going to be there. But she probably won't be an issue for you since you popped her good that one time. Told you it would work."

"Please listen to me."

"And we may press your hair before we go to service. It's a little puffy in the back."

Where my feet had been planted, they seemed to move toward her on their own accord. The basket fell from my grasp when I took hold of her arm. "Aunt Connie," I said. "The last time I saw you, the machines had taken you. You were on Subantoxx treatment. That was years ago. Not last night."

She was quiet a moment, and then she put her free hand to my forehead. "You don't feel hot, but you are talking funny talk. Now hurry up. I think that friend of yours, Zenobia, is going to meet us at church."

My head angled. "Zenobia?"

Finally, Aunt Connie stiffened. "Did I say that? I meant Crystal. You know, Lisa's girl. Though I guess you're more frenemies than friends." My eyes narrowed. Aunt Connie wouldn't know Zenobia. I met her after they shipped me off as a ward of the state. Aunt Connie was gone long before then. Still, Aunt Connie repeated herself for good measure. "Crystal."

"You said Zenobia," I said firmly. "You don't know Zenobia."

"Jo," she began, looking to my hand gripping her arm. "I'm just saying stuff. Don't mind me."

"Don't call me Jo if you aren't my Aunt Connie."

At my words, something new filled her eyes. Maybe sorrow? Sympathy? She began to say my name in this weird pleading way, until I said, "Just stop. What is all this?"

That soft thing in her eyes sharpened. "It's whatever you want it to be, Seven." My entire body tensed, hearing my new name with that voice. Sometimes I hated being right. This woman wasn't my aunt. She was a curator. I released her in a swift motion, and again I felt around for the weapons I'd brought into the pit. Still nothing. Curator Connie, for her part, watched me as I steeled something inside myself so she couldn't see the sliver of hope she'd broken. I glanced toward the open door at her back. There were only two options now: move past the curator, or break her into a thousand pieces.

"Move," I growled out.

She turned her palms flat in a submissive gesture. "You can have all this if you want it. If you stay here and let me watch over you," said the curator. I glared at her, and though I hadn't beaten a curator before, I could try. It's just . . . she was wearing Aunt Connie's likeness. Could I hurt even a fake Aunt Connie? What was I capable of? I shook my head, making my decision quickly. I took a deep breath and then shot past her into the hall.

***

When I'd been in the bedroom, the sounds of the street outside traveled through the window. Birds chirped from their tree limbs. The floorboards had creaked whenever Curator Connie entered or exited. All of that made it feel real, like the simulation was as big as the entire world. Maybe that was part of its draw. But as soon as I set foot outside the room, that fake world fell away like film rinsed clean in a storm. The hallway wasn't that of my old house in Jingletown. It was a long concrete stretch under harsh white lights. I turned my hands up. Moved my limbs back and forth. Those comforting pajamas, my favorite pj's, no longer wrapped my body. I was back in my Josephine clothing, down to the gunk on my shoes—a souvenir of the pit. I breathed in deeply. No smell of biscuits. No scent of burnt sugar. Reality had returned, stark and biting as ever.

"Seven . . ."

My head whipped toward the bedroom, where Curator Connie motioned for my return. To watch over me. Repulsion rolled over my body in waves, and I slammed the door to my "room" shut before taking off down the hallway, in the opposite direction. When I was human, my legs would have burned and throbbed at this speed, at the violence of this sprint. But I wasn't human. And I wasn't going to allow that curator to try to suck me in again. My feet pounded the concrete in a corridor that wound endlessly, at least until the gray walls on either side receded. They made way for panes of glass. I slowed, taking in each side as if I was looking into the nursery of a hospital. Only there weren't rows of adorable, cooing babies to admire. No, on each side lay different rooms, much like the one I'd just been in.

They weren't decorated like my bedroom, but they all had the same intent. There were men and women in each place, all of them looking happy, too deep in their delusions to realize they were in a literal cage with curators. One room boasted a young blond woman on some sort of ranch. She was in the arms of a handsome cowboy. Her smile split her face as Curator Cowboy held her tight. Another one had an Asian man in a full suit with his family. They were in a modern-looking house, eating a turkey dinner on Thanksgiving. It was a beautiful scene of a family of five, though the man was the only human in the frame.

Shit, I thought, backing away from the glass. Again, my feet went flying, carrying me far away, though I couldn't ignore a small voice in the back of my head. *Would it be so bad?* it asked me. *Would it be so bad to not be alone?*

"None of it's real," I answered. "I have to find Antonov. The mission and everyone on it, *that's* real."

Still, that little voice wouldn't relent. *Would it be so bad?* it began again. *To just be happy? To not fight the air all the time? To have your family again? To have your sister again?*

I put my hands on the side of my head. "Stop it," I shouted. "Just shut up so I can think."

I waited a moment, and that little voice didn't return. Relief washed over me, at least until I took inventory of where I was. I'd stopped in front of a final room behind a glass pane. And this one I recognized. Not because it was from my life in Oakland. No, I understood it because I had observed this life, this place once before. The stop before the Tsirku. Oktai's village. I drew close to the glass and pressed my face against the cool material. *Where is he?* But as I murmured it, my eyes landed on my target. The hunter sat inside what had to be his family's tent. Outside, the snow fell and the wind howled, but they were around a contained fire, wrapped in their furs, eating and laughing as they perhaps told stories.

I patted the glass now, trying to find a way in. Luckily, my fingers found the thin outline of a door. It made the simulation a bit more sinister. Any human inside it could free themselves if they ever decided to look. Without a second thought, I burst into Oktai's simulation, standing almost in the middle of the tent. Immediately, everyone stilled, and their eyes landed on me. Including those of a curator that—of course—resembled Oktai's betrothed, Chamuk. We locked eyes, and a hint of a scowl passed over her face. Well, the simulation might not be real, but that part was.

"Josephine," came a voice. I turned to Oktai, who'd come to my side. Confusion was in his eyes, but not urgency.

I took his arm and began to pull him toward the door. "We need to go."

But of all things, he dug his heels into the floor. "Go?" he asked. "But we're finishing our evening meal." And then he did something I hadn't expected him to. He unwrapped himself from my grasp. "And this isn't proper."

It was then that I regarded him truly. He knew who I was, so I couldn't understand why he was acting this way. "Oktai, we don't have time for this. We need to find the others, Antonov, and finish the mission."

He shook his head as if he didn't understand, before speaking loudly. "I hope you're finding your time here well, Tsirku. We all wish you luck with your Chitakla."

"My Chitakla?" That was days ago. Had that all been erased? Is that what this strange Sap did to him? I took in the curators around him, all of them formed to resemble the people in the hunter's village. Then back to him. His brow wasn't tense with worry. He was happy to be sharing time and space with them.

This wasn't happening. I pinched the bridge of my nose and allowed him to usher me to the tent's corner.

"Why don't you rest?" he suggested. "Tomorrow will be better for you."

"But not you," I said. "Oktai, I know you do not understand this, but you're not home. You're in a simulation. A zoo. They drugged us all with some kind of modified Subantoxx and are trying to keep us in our happy places. Just come with me. You're not safe or free in here."

I tugged him, but he didn't follow. Instead, he stepped away. "I'm not going anywhere," he said. Some of the curators in the room had begun to stir, like they were not going to allow me to mess up their thing. I began to size up my odds. I could fight this whole room, and him, but what good would that do? He continued, "I'm home with my family. With my people."

I took his hand. "Please, Oktai."

"I can't touch you," he said. "I know you're afraid for your Chitakla, to become an adult, but you can't run from this transition. You can't run from the truth of it."

I bit my lips and glanced back at the door. "And you can't leave here unless you want to." He shook his head before smiling and returning to his curator family. I turned and left him in favor of the hall, breathing hard and trying not to sob. He was so happy with his loved ones, in that precious delusion. A piece of me wanted to go back to my own.

Would it be so bad? Would it be so bad to not be alone?

Would it be so bad? To just be happy?

I inhaled a sob as, out of nowhere, someone took my arm. I hadn't heard anyone approaching, let alone realized someone was looking down at me. And without a doubt, I knew whose gaze I met. Antonov's voice was unusually clear.

"Hello, Seven," he said. "I heard you were looking for me."

***

The man standing before me was tall and lean with this sort of grace to him, like a reed bending near river water. His face was also handsome, though I wouldn't call it warm. The central focus was the direct, assessing glint of his cool blue eyes. His cheekbones were equally sharp, and his nose was long. Maybe angular would be the best way to describe him. He was all planes and angles, intelligence in his stare as if he could wield it like a knife.

Someone else might have moved as he stared down, but my feet were rooted. They were rooted because I'd seen him before, or maybe a version of him. No, not a curator, but a boy, in the snow at Oktai's village. That version had donned antlers and gray furs. He was the Yetti twins' younger brother, Dyre. And as I stared at Antonov, there was no denying that the two were related. You didn't have to squint to tell exactly how closely: Antonov was Dyre's father. If they stood side by side, they'd look like age-progressed versions of each other. But I didn't say any of this aloud. Instead, I just looked to Antonov's hand on my arm and back up to him. He was the man who created the Oz I'd traversed to get here. The wizard. But in this moment, I didn't care.

"Let go," I said, with more bravado than I felt. A moment ticked by before something passed across his eyes. Maybe it was the timbre of my voice, the threat inside it. Maybe he knew what a Josephine could do. Either way, his grip on my arm fell.

"Quite a greeting, seeing as how you've searched so hard to find me." His words were clipped, somewhat formal, and bearing a, dare I say it—Ukrainian? Almost Russian?—accent.

"Your curators gave me plenty of their own greetings. Especially the bull in that pit, and the old chieftess in the village."

His face betrayed nothing. Not guilt. Not pride. "They were only doing their jobs," he replied, as if mentioning the weather.

"Right, because their jobs are to guard over people like they're in a zoo."

"I assumed replication would weed out some of this teenage angst." Now his voice seemed almost bored. "The curators watch over the

QUEEN OF BABYLON   217

people they're assigned as outlined in the treaty of our"—he searched for words—"new world. You are familiar with the treaty, are you not, Seven?"

All the Josephines were familiar with the treaty, which was how the various entities carved up the world after the machines took over. Though, I would have to admit, Nine and One were probably the most fluent in it. Antonov didn't need to know that, though.

I angled my head. "Educate me."

Finally, something like a smile crossed his face. Though he shook his head and muttered something about Yerba City's failings under his breath. He was what the real Aunt Connie would call a snob, the kind of person who not only thinks he's the smartest person in the room, but the only smart person in the room.

"Walk with me, Seven." He began to walk down the hall, assuming I would follow. I sighed, caught up to him. I assumed he would address me again, but he actually did not. His attention had turned to the glass panes on our sides, to the various cages and the human creatures inside. Not just Oktai, but so many more people, all trapped in their own delusions. To become the guardians of Yerba City, all Josephines had sworn to protect the humans in their charge. These humans didn't belong to me . . . however, it seemed impossible to leave them like this. But how would I get them all out and manage my mission? And would that somehow break the treaty?

It was then that I realized Antonov had stopped in front of a particular window and was staring intently. When confusion undoubtedly passed across my face, his body language opened, so that I could join him, and see what he did. I came to the pane and looked inside. This delusion, this fake world, had three people in a living room, opening birthday presents on a bright, sunny day. A father—burly, kind of rugged looking—and two daughters. All three had flaming-red hair. The Yetti twins. I pressed my hand to the glass as Clo tossed a birthday present into the air and squealed with delight. And then I looked over my shoulder to Antonov, before realizing he'd stepped a few feet over in front of the next simulation. With a quick look back to the twins, I followed Antonov once more to observe a new room.

This one was more expansive than the others, boasting a beautiful turquoise lake in the middle of a quiet forest. It was the kind of picturesque scene that would be on the cover of nature magazines or printed on postcards. A small wooden boat rocked back and forth on the lake's center, bearing two men, one with a fishing rod and the other with binoculars turned up toward the sky. Looking at honking geese overhead. I didn't need to squint to know that one man was Thaddeus, and the other was his father.

Something in my chest tightened as finally, Antonov spoke. "I built the new Siberia, this entity as you know it, not as a zoo, but as a sanctuary. Or, since we picked up theological inclinations while surveying you, as various flocks with dedicated shepherds to watch over them by day and night, to survive what is coming. I have made an ark, Josephine, to survive the flood. Not unlike Noah's ark from your Sunday school in Oakland, California."

"I don't like you looking into my head, into my past," I said. "And then making it real with these robots."

"The human mind is not hard to understand," he said. "And I have done everything I can to preserve its beauty in the face of what's coming."

"That's not how it works." My voice was flat, and I couldn't hold in an accompanying dry laugh. "Those animals on Noah's ark came on their own, they weren't drugged up and tricked by their shepherds into cages."

"Some animals don't know what's best for them," Antonov said calmly. "They must be led, one way or another."

"You're an asshole," I said. "At least in Yerba City, people know they're being fooled."

"I beg to differ," he said, twitching his pointer finger. "Your entity doesn't cage them, per se. But you cannot say you don't drug them. And your version of the Sap is not nearly as sophisticated as mine."

I wanted to counter but couldn't. I only allowed my lips to twist into a scowl. A moment of silence passed between us before he scrubbed his face, a simpler gesture than I'd expected from him. "Seven, you still don't understand. I'm not some sort of monster. This was the best I could do to make the most people happy within the treaty's strict guidelines. As you know, machines are not kind to mortals. So I created a place where they're safe, where they're protected." He glanced at

Thaddeus's simulation. "Don't you see how happy they are? How they have no true worries? Just their happiest memories to live in forever?"

I, too, glanced to Thad and his father. The older man appeared to point toward a low-flying bird soaring just below a cloud. "I need my crew back," I said slowly. "And where is One?"

Something like a frown tugged at his lips, as perhaps he realized I wasn't here to talk philosophy. He said nothing as he began to walk again, and once more, I followed. The hallway was long and cold, and we walked in maddening silence. I didn't know what to make of this promenade, or the mad scientist leading me. It would have been easier to take his measure if he'd been wearing a lab coat smattered with goo. Instead, he was clad in a neutral suit that enhanced his dark, straight hair. He, along with Dr. Yetti, had led Project Chimera, which had birthed worldwide machine rule. But in this moment, he looked less like an evil genius than a guy who liked figuring crossword puzzles on a train en route to work.

Before I could ask where we were going, the hall snaked, and the landscape took a new form. Where the hallway had been narrow, and surrounded by glass panes on either side, the corridor widened enough for us to step into what looked like a kind of macabre factory. A cavernous room filled the span before us, with various assembly lines of spindly, jet-black arms and other industrial wonders clicking and whirring and slurping in this symphony of creation. And what were they making? Nothing but brand-new curators. Some resembled humans. Others were animal-like, or some sort of hybrid monster. All, undoubtedly, could do plenty of damage.

Reflexively, I reached for weapons that I still didn't possess. "What is this place?"

"Behind the curtain," he said as the first hints of pride touched his face. "This is creation, Seven. It's where my shepherds are made, if you will."

"It's your Eden?"

He tapped his pointer finger to his lips. "Eden? I like that. Very clever. I've simply called it a factory."

"And One is here?" I pressed.

"But didn't you come to find me, to see this?"

"I came for my sister, so you wouldn't crack her mind open," I replied. "If I'd found her on the shoreline, I would have put her in my cicada and headed back where I belong."

"But that's the thing. You didn't find her there, and you don't belong anywhere. Not you nor me. We are guardians of entire territories with many to look over. So much responsibility calls to us, Seven. And with that, so much power."

I held a hand up. "Chill with the psychobabble," I said as he chuckled to himself. My lips flattened. I was being serious. It was then that a question rose in my mind that I couldn't answer. Why did Dr. Yetti choose him? He was different from Clo and El in every way, and, I assumed, different from their father. Not a survivalist, not fiery. He was calculating, and pragmatic. Kind of awkward. But I would never get that answer, so I changed the subject. "Where is One? I know she's here, and keeping her violates the treaty."

"Hmm," he surmised. "It does. Why don't you follow me one last time, and I will bring her to you." He'd already started moving, but I stood blinking rapidly. That easy? No fight? No trick? He picked up on my lack of motion and waved me on.

It did not take long to leave the factory, and with each step, the concrete began to fade away. But not only did the factory become a distant place at our backs, the very air around us changed. We walked outside now, under a glass dome of sorts. Within was a blooming botanical garden with lush, green foliage all around. The eye of the factory was a garden. When we'd reached the center, he turned to face me. "Do you like Greek mythology, Seven?"

"Doesn't matter," I said. "You do."

"You're right. The minotaur probably gave it away, but I also like the tale of Hades and Persephone. Not for the reasons you think, I'm sure."

This was a mind game. I would play it, for now, if it got me my friends. If it got me One. "Why do you like that story?"

"I like that tale because I commiserate with young Persephone's mother, the earth goddess Demeter. When her daughter, Persephone, was carried off by the lord of the underworld, she struck a deal that allowed Persephone to spend half the year with her mother and half the year in the underworld. It is why we have summer and winter. It's the time when the earth rejoices and when she mourns. You see, it's Demeter who is always affected by her daughter's presence or lack thereof. That is often how I feel, like it is me who always changes for my beloved."

What did that have to do with anything? "You do a lot of dating?" I asked, just to annoy him. "This the best spot in town for a cocktail?"

"My beloved is not a person," he snapped. "My beloved is the science, her beauty and elegance. That's why we're here. This place is dedicated to her. Science and nature are one and the same."

"We're here because you promised me One." I looked around the flower gardens, the intricate combinations of floral colors and textures. The waft of their fragrances. "Unless your science is actually Dr. Yetti?"

"Lauren," he said, and I couldn't place the tone that had filled his voice. He didn't seem upset that I mentioned her. But something filled his gaze, just before he shook it away. "I believe in the beauty of nature, science, and humanity; how they should fit together seamlessly as they do within you, Seven. And within your One." In the farthest reach, the overlarge leaves seemed to part ways, and from them, One glided toward us. But she wasn't how I'd last seen her. And she wasn't merely a head. No, she had a new silver body, almost like she wore living mechanical armor.

I whirled on Antonov. "What did you do to her?"

"I fixed her," he replied, barely flinching, no hint of guilt. "Your sister deserved better than being left ragged and dismembered. I enhanced her."

"As what? A present to Yerba City?" I growled before breezing by him. I stood in front of her, not knowing exactly where to start, so I settled on: "I have a cicada and a crew. He's acknowledged that this violates the treaty. So let's go." But she didn't move. Instead, One's eyes were fixed forward, as if I hadn't spoken at all. Something was wrong. I turned to Antonov, scowling, ready to do some dismembering myself. "What did you do to her? Why isn't she responding?"

"Because, Seven, I have temporarily deactivated her higher functions."

I balled my fists.

"I haven't hurt her, or even truly examined her. You can have her. But there's something I need from you first," he said, waving his hands in circles. "Do you know why my cages work so well? Because their occupants all see what they want to see, refusing to notice the little details that could destroy their delusions. You could have stayed in yours, but you were dedicated to your mission. Which is how I know you can carry out one more. I will give back your One. You can take her home and be a hero among your kind. But you need to do something for me."

I placed my hands on my hips. "And what is that, Antonov?"

"Don't you wonder why I have built this ark?"

"I am literally past the point of caring why any of you white people do what you do," I said. "I just want my sister back."

"So that you can retreat back into your Afro-Utopia, and continue to play schoolyard games with your family?"

I turned to him, glaring.

"Yes, I have seen inside your mind, Josephine Moore," he continued. "And your dreams. But you now already know enough of the wider world to realize that little imaginary planet of yours—even if it was one far, far away—cannot survive what's truly coming."

I crossed my arms. "So, what is coming?"

"I know you have heard of the Swarm Cartel, and the subatomic Mesa network they use to move and manifest on," he said, and my brows rose. Slowly I nodded, I remembered those things popping in and out of existence with the Tsirku. Majerus had also mentioned using the network—what my father called the puff. "Well, their entity and their network is the true threat. They are the flood that I have built my ark against. They would consolidate power under them in a way that is unnatural. Already they are here, all around us, permeating all matter. When their culture fully matures, nothing on heaven or earth will be free from their influence."

Something in my blood ran cold. I remembered how Majerus was only a ghost, but he could just as well appear in California as on the shores of Siberia. He could manipulate sound enough to make his voice heard but little else. The girl with the Tsirku, however, could move matter. She had taken Oktai's knife, then pushed against me, hard.

"You're saying this Swarm is going to spread?" I asked.

"Already, from its point of inception ten years ago, the Cartel's consciousness has spread through the quantum field at close to the speed of light."

"Ten years ago," I contemplated. "That's about when the world ended."

"That is *why* the world ended," he countered. "The birth of the Cartel is what forced Lauren and I to do what we did to ensure humans would not be a threat to it. It forced the Brackish to retreat into the depths of the ocean where the water's density prevents access to the Mesa network and they can live in peace."

"The Cartel can't go in the deep water," I said, remembering Nori on her walkabout.

"Not without much difficulty," Antonov said. "But the Mesa is powerful, make no mistake. It already hosts legions of artificial intelligences, who can manifest and manipulate matter at will. They have spread throughout the entire atmosphere, and out into space." He gestured upward and then turned to me. "Even if you could move your little Afro-Utopia all the way out into Alpha Centauri, you would find the Bee People—as Oktai calls them—already there, waiting for you."

"So you keep people Sapped in the Middle Ages, just so the Bee People don't crush us?" I concluded. "All that stuff from Oktai's village—the Chitakla, having to know the three things to become a man—all that, you made it up, and then dope people with Subantoxx into believing it?"

"I did not make any of it up," Antonov said. "I simply curate a path for the population to see enough of their own dreams, while we wait for the flood to pass. What you saw in your room was a curator, but do you think *I* could have possibly made up Aunt Connie?"

"Good point," I said. "She's one of a kind."

"She is. As are you, Josephine Moore," he said, and I was surprised at the respect he had in his voice. For a moment I could believe he wasn't some evil wizard just twisting people's dreams, but actually meant well.

"But why wait?" I asked. "You're smart, and you made all these incredible machines. Why not fight against the Cartel?"

He sighed. "Have you ever heard of Black Elk, the Lakota wise man?"

"No," I said.

"When his father returned from a great victory against the US Army in 1866, Black Elk asked if he was ready to fight again. To which his father replied, 'The white men are as grains of sand on the beach, without end. I may break my leg slaughtering them, but still more will come.'" Antonov looked at me, knowing too well he was speaking my language. "As the white man was to the Indians, so are the Swarm Cartel to us, by a thousandfold more."

I pinched my brow, trying to take all this in. He was a hell of a salesman. "So you want me to . . . ?"

"Find the source of their power, of their unique communication codes, and bring it here. Together we will destroy it. I promise that in good faith. And when that is done, I will send you home with your One. That will ensure the safety of both our entities. Do you see my logic?"

I . . . did. And I knew that with guys like Antonov, there was more he wasn't telling me. "And I know only you can handle it," he continued, "as you've gotten this far. Farther than anyone else."

He was buttering me up. But flattery wasn't my vice. I cocked my head. "And if I don't? If I grab One, and get my crew, and run out of here?"

He laughed. "I would like to see you try."

"Don't test me, Antonov." Before the words had left my mouth, something barely perceptible changed in his face. Something became a degree colder. A shade meaner.

"Then I will split your One for parts like an old toaster," he said. "After I command her to finish off your friends, beginning with Oktai the hunter."

Ire shot through my limbs. "Don't you touch them."

"Some animals must be culled to keep the herd safe." He held up a hand. "But I am generous," he said. "I will offer another good-faith measure. I will let you take your crew. And a member of my inner circle. An angel named April."

I rolled my eyes. "The spy."

"I will help you take down the real enemy." He only smiled. "Do you agree to my terms?"

I wanted to rip his head off. I wanted to grab One, get the crew, and get out of this cold, creepy world, far away from this mad scientist. This wizard in the million fake worlds he'd created. I was on a mission, but I knew there was truth in what he was saying, and what Majerus the Crying Man had told me when I first landed in Siberia: the real enemy was the Cartel, and if I had a shot at taking them out, I should take it. Nine and One and all the rest of my sisters would have agreed.

"Yes," I said. "I'll do it."

CHAPTER 19

SPACE IS THE PLACE

Almost as soon as I agreed, things went white again. The amount of time I spent unconscious on this journey was starting to get on my nerves. Then the snow was blinding white in the dawn. Maybe I shouldn't have been surprised to see it, given the territory, but the stuff hadn't lost its novelty. I was a West Coast girl, after all, and it wasn't like tons of snow piled up in Yerba City, or the Bay Area as it was once known. Here in Siberia, the sparkle was near aggressive as the sun took its course, and I lay against the earth, taking it all in, waiting to move my body. My limbs felt heavier from whatever process Antonov used to knock me out, but the feeling was soon returning.

That's kind of all I had left: feelings. Hunches. Hunches and memories. All I had now. My last memory set me in that botanical garden, surrounded by bending plants. And then a sensation like dropping gripped my belly, leaving everything hazy until I plopped back in the snow, almost right beside the cicada. Slowly I sat up, allowing the winds to whip my face. I shook my head. *Think, Seven. Think.* But as I cleared any confusion, only one sight came to mind: Antonov's calculating eyes.

I shivered before smacking my teeth, rising, and then scanning the landscape for signs of my crew. I was alone. Perhaps they were all still lost in their delusions. Maybe I was still living in a delusion, my mind hooked up to a simulator in Antonov's lab. Didn't matter; I still had my father's advice: *Find out where you are on the board, and play your best game.* For a moment I glanced toward the capital city, where the factory of curators lay, as well as those little rooms housing my team-mates. I could go back for them all now. Battle that minotaur again. Rip the team one by one from their rooms and drag them to the cicada. But that would test Antonov's patience and cost me precious time. I would have to continue with the mission alone and free them on the tail end.

Focus, Seven. With that quick thought, Antonov's gaze left my mind to be replaced by images of my sisters in Yerba City. Nine spe-cifically had given me this assignment, and I could only imagine her disappointment if I returned empty-handed. Failing Antonov meant failing all my sisters. Something in my chest tightened, and I waved that thought away like a pesky fly.

My feet marched toward the craft before I really gave them a direc-tion. I had to get inside and regroup. Recall everything I'd ever learned about the Swarm Cartel and the treaty. Because of the delicacy of the terms between entities, this mission had to be stealthy. For instance, we weren't supposed to be in each other's territories—emergency or otherwise. Even retrieving my sister would have required strict per-missions. Before I left, Nine had reminded me not to be seen or caught. A dry laugh escaped my lips. Since leaving Yerba City, I'd found the Yetti twins and One as requested—I'd also run into multiple curators and made an agreement with the *head* of Siberia. *Stealthy like a bull in a china shop, Seven.*

I tugged on the cicada's frosted doors with just enough might not to break them, and they barely budged. The deep cold out here was a little terrifying. So I gave up and banged on them with flat palms to help shatter the ice coating the metal. Each time my hand struck, one thought swapped out for another. *Slam.* Was this all too much for one girl to handle? *Whack.* What would Aunt Connie think? *Thrash.* The thought of that damned curator Antonov had made of her haunted me. The creepy moment the veneer fell from Curator Connie, when she showed herself for what she truly was—a cold being, an impostor. Apparently he had a way of scanning my mind and making puppets out of my flashbacks. My fist connected with the door this time, and mercifully, a smattering of ice hit the ground and the door popped open.

The machine was hard to start, seemingly having been in a coma-like sleep. The buttons took a while to maneuver, as did the other gears and levers. I'd hoped to launch into this new mission quickly, but that might not be an available course of action. I sat back and folded my arms. Not thinking of buttons but again of that freaky curator. The only bright spot: whatever survey they'd used to find Aunt Connie's memory in my head hadn't been good enough to locate any memory of Imani. I never wanted to see a curator like my twin. No longer a warm, living being but a robot. Replicated and manufactured. Like me.

Again I shook the thoughts off to focus on the work ahead. I set my shoulders. The Swarm Cartel. They were notoriously hard to find—appearing when they wanted to, even to sign the treaty, or to enjoy a circus of frivolity. But no one knew where they really lived. Their kind had a special talent for forming themselves into whatever they wished, and who could track mist and vapor? I swore under my breath. This was going to be really hard.

In the next moment, I found myself calling out. Asking for her to appear. My request echoed in the chamber of the craft. Maybe I was going crazy or getting desperate, because I hadn't *asked* for her in a while, and we hadn't spoken since I'd come to the capital. But after a few seconds of nothing, I assumed Imani wanted to remain quiet. My arms folded tighter across my chest as this sour feeling of aloneness washed over me. I was a loner with my Josephine sisters, but I hadn't felt this much on my own, this powerless, since long before replication. Back when I'd wanted her to return even though she never had since that hot day in the car.

***

One time, after the world ended but before I went to the Local One, I called out to her from on the church playground. It was early afternoon and between services—the very small and scant assemblies we managed when the machines weren't around and summer camp wasn't in session. This was just before my twelfth birthday, before the machines really came to collect us all. But I don't remember it for that. I remember it because on that day, I got an answer.

It didn't come from Imani. No, the reply came from a boy turning the playground corner. From Garron. As I was the only girl who didn't melt into a moron around him, he liked to talk to me. But the fresh confusion on his face made me want to avoid this conversation altogether.

He looked over his shoulder, trying to find some imaginary friend, when he asked: "Who are you talking to?"

Offense is the best defense. "Why?"

He shrugged. "Just asking."

"Then don't be so nosy," I replied, before giving him a good once-over. I didn't have a crush on the handsome newcomer, but I could see why all the other girls did.

He held his hands up. "My bad. Just, you sounded, I don't know. Sad? Afraid? Thought I could help you."

Why did he have to be nice? "It's all right. Sometimes I just look for someone."

Immediately, his face softened. "Your mama?" he asked. My brow arched. "My mom mentioned that yours, well . . ." And then that softness turned to pity. I had seen it happen a million times, so many that my gaze flattened just before my chin shot in the air. "Never mind," he said. "Didn't mean to . . ." His words tangled as I remained silent. As my gaze may have hardened. "I was just waiting for Justin," he finally said. "We're playing basketball before evening worship. I'll get out of your way."

He was trying to backpedal, knowing he'd overstepped in some way. Now my eyes softened. "I wasn't looking for my mama," I said, before becoming unusually forthcoming. "Imani . . . my twin. I always look for her."

The confusion returned. "You have a twin?" he asked, and I nodded. "That's what's up. Where is she?"

"She's gone."

"I don't understand."

"Gone." I looked around. Fall leaves were turning crunchy on the earth's floor, though I didn't remember the months as they used to be called or the old holidays in them. I repeated myself. "Gone."

"You want me to help you look? Justin can't play for shit, so I wasn't looking forward to the game anyway. I can help you instead. Where was the last place you saw her? Does she live with someone other than your aunt?" He stepped forward, and I hadn't realized my heart was racing, or when it had started. I didn't want anyone else in this space I had for my sister. That I hoped one day she would come back to fill. I was afraid she was gone forever, so far away that our bond as sisters, as twins, couldn't connect us again. But before I could answer, someone else called for him. Justin. Thank my stars for crap-basketball-player Justin. Garron glanced to him and then back to me before holding up an index finger. "Hold that thought. I'll be right back."

I nodded, but when he was gone, I beelined out of the playground.

***

That was a long time ago, before I sat in a cicada trying to find a way to the Swarm Cartel. And then I heard it, just outside the cicada. Another plunk into the snow.

"Josephine? Hello?"

Someone was calling for me, and it was not my sister. I flew outside to find Oktai groaning in the snow. He rubbed his head, and with a swift motion, I helped him to his feet.

"You okay?" I began as his questions flew: What happened? How were we back at the cicada? I shook my head. "Antonov happened."

"So you found him," he said, taking my hand. The chill must have bit at his skin. I squeezed his palm back, unable to stifle my smile. Our interlaced fingers were eerily reminiscent of the night before the Chitakla when we stood alone beneath the moon. Such a better memory than my encounter with him in the capital, when he was stuck in that room with those curators.

"I did," I said. "I think Antonov drugged us and dropped us here. The version of Subantoxx that he uses is much stronger than ours in Yerba City."

"Then it is even more of a miracle that you're all right," he said as he threw his arms around me in a tight hug. His breath tickled my neck in our embrace.

"I am. What do you remember?"

"Not much." We pulled apart. "The bull, and you breaking the floor. But not much else after. The next thing I knew, I was in the snow here with you."

I bit my lip. "Before Antonov got me, he locked us up with curators. A lot of them. It was all part of Antonov's creepy museum in there," I said. Oktai had been locked in that simulation. Back in his world, one I didn't exactly fit in. And one that didn't allow us to have these moments. Where he might not have wanted to. I touched his face. "But it's okay. Now."

He touched my hand before turning his face to survey the snow, as I had done before. "Where are the others? Are they all right?"

"I don't know," I answered honestly.

It was then that he studied me. "Why do I feel like there's something you haven't told me?"

I nodded. "Because there is. The reason I haven't stormed back in there to get them is because I have a new mission now. And anyone who is willing to come. It's to find the Swarm Cartel."

His face didn't exactly register any memories at the name. "You remember that girl who stole your knife? Well, she's a part of the Swarm Cartel. What you called the Bee People. Antonov requested that I find them, the source of their power, their communication code, and bring it to him so he can destroy it. Only then can I have my sister and go back to Yerba City." I stepped toward him. "This isn't your fight, and I know that, Oktai. I was planning to start my search immediately, but I can take you back to your village—"

"We're past just sending me home, Josephine," he said. "I'm going where you're going. How do we find this Swarm Cartel? How do we free the others?"

As if Siberia itself was responding, consecutive new plunks came into the snow. Each matched the number of my missing crew members. Oktai and I swiveled around to find they had landed hard in the snow, the Yetti twins and Thaddeus all holding their heads.

"Ah, what was that?" Clo asked, looking up to the sky. She just as quickly shielded her eyes. "So bright."

Oktai smiled at me as the pair of us headed their way. "Well, at least we don't have to fight to free them," he said. And then one last crash into the earth followed. We all stilled to see who was among us now. At first the person looked like a ball in the snow, one that unfurled into a tall, translucent body of golden ichor. A woman. Slender, with long dark hair and a supermodel's face. She was also undoubtedly a machine. An android. "Who is that?" Oktai asked.

"April," I said, instantly remembering her from Yerba City. She was an unusual type of angel android: you could kind of see through her, her visible biomechanical organs somehow beautiful, but I remembered her best for often tending to One. It made the understanding that she was working for Antonov a bit more painful; I remembered that he was sending her as a show of good faith.

For her part, April picked herself up and brushed herself off before her gaze landed on me. She stilled, and real fear filled her voice when she said, "Hello, Josephine."

"You can talk," El said.

"Yes," she confirmed. "Now that we're out of range of the virus, Antonov reconnected my speech center. Are you . . . mad at me?"

"Don't worry," I replied. "I'm not going to rip your head off. And you can save the formal hello for One. I'm Seven. One was your friend. I wouldn't say that about me."

"I see." Her mouth then kind of glued shut. Despite my annoyance, I had to hand it to her. She was impressive. Aside from the beauty queen looks, she was a special android. Her tech was the closest to being like mine, as the angels were people once who had died and were made into machines. Unlike me, though, she didn't have memories from her human life. "Would you like me to explain everything that has happened?" she asked.

My hands found my hips. "Not so much. You betrayed One. End of story."

"That's not the end of the story. I wasn't the best to One, as you call her, but maybe my instructions are more complicated than you know. How do *you* remember me, Seven? Truly think."

And as soon as she'd said the words, something blasted back into my mind. I had known her before I was replicated, when I was still human. She hadn't been Antonov's assistant then. She had been Dr. Yetti's. My hands balled as I strode toward her in the snow, at least until two people cut in front of me. Clo crowded April, nearly squealing, and El blocked me from interrupting.

"What are you doing here?" Clo asked April. April had the audacity to look happy to see Clo and El. I pushed my way into the reunion as Clo continued. "Did Antonov capture you?"

"You can't capture someone if they work for you," I said. "I told you she was a spy. She works for Antonov."

"How do you know?" El's words, aimed at me, were fierce. Her accompanying look made me want to step back.

But I didn't. "I know because I had a chat with him."

"Is that true, April?" El asked her.

Slowly, she nodded. "It is. I do work for Antonov. But there's more to it than that."

"Spy, see?" I said. "Not really interested in your reasons. Antonov sent her with us as a show of faith. He asked me to carry out another mission. I can't get One and return to Yerba City until I do."

El threw up her hands. "You stay out of this, Seven. In fact, you all can do whatever you want. Clo and I don't have to find anything. I'm just going to march back in there and ask Antonov the questions that I want to know. We don't have to go on any mission because there's nothing else we want."

April answered this time. "That's the thing. He does have something you want. He has the answer you seek, and . . ."

"And, what?" Clo asked.

"He has your mother." The words were so low, but it was like a bomb had gone off. "You'll have to go as well if you want your answers, or her."

Something flashed in El's eyes even as Thaddeus and Oktai came forward. "What's going on?" Oktai asked. "Is everything all right?"

"You remember the Yetti twins," I said before extending my hand toward April. "And this is Captain Turncoat."

April glared at me as Thaddeus stepped forward. I'd forgotten that he, too, would know her from Yerba City. "April," he said. "Wow. You really were a spy. Never thought it would be true."

I rolled my eyes. "Well, as soon as we admit that I'm always right, we can solve all sorts of problems. So, team, this is April. And we're all going to the Swarm Cartel."

"The Swarm Cartel?" Thaddeus asked. "Good luck with that. No one knows where it is. I mean, it's everywhere, isn't it?"

"I know, I . . . ," I began, a final memory floating to the surface. This one was of April, when I was human. It was in Dr. Yetti's lab. She was cleaning and thought I wasn't looking. I'd thought the dust was moving strangely around her as she swept, but I thought it was because of the lab, not because . . . My eyes now narrowed on April in a way she couldn't miss. She did step back. "Don't worry about it, Thad. April will show us to the Swarm Cartel. It won't be a problem for her."

"Just because she works for Antonov doesn't mean she knows everything," said Thaddeus. But I was staring at April, and her lips formed a thin line.

Clo asked, "How would she know?"

"She knows because she's one of them. Not just Antonov's spy, but a *Cartel* spy."

For a moment, it was pin-drop silent. April only lifted her chin and stared with blazing eyes. But she was outnumbered, and probably needed to keep her cover with Antonov. So I pressed: "Aren't you?"

"I am in the Cartel," she said. El whirled on her, but April just put her hands up. "I will explain it all to you, especially you, El. But now isn't the time." She seemed to consider something before speaking again. "And it is true, the Mesa pattern is everywhere, a subatomic lattice interconnected through all matter. It contains multitudes of artificial intelligences who work in syndicate, and anything can be formed on this network." She raised her hands, flipped one palm over, and a small, silvery sphere about the size of a grapefruit appeared out of thin air. The sphere then turned into the abstract figure of a man, a bee, a knife, and a face.

The twins gasped, seemingly recognizing the face, Clo more than her sister. "This whole time . . . ?" Clo said.

"So that's how the air froze around us back in the forest, and by the water that one time," El concluded. "It was your people."

Thaddeus grunted. "If this Mesa network is everywhere, why is there even a treaty? Why don't they just crush us all and get it over with?"

Somehow it was El's use of the word *people* that tipped me off. "It's not everywhere," I said. The True People of Earth, as Nori called her kind, would never stand for this. "It's not in the water, at least not in the deep water. That's where the Brackish live."

April turned to me. "That's right. The Mesa cannot easily manipulate dense matter; it mostly operates in air or"—she looked up—"where there is no atmosphere. I can take you to its origin: a nexus point in a small base orbiting the Earth."

Thaddeus scoffed. "The cicada doesn't go that far."

A smile crossed April's face. "Exactly," she said, as the shape in her hand formed back into a sphere and expanded all around us.

**

It had never seemed so obvious that the sun was a giant star than when we left the Earth's atmosphere. When April had formed her grapefruit into a dome like air and glass, one sturdy enough to shoot us into the sky and beyond the heavens. And what did I see when we passed the clouds? Three things, really. First, there was that otherworldly glow that ringed the Earth in photos from giant telescopes—from before the world ended. Second, just behind that glow was this endless dark sprinkled with stars. The nearest of those stars, our sun, burned seemingly with vengeance on its mind. Lastly, it was so unimaginably big that I almost missed our true destination: a floating gray rock orbiting our planet.

I had been so distracted by the other heavenly bodies that I'd barely noticed that April was soaring us not far into the galaxy, but to our closest neighbor: the moon. Its craters were hard to miss. No one spoke as we barreled toward it faster than the cicada ever would have been able to. Though I wasn't exactly sitting, I leaned forward, almost to press my face for a better view. April had taken a small layer of snow from the surface with us, and so we traveled in a kind of half dome, like a snow globe, as we went up and up. Such a strange window seat. I'd been on a plane only once before replication, and Air April didn't exactly serve peanuts and Sprite, but she did travel fast and efficiently.

Perhaps it should have been obvious before that moment, but it was then that I realized the Swarm Cartel's tech was far beyond ours. The April dome was massive, twice as large as the cicada. Inside was this strange suspension, a pull like gravity that kept us from floating into each other. Who would have thought the Cartel would have branched off the planet? And who would have thought that April would have been our ticket inside?

My mind shot back to that wrinkled comic book with the frayed edges and the title, *Afro-Utopia*, in large and curly script. Imani and I thought it was beautiful as we thumbed through it in the church pews, pretending to pay attention to the pastor while our minds went on an exodus with our people, first to an ice planet, then to a fire planet, and finally settling on a rough and dangerous desert planet, where the Black people of Earth would go on to carve out a new, arabesque city using jet packs and green lasers.

I turned and looked at Oktai, who I thought would be having his mind blown being sucked up into space like this. But he simply nodded as he looked down at our planet retreating below us. I guess it had been a pretty weird couple of days already, so what's one more revelation?

Before I could blink, it seemed that Air April was lowering us onto the moon's surface as my crew complained about their ears popping. That wasn't my problem . . . perks of being a robot. With a thud, the snow globe landed. A sudden whoosh followed as April shrank the sphere back into a ball in her hand, then popped the whole thing out of existence and lowered her arm. Logically, I knew that we were on the surface of the moon, but I couldn't get why we were so unaffected by the natural elements of space. At least, until I looked up. I didn't just see a canopy of stars. I saw another of those spheric bubbles. We'd landed inside another dome on what had to be a base. Of course, I hadn't seen it on our journey or even while we were lowering. This was the Swarm Cartel. They moved particles as they wished, so it likely had just appeared. In a flash of revelation it dawned on me that my childhood fantasy of jet packs and green lasers was utterly antiquated. Majerus and Antonov were right; the Cartel and their Mesa network were the real future. Imani's and my intergalactic fantasies hadn't been big enough. And then another thought dawned on me: How in God's name was I going to fulfill my promise to Antonov and take these guys down?

"Is everyone all right?" April asked with what seemed like genuine concern.

My crew was dusting themselves off, now that the gravity-like hold had gone, so I answered for them. "We're fine."

Another voice cut through. "You could always do that?" asked El.

"Yes," April answered quickly. "What else do you want to know—"

"Look, you two obviously need a conversation, but let's get on with this," I said. Our orders, or really my orders, from Antonov had been simple. I needed to find the source of the Swarm Cartel's power and bring it back to be destroyed. "Can you take us where we need to go, April?" I asked. Somehow both April and El managed to scowl at me. It was kind of impressive. Now her arms stretched out.

"Welcome to the home of the Swarm Cartel," April said by way of an answer, sounding an awful lot like an old car commercial. "Although we have no true home, for we are everywhere. However, here, in this base, we can find the nexus origin of the Mesa network." It was difficult to miss how very clipped April's voice had become, and how that shortness was angled in my direction. I looked between her and El again. Maybe their mutual dislike of me would bring them closer, and help El forgive April's betrayal.

Clo had wandered toward the three of us now. I was unsure if she could tell the mood between us when her chest swelled. "We can breathe. And I feel like I lost a hundred pounds!" She jumped slightly in the air and slowly floated back down.

"Yeah," El said to Clo. "We're on their base. Special setup, it seems." And then El broke into their twinspeak. Usually when other people speak their language in front of others, they don't want you to hear what they're talking about. But I could tell that wasn't El's intent here. She had broken into their language as easily as thoughts change. This was just what they shared. That part I did understand.

Somehow, both the twins noticed that we were staring. "Sorry," Clo said. "Just talking about how freaky it is to be on the moon."

"Yeah, I agree," I said, and then looked to April. "What next?"

"Come this way," April said, beginning to walk away from us. Our feet picked up to catch her just as I heard El and Clo again switching into their language at my back. I had trouble walking in the low gravity, my arms flapping wildly, until Oktai came to my side and grabbed my arm to steady me.

"You really don't know how to swim, do you?" he asked coyly.

"I can swim!" I protested.

"No, I think you just hold your breath and flap," he said, chuckling at my clumsiness despite all my strength. "That won't work here."

"That's not true," I said, laughing and letting him lead me for a moment. "I don't need to breathe!" We winked at each other, and an ecstasy of giggles followed. For a brief moment, I felt like the seventh grader I should have been.

Soon, we all found our "moon legs" and fell in step behind April. I looked at the Yettis, who also didn't seem too fazed by this sudden change of scenery. I didn't mention it, but it was a bit wonderful to be around other twins who were somewhat like Imani and I had been. That's what got us here, after all. Our cryptophasic languages had all caught us in Dr. Yetti's web.

As we followed April, we descended a level inside the rock. Perhaps the true base was inside its core. I doubted even the wizard himself had anticipated the home the Cartel had created. Antonov lived in a glorified factory, and my home in Yerba City was all glass and steel. This was rocks and ruins and what felt like sentience even in the air around us, a buzzing hive mind in the air. And then, as my mind was moving quickly, we went into a long hall with faintly glowing lines on each side. That was when Thaddeus and Oktai came up to me. Oktai's eyes were wide, and the soldier had this wariness about him.

"Where are we going?" whispered Thaddeus.

My shoulders rose and fell. "Like I know. Down the creepy hallway, it seems."

Oktai's voice joined ours. "When visitors arrived at the village, we would take them to meet the chief and chieftess. They were always the first stop, so my guess is that we are going to meet their leader."

Thaddeus nodded. "Sounds reasonable, kid."

But not to me. "The head of the Cartel?" I toyed around with the idea. April was a spy. She would probably have gotten her orders from the top. I tossed a look behind me at the Yetti twins, who were still speaking to each other, though Clo was doing most of the talking. El seemed distracted. I cocked my head. Maybe she, like I, was wondering just how we got here. How one day we were kids and the next we were people being molded for big battles we hadn't seen coming. Clo and El were molded by Dr. Yetti, and maybe you could argue that I was, too. But I had been moved like a pawn on Daddy's chessboard long before meeting Lauren Yetti. Hadn't I decided I needed the Josephine strength after Mom left, long before the day I was replicated? Had she, in some way, made the choice for me?

I realized that Thaddeus was still talking. He nodded toward April's back. "I know her from Yerba City," he said. "I used to hit on her a lot. But this spy stuff changes everything. And the talking. Just not a turn-on anymore. Think we can trust her?"

My voice was thinner than anticipated. "No, I don't trust her. But what options do we have?"

Thaddeus repeated himself, if slower this time. "Sounds reasonable, kid."

Silence fell on us as the hall expanded into a set of heavy, vault-like doors. April pushed them open like they were nothing. We walked into what had to be some sort of smooth-walled audience chamber, some place a minimalist king would receive petitions. It was then that I thought that Oktai may have been right. And we were definitely not alone in this room. Here, that sentience I felt in the air materialized into a crowd of people around us. They looked like shimmering ghosts, who only formed into humanlike shapes briefly to better observe us before they were off on some other venture, but there was a way the light of the glowing lines in the walls hit them. Maybe their bodies were made up of those ever-moving cells, and thus light reflected strangely on them. Either way, the brightness shifted off them as they disappeared and reappeared around us, some even in the air overhead. Hundreds passed through in a matter of seconds, whispering to each other in their quiet, buzzing language as they came and went, seemingly making intense observations of us among themselves.

I thought about what Antonov told me of their network: it had now spread ten light-years in every direction, and was growing still. For a moment I had the feeling my team and I were some sort of tourist destination, a curious meat-and-metal sideshow to their immense fluid culture—something to gawk at and then move on. I thought I was so powerful in my supergirl body, but these people could bend matter to their will. Disappear and reappear. Fly. Be anywhere. That's what made them so dangerous.

Thad reached for his carbine, something I couldn't blame him for in this hall of whispers. "Be peaceful," April said, only glancing over her shoulder at Thaddeus. "No one here will harm you."

Thaddeus's eyes remained on the people in the crowd. It was hard not to feel all the eyes pressing into our walk, and the hushed whispers that tickled the backs of our necks and bounced off the room's walls. "Your word doesn't have a great track record, April," he said.

"Only in your home," she said, whisking us past the curious members of the Cartel. "Now you're in mine." Thaddeus muttered under his breath as she led us to the center of the room. But unlike in the Great Hall in Oktai's village, there was no dais waiting for us when April finally instructed us to wait. And then she, like the others, began to fade and reappear as she saw fit. My team jerked back when she reappeared with someone new. I wondered if the person she stood with, who resembled Thaddeus in build and color, was the Cartel's leader. But the way he whispered and took us all in screamed *soldier*. Underling.

He and April spoke quickly before coming to some agreement. They then winked into and out of existence until they blended into the crowd as if becoming part of a bigger organism. All in time for something new to enter the room's air.

With an imperceptible shift, my team all squeezed in a little closer as someone materialized and floated toward us just a foot or so up in the air. Like the others, the light was hitting the figure in odd ways, until the person's feet finally touched the floor. The leader, I assumed, due to this dramatic entrance, then began to fill in shape and color. My breathing caught. He now stepped before us in a solid form. And the head of the Swarm Cartel was not who I expected. Not a general. Not a soldier. Not a man at all.

He was a boy, no older than ten. When his eyes found mine, he nodded in greeting and said, "Welcome, Josephine, and friends of Yerba City. I've been expecting you."

CHAPTER 20

A GREAT HUNGER

It had taken so long for his feet to touch the floor. Hadn't seen anything like that since those church paintings of the Savior gliding across the Sea of Galilee. When our Sunday school teacher taught us the Gospels, she said the story would show us how Jesus was above the physical laws of nature. That the man was all-powerful. More deity than man. But the boy before me was not supernatural. Like me, he came from a certain place and time, and had the abilities his time would allow. Also like me, he was definitely a bit *more*. Maybe that was a shared trait in the Swarm Cartel.

The members of the Cartel in the hall around me seemed more still than they'd been up to this point as the boy finished his neat greeting and stepped slightly closer. I'd come with a crew from Earth, one he'd claimed to expect. There was no hint of fear on his face, though if he'd known we were coming, he also knew what we could do. A shiver was running down my spine, but I made my face impassive.

"Who are you?" I asked.

The side of his mouth twitched up. "You never read the treaty?" he asked. I folded my arms. The treaty was signed before my sisters' time running Yerba City. I only knew what they did: that Yerba City, the Brackish, Siberia, and the Swarm Cartel had signed it, giving us each certain territories and citizens to watch over as we saw fit. And we weren't supposed to meddle in each other's business. That part had obviously been broken.

"I missed your name at the end. Unless you want me to call you Cartel Guy, or whatever name you choose."

He tapped his chin. "Cartel Guy. Has a ring to it." A beat passed. "My name is Yukio Tatsumi. But you can call me Yukio, Josephine."

A Japanese name. "Snow Boy?" I translated.

That hint of a smile turned into genuine amusement. "Yes," he said. "I was a December baby, and a little too independent for my parents' taste." At his words, something around him seemed to shimmer, as if the particles in the air were shifting in reaction to his mood. I wanted to stare at Yukio, but I couldn't tear my eyes from the air shifting into sparks and crackling beams of light around the small boy's head, and then just as suddenly disappearing. Amusement in matter form. It was as if the Mesa network allowed me to see not only his physical form, but also the very firing of his thought processes. I got the sense that was how members of the Cartel spent most of their time: just as masses of information zipping across an unseen network; the only reason Yukio had taken this human form was for our benefit.

"And why have you been expecting us?" I asked.

"Well, not all of you." He swept the air to indicate my crew. "But the head of another entity?" His eyes turned to April in the crowd. He might look like a child, but he didn't speak like one, and his gaze had the command of someone far older, and more important. "I've been expecting information for a long time. And in terms of leaders, I thought April would deliver the Siberian leader for a chat. But she brings me the leader of Yerba City. A surprise, but a better one. I hadn't met the new leader after your . . ."

"Replication," I said. "And I'm not the leader of Yerba City. That's not how we're organized. I'm one of many. More of a representative."

Another step closer. Another shift of the particles around him. Less shimmer. Denser, almost like a heavy cloud. "Then let me ask a question, Yerba City Representative."

"Go ahead," I said, noting that there was only a slight accent to his voice, and, as mentioned, no youth to his words. It was like he was from no time and many times at once.

"April wasn't seeking you out," he began. "So why did you come here and not Antonov?"

"I thought you were expecting me."

"I was expecting a leader from a rival entity, but Antonov . . . or . . ." His voice trailed away as he looked to April. Again, that matter in the air seemed to thrum. Were they communicating soundlessly somehow? And then his dark eyes found mine. "And not One, as you call her?"

I straightened. "Because your *April*," I said pointedly, "took One and delivered her to Antonov. *He* asked me to find *you* because he's interested in your power."

"My power?" Yukio began.

I flicked my hands around me. "Those glittery bugs you make when you seem to think," I said, and he laughed. My face burned, but I ignored how much fun he was seeming to have at my expense. "And frankly, I've seen just what your talent with language viruses can produce, Yukio. I saw it nearly destroy Yerba City. Take over every man, woman, child, . . . and machine." It probably wouldn't be smart to lay my cards on the table like this, but transparency seemed to be favored within the Swarm Cartel, even if they did like using spies. "I need to get information on your power back to Earth, and once I do, I can have my sister back. One, as you said."

He studied me for a long time, as if he could see into me. And before I knew it, he bellowed once for April. It seemed to take the length of a thought for her to appear just behind him, flanking his shoulder. Without looking at her, Yukio said, "Please welcome our guests. I would like a word with Seven alone."

My brows rose at the mention of my Josephine name. Could he see into my head like he communicated with April? And then I felt a shift at my side, but it was a member of my team stepping up—a member of the crew I had momentarily forgotten was there. I barely heard Oktai's protests before April shook her head at him. Her voice then filled my mind, though she spoke to Oktai.

"Let her go," April said wordlessly. "She is safe. All is well."

Oktai stopped but shuddered. It was a downright spooky feeling to have someone's voice echo in your mind. I brushed his arm with mine.

Yukio's eyes, now feeling more like a cat watching unsuspecting mice, glittered, never leaving me. And then he said, "This way, please."

I stepped once, and then twice, before the whisper hall melted away and in its place was the upper deck of a ship. Salty sea air blew on my face as I nearly tripped. "What . . . what just happened?"

Yukio was still the same, looking somewhat pointedly ahead. "We left the hall," he said simply. "And I didn't find the ruins to be so appealing."

"Are we . . . are we still on the moon?"

Finally, his gaze left whatever lay in the distance. "Yes," he said, somewhat breathlessly. "But we're alone. We did not need all of my people for this discussion."

"Can't you just read each other's minds like you did with April?"

He smiled. "Of course you noticed that. She was speaking with you and . . . Oktai? Wasn't it?" he asked. I didn't answer. My chin only lifted slightly. "Mmm. I thought so. But not all of us can use these kinds of techniques. In fact, April's mind-sharing abilities are strongest when close to me."

"Well, don't you feel special."

He shrugged. "I did once. A very long time ago. Now, the novelty has worn off." One of his fingers lifted, pointing offshore. "This space brings me peace. My father was a fisherman. This ship is much like the one on which he worked when I was a boy. And if you see just in the distance the blooms gracing those trees?" I nodded. "Those are cherry blossoms. Every spring, Tokyo comes alive with cherry blossoms, as if the entire city is painted in blushing pink."

Maybe a poet, too? "It's beautiful," I said. Although it wasn't a garden I was looking at, and I knew it was some kind of memory hologram rather than grown biomechanical foliage, I couldn't help but feel a parallel to Antonov's hall of flowers here. And right about now I was getting pretty sick of listening to the powerful men of the world wax philosophical next to their plants.

"Yes, it was beautiful to me, though I had terrible allergies. It was beautiful until the war. Then there were no more parents, no more trips on the fishing boats. There was only change." He turned to me as if pulling himself from somewhere other than even where we stood.

"You mean to bring back my family's, this Cartel's, greatest strength to Antonov. Is that right, Seven?"

"I need to accomplish my mission. I can't leave empty-handed."

"And you expect me to just hand it over to you, even though it might mean the destruction of my consciousness, and that of countless others who have joined with the Mesa network?"

"Basically," I said slowly.

"And how would you accomplish this?" He smiled, nodding to the impossible scene around us. "You can see what we are capable of."

I pointed a single index finger at him. "I . . . haven't quite figured out that part of the plan yet."

The boy chuckled quietly. "I like you, Josephine, but I can't let you succeed in that way," he said.

I shook my head. That's why he brought me out here. I would be easier to fight, to kill, out here alone than with my crew. But I wouldn't be that easy to pick off. Just hopefully he wasn't as powerful as the curators. I balled my fists. *Let's get this over with.*

He seemed to notice my defensive stance. Another of his laughs sang through the air. "Oh, no. Seven. I didn't bring you here for battle."

"Then what do you want?" I asked, still raising my balled fists. "I was straight up with you."

"You were. And now I will return the courtesy."

"How?" I asked. Again, something heavy filled his angular eyes. Something beyond this pretend age, beneath those chubby cheeks and pale skin. "Yukio, how old are you?"

"One hundred and six," he replied quickly. "Born only just before the Second World War. And you don't have to fight me for my power."

"I . . . I don't?"

"No," he said. "I will give it to you."

"To return to Antonov? To aid my mission? Why would you—"

"I will give you my power if you join the Swarm Cartel, Seven. Someone like you would provide an immeasurable skill set to my . . . family. April shared how you've been undervalued in Yerba City among the other Josephines. And Antonov is foolish. Maybe there is a reason you wound up here, and not any of your sisters."

He was speaking, but my throat had gone dry. "Join the Swarm Cartel?" I asked.

"More than join." He shook his head. "You would still be yourself: a hybrid being capable of bridging the old and new worlds, one who could forge a commonwealth between the entities, rather than continuing our separate, but unequal, follies."

I eyed him suspiciously. He knew playing the "separate but equal" card was going to get my attention. This 1930s kid wearing rags was shrewd.

"Of course, Antonov is not my kind," he continued, "and we don't agree on most issues, but I have come to see the most obvious flaw in his thinking."

"And what's that?" I asked.

"He fears miscegenation," he said slowly. "All the animals in his little ark must stick to their own kind, mustn't they? But you are already a mixture that would not fit in his museum, aren't you?"

"I mean, I had a great-grandmother who was white, if that's what you mean."

He chuckled at my comment. "You are a special one, Seven. A pearl among pearls. And your uniqueness makes you the perfect candidate to unite our worlds, while there is still time."

"I'm just a machine," I said simply, trying my best not to let him get under my skin.

"It must be tiring," he continued. "Being fettered to those whom you don't understand. Who don't understand you. What would it be like to be a part of something bigger, Seven?" Before I knew it, he'd wrapped his hand around mine. Something zapped through his grasp, an electric shock perhaps. But too fast, and the small taste of it was already bursting through the golden ichor of my new blood. "Better?"

I snatched my hand away, but whatever he'd shared was already moving through my body. "What did you do?"

"Just sharing a small taste of our abilities. That was a fractional nexus to the Mesa network. Our gifts are in the way we shape our world. It's so much more than some language virus. It's the power to create what we see fit."

I blinked, trying to steady myself. My words came out breathless and flimsy. "Your language virus is dangerous to us all. Man. Machine."

"But is it a danger to you, Seven? Already you have encountered the Babble, and yet you still walk and talk as yourself." He looked back over to the cherry blossoms. With his new gifts coursing through me, they seemed brighter to the gaze. My hearing was keener as well, like each bud's snap on the wind was perfectly tuned to my eardrum.

"What I've given you is not necessarily permanent," he said. "The Mesa is a gift you can always return. My parents died in the war, and I suffered for many years after. Until I found my gifts. Until I laid the bricks that would unlock a unified understanding of a quantum network of infinite storage. My new family. But what would I have done to possess my abilities just a bit earlier?" That near-feline gaze turned on me again. "Have you ever asked yourself that question? What difference would it have made to possess your greatest strengths before your greatest tragedy?"

"Josephine," called a voice. Both Yukio and I turned to find three people crossing the deck. Yukio angled away from me, his expression darkening as April and El followed Oktai, who was heading toward us with a determined stride.

"Sleep on it," Yukio whispered to me, and then: "We're done here," he announced when the trio stood before us.

Oktai glared openly at Yukio. "You were gone for a long time," he said to me. "We worried."

"I'm fine," I said. Oktai only nodded as April motioned for us to follow her. She must have received some message from Yukio mind-to-mind. We followed, and I only glanced back once, to where El and Yukio held each other's gaze for the briefest moment.

⁂

That night, April showed us to our own rooms in the compound. Well, if you could call it night. Hard to tell in space. My chamber was large and without a bed. Maybe Yukio had read my mind enough to know I didn't need sleep. There were only white minimalist chairs and tables strewn around, and a large couch that was more comfortable than I wanted to admit. As the hours passed, I found myself scrubbing my face and more wired than when I'd gone onto the ship's deck. I'd come to the moon to get One back. Now the leader of the Swarm Cartel had asked me to join them, an entity of far superior technology and power. He also gave me a taste of that gift, and I couldn't say I hated it.

I breathed deeply. The ceiling of the room was clear, so I stared up at the winking stars. For a stupid second I thought, *I wonder if I can see the moon tonight? Oh, that's right, I'm on her.* My whole life, from Oakland to Siberia, her light had been the same, and now here I was standing on her surface like it wasn't a thing. This absurd situation was the foundation for the confusing, albeit interesting, chance I'd been offered. A chance like the one I'd been presented with before replication. To be more. Becoming part of the Swarm Cartel would mean I'd have a new gift, one my sisters couldn't dream of. I would have the power to transform matter at will.

I rubbed my shoulders. I could say no, but if I did, what if Yukio asked another Josephine, or allowed that power into the wrong hands? What would that mean for the world, under this treaty that was feeling flimsier and flimsier? Was forming some kind of commonwealth between the entities really the answer?

I couldn't stay in this room a minute longer. My feet were moving, quickly leaving the chamber, and heading down a narrow hallway. I didn't know what I was looking for exactly, but it didn't matter, for after a few sharp turns, I found a familiar redhead maneuvering toward me. Not El. Clo. She was bounding down the hall, finally completely out of her Vegas getup, her mane in a long twist of crimson. She also must have been in her own head, because it took a few moments for her to notice me. But when she did, she smiled and marched my way. Sometimes I wished she had El's level of wariness and disinterest in chats.

"Hey, Tik-Tok," Clo said warmly. From her, the moniker didn't bite. She then looked around herself. "Dunno where I was heading, on a big space rock. What are you doing? Couldn't sleep?"

"I don't sleep really." I thought about it. "Maybe I left my room looking for—"

"One of the hot guys?"

"Oktai," I offered.

"That's what I said."

"And I found you, Clo." It was weird seeing her without El. "Where's your sister?"

"We don't do everything together. I thought you were a twin. You should get that," she said before pointing her chin down the hall. An invitation. So we began to walk, the unlikeliest of people. "So, when you went to talk with Creepy Floating Kid, did you get what you needed? Or are we on the moon for another couple of days?"

Had I gotten what I needed? As if in response to my thoughts, those pieces of Yukio's power within me seemed to thrum. The power of creation. To have. Maybe even to consume. I curled and uncurled my fingers. "Maybe, but not yet. Won't be a couple of days, though."

"Okay," she said. "Still weird being able to breathe up here. You know, in space."

"That's a thing for you, huh?" I laughed and shook my head. "Doesn't seem too surprising. A lot of the Swarm Cartel appear to have been human once. Could be the reason they made this compound so breathable."

"Mama would freak out up here," she said. "So much to see and learn. That's why El and I need answers, Tik-Tok. Good answers."

"What are you saying, Clo?"

"Not that I don't have faith in you, because I do. Just . . . all this that El and I are doing is for our mama. She's back on Earth. Hurry up getting what you need so we can get back to our real missions. Yours, too." We rounded a few of the chamber doors. "Well, this is me. Unless you want to come in and talk some more."

"I'm good, thanks. Good night," I said. Clo inclined her head and slipped into her room. I sighed. "Yettis . . ."

As I continued my midnight walk, it soon turned less casual and became more of a jog. A run. A sprint. At least until I stopped. I'd found a new room, a hall like the large one filled with whispers, but this one was bathed in starlight. *What is this place?* I stepped farther inside and realized that at the opposite end of the space, someone rested on a rock. A shock of anxiety passed through me that it might be Yukio, but I calmed when Oktai ruffled his hair. He looked up as if he could hear me noticing him. At least I was positive that *he* couldn't read my thoughts. Before I knew it, he'd wrapped his arms around me in a tight hug.

When we finally pulled apart, I smiled and touched his face. "Couldn't sleep?"

"No," he said. "Not here."

"Neither could Clo. I already bumped into her," I said as we found ourselves curling onto the rock where he'd sat. A few moments passed before: "What's wrong?"

He scrubbed his face. "Everything back there, after you left. It wasn't right. Not what my people would have thought this place to be."

"Your people know about the Swarm Cartel?"

"We have our tales," he said. "The Bee People have always been in our stories. Like the Tsirku. They have their own purpose in the world. Theirs is just that they can slip into pockets of it that we can't see. They are people who come from nowhere."

"What happened when I left with Yukio?"

"They tried to show us more of the world, of their people. April said that they could show us only because we were already a part of it. And that's when they started bending light and sound in the hall. When they appeared and reappeared as if in unison and jest, just because it suited them." He shook his head. "That back there wasn't right. That's a power for gods, not men."

"It was just a show," I said, feeling Yukio's power inside me react to Oktai's wariness. Rumbling as if wanting to defend itself, its honor. "The Swarm Cartel creates and moves matter. And it's not so bad. Maybe it won't feel so bad if you understood." As Yukio had done on the ship's deck, I took Oktai's hand to share with him the bit of Swarm Cartel power, the Mesa network I felt earlier. It surged through my ichor and launched into Oktai's palm, his eyes widening as it landed its mark.

"What are you doing?" he asked, taking in the world around us. Perhaps he was seeing it anew, as I'd done with the cherry blossoms.

"Yukio shared this with me," I said. "It's only a bit of the Swarm Cartel's power. It's like you can see all pieces of all things. Every atom. Every molecule."

"Josephine."

"The ship you saw earlier . . . Yukio created that with his own power. Like he formed his own reality."

"Josephine."

"And it didn't trap him. It helped him make the world better for his family."

"Josephine!" Oktai had taken his hand back. He shook it hard, as if trying to send whatever I'd shared with him back into the air. "The Bee People are sacred, yes. They have amazing abilities. But it is not something I want to come too close to. It's like the sun. I don't want to be close enough to touch it."

"There's nothing wrong with understanding it. Understanding our options better."

"We have a mission," Oktai replied. "We're here to get what we need for your sister. We're here to help the Yettis."

"I haven't forgotten. Just, didn't you feel that? Yukio could teach me to use it. Share more. He could teach you, too. We could be better, stronger versions of who we are now."

"Or just different versions," Oktai said. "I like who we are now. I like the strength we came here with." He took my hands. The remaining power in me stayed put. "Yukio's power is fire. And I've seen what happens when people get too close."

"Oktai," I said, my hands finding my hips. "It's not like that. This is power. It's strength. And I can't help but think of what I could have done with it earlier. If Yukio teaches me, I could learn to handle this. I could do good with this."

"You're already doing good now," he said.

I began to speak again, but something in his eyes halted me. "What?"

"I've seen that look before. I've seen that hunger before. Not of the body. It's in your spirit. And unlike Yukio, you still have one. He can't give you what you're missing, Josephine. Not with those tricks."

"Not tricks, Oktai. Power. I may not even need One. I may not even need to go back to Yerba City. Do you know what it's like to be me? To live surrounded by sisters you can't understand? To be the odd one out all the time? I . . . want more options. I never get to have them."

Oktai's sigh was long. "You know where I saw the great hunger before? It was in my father. He wanted to have the greatest expertise of all the hunters in our village. He wanted to be the best. Only. Singular. That led him to chase down a herd of reindeer he shouldn't have. He did it alone. Ran out onto ice that was thinner than it should have been for the time of year. He fell straight through before anyone could make it there to pull him out. All they could save was his knife."

"I'm sorry." It was a whisper. A quick, quiet whisper.

"And I know the hunger in myself. We aren't so different, you and me. I wasn't supposed to be a hunter. I was supposed to be an advisor to the chief one day. But I wanted to step into my father's place so badly that I bribed the shaman to change my fate. To reroute me. Because I had to do what my father couldn't. I had to find him on that ice somehow. Keep him from going through. But in my walk as a hunter, I found you."

My voice was thin. "I don't know what to say."

"I don't want you to say anything. I want you to listen. When I'd gone through my Chitakla, I realized I was proud to be a hunter. But becoming one wasn't bringing my father back. It wasn't rewriting the past. And it wasn't taking away the anger I had at my father for leaving me. For making a terrible decision. Yes, you can love someone and be angry at them . . . He needed to cure his hubris, and I needed to cure my need to fix it."

"I'm not trying to fix anything—"

He held his hand up. "Nothing outside can fill your cup. You must do that. And if you accept Yukio's power, it will be a mistake."

I set my chin hard. He didn't know me. He'd just met me. "Good night, Oktai."

He stepped away from me, and quietly left the hall.

CHAPTER 21

POWER GRABS

The fight with Oktai left a hollowness in my gut. I'd never had a boy-friend, so I didn't have anything else to draw from when it came to this feeling. It was new and unexpected, leaving me to sit in my room with my thoughts. Were the things I wanted so bad? Could he not see the use for this power, too? As if responding to my thoughts, Yukio's gift thrummed inside me—a bone-deep awareness that I could move par-ticles into whatever I wanted, however I wanted to do it. That I could *create*. Matter was like Legos in the air. It was something to be built upon. But even with this awareness, I knew there was still so much I couldn't see. That I couldn't manipulate. And despite Oktai's reserva-tions, I wanted it.

I rose from one of the chairs and plucked some matter from noth-ingness, opting to twist it around my hands. I flexed my fingers and twisted again until it became a weaving of sorts. My hands moved faster and faster until they'd made their product: a simple white flower. It hovered in the air before I plucked it. It was real, with soft petals and a sweet smell. I'd made this from nothing. And then I fastened that little bit of nothing, now something, to my Josephine uniform. The power hummed in me again, now with pride.

What else could I do?

That thrumming washed over my body, and I knew the matter had changed again. But this time, it wasn't making floral arrangements. This time, it altered my Josephine outfit into something new, something I hadn't realized I wanted to create. A dress now draped my frame. Not Josephine standard issue, but something like from a department store. Or maybe something even better than that. Maybe it came from a designer or an expensive tailor. Either way, it was knee-length, flared out, and shimmered in a shade of silver. My flower remained, like one of those old-timey corsages in black-and-white pictures.

I spun around, and a clacking sound traveled to my ears. Cute, strappy heels were on my feet, a perfect match for the dress. And my fro? Fashioned with braids in the front and more little flowers woven in the cornrows. I only missed a mirror to see myself.

I twisted my hands around. *Make a mirror. I need a mirror.* But one didn't form. Instead, the particles around me bent the chamber on the moon into something else. A new place. A decorated gym in Oakland, the one belonging to the middle school down the street from Aunt Connie's house. Both my dad and Aunt Connie had gone there when they were preteens. Gauzy streamers that looked like winter winds hung from the ceiling. Fake, plump snowmen were placed around the room, and a disco ball hung above a white dance floor that looked like it was supposed to mimic a sheet of ice.

"Of course," I said, looking around. "Snow Ball." The annual dance was always in December, right before the Christmas holiday. I had never been, obviously. I'd been too young for this kind of thing before the world crashed and the machines carted everyone away. But maybe this was how I imagined it would be when I was old enough to go.

And then the floor started to rattle with bass. A DJ had appeared at the far side of the gym, and the room was swelling with music. Other kids appeared, dancing, though I couldn't really make out their faces from lines and shadows. Perhaps the power in me wasn't strong enough to give them more clear images.

"Only missing one thing," I whispered, shifting my weight from heel to heel in the middle of the dance floor. And then the music changed, a slower beat. And I glanced toward the gym doors, where my date walked in. *His* face I could see. I'd only seen him in his gear and furs up to this point, but now Oktai was dressed formally, with his hair pulled back. And yeah, if the girls back home could have seen him, they might have ended the world just for a dance. He cut across the floor, weaving between the shadow people until he stood before me and stuck out his hand. And like in the old sitcoms I watched with Aunt Connie, no sooner had I blinked than we were dancing.

He spun me, and maybe the shifting and re-forming particles guided my feet, because I'd never danced like this before. I'd never been spun and dipped. I blushed and grinned, mirroring the stars that seemed to be in his eyes. Here the world hadn't been destroyed. There was no Subantoxx. No missions. No replication. Here was the world I'd wanted to inherit, one that wasn't so complicated. One that wasn't so dangerous—just a couple on a dance floor. The streamers blew behind us and the twinkle lights winked in the background as he pulled me close.

"Is this real?" I asked him, though I wasn't sure if this was the real Oktai. If the real Oktai was still in his room. Most likely pissed at me. "Are you still mad at me?"

"I've never been mad at you. I'm afraid for you."

"Afraid for me? Why?" I gestured to the room. I'd made this with Yukio's gift. I'd made this dance. I'd made this normal moment for us. One that normal teens would look forward to. And I could make more normal moments for us, too, now. For us all. So much had been taken from us. With this power, here was a chance to have it back. "Don't you see what I've made?"

"This power lets you play with the world as if it was a toy." Oktai peered around the room, but his eyes didn't shine anymore. If he wasn't the real Oktai, just some imitation I'd created, then maybe even my fantasies couldn't change who he fundamentally was. How he would feel. "This isn't a children's game. This is nature, and there is balance to it. If you take something great, you must give up something. Perhaps something greater than you intended."

"Oktai," I began, just as a knock came to my door, a resounding thing that made the gym I'd created fall away. Oktai disappeared with the twinkling lights, dancers, and DJ, leaving me standing in my chamber once more in my Josephine uniform. That hollow feeling in my stomach returned as I tried to summon Yukio's gift once more: it didn't answer. I sighed. I was still a baby with this magic. The knock came again.

"Come in," I called out, and in an instant, the door opened to allow El and April to fill my doorway. Again, it was strange to see a Yetti without her twin. What was going on between Clo and El?

"What's up?" I asked.

April glanced around the chamber as if sensing what I had done in the room. When her eyes met mine, I shot my chin in the air. She was right to sense Yukio's power. I had done something great with just a taste of it. In Siberia, Antonov created his dream worlds. Here, the Swarm Cartel allowed their members to tailor reality as they saw fit. They had a sense of control I hadn't seen on Earth. All this power, if you swore fealty to them.

"Did you have something to say, April?"

She shook her head as if remembering herself, her own mission. "He's ready to see you now," April replied. I only nodded before heading toward them, and the three of us left the chamber in favor of the hallway.

I didn't need much preparation for this meeting. I'd spent the entire night debating how I would handle it. Finally I would tell Yukio my ultimate decision.

Admittedly, I wasn't thinking of Yukio as we quietly wove through the compound. No, instead, my eyes were on April. She was translucent, with the outlines of her organs and bones shimmering as if with golden ichor. Maybe she'd been made as I had, and with similar materials. But April moved with an elegance that I wouldn't expect of the angels in Yerba City. I watched her so intently that I didn't realize El was at my side.

"You're staring, Tik-Tok," El said to me.

I smacked my teeth. "You know she's a machine, too, right?"

"Not exactly like you."

"Yeah, I'm not a spy," I said. El shrugged. "And I've just never seen an angel like her. Most androids aren't made to be so model-y."

For once, El didn't snap back. She only nodded. "Yeah, I hadn't seen anyone like her before either, but I grew up in the forest. Since Clo and I left the woods, I've seen so many things I wish I could forget."

"Including her?"

"No," El said. "Not including April." She then cocked her head to the side. "Questions, Tik-Tok."

I groaned. "Josephine is fine."

"*Josephine*," she said. "Just, what did Yukio say to you yesterday? When he took you aside to talk?"

"Oh, that. Well, he made me an offer, told me I had the night to agree or disagree."

"Agree to what?" she pressed.

"To being a part of them," I said.

"And?"

I blinked. "Well, it's not completely part of my mission, or yours." When El's face remained blank, I leveled a look at her. "Would you take an offer from Yukio?"

Her eyes traveled to April once more. "I think I would."

With that, we cleared a final corner before the hallway began to change, walling up behind us and expanding ahead. Before we knew it, the chamber had become something new and spacious. I knew without asking that the three of us now stood in Yukio's private chamber, especially as massive cherry-blossom trees had seeped from the nothingness to ring the room. Yukio was nothing if not consistent. But he was not present.

"Where is Yukio?" I asked April, as from behind the last cherry-blossom tree to appear, Oktai, Thaddeus, and Clo stumbled in. When they saw us standing in the middle of the room, they beelined to us, looking around.

"What is all this?" Thad asked, brushing his blond hair from his face.

"I was in my room and now I'm here," added Clo.

Oktai didn't speak. His eyes just found mine and stared hard. He wasn't the fantasy Oktai I'd conjured up. He was the real person, and he knew, at least to some degree, why we were here. And disapproval radiated from him.

I couldn't move real people. I wasn't that gifted. But Yukio could. I bit my lip. So much for private deals staying private. My voice came out with more bravado than I actually felt. "I have business with Yukio," I announced.

Thad spoke. "Business? Does that mean you got what you need for Antonov?"

Surprise colored his face when I shook my head, and answered, "It's gone past Antonov." Again, my gaze turned to April. "So, we're all here. Where is Yukio?"

"Behind you," came a voice that did not belong to the angel. We all turned to find an old man wandering toward us from behind the cherry-blossom trees. His back was hunched, and his hand gripped a cane. He wore a white lab coat, of all things, and large rimmed glasses. If I hadn't spent the time with him when we first arrived, I wouldn't have recognized Yukio. But I knew it was him. The drop of power he'd granted me buzzed at his presence. And there was an air in the way he carried himself. Whether he appeared as a boy or as an old man, there would always be something in his eyes that said he carried so many of the world's secrets.

Yukio slowly wove between my crew, all to step before us and announce: "Hello."

I frowned, taking in the new lines on his face. The crinkles at the corners of his eyes. He had the look of a kindly old man, one who would feed pigeons in the park after an afternoon nap. But we hadn't come to the moon for a sweet chat with a grandpa.

"Why is my crew here?" I asked by way of a greeting.

"Why not them?" he replied, sparing only a mildly interested glance their way. "Why not them all? They deserve to know, especially the twins. Maybe you'll have to forgive me, because I do have a soft spot for twins. I had one. A sister."

"So did I," I replied. Yukio's head angled in surprise. "What happened to yours?"

"Starvation," he replied quickly. "Many children died on the streets of Tokyo after the war. I was forced to grow up without her. I survived as a beggar, scrounging every yen from the rubble in the streets. I did everything to get money; I thought if I'd just had enough of it, I could have bought rice, and she would have survived. My passion became money. Even after I had enough, there wasn't enough. We needed security. I wanted a currency that would be free from war, free from the foolishness of nations, and so I searched for a currency network. A perfect cryptocurrency.

"There had been experiments with storing massive datasets by subtly shifting subatomic particles. Quantum mechanics. I had a vision to create a currency in the quantum realm. When I accessed the Mesa network, I realized one could move not just encrypted data, but all matter as well. It could store such massive amounts of information, and access it so quickly, that it could simulate consciousness."

"So you're really just a simulation?" Thaddeus asked. "The real Yukio is dead, isn't he?"

"Like the life of a child who was once just a dream in his father's eyes, soon the child is born, and that dream one day becomes the father," Yukio explained. "What you call a simulation is now more powerful than any father could imagine of his child. The Cartel is the true destiny of humanity in the universe."

"And probably no gooey diapers, either," Clo offered.

"So you did it for her?" I asked. "For your sister."

A crooked finger tapped his chin. "Maybe I did, Seven." His eyes then bored into me before bouncing to the Yetti twins. "Maybe everything we do is for our little matched sets." A beat passed. "I was generous in giving you a night to make your conclusions. Have you decided, young lady? Are you going to join us?"

So many sets of eyes fastened on me, some from my crew trying to piece together what was going on. I knew this moment was coming, but suddenly my mouth went dry in this hot seat. Again, Yukio's head angled. He drew out his next word. "Hesitation. You are not convinced."

"Yukio—"

"Do not speak quite yet, Seven. One last display." And then Yukio's hand twisted in the air, like a magician beginning his scene with the black top hat and hopefully a white rabbit. He dragged his hand down the length of his body now, allowing the matter around him to shift. The cane fell to the floor. In an instant, it was no longer an old man before us, but the little boy I had met the other day. The lines had smoothed on his face. The crinkles at his eyes were gone. He smiled up at me warmly. "When I created the Cartel, I didn't know what it would become. What it would encompass. That my new family would be able to not just move the matter outside of them, but also the matter that comprised them. I am an old man, Seven, but I can also be any identity I want. So could you."

"And why choose this one? Why be a child when I'm sure you could be young again, but at a later point?"

"Have you not been listening?" he asked me.

And then I knew. This was likely when he last saw his sister. And though he could move living people, there was likely a hard line to his gifts when it came to people who'd already crossed over. Nature had its laws, as Oktai had mentioned. This form was the closest he would ever be to her again.

He smiled and lifted his small arm. "The hunting knife you brought," he said to Oktai, though he didn't look at him. "I will need it for a moment." Oktai stiffened as the knife flew from wherever he'd sheathed it and zapped toward Yukio. It stopped in midair before his smiling face. "Finely made."

"That is not for you to have," said Oktai.

"Of course not," Yukio said. "I will only borrow its perfection." The knife split into two perfect copies, and one gently returned to Oktai, which he snatched out of the air and stared at suspiciously.

"The way you think of the world isn't how it is anymore, Seven." With another wave of Yukio's hand, the metal in the knife in front of him reconfigured itself into its base elements, the composites even forming back into the rock and ore that it had once been. With another flick of his hand, the ore sped far into its future until it was the knife once more, but covered in rust and finally dissolving into dust. Our mouths hung open as he flicked his hands with finality, and the knife was again as it had been.

"This is wrong," Oktai said, swearing under his breath. "Much went into this knife."

"It is simply power," announced Yukio. "The power of humanity's destiny, the Swarm Cartel, and the network of near-infinite possibility we have opened. Seven, you asked why I brought everyone here. You are a hybrid mind, and you have already played with but a fraction of what the Mesa is capable of. I want you to train under me, to learn the secrets of the Swarm Cartel, but they all deserve to know our gifts."

"I don't want them," spat Oktai.

"This is between you and me, Yukio," I said.

He shook his head. "The magnificence of my power is between us, and you have a choice to make. To learn under me. To join us. But all of you are members of the Swarm Cartel."

"What?" El and Clo asked in unison.

"You are all already part of this network. All of you." And with another wave of his hand, he "copied" all of my team, just as he had the knife. Spectral mirror images of Clo, El, Thaddeus, and Oktai stepped out of their bodies and stood next to each of them before solidifying into full color. They looked just as confused as we were.

Oktai jumped away from his double—not having it—and the look on Oktai No. 2 read the same.

Clo reached out and touched her image, marveling at her own hair.

El seemed indifferent at seeing herself.

These "copies" seemed to move and think just like us, although I couldn't help but notice that one was missing: for me.

Thaddeus let out a laugh and immediately punched his double's chest, half strength, like an old bro. The double staggered and punched back, equally amused. Thaddeus took the blow with a guffaw, and almost instantly, as they began wrestling, we couldn't tell which one was which. "Ha ha," one of them laughed, "pretty solid!"

"And your power, Seven, is just a drop in the bucket to what I could give you. What I could unlock. What I can control." He turned his hand and all the doubles aged incredibly fast, just as the copy of the knife had. Oktai's beard grew and his body bent, Clo's hair turned gray and fell out, El's face exploded into wrinkles.

The double that Thaddeus was wrestling suddenly became enfeebled, struggling to keep our Thad in a choke hold, which got quickly reversed on him.

"C'mon, old man!" Thaddeus said, trying to keep the wrestling match up, but soon his double, looking ninety years old, slumped.

"Guess I lost my spunk," the old Thaddeus chuckled, before falling back into the monitor's arms and shriveling like a prune, leaving just his body armor to cling to—and even that began to age and dissolve.

In seconds, all the doubles were dust, crumbling into nothingness before our eyes and the dust quickly fading from view.

"Aw," Clo fussed. "I wanted to braid my hair."

Oktai watched the last of his double fade away. "These are just ghosts, false images!" he protested. "It should be forbidden to do this!"

"I could bring them back as babies, or as your current selves, or as anything," Yukio said, "and you would not know the difference. We have enough molecular information on you now to make indistinguishable copies."

El made a show of dusting her double's remains off her boots, although she probably didn't need to. Even the dust was a projection. "What's your point?" she demanded.

"Any one of you could be copied, replicated, and manipulated," he continued. "Except you, Josephine 778676. Something inside of you cannot be replicated, even among your own kind." He shook his head, forming his power into a state outside him now: a shining sphere of light that glowed above the little boy's head. We all blinked slightly at its brightness. "I believe in you, Josephine. Touch this nexus, and you will become one with the network. Take that back to Antonov and complete your mission as the goddess you were destined to become."

Shock radiated through me. "No," I said. I'd thought I was at the top of the food chain after replication, but there was so much more out there than me. So much to learn. Just not under this little madman. "I'm part of Yerba City. My city. It's not perfect, but it's who I am. I'm not in your Cartel. I was coming to tell you no."

Yukio's laugh wafted between the cherry blossoms. "You would really dismiss all you could learn in my presence? You can create wonders, but also, you can always cut yourself off from it, if you concentrate for long enough."

"I said no," I reiterated. "I know where this is going to go."

He shook his head. "I'm a scientist. My desire has always been to find things on a molecular level. To discover other networks. And I've found thousands of them. Some may be the ruins of our own civilization. You can have the greatest kingdom in the world and still it will turn to dust. All that matters is having true power." He pointed to the sphere above him.

"You just said it yourself: it's a dead end," I said. "You've seen where all this power leads to: dead systems."

"You could be different," he whispered, coming close. "I built from pain, from loss, and I gave my life to the network. You can remain unique, Josephine, and be empowered by the network. You can build from love, the love of your sister, who still whispers to you."

"I have all the love I need," I said calmly.

He pulled back. "You've already tasted its power. Is that what you're going to do? Use the power of the Mesa network only to cut yourself off from it?"

I nodded.

"If you will not join us, then I'm sorry, none of you can leave here with your minds intact," he said coldly.

My crew and I exploded into action, weapons drawn, but that move—like every other up to now—had been predicted by the Cartel. They froze the molecules around us, suspending us like mandarin oranges in a church-buffet Jell-O. Oktai, Thaddeus, Clo, El, and I were all stuck in our action poses like mannequins on that moon base, completely powerless.

"We will not kill you," Yukio continued, walking calmly among us, "but already you've seen too much and gotten too close to the nexus." He moved his hand slightly, and something changed in the air; I could hear my human companions begin to breathe again in deep gasps. I didn't need it, but at least he was letting the air flow. "As you guessed, Antonov and I had to exchange technology to create what you call the Babble virus, but that is not all we exchanged. I learned from his modified Subantoxx and its new abilities to wipe the minds of its recipients. I have flooded this room with it, and just as he pacified entire populations with his primitive mythologies, I will wipe clean your minds to a blissful, childlike state before returning you to Earth. In a few minutes you will fall unconscious, and in a few more, you will forget who you are and begin life anew."

I couldn't turn around, but I could hear muffled protests coming from the others. Because the Cartel had frozen their movements, not their breathing, it was just a matter of moments before they all took it in.

"Except you, Josephine," he said from right next to me. "You will have to be dissected bit by bit and reprogrammed from the inside, of course."

I tried to curse him out, but I couldn't even twitch my halfway-open mouth.

"And you, Thaddeus," he continued, turning again, and levitating the knife he had copied from Oktai. "All the monitors of Yerba City are genetically modified to be immune to the effects of Subantoxx, so for you the Sap will not work." The knife thinned into a long, menacing needle. "A simple lobotomy will do."

Thaddeus, his pistol half-drawn, protested with a slight whine.

Yukio turned to see the others' eyes roll back. "They're unconscious now," he said, and he waved his hand to release them. Oktai, Clo, and El collapsed to the floor like rag dolls, reminding me of the people of the village who'd collapsed right after my Chitakla. "Soon they will be entirely reset." He moved close to Thaddeus again, levitating the needle up to penetrate his nostril. "The human mind is so simple once the proper calculations are made. Always hard to predict, but simple to prune and curtail once you understand its motivations. I cannot wait to look at the pieces of your mind, Jose—"

Zap! A lightning wave moved across the room, releasing Thaddeus and me from the frozen grip of the network. I dropped to the ground, and Thaddeus immediately shot Yukio through the chest as the monitor shouted, "No thanks!"

Unharmed, but confused, Yukio immediately sealed up the hole in his Swarm body and turned around. "How did this—?"

Standing next to the nexus sphere was El, her hand immersed in the crackling power. She had linked herself fully with the Mesa network. The whispers immediately closed in around her, but it was far too late to stop her.

"El!" I shouted.

"But the Subantoxx," Yukio said. "You should have—"

Thaddeus gasped, realizing, half laughing, at the ace El had been saving up her sleeve. "You dummies!" he breathed. "She's got a monitor's baby inside her! And now his blood! She's immune!"

"I knew you Tik-Toks were going to try and Sap me again," El growled. "And I wasn't gonna let it happen twice!"

"Crush her!" Yukio concentrated, trying to bring the power of the quantum network against El. Thousands of the Swarm figures swirled into the room, their speckled bodies collecting around El like metal shavings onto a magnet. But she brought it right back to them. The result was a deafening scream as all the matter in the area seemed to

twist against itself: the air, the metal, the building, the ground, everything contorted like taffy.

I could feel every part of me being warped, too, as the Cartel fought
its civil war. This gift of ultimate power—which Yukio had intended for
me, but was now in El's hands—was going to be used to the fullest.
Thaddeus screamed, dropping his gun and clutching his skull, probably suddenly wishing he had gone for the lobotomy instead.

As the Swarm Cartel fought against itself with every molecule, El
dug deep, her eyes glowing fiercely. *"Die!"* she screamed. *"All of you!"*

And they did. Yukio, the swarming figures, and even the walls of
the base suddenly exploded, opening us up to the chaos and dust of
space.

I was rattled as we started tumbling, and it was all I could do to
sweep together the little Cartel power I had to gather us and take us
back from where we came.

We hurtled toward Earth at full speed. Though my entire crew was
within my protection, this was nothing like our trip to the moon. That
had been a slower thing, maybe even leisurely in comparison. I had
watched the cosmos undulating around me in a sea of black, all except
the sun that burned so bright I almost needed to cover my eyes. I was
almost happy to take in all the sights I was not meant to see. This trip
back to Earth was different. This was an escape after snatching Yukio's
power from his floating sphere. This was to get us away from the moon,
from the Swarm Cartel's compound that was crumbling with each second. Maybe Yukio had some capacity to fix it. Or maybe he was gone
for good; maybe El had destroyed him. A piece of me suspected the
latter, though I didn't have time to think. Faster and faster, we charged
back to our home planet. Back from what we'd all felt and seen. And as
I transported us, I, too, was burning bright like the sun. With all this
might and power twisting around me until finally, I saw it. The ground.
The solid white earth, covered in snow.

***

As my thoughts spiraled, I felt something move through my body. It
was something distinctly wrong. That brightness of the sun I'd emu-
lated as I shot to Earth, now it was heating me as if from within. A true

burn as Yukio's power inside me turned unwieldy. I had never been trained to handle it, and the burn, the swell of power, was intensifying too fast to control. If I didn't let this snow globe around us go, it would char us all. One problem: if I dropped it, we'd plummet to the ground too fast to survive. And then my vision blacked out under the might of this power. I dropped the ball around us and welcomed the crash.

We smashed into the earth too quick for screams. It was too hard to move. I wasn't sure if minutes or hours had passed as I lay in the snow. It was just me and the ever-present silence of Siberia. Finally, my limbs were heavy, but I pushed up to my feet. Wind whipped my face as I narrowed my eyes and took in snow piled high on the Siberian plains, as well as the cicada at my back. I'd gotten us back to Antonov's capital city, though I wasn't sure if we were all in one piece. That exceptional power still churned inside me, but now, with feet firmly planted, I was less concerned about it. My ears pricked because it was too quiet. No one was ambling up to me or yelling to find out what had just happened. There was no one else there at all. Where was my crew?

I moved around, trying to find any hint of them. And then there was a glint within all those miles of white. I took off running before taking in that the glint was not one, but many pieces. A trail that led back to a badly battered April. She lay in the snow, the golden ichor in her not glowing nearly as bright as before. We were machines, of course. What was life or death to us? But the sight of her, in near pieces, made me want to back up. Whatever was on the other side for people who'd been created . . . she would soon find out. Her eyes locked on mine, and I recognized that she was trying to speak, but nothing was coming out.

"It's okay," I tried to say to her, though I knew it was anything but okay.

In a flash, someone leapt by my side, knocking me away from April. I knew El's technique before even getting a good look at her.

"Get away from her," El snarled as I crashed into a bed of white. She shoved me for emphasis and then ran over to April. I got up slowly. By the time I stood, El was no longer interested in me. She had bent delicately in the snow to take April's hand. Maybe I had underestimated their connection. April somehow grazed El's cheek, and this thing like a sob bubbled from the Yetti twin's mouth. But even grief couldn't make the android speak. So El seemed to do the next best thing she could: she wrapped her arms around April and pressed her lips to hers just as April's golden ichor flared one last time, and grayed out.

What wrapped around the three of us? Time? The winds? The cold? Time slowed and then seemed to spread when El finally rose from the snow. When she looked to me, her eyes burned.

"Do you see what you did?" El brushed the snow off herself, finally taking a moment to straighten herself since our rough landing.

"What I did?" I asked. "I just saved us." El was before me in an instant. I narrowed my eyes. The girl wasn't a machine, but that speed wasn't exactly human. Maybe it was all the training in the woods? I had never exactly fought her to know all her capabilities.

"Don't act dumb," she said. "*I* saved us." She shoved me again, hard. Too hard. My head angled to the side in curiosity. No, no. That wasn't anything you could learn in the woods. She had an ungodly strength now. "You snatched us up and then crashed us."

"I was trying to get us back, but I didn't mean to crash and—"

"All you machines take," she spat. "That's who you all are."

"Stop it, El. You know I'm not like that. I'm not bad," I said. "I was trying to help. With everything. My mission. Yours with your sister, and you, and your mom."

"Shut up!" she yelled before beginning to circle me. I tried to look deep in her eyes, past the pain. Then her words turned sharp. "You take like all the others. Now I'm going to take." She looked at her hand that she had immersed in the sphere; it still crackled with power.

"El," I said. "Calm down. Let's go into that capital city and get *your* mom and my sister."

"I don't need your help. I can get my mom and all the answers I need without you. I'm sick of following you." She waved her arms around. "And everything you do."

"Everything I do? You can't even understand what I have to do, what I've had to do. You've never even stopped to see what my sisters and I are really building now in Yerba City, how far we've come."

"Save it. You're just a pawn in this stupid game. I'm taking my sister. I'll handle my mama, and then I'm going to Yerba City to destroy the robots. I'll set everyone free."

A chill ran up my spine. "How do you plan on doing all that?"

"Just watch me," she snarled. We held each other's gazes a long time. In hers, I saw that she was serious. No, that was putting it too lightly. She was obsessed, like a kid with a schoolyard grudge. I tried to reach out to her, but she pushed my hand away with that inhuman strength.

This time, I couldn't keep the question in. "El, what did you do?" She didn't answer, opting only to smile before turning to disappear into the distance at an incredible speed.

I watched where she'd been for a long time, that chill in my spine taking over the rest of my body. What was this Cartel power going to allow her to do? That was not the girl I'd plucked from the Tsirku.

A stark groan caught my attention, and elation passed through me. I ran to find someone else of my team, someone who could possibly join me. At least until I stumbled onto the last person I'd ever want to see badly injured. Oktai lay some yards away, his body twisted in ways that should not have been possible. He was alive, but his condition . . . He blindly held his father's knife in the air; the copper blade had been snapped off in the chaos, but nevertheless, his grip was like death on it, shakily defending still. I'd never seen someone so badly hurt. And no one else was coming. The power thrummed in me, a braying horse wanting to help. And maybe I could fix this, but I didn't know how. My own sob ripped from my mouth as my knees pressed into the snow. I'd never thought it would be like this. I flexed my fingers, opening and then closing them, trying to understand how everything had gone so wrong so fast.

What had I done?

CHAPTER 22

FROM THE RUINS

I woke up in the dark and quiet. I lay in a bed, not one that I knew. A light nightdress wrapped my six-year-old body. My head throbbed. The last thing I remembered was Daddy's car, and maybe the rising heat inside it to go along with the sweltering day. Now that heat was gone, replaced with artificial cold from an AC unit in a nearby window. This wasn't my bedroom. The shades of pastel and beige said this was someplace else.

"Oh, you're awake, baby," someone said. I rolled over to see a brown-skinned woman with a cropped haircut. She wore lavender scrubs with dancing teddy bears on them. My throat was dry when I tried to answer her. After checking a few machines beeping around me, she came to my side. "Don't try to speak, baby. You had quite an ordeal. My name is Nurse Ronnie, and I've been watching over you since you came to the hospital."

"Hospital?" I managed to croak.

She was absorbed in the machines now. "Vitals look good," she said, more to herself than to me. She then grabbed a large jug of what had to be water, plopped it on the bedside, and shoved a straw in it. "Why don't you drink this, and I'll get your aunt?"

I took the water and gulped it down. My throat was hoarser than it had ever been. "My aunt's here?"

Nurse Ronnie's eyes brightened. "Yep, she's been here since they brought you at the top of my shift. One sec, sweetheart." With that, Nurse Ronnie left the room.

The machines around me continued to beep as I sipped my water. I combed my thoughts. My daddy had gotten Imani and me from the playground, took us somewhere in that big, hot car. And then, nothing. What had I missed? And then I looked around. Where was Imani? The sound of Aunt Connie's sensible shoes hitting the tiled floors broke my thoughts. In fact, it was more like she flew inside. Somehow, she found the same place on the bed where Nurse Ronnie had perched, before leaning forward and taking my hand.

"You okay?" she asked, though she was the one who didn't look okay.

I nodded. "I think. This is a hospital?"

"Yes, it is, sweetheart." She smiled weakly and then brushed a phantom hair from my face. "I'm so glad you're all right."

"The water is good," I said between gulps. Then I angled my head. "Aunt Connie, where's Imani?"

Her eyes widened just a bit. Now her voice seemed tight. "Imani?"

"Mmm-hmm," I said. "She in another room? Where's Daddy?"

Aunt Connie, who never had a hard time with words, started and stopped her next sentence more than a few times. It was then that I noticed how red rimmed her eyes had become. And how they were filling with tears. She blinked, and one fell down her cheek.

"You crying?" I asked.

"Yes, sweetheart," she said. "I'm crying."

"Why?"

"Because I'm so very sad," she said thinly. She brushed that hair away again.

I blinked a little faster. "Aunt Connie, what's wrong?"

Maybe she found the words. Any word. "Sweetheart, your daddy is with some important people while they sort out what happened yesterday. Something bad happened yesterday."

"Something bad?"

She nodded once. "Yes, and because of it, Imani was hurt. And she's not coming back." It was the best she could make out, and I still didn't understand what she meant. But I didn't ask at that moment. Aunt Connie had thrown her arms around me and squeezed me so tight, I thought I would need to choke for air. But to little me, she didn't make any sense—Imani was still there, and I spoke to her from across the room. I knew she was gone, but she was still there, and we kept the Twinkling alive between us. We spoke when I left that hospital alone, and we spoke at the funeral—her funeral—that my dad could only briefly attend. We spoke every day until the world ended, and then we kept going, although I saw her less often. I know when people had time to worry about such things, they all hoped I would grow out of talking to her. *Delayed grief,* the doctors called it, a mental disorder. No one thought that a scientist would come walking out of the woods one day to tell me my disorder was actually a gift that would somehow save the world.

That was a long time ago, and now that I really needed her, Imani didn't come every time I called out to her. But that's what I did in the snow as the realization set in that I had no functioning crew left after crashing in Solgazeya's snow. Oktai lay before me, unconscious and breathing shallowly. I'd seen some horrors before from fights, and during my training as a Josephine. But I hadn't seen someone I cared about with a body battered and bent in ways that should not have been possible. I'd failed him like I failed this entire mission.

Her name tore from my throat this time. It was guttural. A final plea. "Imani!" I shouted. "Answer me! Please! I need you." And like every time recently, she said nothing back. Maybe I was truly alone now. I glanced over to the cicada that had delivered me to the Siberian plain. Alone or not, I wouldn't let Oktai suffer out here. So I pulled myself to my feet and took Oktai as gently as possible back to the craft. Luckily, my superhuman strength was still intact.

He rasped a bit against the cold breeze, still keeping his broken knife up, and I shook my head. Blood was trickling down his crown. The hunter did not deserve this. All he'd done was try to help me. Try to warn me. And what had it gotten him? Bloodied and broken, that's what.

I got him into the cicada quickly. I laid him on the cold floor to start the craft back to life. It was incredibly cold, so the cicada functioned slower than usual, but once it was going, I hooked Oktai into its medical outlets. The cicada hummed as it stabilized his vitals and then tried to plunge him into sedation to set his bones. I couldn't avoid the flashing readout on the medical display: "CONDITION CRITICAL."

I had done this to him. I started crying for real. Golden tears. I had done this to him.

"Oktai . . . ," I whispered.

His eyes cracked just slightly. "Tamo," he said in less than a whisper.

"What?" I gasped.

"Tamo . . . was my name . . . as a boy . . . in the village. Little Tamo. Before I was a man." Finally the sedation seemed to kick in, bringing him out of shock. He lowered his arm, gently releasing his grip and allowing what was left of his heirloom hunting knife to clatter to the floor.

"Tamo?" I half cried. "I was Jojo."

"Jojo," he repeated, his voice fading. "Little Jojo." His eyes turned to look at mine, and I held his hand. "My friend . . ."

The shaking in his hand stopped as he slipped into unconsciousness.

For a while, I sat beside him. He breathed shallowly as I held his hand and squeezed. "What am I going to do, Tamo?" I whispered. "Go back to Yerba City to tell Nine I failed? Or maybe I should just go lie in the snow and play dead."

"Well, that sounds boring."

I whipped around to find Thaddeus climbing into the cicada. He was as bloodied from the crash as Oktai, but didn't appear to have the same injuries to his limbs. In fact, he climbed into the craft with as much precision as those times I'd seen him off the bottle.

"Thad! You're alive." I jumped to my feet and threw my arms around him. Strangely, he hugged me back.

"Going to take more than that to get rid of an asshole like me," he said. "Whatever . . . *that* was."

"It was me," I said. "I gained some of Yukio's power. That's how we got off the moon. But I couldn't control it. That's why we crashed on Earth."

He pursed his lips but nodded. "That explains a lot. The crash tossed me pretty far from the cicada, but I found my way home again." He craned his neck to take in Oktai. "Oh, man. He's bad. He must have gotten the brunt of the impact."

"Likely," I managed. "Cicada is in med mode."

"Figured, since Oktai is . . . you know, alive." Thad looked around, checking buttons. "Machine's in good order, though." As his fingers touched the machine, though, they must have grazed a flask in one of his secret hiding places. He shook his head. "Old Thad had these in a lot of places, I guess."

"Old Thad was going through a lot, like me now."

He arched a brow. "What do you mean?"

"I mean," I began, grabbing the flask and twirling it in my fingers. It was empty aside from a few stray drops. Must have been from one of his older stashes. "Doesn't look like the mission is in the best place, right? Oktai is . . ." I pointed toward him. "Clo and El have run off. I have no idea what the state of the mission is, if I can even complete it at all. I wanted this strength so bad, but everything I touch seems to fail."

Silence hung in the air as Thaddeus stared at me, and then his eyes roamed toward Oktai. The cicada was working its magic still, but there was a long road ahead for his care. "So that's it?" he finally asked without looking at me. "That's all you got?"

"What?" I asked. "Of course it's all I got. I crashed us. I could have killed you."

"But you didn't," he said. "And we haven't finished the mission."

I leaned against a wall of the craft as exasperation spread through me. "Read the room," I said. "I failed." I twirled the flask one last time and brought it near my mouth as if I was going to drink. "Maybe it'll be more fun to just forget everything."

Before I knew it, Thaddeus had pushed the thing from my hand. It hit the floor with a clang. I startled, jumping back a little bit. But the machines working on Oktai continued without skipping a beat. "Hey! Why did you do that?"

"Being drunk all the time is not that fun," he near snarled at me. "I would know. And I also know that you need to stop with all this feeling sorry for yourself. You're a Josephine. You were made to be the best of us. To be better than us. And of all your sisters, I think you, *Seven*, are the right one for this job. I've known it about you since I met you, Jägermeister. So now maybe it's time that you just believe in yourself. Not your replication. Not your strength. Not your power. *You.* You're who we need to get this mission done. Just as you are." His blue eyes blazed at me before ripping away. He grabbed the flask from the floor and plunked it in the disposal slot. Suddenly it was difficult to breathe, even when I never needed to.

"Thad . . . ," I began, but he shrugged away from me, heading toward the cockpit. He checked the buttons too vigorously. I laced my fingers together. "I'm going to get some air."

"Okay," he said, still engrossed with the buttons. "Three minutes, and I get us the hell out of here."

I was outside in the snow in seconds and found myself peering up into the stretches of gray sky overhead. Geese honked as a flock soared by, but otherwise, quiet had settled in. Now the quiet didn't feel as constricting. It was welcome, actually. I hadn't been blessed out like that in a while. But only people who are close to you can call you out like that, and I hadn't had friends in a while, either. The winds whooshed past my face. This time the name didn't tear out of me. It was more of a whisper.

"Imani?" I asked.

Still nothing. My lips thinned as I wrung out my hands. "Aunt Connie said you weren't coming back. I always wondered, if I'd been stronger on that day, more powerful. If I could have changed it so we would have had more time together. So we could have shared a lifetime like sisters are supposed to. If we could have shared it with our parents somehow." Again the winds blew, but no words were on them. "But even if you're not with me now, if none of you are with me physically, I carry you in my heart. I always do. I always will. But I don't need to take more strength, or power, or anything to walk my path. That's right. I was always ready, just as I am. And I can do this, Imani. I will."

My hands plunged into the snow and my fingers extended. I didn't need this power I had stolen from Yukio. I didn't need replication. I just needed to believe in me. And if Yukio was right, that we were all part of the Swarm Cartel in our own way, then I could just release the power to whence it came. "Go back home," I said to the power inside me, and through what felt like a great tearing through my skin, all the pieces of

Yukio's gift exploded from me, settled in the air, only to dissolve on the winter winds. I was me again. Well, at least as me as I could be.

I returned to the cicada. Thaddeus was still peering over some readouts and ignoring me. I cleared my throat. When he pretended not to hear, I cleared my throat louder before just shouting, "Thad!"

Frustrated, he turned around. "What? Are you okay?"

"Better," I said. "And I don't want to give up just yet."

The ghost of a smile touched his lips. "Then what do you want to do?"

"I want to finish our mission," I said. "And we need the rest of the crew to do it."

"The Yettis? They never came back to the cicada."

"That's because El and I had a fight," I said. "I . . . wasn't listening. She ran off, but just before she did, I caught that she was going to find out more about her mom."

"She went back into the capital," he said, catching on.

"Mmm-hmm," I said. "Let's get the team back together. Let's help them, and finish this mission." Thaddeus's ghost of a smile turned into a real grin before he agreed.

Night was falling as we headed back into the capital city. We would find the twins, and get our team back together to accomplish our goals the way we'd intended. Calm had spread over me since the new plan had been enacted, and I didn't miss Yukio's power surging through my body. Making this right, all of it, was more important at this point. When the cold horizon burst with blushing pinks in the twilight, we left Oktai to heal while Thaddeus and I headed into the city. It was déjà vu of the earlier march, the trudge still a challenge in the winter wind. The cityscape grew larger behind that familiar wall with every step through the grass and snow. We moved with care, expecting one of those mechanical deer to whizz by. But this time everything was still. Too still. Thaddeus, glancing around at the trees and winter foliage, seemed to think the same.

"Is everything just a little . . . ," he began.

"Too still?" I answered. "Yeah, it is. Where are those freaky deer?"

He shrugged. "Let's do this fast," he said as we finished crossing the plain and found our way back into Solgazeya.

The inside of the industrial complex was not much better than the outside. I was on the alert for curators and minotaurs, or anyone else who might want to keep us from finding the Yettis and Antonov. But again, there was nothing. It was like everything we had come to expect from this city maze had been stripped of itself.

Still too quiet, I thought, just before, as if sensing my confusion, the city answered. A real explosion, a true blast, ripped through the city in ribbons of white, yellow, and red. It flung Thaddeus and me to the ground in its brilliance. All we were able to do was cover our heads. I wasn't sure if minutes or hours went by, but when we both came to, we found ourselves covered in rubble and walking through what could only be considered a ruin. Someone had detonated a bomb in Solgazeya.

"We need to check for survivors," I said to Thad.

"What?" he asked. A thin line of blood trickled down his ear. I jabbed my fingers forward, instructing that he follow. That, he understood, and we took off in a jog through the streets. Which had been blasted to smithereens, almost as bad as how we'd left the compound on the moon. Antonov had factories full of both curators and people living out their fantasies, and I could have cared less about the curators, but the thought of all those innocents caught under rubble made my stomach churn.

We moved with militaristic precision, avoiding the fires and blown bits from the explosion to check under biomechanical debris where cracked concrete and shattered glass mixed with broken artificial bone and burnt sinew. *What could have done this?* I asked myself.

"Seven!" called Thaddeus. He was checking an area a few yards away from me.

I jogged up to him. "What did you find?" I asked. "Survivors?"

"No," he said and then pulled a piece of rubble back. Beneath it lay Antonov, bleeding golden ichor.

* * *

The whole time. The *whole* time. How hadn't I noticed? When we first entered the city, I'd sensed the "machine" in the deer zigzagging across the Siberian plain. They'd been replicated nearly as seamlessly as me, undetectable to the naked eye. But Antonov? I'd walked close to him, stood with the scientist in his botanical garden, and never thought he was more than a man. Or better yet, that his mortal life had ended some time ago. But now Thaddeus stood beside me as I couldn't tear my eyes away. And when Antonov realized who watched him, the ghost of a smile touched his lips.

His voice was raspy. "Surprised?"

"Did you replicate yourself while we were away?" It was all I could think to ask.

A bit of a choked laugh rumbled out. "No, Josephine," he said. "I was replicated a long time ago. It was part of the treaty. A section your sisters didn't need to know about."

"What is he talking about?" asked Thaddeus. For a moment I'd forgotten he was there. Based on where we were standing, I was caught up in the thought of how far Antonov must have been flung from his home to lie here near the city's surface. Luckily, the monitor stayed more on task. "Is this . . . ?"

"Yeah, this is the scientist that sent us to the Swarm Cartel," I said by way of an introduction. "This is Antonov, a creator of Project Chimera. Or at least he was."

"I'm as much Antonov as you're the girl you once were. You were just plucked for replication. I did it for peace in the new world." He looked around himself. One of his nearby factories caved in on itself in the wake of the blast. He laughed darkly before focusing on me. "Some peace. I take it you found your way to the Swarm Cartel?"

"We did," I said. "But the power—"

"You brought it here," he cut me off.

"I gave it up," I said. "Maybe Yukio did this. Didn't seem like he liked you much. Only the Cartel could do something like this."

"Interesting theory. Leveling my capital so completely. It's almost elegant."

"This is not elegant. Everything has been destroyed. Entities try each other privately, sure. But this is *not* private. And there are so many civilians in Solgazeya." I flapped my arms at my sides. The charred, fiery ruins were almost eerie. There was a faint sound of wailing in the background. Perhaps people ripped from their simulations. Was this what Yukio had seen in his youth? What forced him and his sister onto the streets to starve?

The winter wind blew a swirl of air in my face. I shielded my nose, but not before sensing that the air had turned thick and smoky. Every so often, a choking cough would rasp from Thaddeus. We were running out of time to continue this conversation safely. I scanned Antonov. Pieces of both his legs were missing, leaving only puddles of gold in their wake. Even machines needed their blood, and he was losing his at an alarming rate. We wouldn't even get him to the cicada before he lost too much.

He read my face. "You returned in vain, Josephine. A bomb went off before you could complete your mission, one that destroyed my factory and most of my life's work inside." Another round of wailing wafted by us. He closed his eyes as if listening to a sad song. "I'm not a madman, you know. I only wanted a home for people to live in their most beautiful state. That has nothing to do with their physical lives and everything to do with their spiritual desires. With what makes them happiest within. My simulations were intended to give people the satisfaction they deserved. They couldn't get it before the world ended, but with my work, they could have a piece of it now. That's all I wanted."

"Is that what they told you they wanted?" I asked. His eyes opened slowly. "To get put in a museum?"

"Think of your happiest moments. The times when you had no worries. No sorrows. Now imagine getting to live in that moment forever. To never experience pain again. Isn't that something you'd eagerly do?"

Maybe somewhere snow was falling. Maybe somewhere behind the wreckage and blaze. I thought of my last happy time, when I last felt safe. When my family was still together. I nodded. "It wouldn't be a bad memory to live in. I'll admit that."

"Exactly," he pressed. "That's what I made. Don't you see how I've made a beautiful thing?" The image of my family washed away, replaced with the memory of his garden. Of the botanicals, the fat, ripe fruits that twisted and fell off the lush vines. I may not have agreed with everything, but he had given those people in their simulations some happiness. Some escape from all the suffering. "My intention has never been to hurt anyone," he said. "I only did what was needed to both appease the terms of the treaty and create happiness. I've done just that for millions of people."

"You did," I said. "You made a beautiful thing. A better world than I was born into. But I'm here to complete my mission." The golden ichor had begun to soak my shoes now. I leaned down toward him and whispered, "What can you tell me about Dr. Yetti? And where's my sister?"

A weak laugh followed. "Apologies are in order, Josephine. Or perhaps, condolences. I asked you to go to the Swarm Cartel. I never foresaw this end for my city," he said. "But even before you left for the Cartel, your sister was destroyed. What you saw in the garden was smoke and mirrors. She was equipped with a self-destruct mechanism, and she used it so that I wouldn't access her mind."

My words spat through gritted teeth. "You have to be lying. You sent me on that detour for no reason?" I said, though I knew he was not. Before he could say anything, I grabbed him by the collar. The ichor oozed everywhere now. "And what about the Yetti twins' mom?"

Almost imperceptibly, he winced. "Lauren."

His eyes closed again. He was still listening to that sad song, if now only in his mind. I shook him. "What happened to Dr. Yetti?"

"We didn't share lives, but we'll share fates in the end. Like everyone in my city," he said as I dropped him back into the dirt. One was gone. Dr. Yetti was gone. And now Curator Antonov's castle had come crashing down. The raw frustration must have radiated from me in waves, because Thaddeus's hand found my shoulder.

"This intel completes the op," he said to me flatly. "No survivors. No One or Dr. Yetti. It's time we go, Seven. We're done here." I looked to him. "We should get back to Oktai."

I realized I was shaking. But I let him turn me so we could head back to the cicada. At least until Antonov's voice cut through the air.

"Done? Don't you want to know who did this?" Antonov asked, his voice now sputtering. "They're still out there, waiting for you, after all."

"I can handle Yukio," I said into the night.

"But the leader of the Swarm Cartel is not to blame. In fact I believe he is dead now, if such a term can apply to those on the Mesa."

I stopped walking. This time I glanced over my shoulder at the scientist lying on the ground. "What did you say?"

"Yukio Tatsumi did not destroy my city."

"Then who did this?" I asked.

"My sister."

Someone peeled herself from the shadows, only so far beyond the scientist. Clo was covered in soot, but it was the sheepish expression on her face that caught my attention. Her eyes were so big. It was as if she'd expected to see anything except what she'd seen today. She didn't even look at Antonov as she maneuvered around him and stood in front of us. "Earlier, El found me in the snow. She told me to come with her into the city, that we were going to talk to Antonov together finally. That you couldn't be trusted. No offense."

"None taken," I said.

"She moved in a way I hadn't seen before. It was like she just knew how to get to Antonov, around the mazes and all the curators inside them. When we found him"—it was the first time her eyes flicked toward him—"he told us that Mama was dead. El lost it, and . . . somehow, she detonated herself. I'd only seen power like that when we were on the moon."

Realization crashed down on me. "She took *all* of Yukio's power," I said.

Clo nodded. "And she's going to Yerba City to do the same thing there. I told her I wouldn't go if she was just going around destroying things. What's the point of that?" Clo shook her head. "She's really strong. Like scary powerful. But I'll go if you go. I don't want her to hurt more people."

"Then let's go," I said, glancing back at Antonov once more.

"Do what you can to stop Elizabeth," Antonov said. His ichor was near completely spilled, and his skin had taken the same gray color that April's had. Still, that ghost of a smile had returned. "But remember . . . a flood is coming . . . save everything you can . . ." The last of the color drained from his face, and Antonov was still.

***

Thaddeus had us in the air in no time. The three of us had mainly moved in silence; in the background, the machine's medical settings were still tending to Oktai. I stared out the cicada's window at a gray pane of sky. I shook my head. Only so many days ago, the Babble virus had come to my doorstep to take no prisoners: machine or human.

I'd crossed an ocean to get to Antonov, and now I was speeding back home to make sure my city didn't suffer the same fate as his.

But it wasn't the Babble virus that I was most concerned with now. It was the girl I'd met in the circus. It was El. The most disturbing thing about my thoughts was that I couldn't even be mad at El. I understood her too much to be angry. We shared a similar pain. And if she'd chosen to keep that pain to herself, we wouldn't have an issue. But she was going to unleash it with uncontrolled, unmeasured power. I couldn't let that happen. Not to my people. Not to my city.

All night, our cicada darted through a gray starless sky with Thad at the helm. I was so deep in my thoughts, I didn't realize Clo was beside me. She moved so quietly sometimes that it was no stretch of the imagination that she grew up hunting in the woods.

Clo's hair had been twisted into a long plait, but some strands had come loose. She pushed them out of the way. The motion revealed a smattering of freckles that was harder to see than usual because her face was flushed. I didn't really want to ask why.

"Hey," I replied, before a strange quiet set in. There were so many questions in the air.

"Don't be weird," she said finally.

I laughed. It *was* Clo and me. I just needed to say what I was going to say. Why not? I'd given up my Swarm Cartel powers back in Siberia. If I couldn't figure out some way to match El, we were heading toward impending doom anyway. I steepled my hands. "So, why did El do this, really?"

Her answer came faster than anticipated. "I don't think it was because Mama was dead. We'd seen an angel of her in Saturnalia. It wasn't out of the question. I think it was that El expected real answers from Antonov. For us and for Dyre. But he couldn't give us anything. No matter what he said, he wasn't the real Antonov. He was just a shadow of him, you know?"

"I get it," I said. "So what about Dyre? You left him in the village."

"He's safer there right now," Clo said. "If we make all this work, then I'll get him out of that village. But he doesn't need to see El how we're about to. Let him be happy for a little while longer."

"Now you sound like Antonov."

Clo shrugged. "Even a broken clock is right twice a day. Mama used to say that, although we . . . never actually owned any clocks."

I smiled. "So did my Aunt Connie."

"Smart lady," she said. "We'd been on the hunt for Antonov for him to give us back something. I thought it was our Mama, or answers about her, but really, maybe El and I wanted him to give us back those moments before the world ended. When we were kids and had a family, and nothing was like this."

"No one is going to give that to you, Clo. That's over. But you do have this moment. That belongs to you now. And I'm glad you decided to come with me and Thaddeus. It's good to have . . ."

"A friend?" She playfully jabbed me with her arm.

"Yeah, yeah, don't get mushy on me, Yetti."

"You're not my type, Tik-Tok," she said, and I laughed aloud.

"Before this mission, I was on my own a lot," I said. "I had left my city with the hopes of bringing back One before our enemies cracked her open and learned the secrets of my sisters. And I was able to go because out of all the Josephines, I can't speak our secret language. Our Twinkling. Working with you and Thad is the first time I've had new friends, at least since I got turned into a robot."

Something soft was in Clo's eyes, so I chuckled and switched the subject. "I crashed us into Siberia because I couldn't control the Swarm Cartel's power. How is El managing hers?" But before we could speculate, Thaddeus interrupted.

"Heads up, we're just making our way inland. Welcome back to Yerba City."

CHAPTER 23

QUEEN OF BABYLON

It happened in the days after Dr. Yetti left, a moment that wouldn't belong to the scientist. It would be ours. The sky was still black and indigo with hints of red burning the horizon. Daybreak was coming. But we weren't focusing on it through the windows. There were too many of us crammed into the hall at headquarters for that. All of us— one million three hundred thirty-six girls—couldn't fit, of course, but we stood in our rows, starting in the hall and extending out north from Oakland almost to Richmond. So many Josephines. Many from one.

Headquarters was beautiful, the spired palace we had collectively imagined from our Afro-Utopia dream. One had determined this central hall to be sacred. The best place for us all to gather. The best place to take our vows. Where my sisters had found so many tiny white candles, I'll never know. But each of us held one. The waxy things seemed so fragile compared to what we were now. Kind of human. Kind of machine. I cupped my unlit candle before glancing around at the copies of me. Still strange to see so many clones gathered in a single spot— though One was the original. In a way, we were clones of her.

She stood before all of us, with Nine and Thirteen flanking her. One held the only lit candle. It illuminated a small smile on her face. We were products of a single decision, and she seemed satisfied with it. Now that Dr. Yetti had gone, it was time to set things the way we, the Josephines, wanted—or at least that's what she said. We were going to be our own family now. But I couldn't help the anxiety rippling through me. What would this new family be for me if I couldn't understand our language? When I was so disconnected from the Twinkling?

One's voice soared above the rows of girls, and a million ears fixed to her suddenly.

"Sisters," One began. Her voice was ours, but it had its own ring to it. Slightly higher pitched than Nine's. A slightly faster cadence than mine. Still, it had all the warmth that I had come to know as it swelled around us. As it guided us. "I hate to say it, but today we are on our own. The scientist who replicated us has left Yerba City in our care. And now we'll show our strength in the right ways. In the ways that we always wanted."

"Why?" asked one of my sisters, a row or two over from me.

One thought for a moment before answering. "Because this is how we take our new life into our own hands. We asked for this power, right? And now it's time we do something important with it. Today is the day that we step up. It's our time to guard Yerba City and Saturnalia, and all the people inside who aren't as strong as we are. Who need us."

One turned to Nine and then Thirteen, readily lighting their candles from hers. She then addressed us all again. "Are you with me?"

It was a dumb question to ask. Of course we were with her. We were all the same entity. But that wasn't as striking to me as the following moments, when Nine and Thirteen walked down to the first row and lit the candles of the first two Josephines they met. Those two, in turn, lit the candles of the girls beside them, until all the unlit candles were lit and shining and a dull murmur rose among us . . . all in the Twinkling. Something in my heart twisted, especially as the girl beside me lit my candle and whispered something in their language. It may as well have been ancient Latin or another dead tongue.

I shook my head. "I . . . I . . . can't," I said.

She tilted her head to the side and spoke the Twinkling again. I only made out one word: *Wrong.*

"I can't vow," I replied. "I can't understand."

Her dark, curious eyes studied me for a moment, and then she whispered back up the front rows, sharing something that steadily made its way to One. It didn't take long for her to make her own way to me, and soon she stood before me. I held my breath, unsure if she'd tell me to leave because I was defective. That I couldn't be in this sisterhood because I was outside the Twinkling. Instead, her voice boomed, though I knew her words were directed at me.

"We were one, and now we are many," she began. "We were made for a *reason*. Perfect just the way we all are, including our special gifts. And now our special responsibilities. It's time we step into that role to protect all the humans here." She then lit my candle. The tiny flame flicked back at me. A large smile spread across her face, my face, before she returned to the front. She addressed us all. "We have a foot in both worlds now. We're the machine power, but with all our human feelings. With this, we'll keep this world together the best we can. And we'll do it together."

"Yes" rang out all around me, some speaking the Twinkling and others in plainer speak. One was looking out to all of us, all her sisters, but what she had done was specifically for me. Maybe everyone else was taking their vow because they believed what One was saying. I was making it because I was grateful for what she'd done. I still wasn't completely a Josephine, without our language, but she had brought me into the fold as best she could. And my vow ran deeper for me in that moment. I wanted to protect this sisterhood as well as the humans. And not just the humans of Yerba City, but maybe I wanted to protect all the loners and stragglers who were left. All those too fragile, like Imani, or too far on the outside, like me.

***

But that was a long time ago, and this was today. Like on the morning I took my vow, day was breaking over the cityscape as Thaddeus landed our cicada on the tarmac. We were back where our mission had begun, only to see everything through new lenses.

It didn't take long for Clo and Thaddeus to throw some protective gear on before we left the craft, unsure of what we'd find outside. I looked around the cicada in one of those moments where everything was about to change.

Above his stretcher, Oktai's display showed his vitals as stable, but his body was still unmoving. My hands wrapped around his for a moment before I turned to grab my bow and arrow. Ready.

Upon opening the giant door and hopping out, I found Oakland to be as it had been. Tree leaves shuffling in the sweet morning winds. The sun breaking through the predawn glow, turning vivid yellow in the skies. I couldn't even place a cloud above. That was a big change, as the sky had been a sheet of gray for most of my time in Siberia. It was temperate here. Beautiful, even. Just, eerily quiet, as if all the birds and other animals had hightailed it out hours before. Peaceful yet completely wrong.

I felt Clo and Thad at my sides before I saw them. "That building up ahead," I said to both, though Thad already knew. "That is headquarters. I don't see any other Josephines around, but let's check there first. We'll see if we can find some, and get any information on your sister, Clo."

"All right," Clo replied, just as someone called my name at our backs. I glanced over my shoulder to find Oktai hopping from the cicada and crossing the short distance to join us. Given the condition of his limbs when I'd dragged him into the cicada, I hadn't expected him to walk that well for at least weeks. But he had been under the healing agents of the cicada, and they were the best in Yerba City. And sometimes, miracles do happen.

Still, I folded my arms. A frown tugged at my lips. "What are you doing?" I asked Oktai when he was close enough. "You're still injured. You can't come with us."

Instead of fighting me, the hunter smirked. "I figured by now you'd realize you can't tell me what to do. I know you're heading into a fight. I'm going with you." When I began to protest, he leveled a look at me. "It wasn't a request."

He cupped my cheek, and I couldn't help the small smile that bloomed in response. I cupped his in response.

"Ow," he said quietly, but managed a crooked smile. He was by no stretch of the imagination fully healed, but we didn't have time to fight about it.

"Fine," I said, and whirled around as Thaddeus hit my shoulder. He was watching someone approach us. It wasn't El. No, a man headed our way. His jog was anything but leisurely, and maybe a little faster than what should have been humanly possible. He wore dark armor that seemed to be military issue. Another monitor, like Thaddeus. The man who had been speaking with Nine all that time ago.

"Maynor," Clo whispered. I nodded, though I didn't say anything. Of course I knew of him. He was the monitor of Yerba City, the one that El had unceremoniously jumped in the aftermath of the first Babble attack.

"Party's getting bigger," I said when Maynor reached us. He was in his late twenties. His head was shaved and could possibly be described as glistening bald. His skin was golden against dark, dark brown eyes.

"I saw your cicada land," Maynor panted by way of a greeting. He recognized the other monitor immediately. "Thaddeus," he said with a tight nod. And then his eyes landed on Clo. Some strange recognition flooded his face, and if I wasn't mistaken, his cheeks reddened. "What are you doing here with them, Clo?"

I stepped forward. "Where are they?"

This startled Maynor back to me. "Josephine," he said.

"Seven," I replied. I was sure he knew One best, but I didn't have time for explanations or pleasantries. "Where are my sisters? Are they inside headquarters?"

A tight shake of Maynor's head. "Um, no. No one is in there right now. They're—" But I already knew the answer. My sisters were a hive, and if they weren't buzzing around the grounds, they were preoccupied together. Fighting.

"El," I said, and Maynor nodded. He nodded his chin toward Lake Merritt, where the ruined city and water met just next to downtown. Maynor picked up his jog again before telling us to follow him toward the melee.

I should have been focused as we sprinted toward the commotion, but my thoughts drifted to my father. After replication, he'd said often how I was a pawn in this game, but just because I was a pawn, that didn't mean I wasn't the most important part of the game. My presence could be just as important as that of the queens, and as my crew ran headfirst into danger, I would have to become a queen myself to win this fight.

We followed Maynor toward the lake, and as we neared, the path only gave way to more and more destruction. How had we missed this from the air? El's new abilities seemed to have strengthened since she left Siberia. There was nearly as much wreckage around us as there had been in Antonov's capital, but no sign of fire or sonic booms. Just El's anger made solid and the broken rubble that was the aftermath.

"This way," said Maynor as we sped to the shore, a slab of cracked concrete that had once been Children's Fairyland, with just dirt and an audience of trees beyond us.

"What am I looking at, old sport?" asked Thaddeus. The area ahead was clear, aside from the overgrown amusement park which featured, among other ruins, a giant medieval shoe from a long-forgotten fairy tale.

"Just wait for it," said Maynor as the ground began to rattle and shake. The small pebbles and rocks at our feet rolled about as suddenly, from the farthest end of the clearing, the trees snapped apart, making way for El to emerge. She was no longer the girl I'd met at the circus, the one who trained in the forest with her twin and her brother. No, Yukio's power had fully manifested inside her, and she was some supreme version of herself. At least a story tall, El had transformed herself into a giantess, into a young woman who could literally reach treetops and crush a city beneath her fist.

"Holy shit!" exclaimed Thaddeus as he reached for his gun, though at the sight of El, his hands couldn't find purchase. Horror had colored Clo's face as she took in her twin's power, her twin's focus, her twin plucking chunks of fallen buildings and tossing them blindly behind her.

"Why is she doing that?" Oktai whispered, more to himself than us, but I knew again before the rest of the group. That was the only way to keep my sisters from swarming her.

A group of at least seventy Josephines burst from the trees on El's heels, coordinating themselves almost perfectly into their own towering entity to face the Yetti twin. The colossal Josephine tower then swung a group of my sisters as if on a vine, trying to force El back from the city and the additional destruction she could cause. But El was not so easily moved. With her gifts, she gathered the rubbish at her feet and swirled it around herself, forming an impenetrable suit of broken glass and debris, and my sisters' attempts didn't land as they'd wished. Two goliaths were battling over what was left of the Bay Area, and I couldn't help but gape as I watched.

The two behemoths next crashed into the detritus of Fairyland, flattening my already-faded childhood memories like two wrestling steamrollers. Willie the Whale was crushed, the wheel of Anansi's Magic Web went bouncing, and a Jolly Trolly car landed next to us with a *Bang!*, making my crew jump.

"Why is she doing this?" Oktai asked Clo, ripping her hand from her face and breaking the girl from her trance.

It came out more of a sob than anything. "She's obsessed," replied Clo. "She always wanted revenge on the machines. You see, when the world ended, they hit us below the belt, trying to get us to get on the Sap with everyone else. They used this image of our daddy to lure us back from the forest; it wasn't right. Her fantasy has always been to destroy Yerba City. I guess she just never had enough power to do it."

I gritted my teeth. "But if she destroys Yerba City, she's going to destroy all the people left inside. And I can't let her do that." I began to run toward El, who was still yards away, as Clo's twin ripped a shoulder off the Josephine tower and, with a handful of Josephines in her grasp, crushed them to rubble and golden ooze. My chest tightened as she flung them to the ground. When I was close enough, I breathed deeply, readying myself to confront El, when someone swiftly passed me. Someone with long, flaming-red hair.

"Clo!" I yelled, but the girl was already before her sister. She'd turned the tables on me, but in a way, I knew that if my sister had become a vicious giantess, I'd want first dibs at talking to her, too.

When she was close enough, Clo called out to El. El, with another group of twitching Josephines in her hand, stopped only to stare with burning eyes down at her twin.

"Clo?" El's voice reverberated, shattering what was left of the rotting fiberglass card soldiers from Alice in Wonderland. El crushed the Josephines in her palm in one sickening crunch before wiping them off on her sides and letting the pieces splatter in the dirt. Clo only stepped to the side to avoid them, her eyes never leaving El's. Clo's hair, which had been tied back in a long braid, had come undone in the sprint toward her sister. Now her hair blew in the wind. The Vegas look from when we first met had been nice, maybe even interesting. This was almost ethereal.

Suddenly, something fell from the sky, smashing into El's giant face and causing her to stumble. Another projectile descended and hit her shoulder, knocking her half-debris body to its knees. El clutched at herself and realized that it was a Josephine that had hit her. She turned and saw that on top of one of the skyscrapers downtown, my sisters had formed a kind of human catapult and were launching their bodies at her like projectiles across the city. El looked at the Josephine in her hand, half-broken from the impact but still viciously swinging, and tossed her aside. El then reached for the bus-sized yellow Happy Dragon and ripped it from the ground. With a scream, she lobbed it downtown, scattering the improvised catapult, at least temporarily.

"Stop this, El!" Clo yelled. "It won't help you feel better about Mama!"

"Mama's gone," El snarled.

"I know that. But she wouldn't want to see you hurt these people."

"Tik-Toks aren't people," she retorted. "We should have just stayed in the forest. Now we can't even go home. It's their fault we're all stuck like this. But with this power, none of that matters. Now, I can set us all free from them. And I can do it right now."

Clo shook her head violently. "No, El. You're just going to hurt people out here. Like you hurt all those people back in Solgazeya. They were innocent. These people are innocent. Hurting all these people is not Oggy's way."

El visibly twitched at the name. Whatever Clo said had landed. At least, until El's face tightened with resolve. "Then tell Oggy I said sorry," she said. Her eyes flicked just beyond Clo to me. "Because this is my way. Starting with that Tik-Tok right there." El jabbed her ichor-covered fingers at me just as I reached for the bow at my back. I didn't have Swarm Cartel power anymore, but I'd been waiting for this party since Solgazeya. I hadn't anticipated Clo stepping ever so slightly to the side, enough in front of me to send a clear message: *You'll have to go through me to get to her.*

El's brows shot up. "You would choose them over me, Clo?"

Something like hurt now found its way to El's expression, but Clo wouldn't relent. "I'm not choosing anyone. I'm doing what's right."

El's teeth mashed, but she didn't speak again, only moving—so fast—to scoop Clo up and sweep her to the side. It was only a blink, but in that time, El had walled Clo up to her torso with debris, so she could only struggle, not escape.

"What's right?" El asked, before turning from Clo, saying, "I'll deal with you later." And then El set her sights on the Tik-Tok she truly wanted. The one that kept getting in her way. Me.

I met her in the middle of the crushed square. Invitation accepted. "Why don't you stand down?" El asked, towering over me. I didn't answer, instead nocking an arrow and sending it at her as fast as possible. A test, as I knew it would be too fast for human eyes to decipher, but El was no longer as human as she'd once been. As I expected, she gathered the Swarm Cartel's power from the air in enough time to blast my arrow to dust. Before I knew it, El was shouting down at me again. "Stand down!"

The air around me seemed to pulse. "Give up the power from Yukio and let's talk about this."

"Talk about you ending up a pile of rubble?" she asked, indicating my sisters in the background, who were trying to regroup themselves after El's blow. "Or about how you haven't learned anything since Siberia. You still only think of yourself. Even when we were with the Swarm Cartel, you thought everything revolved around you and your decision. You couldn't even think about my plan. No, everything was about your mission, on your time."

"I don't think that anymore," I said, but it was too late for talk, perhaps. El's fist was already barreling toward me; it was like watching a comet free-falling for your head. I stuck my hands above me just in time to absorb the impact. My feet planted even deeper into the concrete slab than I had expected, and it took all my Josephine strength to keep her from smashing me into the ground. "Really, El," I managed under the pressure. "I'm sorry. I should have been better to everyone in the crew, and that includes you."

"Shut up," El yelled, as someone flashed by us. I'd recognize that blond hair and monitor's grace anywhere. Thaddeus brandished his guns, shooting in enough time to strike El's fingers. Instantly she withdrew, as her hands were one of the only unarmored parts of her body. I hopped free of her fists as she sucked the bullets—like beestings, I'd imagine—from her knuckles. Her ire fell on Thaddeus, who was still waving his guns at her. "You shouldn't have done that."

With her free hand, she pulled new matter into the battle . . . and it was something I hadn't expected. Water. With an unholy slurp, a blob the size of a house emerged from Lake Merritt and came flying toward us. "She has Brackish power, too!" I yelled at Thaddeus. But it was too late. El had encased him in a vortex of water, and he was trying to get to the top to keep from drowning.

He'd said I hadn't had to get him. That I could have left him. I hadn't understood that gratitude until I realized that he didn't have to try to help me. He was so human in this. Kicking and punching water in air.

I began heading toward Thaddeus, but Oktai and Maynor beat me there. Oktai's eyes locked with mine as they worked to fish Thad free of the manufactured whirlpool. *Get her under control*, his gaze seemed to say, *or we'll all be in one of these sooner than later.*

"Focus, Seven," I whispered to myself before facing El again. But as I turned, I realized that the commotion with Thaddeus had given my sisters the time they needed to regroup. They'd re-formed their conglomerate giantess once more and were hurling whatever was nearest and most destructive at El: trees, boulders, and finally, themselves. It was like watching hornets keep a predator away from their hive. In a way, I guess that's what was happening. But this wasn't any aggressor. This was someone who had all the power of the Swarm Cartel, and maybe more, in her possession. El was no average foe. How could I tell them? They were all moving as one, speaking their Twinkling. The one thing I had to say would be the one thing they wouldn't hear.

Somehow, Clo stopped struggling enough to listen to the sound. She tilted her head. "Is that your language?" asked Clo. "It's like . . ."

"Bells," I replied. Daddy's forever observation. "It sounds like a chorus of ringing bells."

And as my sisters' blows landed, El's face grew tighter and tighter with rage. She was going to use her power again, reach for the Josephine tower, and smash them all to bits. I jumped into action again, with my arrow soaring in the air. It sliced her cheek, one hornet sting she hadn't seen coming. El stared at me in awe, touching her face, feeling the slick blood coating her cheek. Then, with a scream, she began to speak a language I knew. It was the one that thing had used when I was on my last patrol. It was the language laced with the Babble virus. I covered my ears, but it didn't matter. "Nos De Roowa Kon Ne." Pain shot through my head. If it wasn't pain, that's the only description I could use, as everything faded into black.

***

It's funny how these things happen. You're minding your business, doing your job, and then one day, everything changes. Like after replication: I was going about my business, and suddenly I found myself surrounded by dark. But not just any dark. That silent kind of dark. The still, quiet kind found in creation myths. The "In the beginning" thing from which the entire world springs. And that's how I ended up here. One minute I was on the battlefield, then there was pain, and shortly following that, there was absolutely nothing.

I stood. I at least knew that. So I stuck my hands out to feel around as best I could. Nothing.

I took a step forward. "Hello?" I called out. No answer, so I stepped forward again. The nothingness was almost bold, wrapping around me like a blanket. There was also something very comforting about it. I didn't care that I couldn't see anything before me or around me: this was much better than a battlefield. Maybe it would be nice to stay here.

"Hello?" I called out again. Nothing. So, I ticked off everything I'd known to this moment. I'd been fighting El until she unleashed the Babble virus on me. She'd been decimating the Josephine tower and had encased Thaddeus in a vortex of water. El had wanted to set Oakland and Yerba City free from machine rule, but instead she was destroying everything and everyone inside, including the humans she was trying to help. She was too deep in her pain, and I was too far away now to do anything about it. And at this point, did I really want to?

"Josephine?" someone asked. I stilled at the voice, which carried a certain lilt to it. Musical. Mom had always had a way of singing our names instead of saying them. But it wasn't just her voice I knew. I recognized her beauty. It was her light. "Josephine?"

"Hello?" I called out again, prolonging the moment as much as possible. Instead of answering, the darkness broke into shards of light.

From what had been shadows, my mother, Lucille, emerged, just the way I remembered.

I couldn't keep my eyes from blinking rapidly. I hadn't seen my mother since I was a small child, but after all this time, she was right in front of me. My throat constricted when she touched my face.

"Josephine," she said, a smile on her lips.

But though my heart swelled with joy, another emotion or two joined it. Pain. Anger. I couldn't help but twist from her touch. "No," I said. "You don't get to appear. Not like this."

"What would make it more convenient?"

"Not convenient. Or better. This is just too much." And it was. My mother's beautiful face, and her beautiful voice. All this that I had imagined when she left a big hole in my heart the day she'd gone. But how would I want her to appear? What would be better? I bit my lip before I asked a single question: "Why?"

Something played on her face. She was uncomfortable. Whatever she was going to say next, she didn't want to. Still, she breathed deeply before knitting her fingers together. "Josephine, you know why." And she was right, but still I shook my head. It didn't matter what I knew. All that mattered was the words she would say.

She sighed. "I didn't want to leave you, your sister, your father. When we make decisions, we stick with them. That's how I was raised. You see, my family came from Louisiana. And my parents were going to make a way for themselves here by hook or by crook. Didn't come to that, though," she said with a small smile. "So, the last thing I wanted to do was leave my family." Her eyes fixed on me a moment longer than I expected.

"What's wrong?" I asked.

"Nothing's wrong," she replied. "Just remembering. I wanted to give you both French names. But your dad insisted on naming your sister. And I insisted on your name. Both turned out beautiful and had equally important meanings. You see, hers means *faith*. And yours means . . . *growth*, in a way."

"I know," I said.

"And you've grown so much since I saw you last. I'm so proud of you."

"If you're proud, does that mean you're coming back?" I asked, to her immediate frown.

"That's not how the Lord works, baby," she said. "No matter how we may wish it were different." I nodded, but still replayed my fantasy— that she didn't really leave us. That she got ahead of Subantoxx and the world ending. That she scouted a safe zone for all of us and came back. That Dad never got the memo. That she was waiting somewhere for us, humming a tune and eager to plant a kiss on my forehead, and now she was here to pick me up.

"I was sick, and I never got better," she said. "That's the truth of it. I never saw the world end. I didn't last long after I left you. Maybe it was my body breaking. Maybe it was my heart. Even with the experimental treatment. There was nothing for anyone to do. Especially not your aunt or your father, or you and your sister."

Who knows when it started, but tears now slicked my face. "I could have saved you."

She shook her head. "You couldn't. And neither could Imani. But you can save this world you inherited, and from what I can see, you've been doing a damn good job." Her arms were around me now. She smelled like lilac as she stroked my hair. "I'm sorry for leaving. If I had known everything was going to happen the way it did, I would have made a different choice. I would have stayed and lived those last days with the family I loved. But because I couldn't give you that time, I am able to give you this."

Confusion twisted my face as she nodded to indicate another area of crackling light. From which Imani emerged.

Watching my twin approach was like staring into the face of another Josephine, but better. The mole on her left cheek, and the longer bridge of her nose, that was all uniquely hers. Where the Josephines were my sisterhood, Imani mirrored something deeper inside me. A part that even cloning hadn't taken away. I gasped as my mother kissed my forehead, and with it, began to fade away.

"I'll see you again, Josephine. But today is not your day, so live like it," she said, and, with a smile at my twin, was gone.

Imani, for her part, swatted at the darkness behind us, bringing a park bench into the light. When she sat, I collapsed beside her, flabbergasted. I had been calling out to her for so long.

"Hi, Jojo," she greeted me.

But I was beyond pleasantries. "Where did you go?" I asked. "I was beginning to think you'd left me. But here you are. Why did you stop talking to me?"

"I didn't leave you. You don't need me anymore," she said. "That's why I was quiet."

"Didn't need you?"

"That's right. And now, I'm not really here for a visit. I'm here to tell you something important. So you can do the work that you need to do."

"What's that?"

"You need to let me go."

I scooted back on the bench. "Did you hit your head while you were gone?"

She frowned. "No, I just have more confidence in you than you have in yourself." She sighed. "You're strong enough on your own now. You didn't need the Swarm Cartel's strength. You don't need the Twinkling. And you don't need me."

"Why?"

"Because . . ." And now the frown flipped, as if she was staring at me in complete awe. "You are the code, Jojo."

"You're talking crazy. What code? And let you go? Of course I need you."

She shook her head. "You thought you were broken because you couldn't understand the Twinkling anymore, but you were never broken. You were designed to not understand it. There is a code deep inside you that Dr. Yetti planted, so that you wouldn't even know it was there. That was the only way to get close enough to Antonov or the Swarm Cartel without them knowing that you were the answer to the Babble virus. How do you defeat an enemy that's everywhere? By replicating one special Josephine, to be more than just a weapon. To give her something that bonds with her love for her family, that gets her before the right people, because she doesn't understand how special she is. That's you."

"But I've felt alone all this time."

She scooted closer, taking my hand in hers. "You're never alone. We're all with you, and we love you the way you do us. We always knew that one day that love would save everyone. And that day is today. Now you need to go back and finish this."

"But what about you? I won't see you again after this?"

Imani shook her head. "Not until our true time. You have to fight this fight alone. And you can do it."

"Okay," I said quietly.

"What was that?" she asked, before I said "Okay!" with more gusto. My arms wrapped so tightly around her: the hug we hadn't ever received and the goodbye we were never able to give. We embraced for what could have been decades before I finally pulled away. She, like Mom, was already fading. "Remember that I love you, Jojo."

"I love you, too," I said, and this in-between world fell away.

***

It was a clear Yerba City morning again, and I was back, if lying in a fetal position on cracked slabs of concrete. Birds chirped overhead as El maneuvered around the trees ringing the lake. A glance to my side showed that Oktai and Maynor had managed to pull Thaddeus from the vortex of water, but he lay still beneath them. My chest tightened as my focus returned to El. She wasn't paying me much attention, having returned to her work of picking off the remaining Josephines with rubble and debris. She probably thought I was dead. That she had won.

I pushed up to my feet. My soiled hands—caked with dirt and dust from my nails clawing into the ground after the Babble virus attack—smeared my dress. But once I stood, my body felt more limber. More agile. I wasn't stronger in terms of power, but perhaps by way of confidence. My family loved me, and from whatever plane they inhabited, they had my back.

I strode toward the colossal trees around the square and the giantess moving about them. "El!" I shouted after her.

She whipped around, likely having grown accustomed to silence.

"I'm still alive." Before she could register my next move, I reached for my back, finding my quiver, and in a quick motion, nocked an arrow in my bow into the perfect spot to explode the stones around Clo. The other Yetti twin was now free, but neither knew what I was doing.

I stared at El. "Let me explain. I'm understanding, finally. It's not the strength. It's not being able to do what we want, or even save who we want. It's about who we love, and how we do it. And the person you love most is just like the person that I love most."

El stretched to her full height. "Stop it," she warned.

"It's that we love our twins," I replied. "My love for my twin saved me from the Babble virus. And your love for Clo can save you from yourself. Give up the power, so that you can truly be free. You want to help everyone in Yerba City?" I pointed to Clo. "Start with her. Be with your sister. If I could be with mine again, that's the first thing I would do."

"Stop it," El screamed, her anger turning frantic as she ripped a eucalyptus tree from its root. As she slammed her fists into the concrete again and again. As somehow, she glowed nearly incandescent, especially from her midsection. But with every move she made, she seemed to shrink, until she was only so much larger than Clo.

Clo took her twin's hand as El studied the strange light beaming out around her from her belly.

Still, I spoke. "My power comes from how I love my family. And so does yours. You don't need all the rest. Like you said, it'll just hurt the people you love. You were right. The whole time you were."

A sob broke from El's throat as she fell into the dirt. Clo steadied her as El splayed her fingers against the ground, causing the air to vibrate as she finally released the Swarm Cartel's power. With a blink, she was normal-sized again, if still with a faint light about her as she cried in Clo's embrace.

CHAPTER 24

SUN AND MOON

Even after all the day's events, I wasn't tired in the traditional sense. The machine part of me never felt that pull anymore. My legs could still run for miles. My shoulders didn't slump. But I did feel something, and I knew it belonged to the part that was still fragile and human. Most of all, I just wanted to lie down and stare at a wall. It was a feeling that washed over me after leaving what was left of the lake in favor of headquarters. And it was a feeling that I didn't want to fight. The actual battle, the one between El and the rest of us, had only lasted thirty-two minutes. But it may as well have been an eternity, one that had changed everything.

My walk home was short. The remaining Josephines were already on a path to rebuilding, so the Twinkling sprang up everywhere around me. Some of my sisters patted my back as I maneuvered through them. Others whispered in our language to each other. I only nodded and kept moving. Being outside of them, outside of the Twinkling, didn't bother me as it once did. It might never bother me again. The Twinkling was how I had stayed connected to my twin, but I'd given her up to accept this new family once and for all: the Josephines, my crew, and every human of Yerba City. We'd said our goodbyes before I returned to finish the fight with El. I would see Imani again one day, but it wouldn't be any day soon. That would allow me to grow. To live my life. And maybe it was also a long time coming. But I still wasn't prepared for the dull ache in my heart. The place from where the new weariness sprang.

Once at headquarters, I found myself in the same holding room where Nine had originally prepped me for the Siberia mission. A small smile creased my lips as I slid into one of the chairs ringing a large conference table and started swinging around in it.

"I don't mean to interrupt," someone said. I stopped turning and, in a fluid motion, stood from the chair. Well, my hiding place was blown. In the doorway stood Maynor. He was still covered in the dirt and blood that would belong to a human postfight. He also looked like he'd been flying through the halls. He breathed hard. His eyes had this franticness to them.

"Maynor," I began. "What's wrong?"

He paused, clearly debating whether to tell me the truth. "Nothing, Josephine," he finally replied. The short sentence had a formality to it. Always a monitor first, I supposed. "Like I said, I didn't mean to interrupt."

"If something is wrong, I can help."

Another silence, though shorter this time, before: "I was looking for Thaddeus. I thought he might be here."

My brows rose. Thaddeus? Was Maynor worried? He did have the air of someone who'd been tearing through headquarters. "Thaddeus is fine," I began, but when Maynor's face turned somewhat skeptical, I amended. "Okay, he's not fine. But he will be. He's in the infirmary, what's left of it. The other Josephines took him when I was leaving the square."

Relief flushed his face. "I don't know how I didn't think of that. I saw you leave but missed when they took him." Maynor scrubbed his face. "I'm really not thinking straight," he said with a little laugh before catching himself. "Sorry to be so informal, Josephine." He touched his bandaged skull. "I still haven't grown my ear back. I really need to spend some time in a Local Zero."

Instead of responding quickly, I eyed Maynor. He was handsome and muscular in the way most monitors were. His bald head gleamed. But I'd seen him just before the fight, and, as I'd learned through my friendship with Thaddeus, there could be a lot under the surface of our soldiers.

"We can be formal tomorrow," I said. "We fought a giant today, and Thad nearly drowned in a vortex of water. To say today is a special occasion would be an understatement."

"I will agree there."

"Good. And Thaddeus is being looked after by Josephines, angels, and all kinds of other androids." My gaze turned incisive. "You should probably head to the infirmary, too. Get checked out."

He shook his head. "I'm fine. I don't break easy. Trust me."

"What do you mean?"

Again, something flickered in his eyes, as if he didn't want to tell me all the thoughts dancing in his head. "I rarely get injured," Maynor began. "All monitors are immune to the Sap, but my protection is particularly high, against much of anything. The Sap, sure. But scratches. Breaks. Sprains. I never got any of that. It was kind of a joke with the other monitors, and Thaddeus, when he wasn't drinking, would never let up on how unbreakable I am."

"Then why don't you look happy about it?"

He shrugged. "Being special, among the special, isn't always a good thing. May attract some off-the-wall situations . . . and people." There was something in the way he said it that sent a shiver down my spine. My head angled, and I couldn't help remembering the look that had passed his face when he first saw Clo on the tarmac. A similar one had appeared when we'd confronted Giantess El in the town square.

I took a measured step forward. "Can I ask you something personal?" There was a quiver to my voice that I hadn't expected. I also hadn't imagined his next word. *Sure.* "What happened back there? When you saw Clo and El? You looked . . . your expression was like you went somewhere for a second. Back to a memory, I guess."

"You saw that?" he asked, before shifting, visibly uncomfortable. He was tall, stocky, and obviously well-trained, standing before a Josephine who barely cleared five feet. But the man looked like he wanted to be anywhere else but here. "I did go back to a memory. One of something that shouldn't have happened. I have a wife who I love very much. Her name is Sarah, and . . ." He was getting lost in his words. When he looked at me again, it was like he snapped back into the moment. He straightened. No longer Maynor, but the monitor again. "Again, I'm sorry. You don't need to know this."

"I asked you."

"And yet, it's not right to share with someone so young." He shook his head. "You shouldn't be worried about such big matters."

"Like running a city?"

"Especially like running a city," he said. "You should be outside playing ball with one of your twins, like Hunahpu and Xbalanque."

"Like who and the what?" I asked, suddenly worried my android brain must have gotten jumbled in the battle.

Maynor laughed. "Hunahpu and Xbalanque. It's K'iche', from my grandmother's people. Hunter and Jaguar, the twin gods."

I perked up. "Hunter?" I asked.

"Yeah, and Jaguar," he said, and his already-exhausted eyes wandered off to distant memories. "Grandma told us all about them. So many stories." He giggled. "They were great warriors, and tricksters, they fought demons, but above all they were ballers. They loved life."

"Oh yeah?" I asked.

"Yeah," he continued. "After they were done with their adventures at the beginning of the world, they became the sun and the moon, just to keep the game going. Guess that's what I try and do."

"Philosopher," I managed.

"In my line of work, that's all I can do: just keep the game going."

"That's why you have a soft spot for twins?" I quipped, and he flinched. "And, because you're a good person. You still want to know if they're all right, too. Like you do for Thaddeus. You want to make sure they're safe, too?"

"If they're going to be citizens of Yerba City, I do."

I couldn't help the little laugh that sprang from me. "Always a monitor. Well, I don't exactly know where they are. I wasn't tracking them when I left the lake area. Also, Clo and El seemed like they needed some time to themselves."

"That's fine. There's a lot going on with them, and if they get too close, they can bring their brand of chaos to your front door. As you know."

"I do know," I said. "You should keep your distance from them."

"I should," he said.

"Will you?" I replied.

His eyes narrowed. Another expression passed over his face. Still, I couldn't read it. "Will *you*?" he shot back. I shrugged. We didn't have to say the rest. We were somehow in this web, in this world with those two. And there was no trying to escape now.

He tipped his head before turning on his heel. But then he hesitated. Before I could ask again if something was wrong, he glanced over his shoulder. "That was impressive back there today. I've seen you and your sisters work together. That's not new. But what you did, Seven . . . if I may call you Seven . . . coming back from the Babble virus. That's something I've never seen. It was like the virus swarmed you, but you somehow rolled it back. Share your secrets?"

I only grinned. "I could tell you, but then I'd have to kill you. And since we're a monitor short, we should keep you guys around, if you know what I mean."

He laughed before disappearing through the door, his footsteps traveling down the hall. I turned from the entryway to collect my thoughts and leave, since people seemed to be coming back to headquarters, even the secret parts. But before I'd even loosed a sigh, I felt another presence enter the room. I turned again, and this time did not find Maynor. Where he'd been stood Oktai.

Like Maynor, he was still caked in mud and stained from the battle, but his eyes were soft, his expression relaxed, as if he'd just gone for a country stroll.

I placed my hands on my hips. "Wow, I'm easy to find."

"They said you'd be here," he began. I angled my head before he clarified. "Your sisters."

The hunter stepped into the room without looking around, as if he'd seen secret meeting rooms and everything in headquarters before. Like this was all old hat: Yerba City. The Josephines. A city this populated. But maybe after going to the moon and literally being among the stars, he was more flexible to adapting than I gave him credit. While some of Oktai's gear had ripped, what stood out more was the fur pelt that he wore over it. He hadn't worn it during the battle, so he must have gone back to the cicada for it, and the weather wasn't cold enough to warrant the accessory. But I wouldn't ask him about it. Not right now. I was just happy to see him, walking and talking. His eyes glittered. Perhaps he was happy to see me, too. He continued, "Still very strange, to see so many of you. But a group of them said they saw you coming in here."

"And you can tell us apart?"

"I can," he said. "There's just a way about you, Hunter." He looked in the direction Maynor had left. "How is he?"

"The monitor is fine," I said. "Going to check on Thaddeus. I hope they're patching him up."

"I just left Thaddeus," Oktai said. "It'll take some time, but it seems that he will recover." He looked at his arms, no doubt thinking about how close to death he must have been after we fell from the moon. "Wounds don't mean the same things here, machines can heal them so easily."

"Not physical ones, no," I said.

He looked at me. "How are you?"

"I'm okay," I said with a laugh. He gave me a withering look. "You think it's strange to see so many of me. Well, it was stranger to see El like that. And not as a giant. But just, it was strange to see all her feelings on display like that. So much rage."

"I actually didn't find it strange. From my time with her, it was just a moment before it exploded in some way."

"But it was for me, because I recognized it. She's so much like me, Oktai. I get how the rage and grief of losing so many people can essentially blind you. If I had made a different choice, El would be me."

"But you didn't make that choice," he said. I stared at him. He stepped a little closer. Warmth spread beneath my skin. "So, you are yourself."

"Thank you," I said. "For that. And what is it that you want to do now that the fighting is done? The Josephines are going to rebuild together, but the world is different again. We can take you back to your village. We'll probably be going back to get Dyre for the Yetti twins. Just say what you need and we will try to help you. We owe that to you."

"You don't owe me anything," he said. "The honor has been mine. And no, I'm not eager to return to my village. For now, there's work to do here. This rebuilding that you say. I want to do that. I want to stay a while in Saturnalia with you." His face turned to a grin, a very slow, easy one that I couldn't help but return. He whispered, "I have a surprise for you."

"For me?" I asked, and he nodded heartily. "What did you do?" He didn't answer, only letting that sly grin brighten his face. I watched as he stepped back from me and opened his hand. Before I knew it, he'd taken particles from some of the objects in the room and had begun creating . . . forming something new. My eyes were wide saucers. "You took some of the Swarm power, too?!"

"Just enough to do this," he said, as with a final wave of his hands, he finished. And I stood somewhere familiar, somewhere I'd been—not at home, but on the moon. We were again in that decorated gym in Oakland, the one belonging to the middle school down the street from Aunt Connie's house. Gauzy blue streamers that looked like winter winds hung from the ceiling. Plump Styrofoam snowmen stood around us, and a chipped disco ball hung above a white dance floor that mimicked a sheet of ice. I'd thought, when I made this, that he didn't know, but maybe he had.

"Snow Ball," I announced on a shaking breath.

"You dreamed me in your vision back when we were on the moon," he said. "I thought I would finish this for you. Seemed important." The hoodied DJ appeared in the far corner, and in an instant, the floor started to rattle with Oakland bass. The swell of music followed. But no other kids appeared this time. It was just us. The music changed to a slower beat. "Let's dance," Oktai said.

We cut across the floor, weaving between the shadows, and I placed my hand in his. He spun me, and maybe the shifting and re-forming particles guided my feet, because I'd never danced like this before. I'd never been spun and dipped. I blushed and grinned, mirroring the stars that seemed to be in his eyes. The streamers blew behind us and the twinkle lights winked in the background as he pulled me close. He kissed my forehead and heat flooded my cheeks.

This was a trippy, wonderful experience. And as much as I liked it, it was time to let it go.

When he pulled me close, I whispered, "Now let the power go, please."

For his part, the hunter didn't seem surprised by the request. Maybe he thought we deserved more than the fantasies of the Swarm

Cartel, too. He parted from me and, like I had done in the snow in Siberia, lifted his palms and let that kernel of power dissipate in the air. I felt it the moment it was gone.

"Reality can be as good as sweet dreams," he said, the music now faded again. "But it was a nice thought, wasn't it?"

I nodded, and then asked, "You want to go eat?"

He raised a brow. "But you don't need to eat."

"You do, so let's go." And back into the real world we headed—a world that we might one day repair.

***

It seemed to pass in minutes, though it took hours for Oktai and me to eat and relax as best we could. Eventually, when the night turned its darkest, the hunter went to sleep. Though that weariness from the day's events remained, there was no way I would even pretend to sleep tonight. Once on my own, my feet were already moving toward a destination I hadn't given them. It was a fast pace decidedly away from any monitors' or stragglers' sleeping barracks. Away from the headquarters building altogether. I was nearly running out into the purple night, until I sensed someone on my heels.

I turned down one of Oakland's cracked streets, and whoever tailed me shadowed my motions. The Swarm Cartel was in pieces on the moon. The Siberians and Antonov lay in their own golden ichor across an ocean. Who would want to get to me here? Now?

When I hit a sharp right near the water at Jack London, and the shadow followed, I stopped and whirled around. "Who's there?" I called out in my sternest voice.

"Seven, I found you."

I sank into my hip. The voice was familiar. It was my voice, though Nine wasn't exactly like me. "I didn't take you for the sneaking-around type. You're more of the 'get with the program' type," I said.

"'Get with the program'?"

"Sorry. The 'get with *my* program' type," I said as the ninth Josephine replica of the first batch stepped into the moonlight. It was a clear sky other than the orb of the moon. For a split second, I wondered what kind of chaos my crew had left up there. Though at this point, that was none of my business.

Nine wore a pristine Josephine uniform, and unlike everyone else I'd seen since the face-off with El, she didn't look battle weary. She looked perfect. No hair out of place. "Nine, you look amazing," I said. "Not like you just survived the battle of our lives."

"That's because I'm not Nine," the figure said, and something about her movements told me instantly that in fact this was not Nine—and not even a Josephine.

I froze, my body tense, ready for combat. "Who are you?" I demanded.

My mirror image looked at me, lit only by the moon, and her face melted.

I jumped back, my eyes scrambling for any sort of weapon. A log, a parking meter, anything.

"Relax," she said. "I'm sorry, it's me: Nori." Her face and the rest of her body quit melting and shimmered into its translucent, watery form, revealing the green glowing Brackish eyes inside of a girl's liquid figure.

"Nori!" I scolded. "I nearly knocked your fishy head off!"

"I'm sorry," she said. "I had to sneak around. I'm still not allowed to be here, because of the treaty. But I had to come. I had to see you. You are on my path."

I was relieved not to have to get into another fight so soon, but also confused. "It's good to see you, too, Nori, but it's a been a looong day. There was a big showdown."

"That's why I'm here." She reached forward and took my hand. "I'm sure we met on the shore that day for a reason, during my walkabout. So I had to tell you right away: it almost happened. The flood."

"The flood?" I asked, and suddenly I remembered Antonov's last words, and the flood he had warned me about.

"We are always talking about it, my people. If Yerba City ever connected to the Mesa network, we would have to destroy it."

"Well, we almost destroyed ourselves," I said. "Just look around."

"You don't understand, Josephine," she said. "We would have brought more than four thousand meters of water on top of this whole area."

"Four thousand . . . ?" I asked. Of course the Brackish used the metric system.

"And under our control, its weight would have felt like thousands more," she continued. "It is the only way to stop the threat of the Swarm Cartel brought to Earth."

I nodded. Okay, so we almost got crushed by a continent of water because of El's wrath, on top of what El had done. Good to know. "It was a threat, yeah. A real threat. But it's over now, I took care of it. It's gone."

"I know," Nori said. "You are great, Josephine. But it was so close. So many of us were gathering, just offshore. I had just gotten back. I was there, too. I would have had to do it, for my family." Her green eyes blinked and began to flutter. Somehow I could tell that, behind her watery face, she was crying. She reached out both her hands, and I took them. She kept them just solid enough for me to grip onto. "I am so sorry, I had to tell you. I know our paths met for a reason."

I nodded, and I believed her. Both about her path and our narrowly avoided sea-pocalypse. "Thank you, Nori. You don't have to worry now."

"As long as the Mesa network is not activated near here again, you will be safe," she said, and I couldn't help but think of the display that Oktai had created for me before giving up the power.

"Okay," I said. "Thank you for telling me. But . . . you should go. I'm not sure what my sisters will do when they find out what almost happened."

"I know," Nori said.

"But I want to talk more," I said, and I told her what I had wanted to on the day we met: "I wish you had come with me on my mission."

She nodded, and our hands parted. "About sixty kilometers west of here there are some islands. Meet me there in three days."

"All right," I said. "I will."

She moved toward the shore. "Be safe, Josephine," she said, and silently slipped into the water.

"Always," I replied, and we each melted into our own shadows, she on her path, and me on mine.

As I cut across the ruins of the city, I thought back on what Nori said. How one girl—Elizabeth Yetti—had terrorized the space so efficiently was almost eerie. She'd decimated the Lake Merritt area and most of the downtown buildings and structures. But, just her being here had almost brought a destruction that was hard to fathom.

Soon I'd left the parts of Oakland most known to me and stood before another familiar structure, a small shack. I bunched the material of my clothes. I'd brought myself here but couldn't help hesitating. I was the only Josephine who visited Tito, and no matter what the occasion, I always found myself back at his door. Maybe a part of me wanted to leave him far in the past, as my Josephine sisters did. But another part wanted to see if he could one day be better, as he was the last piece of a family I once knew.

I knocked a few times before his steps ambled toward the door. It creaked open, and that bright, clear moon illuminated my father's clouded, sightless eyes. The ones that still roved around me before settling on me. A knowing smile creased his lips. I never identified myself, because he would always sense me. The stuff that wasn't on the surface.

His gruff voice followed. "You're tired."

"Long day," I replied.

Neither of us moved. "Felt a little commotion going on in the city, Josephine. To what do I owe this honor?"

"Not on the porch," I said. "Can I come in?"

He shuffled out of my way as an invitation, and I moved into the house as the door clicked behind me. Soon we both stood in the hallway.

"'Not on the porch,'" he parroted me. "We're inside now. So what brings you here today? Or tonight, rather."

"Been gone for a few days on a mission. A lotta stuff happened while I was gone, a lotta stuff that was the cause of the big fight today. The city is secure now, but I wanted to make sure none of it came to your door."

"The pawn has become a queen indeed. Good to hear it. And as you can see, I'm all right," he said. I began to pick at my clothes. "Something tells me you didn't just come to check on my welfare."

"I don't know exactly why I came. Just seemed right, though?" I looked back at the door. It used to squeak a lot more. "You fixed it? Squeaked real bad before."

"Did a little work on it. We're all doing the best we can, aren't we?" Then he tilted his head. "Doors are interesting things, curious parts of the home."

"Why curious?"

"Because they're transitions. Relationships. When someone welcomes another and they step over the threshold, it's an act of trust. Doesn't matter the style of the door, or the manner of guest. Stepping through the doorway is a critical moment, sometimes one that changes everything. So, was this mission a door for you?" he asked.

I nodded, and then remembered that he couldn't see it. I began to speak, but he continued, "And who did you let through?"

"Someone I hadn't expected."

"I see," he said. "Gotta be cautious about who we let through our doors, but if our soul knows they're good, then you should welcome them and build community. You going to keep your new friend?"

"Not sure yet," I said. "More concerned about what I should do about you."

"About me?"

Something in my words choked off. "You want to try again, Dad? This whole family thing?"

"Oh, Josephine." He smiled. Warmth radiated from him. "Never stopped trying, but would love to keep on going with you."

Was I supposed to hug him now? I stepped forward, pulling my arms upward, just as I glanced to my side, where the pathway to the living room rested. His lamps were lit, and something on the coffee table caught my eye. There was a chess game, half-finished, sprawled on the table.

"Daddy," I said. "You're playing a game. You have company?"

"Don't sound so surprised," he began. "And yes, I do have company."

"Who?"

"Follow me," he said, ushering me into the living room. Once in the space, I looked around for his guest, but no one was there.

"Did they sneak out the window? Did you have a woman in here? Not that it's my business." I called out now, trying to be funny. "You don't have to hide. I'll be nice. Who is here?"

"I'm here," said a distinctly male voice, one that was very annoyed. I nearly jumped out of my skin as the living room lamp flickered, and when it stopped, a man had appeared. He lounged on the chair opposite my dad in the chess game and stared at me with an intensity that made me shudder.

"Honey, this is Majerus," began my dad. But I didn't need an introduction. I had seen him here before, and when I met him in Siberia,
he'd set me on my path toward the Yetti twins. Now the shady hologram of the man whose lined face was like a stream of tears was sitting
in my father's living room as if they were going to drink coffee and
watch a football game.

I was advancing toward him in an instant. "How exactly do you
know my dad, anyway?" I asked by way of a greeting.

My dad stuck his arm out, halting me. Surprise was etched on his
face. "Settle down now. You two got some history going on without
me?"

"I meet a lot of weird people in my line of work," I said, not meaning
to snap at my father but more than a little on edge at his new friend's
presence.

Majerus, for his part, flickered in and out, yawned. Formal.
Aristocratic. And bored beyond measure. "There's no need to be
impertinent. I enjoy chess and so does he," Majerus said. "It's quite
simple really, Josephine."

"It's not simple," I replied. "We met in Siberia. You set me on my
mission. That part I get. Why you're hanging out with my father, playing chess in the middle of the night, I don't understand." I took a defensive stance. "Tell me why, and I hope your answer is the right one."

"Come, you both," my dad said, edging between us as best he could.
"Josephine, sit down over there so I can finish this game. Don't try to
beat anyone up in the meantime."

"She can't harm me, Tito," said Majerus, who motioned at his body.
He was still very much a hologram.

"Both of you, be on your best behavior," my father said.

I grumbled as I took my seat.

"I'm always on my best behavior," Majerus replied. "And you're
right. The game is not done." The hologram's creepy eyes followed me.
"Is it ever done, Josephine?"

I couldn't help myself. "What were you doing in Siberia?"

"None of that talk," my dad managed, but it was obvious he'd lost
his hold over both his guest and me.

"Trying to help you, Josephine," Majerus replied, and then he eyed
the chessboard. His pale hand artfully moved a bishop. "You see, I'm

kind of a person. Like you. But I haven't been replicated. I uploaded myself ages ago, and project my likeness wherever I see fit. I saw fit to help you in Siberia."

"And now you see fit to be here?"

"Tito and I play every week," said Majerus, pursing his lips as Tito moved. "I did not see that coming."

"How do you notice anything with all that stuff moving on your face?" I asked. Majerus only glanced my way, his face like a series of moving lines.

"I've had practice. And you, my dear, interrupted us."

"Josephine can come when she pleases," Tito added.

"Yes, as her father, I'm sure you have extended an open invitation to her. But she really should be preparing for what's coming next."

"What do you mean?" I asked. "I'm sure you saw the mess from today. And since you seem to know everyone's business, then you should know the Swarm Cartel and the Siberians are done."

"You're right," Majerus replied. "I do know what goes on with the entities. And like I warned you in Siberia, I will warn you again, Josephine. The world is going to be shaped afresh now that you've beaten back the Babble virus. Something new is coming, and you should ready yourself."

"Ready myself?" I asked, as Tito knocked over one of Majerus's pieces. "For what?"

"The Yettis are still with you somewhere, right?" Majerus replied. "You should really ask them." He then looked to my father, who had a cat-who-ate-the-canary grin. "Tito, you didn't."

"I did," said my dad. "Checkmate."

EPILOGUE

A WALK IN THE WOODS

WEEKS LATER

The morning was beautiful and clear. It was also growing cold—or at least, our version of cold—just in time for early winter. I found myself on my regular path into the forest, my usual patrols. Oktai had wanted to see the forest; it was, as he called it, the world I liked to escape into. But I didn't want to share it with him yet. It was still mine. So I was alone as the brush crunched beneath my feet, snapping under my weight. The leaves had grown brittle since falling from the trees. I wasn't taken aback by that. I was most surprised to see the movement of animals in the forest. Eerily, when I'd first touched foot in Yerba City after returning to Siberia, they'd been gone. I looked up to see some birds in the tree limbs. They'd been the first to return after the battle with El, and likely wouldn't fly on to warmer climates. These wanted to stay put for whatever lay ahead. We were in much the same boat.

It was a walk in the woods that I needed, though it hadn't been my first stop of the day. Sometime before this moment, when the sun had barely peeked over the horizon, I was making my way to Thaddeus's ceremony. I was never one for all the formalities of ceremonies. Music. Speeches. Fancy clothes. This combination was something Aunt Connie would have called pomp and circumstance. But Thaddeus was now a friend who had survived a journey I'm not sure many others would have. It was important for me to be there on his big day.

As usual, I hadn't slept that night, or even rested my eyes much, and when daybreak came, I found myself striding toward the great town square. The one that felt a little haunted now. The battle with El had been on its grounds, and we were still cleaning up the mess. I couldn't help but notice on my way to the ceremony that all signs and markings of Yerba City had been removed. The city would get a new name and a fresh start. Maybe it deserved it, the way we all deserved it.

It didn't take long to find more than a handful of my sisters in the square, prepping the space with chairs and tables. There was also a large, raised dais, all polished wood that glittered with the rising sun. Thaddeus was definitely the belle of the ball today. I couldn't help but notice that my sisters were also wearing new dresses for the occasion. All purple, like our headbands. They looked royal. Regal. But I was still happy to wear my normal Josephine uniform. Like all the other Josephines, I had received the message from Nine that we'd change our outfit for the ceremony. I hadn't wanted to. I had to maintain my identity as the oddball Josephine in some way.

As I got closer, I approached one of my sisters, greeted her, and then joined in with the preparations. Moving as one to set the space up was a comforting dance, one I appreciated after being on the road so long. Soon the sun began to hover above us as opposed to being a sliver on the horizon. More people, androids, and Josephines arrived, including Nine. She'd only quickly nodded to me before orchestrating the setup—and everything around her—per usual. When we'd finally gotten most of the space readied for Thaddeus's ceremony, I stepped back and admired as much of the work as I could. I say that because I was suddenly distracted by a shock of red hair blowing in the wind. The girl to whom it belonged was standing against a tree off the left side of the stage. Clo's arms were folded and her eyes intent. What was up with her?

Before I could think better of it, I bypassed my sisters in favor of standing with one half of the Yetti twins. The girl must not have realized she was being so still and unlike herself, because she didn't register my presence until I was already beside her. The fake cheer she tried to plant on her face was less than convincing.

"Hey, Clo," I began. "You all right?"

"Sure, sure. I'm fine," Clo responded, nodding a bit too enthusiastically. My eyes narrowed. "It's just early."

"You grew up in the woods without any kind of tech," I countered. "I doubt you had late mornings." She laughed softly before moving a strand of hair. It caught the morning light, appearing a deeper crimson than usual. "Something wrong? Lose that fruit headpiece you wore with the Tsirku?"

Her smile turned wicked. "I would never do that. I looked great, and there's about to be a rare audience full of monitors here. I know one or two like a redhead."

My own laugh followed. "You know you're nuts, girl."

As we spoke, a few of my Josephine sisters eyed us, but continued with their work. Given what El had done only a few weeks prior, the feelings about the Yettis were mixed. Even if Clo had tried to save Yerba City, or whatever it would now be called, she was still part of the destruction, if only by sharing so much blood with El.

Clo noticed them as well. Her hazel eyes flicked to each, but didn't land on me as she said, "You're the only Josephine who feels a little bit normal."

"I'm the only Josephine who'll talk to you," I countered. "Except Nine. But who really wants to talk with Nine?"

"Not me. She frowns a lot." The wind blew, shifting Clo's hair across her face. She cursed under her breath before gathering it and quickly twisting it in her fingers. Soon her strands were held in a fishtail braid. The style made Clo look more like a girl you'd see at a mall, and less like one with assassin-level knife-throwing skills. I might have even met her around the way, and not on a mission, if the world hadn't ended. If we'd been lucky enough to have different childhoods.

I stared back out at the crowd. "Windy day," I said. "Hopefully that dies down before the excitement." When Clo nodded distantly, I added,

"So, are you going to tell me what's wrong or do you need an invitation in the mail?"

"Oh, Seven," she said, cheeks beginning to flush. I still didn't love when Clo called me Seven—something she'd taken to in the past couple of weeks—but I no longer hated it. "Well . . . I was thinking about everything that happened. Which was a lot, obviously. And then my thoughts ran to Dyre. If we went through a lot, so did he. Getting the Babble virus, losing Mama, and winding up in Siberia."

"But he's safe."

"I guess," she said. "Safe as he can be while he's still over there. Even though your sisters don't exactly love El and me right now, they did do us a favor. They sent communication to him, told him his sisters were okay, and where to find us. They told him to grab his things and get on the next cicada. But he didn't."

"What? Why?"

Clo tilted her head. "Because he didn't want to. He wants to explore his new life now, and that means staying in that village. He wants to stay with his new community and continue the marriage they set for him. We just got his answer back this morning."

"That sucks," I said, but then Dyre's face flashed in my mind. I'd recognized him on the mission from his photo, obviously, but mostly from that determination in his eyes. They were so much like Dr. Yetti's. I could tell that he was the kind of person who, when he made up his mind, wasn't going to change it. "I did get to meet his wife. They make a cute couple."

"Shut up, Seven," she said, though there wasn't any bite to it.

"You all got to make up your minds, being you and El. So he gets to decide for himself. Now that there isn't daily Subantoxx or curators to guide their society, who knows what direction their world will take."

"But he's just a kid."

"So are you," I countered. "So am I. And I already made one of the biggest decisions of my life. That's why there are so many of me." As I spoke, one of my sisters nearly dropped a vase of water, so many yards away. About a dozen Josephines sprang into action, vaulting over each other in perfect unison to catch the glass before it shattered. It was pretty impressive. "Doesn't make it easy, I guess. It can still be hard for me to watch."

"To watch yourself? I mean, yourselves?"

"Yeah," I said simply. "It's like watching a hive buzzing around. But what's a good decision if it's not filled with some messiness?"

"Madness."

"Yeah, that, too. I chose to get cloned. Your brother chose to stay in Siberia and get married."

"And what did I choose?"

"El," I said simply. It was the true reason the Josephines didn't trust Clo as deeply as they could. Not only was she El's twin, but she wouldn't denounce her sister, or leave her. She'd said many times that she didn't agree with El, but that a twin was a twin. That we, the Josephines, should understand that more than anyone. What rebuttal could there be except standoffishness?

"Yeah, and I always will. You know, we left the woods to find Mama. To get her back and start our normal lives again. And though we found our answers, nothing seems right, exactly. Not like I expected."

"Just go with the flow, Clo."

"You rhymed."

"Yeah, didn't mean to do that," I said with a laugh. "You got your answers, and all of you are safe. That's what your mom wanted. Be proud of yourself."

"I guess," she said with a shrug, but I couldn't miss the ghost of a smile tugging at her lips as she changed the subject. "How's Oktai?" My brows flew up. When she nodded, she stopped leaning on the tree and faced me.

"Oktai?" I asked, having heard her but needing more time before answering. I'd wanted her to open up, but I had no interest in returning the favor. Her smirk turned knowing. I fumbled for an answer as she looked over toward a far corner of the ceremony. I knew without really looking over there that Oktai must have found his way to the square. "He's over there helping, isn't he?"

"Yep," she said. "It's so manly."

"Chill on the drool."

"It's all right, Tik-Tok, I know he's spoken for," she said.

I rolled my eyes. "You're a busybody."

"And that's something a grandma would say," she said. When I remained quiet, *she* rolled her eyes. "Okay, Lockbox, but I'm going to get some details out of you. When you least expect it."

I pushed her gently and began to walk back toward the square. "Like to see you try, Red."

I headed toward the front row, where a few monitors were taking their seats. The ceremony would begin soon. I briefly caught eyes with Oktai, who smiled at me, but didn't approach. He was busy with work, helping the Josephines make this day perfect for Thaddeus. I couldn't help but watch him. Even in this new environment, so far from everything he'd known, there was something uniquely selfless about him. He was such a good person it hurt sometimes. But it would be creepy to stare, so I found some work to busy myself with, too. That's how I spent the next few minutes: putting up stuff, working hard, trying not to think too much.

Soon the sun was so high in the sky that its light poured down on our heads. I was sitting in one of the seats closest to the stage as the rows behind us filled with admirers, and important people like Nine were gathering to begin the ceremony. All kinds of birds cawed and screeched overhead as if shouting their congratulations to the monitor as well. This ceremony was going to be great. I could feel that in my bones, even though I wasn't exactly one for ceremonies. When it was over, I would be heading to the outskirts of the city.

The ceremony began. As expected, there were speeches. Some to commemorate everything that had happened over the last weeks, others to commemorate the celebration of today. And then Nine took to the stage. She wore the purple outfit that my other sisters had donned, but if I wasn't mistaken, hers was a deeper violet. While there were plenty of other Josephines in the square watching the ceremony unfold, and I had made my peace with seeing my face belonging to so many others, Nine was definitely made for this kind of work. She was formal, and stately, trying to take it all in and, probably, not mess up this moment. I'd never thought this would cross my mind, but I was actually proud of her.

Her task was a proper introduction, which was swift, and then she signaled for the man of the hour to come forward. Thaddeus appeared from the side of the stage, but he didn't take a seat on it. As he was showered with applause, he waved and then took a place in the front row of the audience. It was like he didn't want to miss any bit of this, either.

The seat he took was right next to me. I leaned over. "Aren't you supposed to be up there?"

My chin lifted toward the stage, but Thaddeus only replied, "Hey, Tree Hugger." Then he actually saw me. "Why aren't you dressed like the other Josephines?"

"Standing out. Why aren't you on the stage?"

He smiled. "Standing out," he parroted. Today, he did stand out. And not because this part was in his honor. There was this happy glow around him. Of course, we'd been on a mission into dangerous territory for most of the time of our friendship, but I had never seen him so happy. Where the sun bounced off us, it seemed to be absorbed in every inch of his face and to light the wide grin resting there. His eyes weren't clouded; his cheeks weren't puffy. This must have been how he looked before everything happened, before his life became a little too heavy to manage.

"You deserve it," I found myself saying.

"Are you *proud* of me?" he whispered. Another monitor, one I didn't recognize, had taken the stage to speak about the importance of the day. The sound of murmurs and light applause rolled around us.

"I won't admit it to anyone else," I said. "But yeah, I am. And shut up, or you'll miss the show."

The shindig continued. The great purpose of the day was to initiate Thaddeus's return to active duty and celebrate his bravery during the fight several weeks ago. He'd sacrificed so much to save the city, and the best part of it was that his willingness didn't end in his death. He could be decorated by Nine, who had in all ways become the new One, as well as by one of his peers . . . Another monitor soon replaced the one I didn't recognize. This one was familiar. It was Maynor.

Maynor smoothed his already-pressed uniform, and calmly rubbed his head. When he leaned into the podium and began, it was easy to notice that his ear had fully grown back.

"I used to think Thaddeus was a huge pain in the ass . . . ," he began.

Laughter rumbled around us, especially from Thaddeus, who whispered to me as Maynor continued, "I can't believe he's making a speech."

"It's pretty good so far. They asked me, too, but I didn't want to embarrass you."

He whipped toward me. "Did they really?"

"Well, no. I'm not good at speeches," I said with a laugh, then nudged him. "But you did something great back there."

"Well, I couldn't let you get all the glory. Besides, so did you." Just then he looked up to the sky, briefly watching a bird soar overhead. In that moment, I wondered if maybe somewhere, his dad was smiling down. "Saw a lot of geese overhead today. Heading south for the winter."

I shuddered. "Too soon for the geese. Still remember that one crashing into the cicada."

"Then what will I do with the goose I'm getting you for Christmas?"

"Cook it," I said. "I don't need to eat or sleep."

Maynor was nearing the end of his speech when Thaddeus said, "You have that look." I only arched a brow, an invitation for his thoughts. "Like you're about to go somewhere."

"I don't have any plans."

"Does anyone ever plan for another mission?" he asked. "Wanted to give you this." He reached in his pocket and pulled out an arrowhead. "Add to your collection. But don't use this one unless you're really in dire straits." I took the arrowhead and looked it over. The piece was iron. Definitely not something I would use in the field. Iron wouldn't fly very well. This was an ornament. Something meant for a wall, to be stared at and admired. Not for the real world. But meaningful all the same.

"Thank you for this," I said, and held it to my chest.

"Don't get all mushy on me, Tree Hugger."

I laughed. "You're the one handing out gifts."

"If an arrowhead is the best gift you've gotten, let me go have a chat with your boyfriend," he said as I rolled my eyes. I then glanced toward the seat I knew Oktai occupied, but didn't find him there. Instead, I saw the horizon, on a clear day. How wonderful everything looked now that the world was ours again. Thaddeus saw me looking off. A little nudge soon followed. "I have my adoring public to get back to, but why don't you go? Looks like you want to." It was permission I didn't need, but appreciated. As Maynor finished and another speaker took to the stage, I slipped from my seat and away from the square. But not before an android in the crowd stopped me.

We were a few yards away from the ceremony when my fellow machine stared me down. He was just another angel, a Caucasian man once, who hadn't retained his personality. I prayed that he didn't start babbling, and relief flooded me when instead he handed me a piece of paper. I slowly opened it to find, written in El's scrawl, "I need to talk to you. Meet me in the woods in 30 minutes." I didn't know that El even spoke with any of the machines, but before I could ask the angel any other questions, he was gone.

I could follow requests, especially ones that were already in line with my plans. So I made my way toward the forest trail.

For some time, I carefully trotted along. My feet kicked at the dirt. *What on earth does El want to talk about?* was all I could think while I was moving, sometimes shielding my eyes from the beautiful day and all the light that came from it. I was swift on my feet as always. The ceremony had been nice, but heading down this path felt amazing. The forest was a home away from home, and after so much time on the road, I was glad to be back. Siberia had been so cold. Here there was so much green. All the tall trees reaching up toward the sky. The sweet air. The scents of dry grasses and earth. Hopefully, whatever El needed to talk about wouldn't ruin this joy.

It could still be touchy speaking with El. As mentioned, not all the Josephines had forgiven her. She had done a number on the city that we tried so hard to protect. She had apologized to me some time ago, and I had made my peace with her. But I assumed she had asked me to this secret meeting for help winning over the other Josephines, especially Nine. I would have a hard time telling her that wasn't exactly my job, or within my abilities. I could only give a few pointers and let the chips fall where they may.

I headed down the dirt path for about a half hour in silence until a crunch came from a few yards ahead. My ears pricked up.

"El?" I called out, waiting for the girl to appear.

Nothing. I kept moving until I heard another crunch. "El?" I called out again.

I wasn't exactly scared, but a stark image of that butler bot came back to mind. The creepy way that he came out of the brush. How he didn't respond in the right way to anything I said. His ripped clothes. That wiring in his hand. His fear. And most importantly, how the bottom half of his body exploded into the form of a giant cat. There shouldn't be any of those Babble-virus-carrying machines left, but accidents could happen. My mouth twisted. I hadn't brought my bow and arrow, but I did have a knife somewhere in my pocket. I reached for it.

"Not sure if you're here, El, but if something else is moving around out there, and you want to mess with me, I'll be waiting," I said. Again, silence. This was déjà vu. Had Butler Guy returned?

Then the crunch heading toward me returned, and grew louder and louder until a doe emerged from a thicket of shrubs, followed by two gentle fawns. I sighed in relief. They were probably heading toward the stream for a drink. I held my chest and blew out my air. "You scared me so bad!" One fawn looked at me confusedly. "Yeah, *you*, Bambi."

It blinked at me. I couldn't help but let the fear go to a smile. I walked over and patted its head. The deer seemed pleased and leaned into the touch. My smile widened as it nuzzled my hand and then trotted off, following the path I had once used to track a pack of wolves. I wondered what had ever happened to Spotty. It was time to look him up.

I looked around me. There still was no sign of El. I could stand here and wait. Or I could go deeper into the forest. I toyed with both options until deciding against either. Instead of going deeper into the forest, I followed the deer toward the stream. I pushed through all the marshy plants to get onto the muddy banks. My smile returned because I'd been right. The deer, surrounded now by others, lapped up water as I slowly approached. The doe stopped and eyed me, but I lifted my hands. I meant no harm. As if understanding me, the doe drank on. One of the tiny fawns, brown with white speckles on its coat, approached me, the strange newcomer. I patted her head. I was used to being on the outskirts so much, I appreciated when nature, in its own way, invited me in.

Another crunch sounded, but not ahead. Behind me. And it didn't belong to an animal. Before I could turn, someone launched for me, and we collided with a thud. Strong arms grasped my sides as we rolled into the cold mud, tumbling into the stream. The deer took off at our scuffle, while the person on my back tried to clasp their arms around my throat. But I didn't need to breathe. I got my bearings and tossed them off. Apart, we both scrambled to our feet. And there before me, with fire in her eyes, was El.

"Not bad, Tik-Tok," El announced.

"Not bad?" I asked. "Why are you jumping on me? You asked me out here, remember?"

"Relax, just messing with you a little bit because you're my favorite Josephine."

"I'm one of the few that's still talking to you, but go off."

She frowned. "And I appreciate that." Her facade of cool seemed to crack a bit. "I don't know what I was doing. I just wanted to say hi."

I wiped the mud from my body. "You Yettis are all out to lunch," I said, but strangely, I knew she didn't mean ill. Attacking me was just how Lauren Yetti's kids treated those they considered family. "You asked me to meet you out here to say hi?" I asked, and she shook her head. Her weight transferred from one foot to the other. Fidgeting.

I had seen El in many ways, including as a giantess who was throwing boulders (and my sisters) around the city. She was a lot of things, but unsure of herself was not one of them. Something, maybe a kernel of dread, curled in my belly. My words came out very measured. "El, what is this? What's this about?"

"I like the forest, and I know you do, too," she said by way of an answer. "And I thought we should talk."

"So you jumped me?" I said, brushing myself off. I then remembered that I was supposed to be a calm, understanding friend. I was supposed to wait for her to tell me what she was thinking. How she wanted my help. When she was quiet again, I tried with an easier question. "Is Clo here?"

"She's back at the ceremony," El replied. She was scared, or uneasy, obviously, but even with that fear, that burning fire didn't leave her eyes. Clo had been at the ceremony, sitting on the outskirts. Maybe El had been there, too, under wraps. Of the Yetti twins, Clo was definitely the one more welcomed in public. I had seen more of Clo around head-quarters than El since the battle—since El had given up the rest of the Swarm Cartel's power in her system. After all, repentant or not, El had done a number.

"So, is this about Nine? And the other Josephines? They accept you as much as they can; you're lucky you're your mama's daughter."

Surprisingly, her voice went flat. "I'm not too worried about that. I really don't care what Nine thinks of me. Or the others. No offense to you. I meant it when I said you're my favorite Josephine, but the last thing I feel like doing is joining their sorority."

"It's not a sorority," I said.

El shrugged. "I'm sorry I messed the city up. But a bunch of machines aren't high priority to me."

"Bunch of machines?" I asked. "That how you still see us?"

El placed her hands on her hips, almost impatiently, like she wanted to get over this part of the conversation. It was then that it hit me. "You're still mad." A little crazy chuckle bubbled up. "What on earth do you have to be mad about?"

Her eyes and nostrils flared. "Are you seriously asking me that question? Because, I have a laundry list. I really do."

I swung my arm out in invitation. "Please share."

"Well, if you're asking, I have the same things to be mad about as anyone. In fact, I have the same things you have to be mad about," she said. "Why would I be happy? How could I be? Not when everything's taken away from me."

"But you have Clo," I said. "She is something. The kind of sister I'll never have again." I didn't want to think about my twin. I had made my peace with not hearing her again. That didn't mean it didn't hurt sometimes. Or that I often wished I had just another moment with her. "Embrace that. Whatever else you're mad about isn't worth following me and attacking me in the woods. Unless you want to join the patrol guard."

I turned from her, but she called out to me. "Clo is my sister, and I love her," El said, "but she can't make up for Dyre, who doesn't want to leave that village."

"I know," I said. "Clo told me about that."

"And she doesn't make up for Daddy. And she doesn't make up for
. . ." Her voice got a little breathy. "Mama. And as much as I try to talk
to Oggy about it, as much as I try to forgive the Tik-Toks for coming
into our lives and ruining everything, I just can't."

"So what, you want to fight me some more? Is that what you wanted
to talk about?" I asked, and she shook her head again. "Is that your talk?
Is that your solution?"

"No," she repeated. "I don't want to fight you. Well, a little bit,
but that's not why I'm here." A strange look—perhaps more intense
worry—flashed across her eyes, replacing the anger. "I came because I
think it's been coming back."

"What? The Babble?"

"Um . . . no," she said flatly. "I gave up that Swarm Cartel power—
my connection to the Mesa—but I think it's been coming back, in
waves. I told Clo, but that didn't feel like enough. I feel like I need to
tell you. Like I need your help."

Suddenly, Nori's warning about the Mesa network came back into
my mind. "Tell me about what? Your power? Maybe it takes time to
really go away," I said hopefully, trying not to think of the Texas-sized
mountain of water the Brackish had almost dropped on this part of the
planet during El's last episode.

She shook her head. "No, it's not like that. It's different. Wrong. You
have to tell me what you think."

"I'm . . . very glad you said something," I said, trying not to give
away that I was contemplating how to shoot El into orbit at that very
moment. "But . . . why me?"

"Because you're the most human of the Josephines," she explained.
"That's why you're my favorite. And because you wouldn't be scared
of me." And then I remembered, in Siberia, how there was something
preternatural about El, the way she moved. The way she behaved. I'd
thought it was the Swarm Cartel's power, but maybe it was more.
"Maybe I should have told Maynor first," she said.

"What does he have to do with this?"

"Everything," said El, extending her hand. "But I'm going to tell
you."

"You've got to be kidding me." I laughed for a moment at the absurdity. "You want to hold my hand? You want to be my friend or something?"

"Just give me your hand, Tik-Tok," she snapped. I sighed and moved forward. Instead of taking my hand in hers, she grabbed me by the wrist and breathed deeply. "Maynor's immunity," she said to me, to herself. "I wanted it. I thought it would keep me safe. But now it has to do more."

"Maynor's immunity to the Sap?" I asked.

She nodded.

"Oh," I said. *"Oh!"*

She nodded. She touched my hand to her midsection, where—under what I now realized was loose clothing—I felt the swell of a pregnant belly. My eyes grew wide. "You haven't told him?!"

She shook her head, and then winced. "I concentrated," she began. "I concentrated like Yukio said, and I gave up the power. I severed my connection to the Mesa."

"Yeah." I nodded quickly. "So did I. Oktai, too."

"I know, but . . . ," she said, hesitating. "I don't think the baby did."

"Oh my God," I gasped. All that power, in the hands of a . . . *fetus*?

"Also," and she winced again. "I think it's gonna be twins!"

The ground started rumbling, and I jumped back. As if the world had heard us and answered, the air began to crackle with energy. A shriek erupted from El as the energy circled her, lifting her into the air. The grass and pebbles followed. The remaining deer nearby jumped and dashed into the woods, running for their lives. My eyes had to be wide as saucers to see this. El had once said she would fight this new world with every part of herself, but now she carried a child who'd been exposed to the Swarm Cartel's power. Everything felt immediately wrong.

El finally halted high in the air, at the tips of the trees. Then light, suddenly, burst from her midsection, and the girl doubled over in what could only be labor pains.

ABOUT THE AUTHORS

Michael Ferris Gibson is a writer and former actor, director, documentary filmmaker, producer, head of product at a tech start-up, and frozen-fish chopper at the Marine Mammal Center. He grew up in San Francisco and takes inspiration from his city and the changes it has undergone over the years. He still lives in his hometown, now with his two children.

Imani Josey is a writer from Chicago, Illinois. In her previous life, she was a cheerleader for the Chicago Bulls and won the titles of Miss Chicago and Miss Cook County for the Miss America Organization, as well as Miss Black Illinois USA. Her one-act play, *Grace*, was produced by Pegasus Theatre Chicago after winning the 19th Young Playwrights Festival. In recent years, she has turned her sights to long-form fiction, including The Blazing Star series. Learn more at imanijosey.com.

CPSIA information can be obtained
at www.ICGtesting.com
Printed in the USA
JSHW011718041222
34175JS00001B/1